the Continuum

by TS Caladan

SF

2014, TWB Press
www.twbpress.com

FIFTY-NINE

The Continuum
Copyright © 2014 by TS Caladan

Edited by TS Caladan

Cover Art by TS Caladan

Published by TWB Press

ISBN: 978-1-936991-77-8

Preface

Dark Days of the Galaxy

Middle Ages of the Galaxy

End Times for the Galaxy

Preface

IN THE BEGINNING there was darkness until glimmers of stars shown their brilliance of existence. From nothingness came somethingness. Existence was an unsolvable mystery to the greatest minds of the 'Cosmic Consciousness.'

Big Bang explosions of physical worlds sparked explosions of Life, not as a natural by-product of the Universe but as a structure that produces artificial fabrications from higher dimensions. Solar systems on the physical plane were pure and real experiments from the highest forms of Light-Beings.

The first heat and light from suns began an endless exercise in new life experiments and new forms of life-shapes in the real world of material existence. Countless solar systems through a 'Mainstream' or Color Spectrum forged the playgrounds for fantastic numbers of living-varieties.

Life emerged from other planes onto the physical realm. Now, Time was relevant. Time marched on. Civilizations rose and fell. Infinite combinations flourished, made peace, made war, flickered in a moment of brightness and then faded to darkness. Time changed everything. Now (different from static dimensions) there was entropy. There was aging. There was *change* and ultimately, there was material Death. There was no unifying order to the worlds of living-varieties. There was no organization or Laws in the wide array of creatures in galaxies furiously flying apart. Control and Power were first invented in the minds of the living to rule over the masses that came to exist around many suns. Seeds of failed fascism crystallized in the First Age. During the Second

Wave, power-mongers were primarily not militarists. They did not conquer with war-machines and super armies as was done in the primordial past. A far better method of Universal Control was unleashed upon the galaxies.

A Master Plan of enslavement materialized from 'secret leaders' of each spinning world. There would be order from chaos. Enormous distances between worlds were easily broached by incredible technologies from high numbers of advanced systems. How did one unite galaxies and smaller planetary worlds? How could life forms be controlled and manipulated?

A Cosmic Hierarchy of Life had developed on different planes and levels of dimensions. A type of Life-Pyramid had coalesced with extremely developed Mind-Beings or 'Zogs' on top. Medium-type civilizations, only partially ultra-sophisticated, occupied the general mass-population of Citizens. Then there were the lower forms of yahoos which wallowed on the bottom floors.

Problems were everywhere. Suffering in a material existence was everywhere. Each galaxy needed assistance. Help in the form of a soft, comforting voice eventually came. Creatures of all colors prayed for Galactic Unification. They prayed for a Zog. They wanted salvation from different Zogs of higher orders and it seemed as if their prayers were answered.

A secret 'Committee' of the most powerful Beings in known Universe met and decided that the entire Universe needed to be reshaped. Lower creatures in the power-matrix were totally unaware they were under the jurisdiction of elite authorities who operated from shadows.

The second scheme was simply known as 'the Order.' This was a galactic sweep of every boss, leader, king, emperor, president or prime minister to join the ranks. Planetary nations of every spiral arm were quick to unify with larger forces that appeared to have everything under control. Soon, the Order became a very powerful Federation whose elite Directors had no names or faces to the galactic population.

Whole sectors of space gave in to, not military

intimidation, but a beautiful belief of faith and hope that *this was right; this was good.* Ancient high-tech wars and conflicts were forgotten. Creatures on various planets believed in the Order and submitted to its will, voluntarily. Wars and petty differences between feuding planets were lessened. A strong feeling of a better world approached and great majorities were now willing subjects of the Order. Campaigns of a 'New Dawn' and a 'New Day' were very successful.

Few, and only a few, realized the freedoms that would be lost. There was little resistance when the Order took control of entire galaxies. The exception was from a particular galaxy designated L-MN200 (Trinar's Galactic Glossary). From one of infinite galaxies emerged a 'Wonderful Warrior' known as 'Zog.' Zog would play a crucial part in the History of L-MN200.

The Secret Federation handed down 'rules' along with technological solutions to assorted planetary dilemmas. The alignments were not harsh and Citizens accepted certain restrictions and massive improvements that seemed to come from Nirvana above. Few understood they were betrayed with a web of lies with only an *illusion* of help. Life was better for many solar systems. There was peace. But the Plan was well into effect. Generally, the Order controlled the cosmos. Life forms did not see or *want* to see that resources and minerals were being drained from their lands.

The Order was paid tribute for the technical expertise and a promise of a 'safe-haven.' The higher Hierarchies were becoming fabulously rich while they only gave 'crumbs' to immense numbers of subjects below them.

Zog was a popular belief and grew in popularity. The humanoid on Mineer gained fame on a galactic level. He had vast powers, so said reports. Some claimed 'he' could channel energy and 'raise the dead.' In no time, his fame became a threat to the Federation's Star Chamber and the Order's enlightened members. It was understood among the uppermost of shadow officials that 'The Zog had to be dealt with.'

There were always 'plans within plans.' How would

they continue to enslave the galaxies without Citizens knowing it? It took numerous yarns of deep investigations, computer-models and speculative theories to devise a New Plan. The new concept was to create a universal empire or State Galactic Government. They were going to reshape the already molded cosmos all over again. The word 'Chancellery' spread among solar systems of L-MN200. It was the first time fear or tension was felt from Mystics along space-ways and Wormhole corridors. What would occur if planets refused the State's Chancellery? More out of fear, beings bowed and accepted the will of the new wave.

Zog did not bow.

Dark Days of the Galaxy

Chapter One

RISE OF SARDON

Normalcy was the vibration among the stars. Life forms, in the 'Second Chapter' of Galaxy L-MN200, were complacent. Beings were not naturally fearful. For the most part, creatures did not run to defenses and build armies or Weapons of Mass Destruction. Early wars were not the way of this particular galaxy in Phase II. Major conflicts were aberrations. A type of 'planetary trust' existed that intelligent societies would not construct and use weapons against neighboring worlds. This was true as the Old Days of warfare were nearly gone.

Pyramid power-stations were installed on planets in many solar systems without any defensive barriers whatsoever. Why spend energy on security measures when there were no enemies and only tranquility? Why make force-fields if they were not needed? Consider if full military assaults *were* waged on the wireless pyramid stations, civilizations would utterly *collapse.* Floating cities and flying 'vimanas' would crash. And yet, transmitting towers were left wide open to attack in an age of peace. The non-actions were similar to leaving homes unlocked without fear of invasions.

One benefit from being under the wing of the Order was civil wars were at a minimum. But soon, everything was about to change once more.

Galaxy L-MN200, birthplace of Zog, would become the center of a future controversy. The 'Pinwheel' of worlds would become a *turning point for future events.* Mystic Masters, seers, prophets from the great Color Spectrum and on the highest of levels had foreseen the importance of what was usually an insignificant galaxy. L-MN200 was special. Soon, every advanced Citizen would be completely aware *who* and exactly *what* Zog was. An entire Universe would be astounded!

Has the Zog really returned?

The odd galaxy was christened with a new name. No more was the Trinars' cold classification. In its place was a strange word that appeared the same backwards and inverted. The word was 'Monopdonow.' Galaxy L-MN200 had become the 'Monopdonow Galaxy.'

The Secret Federation, under the growing Chancellery Movement, was more than a little concerned about the 'Chosen One.' The Star Chamber which ruled 'the Order' decided to pay the Zog a visit. The Order's psychics suggested the idea. Could the Mineeran really fly, walk on water, raise the dead, channel the All-Being Creator of Everything and exist as a physical, representative Avatar of Zog in the material world? Was this Zog *the* Zog of ancient legend? The feds or covert 'Committee,' which still went by the name 'the Order,' wanted to find answers.

The historic first meeting between Zog and a large entourage of soldiers and Committee members took place in yarn 798.66. Two hundred heavily armed Order troops with authority from the Chancellery landed on the blue and green planet of Mineer. A few, disguised, elite members and their representatives were in the invading party. What they discovered upon landing was shocking.

[The following translated transcript and description of events were precisely what occurred in Monopdonow History and could be verified by a sub-section of Ran Regale's Cantor Archives, miraculously discovered in yarn 885.64].

The Order's storm troopers dressed in tight black uniforms arrived not far from given coordinates for 'the place Zog dwelled.' The landing of the black craft on Mineer was smooth and without any signs of multitudes. There were no cities or civilizations anywhere near. Clean jungles, lakes, rivers, streams and mountains could be viewed in a fantastic terrain. Colors were brilliant. One yellow sun shined brightly almost directly overhead. There was electricity in the air around spectacular nature.

The Order members were initially confused. How could

a humanoid live so far from civilization? Scans showed no domiciles, unnatural constructions or energy sources of any kind. What they expected was a vast metropolis where 'the Zog' sat on a throne in an opulent palace. They thought there would be throngs of excited followers paying honors and tributes to the Chosen One. The military presence was a security precaution if they had to fight walls of Mineerans opposed to their Zog having any contact from official realms. There was no need for fear on the part of the well-armed troopers.

No one knew what the Zog looked like. There were no films or pictures. The Committee was not even sure if 'it' was a male humanoid. Reports called it a 'he' but there were other reports that the being was female. They knew 'he' was not carbon-based. He did not eat or excrete as some lower yahoo humans did. Zog should not exist by all the understandings of physics from the greatest seers and scientists. Yet, he *did* exist. It was reported that 'the One' could change appearance. Would he emerge in the form of a snake? Would he look like a woman, bird or giant? No one knew as the large mob-army in black approached ground zero, the home of Zog. Weapons were raised.

Before the deadly troopers appeared an opening in the colorful vegetation. Instruments told them that here was where the coordinates converged. This was the exact spot they were to encounter the Zog. It was supposed to happen right now. Zog calmly, without ceremony, walked out of the jungle underbrush and glided directly to the closest official.

The beautiful creature had two arms, two legs, two eyes and one head. He was decidedly male with long, blonde hair and azure skin that was not skin. What immediately struck viewers was the blue locus-line or brilliant aura that perfectly surrounded Zog. The light was not diffused but more like a thaser-line. He did not appear to wear clothing. The humanoid Being seemed to *be* the substance within the blue line. The young, potent figure of a humanoid had a large smile on his handsome face as he spoke the accepted galactic language-standard of 'Lebritz.' The Order's forces were ordered to aim weapons.

Zog stood proudly in front of the 'Powda'me' or the Order's army of enforcers plus disguised Ralian officials. His sweet voice said, "Welcome."

Instantly, pointed weapons of every shape and size were lowered.

The Being emanated love, truth and blue light. He knew everything, almost. Zog had *the* answer. He was willing to show the Order what he could do.

The highest of Chancellery agents was closest to the Zog. Their eyes met. Zog smiled even broader and extended his arms wide. "Sit." With that statement, heard by all, Zog slowly lowered himself to the ground. His arms maintained their outstretched position as he now sat on the soft surface.

Powda'me troops followed the lead of the officials. Soon, everyone was in a sitting position. Zog made the crowd feel relaxed and at ease. Weapons were placed on the ground. They were now going to have a simple conversation...just the most elite of Chancellery representatives and the creature that was reported to be the Zog, the Creator of Everything.

"Welcome. Be at peace." The Zog lowered his arms, took a big breath and broadcasted more love than the effects of a purple Nirvana pill.

"I am Agent Trask, Order Representative, Council Class 3 with the authority to interrogate you." The agent changed to a mellower attitude. He smiled behind official Chancellery garb in black. "We want to ask you a few questions. Would that be...acceptable?"

Zog nodded.

"How can you claim to be the Zog? Zog is myth. Stories from long ago and from many places; it is a *belief*...that, that one being created the exploding-universe Big Bangs? Zog, the Creator of all things...is a *belief-system* from solar systems that should not be connected in any way...that Zog...the ONE responsible for Everything now moved in our physical reality, walked again. Religions, faiths, tribal traditions to modern scientists trying to prove the Zog-Principle...*how can it be you?* How could it possibly be the Architect that originated the universes is now among us as any one of...of its microscopic creations?" Trask smiled with confidence at the blonde being inside blue light. How would the thing respond? Recorder-crystals captured every detail, movement and sound.

"I do not claim to be the Zog. Others said that I am. News spread about the possibility from system to system. I am left alone here because that is my wish. Believers, the humans, on Mineer respect my wishes."

Agent Trask waited for a pause in Zog's words and asked, "Then you are *not* the Zog?"

Zog laughed and quickly responded, "I didn't say that."

Many in the dark crowd laughed, chuckled, giggled, commented and were soon silenced when Committee agent Trask *sternly turned around and glared at them.*

The one in command changed to a more pleasing tone. "Show me...show *us,* what you can do, Zog." Trask attempted to give Zog a test which the thing was not opposed to doing. In fact, he was very willing. A few of the worried soldiers carefully reached for weapons.

Zog happily obliged the agent. The gorgeous 'Wonderful Warrior' closed his eyes and concentrated. He again outstretched his arms and relaxed. A large breath was taken. Everyone's eyes focused on the Zog. Then, the cross-kneed limbs of whatever the substance he was made of began to *shake.* Sitting Zog, eyes still closed, started to rise. The humanoid lifted off the ground about one bar and hung there for a half ya. The blue creature fell back down and breathed heavily as if really exhausted.

That was it? thought the officials and Powda'me onlookers. The moment was gone. *All it did was levitate for a short time?*

Trask spoke the obvious. "Is that the extent of your powers, sir? I've seen better acts at Gambling Houses of Delphino. We heard *walking on water."* The official laughed. "We heard, ha, raising the dead!"

The crowd supported the Committee agent and laughed. "Is that the *best* you have?"

Zog answered as before. "I didn't say that."

In a moment, *Zog became a Woman.* The phenomenal creature got to her feet as the others also stood up off the ground in amazement. There were gasps. She was stunning and apparently made of the same odd material as the male Zog. This one had more curves and was prettier. Storm trooper brutes as well as elite officials could not believe the beauty that rose before them encased in brilliant blue light.

"What *are* you?" Agent Trask asked in wonder and awe. Rather than appearing weak, the agent altered his tune. "These are simple tricks. The natives of Clarion 3 change from one sex to another with a thought. Ha, ha, how did we ever?" Trask was ready to call off the mission to Mineer and report this Zog was a fraud born of exaggerated rumors and their Mystic seers were dead wrong when...

The perfect blonde with long hair *flew over the crowd.* She flew at faster and faster speeds. The flying Zog startled the crowd of over 200 troops. Many aimed their weapons but would not shoot until ordered.

Agent Trask surprised everyone and *ordered* the soldiers to shoot! Most of them obeyed and shot the lovely vision in blue. Electric Howzer-rays struck her again and again. On any other physical hulk, molecules should have been so disrupted as to explode. This did not happen to the Zog-woman who traced fine, smooth, sweeping arcs in the air. Cannon and rifle blasts did not throw her off course a bar. They stopped firing. She gently landed in front of Agent Trask.

"Impressive," replied the agent. He moved closer and got a better look. She was not hurt in the slightest. Nothing was changed. The blue glow of Zog was as radiant as ever. "But, I've seen personal force-fields before."

"That's not what this is, Caladrian."

"How do you know my name?" The high Committee member-agent was spooked. Caladrian calmed down when he realized there could easily have been a simple explanation.

Then he oddly asked, "What is my future?"

The lovely Zog leaned close to one of the prime members of the Order. She sincerely told him about the Commander, "He will be the one who kills me."

Agent Caladrian let out a roar of laughter. That was a contingency with the mission to Mineer. If the one who claimed to be 'Zog' was a powerful threat to the Order and Agenda, he was to be eliminated (possibly the whole planet). Trask decided this pseudo-Zog was no threat. *But, he was going to destroy the planet anyway!* Caladrian signaled his ship by radio. Detonators were activated. The dark, ominous ship contained the capability to *poison* the whole bio-sphere. It hummed in a low vibrato.

"Is that correct? Why wait?" Caladrian's eyes widened and his arm was raised. When it came down, his comrades would have just enough time to depart and be spared the horrific catastrophe.

"I can't let you do that. These are my people."

Agent Trask said, "You better be able to fly away very soon little girl." His hand came down and the *fumigation* sequence began. "Ha! *Can't let me.* There's nothing to stop the countdown." Agent Caladrian believed he had the method of the fake Zog's destruction. He turned to the others. "We're going home."

"You'll be back," Zog assured the agent.

One more laugh was combined with more laughs from those in earshot.

Zog continued, "Yes, Cal, I can't leave. You have to return here in order to kill me. I've seen it."

"Sure, sure," the agent said as the dark mob of Powda'me departed toward the vibrating spaceship. It was at that moment where hidden recorder-crystals registered *one of the most extraordinary visual scenes of all time.* The special Event was later analyzed and restudied over and over for many yarns in certain elite circles. Classic films of 'the event' (from long ago) showed a female Zog who rocketed high up into the air. A wide-angle view caught *Zog rip away the sky!* As if a fantastic curtain that stretched for light-yarns was torn down to reveal:

Super-Giant life forms of psychedelic changing-colors, crowds and crowds of ever-enlarging super-Zog Beings of unbelievable proportions. It was as if Giants watched the whole cosmic display of the lower universe. Galactic clusters were merely 'tables' or 'test tubes' where the smallest and most insignificant life forms of the real world collected dust. *Soldiers and Committee officials fell to their knees with supreme fear in their Centers and begged to be spared.*

What primal recorder-crystals captured were not angry, electric Zogs ready to throw thunderbolts. They were of all colors, changing shapes, laughing, being a receptive Audience, enjoying the micro-universes in front of them, mega-interested and functioning on an incomprehensible level above anything stellar. Then everything drastically changed again.

A starless blackness pervaded the cosmos as the Universe clamped down hard, loudly, and stark terror intensely struck every person of the mission to Mineer. In an instant, their deepest Nightmares were made real (later reported). Screams were heard as the crystals stopped recording.

The 200+ members of the entourage were back in the dark spaceship on course for Ralia. Caladrian remembered the experience safely onboard. He could not conceive of what had happened in the last yams. Was it a dream? No one had a memory of returning to the ship, but everything seemed normal.

Agent Cal Trask did not understand. If what they experienced was truly 'the Zog' with his mega-legions of ultra-Beings, creatures that made their world seem like paramecium, then what did the Zog mean? *He was going to return and kill him?*

How was it possible to kill a Super-Being?

The Committee ship landed on planet Ralia, the site of the future Chancellery. The soldiers' stories were not completely believed by other Committee members. The Committee only partially accepted the words of their top agent.

There were more important matters to attend to and the whole Zog affair on Mineer was forgotten about for quite some time.

Ralia was a small planet or planetoid that contained the most palatial environment in the known universe. Three deep violet suns slowly orbited the planetoid and not the other way around. Staggering violets, purples and hints of complimentary colors gave Ralia a royal atmosphere and the perfect secret grounds for the coming 'Chancellery' concept.

Such extravagance was difficult for minds to fathom. Fabulous nature elegantly blended with artificial structures 'made by the Zogs.' Temples, columns, pyramids, obelisks, monoliths and grand otherworldly architecture were set superbly among scattered decorations of scenic nature.

The entire planetoid, crafted by the highest levels of the Order and the Committee, was near *completion* after numerous yarns. Ralia first began in GST of 625.72 and now as the last shred of statue and shrine was finished, the yarn was 799.89. Wealth in every form contributed to the making of New Ralia. A once picturesque, violet wilderness had been tremendously altered by the Order's Committee.

In truth, the fantastic world (hidden from the rest of the universe by a cloaking-device) could only have been built because of the raping of countless planets' resources. Tentacles of the Committee's 'web' were entrenched within most systems. The web work siphoned marvelous treasures like invisible mining rigs directly into Committee coffer vaults.

Soon, opening ceremonies were going to start at the main temple called 'Majestic Taj' built more than ten times larger and more spectacular than any other on Ralia. Controlling forces had divided into three groups. Most dominant faction and the one that thought they were in control was the Secret Committee no longer referred to as a Federation. The second most powerful group was still called 'the Order.' They were the next generation of descendants incorporated into the family-business. The 'Order' no longer intimidated planets and lost most of their military power with the realization they were actually commanded by or under the higher authority of the Committee. The last group was known as 'the Council.' The Council was the public 'face' to the rest of the Pinwheel Galaxy. They were a band of 'puppets' in galactic Media that ruled *nothing*. Yet, lower yahoos from lesser developed systems assumed these were the ones in charge. They were not.

By the time of the grand and secret opening, there was great confusion among administrators. The long Ralia colonization-plan, which included such astronomical sums of resources, seemed to come together without one director in charge of the project. The ultimate Financiers were very absent from the Committee, the Order and certainly to the clueless Council.

A pre-ceremony special meeting was called to order in the most prestigious Hall of Majestic Taj. Gigantic windows let in violet light. Highest ranked agents of the Committee, the Order and one Council member (phony 'President of the Galaxy') attended the vital session. The expanded, splintered Star Chamber had no idea who was 'running the show.' Who were the 'Supreme Bosses' that produced Ralia and had not shown themselves? Who was secretly draining the Order's coffers as the Committee had been draining natural resources of planets? A larger and larger percentage had been going *out* (computer-books reported) exactly like fascists were putting the screws to various systems.

"Who's in charge here?" a high magistrate spoke out of turn, out of procedure before any introductory rituals were performed.

Speaking out of order spawned others to do the same.

"We're in charge," Old Mal, a crowning Committee leader, responded.

"We *were* in charge."

"Order! Order!" another magistrate barked.

A familiar figure walked to the podium, which turned the chaos into a more orderly spectacle. His amplified words were heard by everyone. Any administrator not understanding the language could plug in for the translation. The man was

Agent Caladrian Trask, now head of the entire squad of agents. He appeared a bit older as the yarns have been kind.

"Order, Chief Agent Trask will speak."

"Hear me! We are but pawns in a game of Zabu. *No one* here is in charge, because the highest of Authority is not present in the room."

Cheers and jeers were shouted inside the violet temple built for kings.

"Hear me!" Agent Cal Trask yelled. "Not only has every structure on Ralia been designed by ghost architects and installed with amazing, robotic efficiency...I ask you, good representatives of the two factions, who created the Chancellery Campaign we have been flogging everyone with over the last 20 yarns in the first place? Order comes to the Order. If the Cosmic Chancellery truly built Ralia as a covert site for their ultimate capital and headquarters, well, *where are they?* You of the higher Committee are too stubborn to see..."

A bell of order suddenly rang and got everyone's attention. The tone signified an important announcement was about to be immediately brought forth to the Committee.

A known courier ran to the long table where the representatives and administrators sat. He whispered into the highest official's ear. Then Mal plugged into the com-system so the others could hear. He said, loudly with a tinge of fear, "They're here."

"What?" Caladrian knew a page would be turned and nothing would ever be the same...as soon as...

The massive jewel-studded door opened wide and a very tall, thin, dark figure slowly crept into the Hall. It took its time. It was twice the height of the tallest in the great Hall. The closer the creature got, the more frightening it became. It wore a wide-brimmed black hat and glared at everyone with blood-red eyes. It had grey skin what little skin was revealed. Its long black coat went all the way down to the malachite floor so that no legs were viewed. The figure appeared to slowly float to the podium. The Financier from some nether underground that never saw a sun was about to address the meeting.

Chief Agent Trask was informed the creature was a SARDON.

Its deep, scratchy voice was electrically amplified. "My home world does not belong in your dimension. Sardon is nearly dust. We were the Children of Sardon and there are only a few of us left. I have been reduced to this size, to your realm, to finally speak with you dylars."

Magistrates were unclear and turned to curiously look at each other.

"We are *ever* so pleased Ralia Project has been completed at 800.00 in the material sense and the Chancellery Charter will be enforced..."

"Sardon?" Mal interrupted the creature, which took everyone to further surprise. He did not know how to call the creature by name. "We've had no communications with Financiers in the last 20 yarns. Committee members realize we've been *overstepped.* There are Directors above us...taking from us...but..."

"But, what?" the Sardon tilted its head and asked with a rough voice.

"But..." Mal, malcontent and self-proclaimed leader of the Committee, said with false authority "This is *our* world, we are the Law here. *We* are the governing body in charge. We were not consulted on a charter. You do not *own* us, Sardon!"

Immediately, the cold and calculating creature of nightmares pulled from its coat an old scroll. "In fact, we own every last one of you dylars." It pointed to the specific place on the rolled document that gave it the official *authority to do anything it damn well pleased to do.*

These creatures had paid for everything.

Old Mal had heard enough. The ancient administrator could not let anyone walk in and assume total control. He stood up and signaled the one Security Agent in the purple Hall to do his job. The agent drew and fired his weapon. The Sardon made the electric Howzer-rays *bend in midair* and strike Administrator Mal. He *vaporized in a messy explosion all over the Hall!*

Other officials were in shock. Some were appalled and some were in the process of cleaning Mal off themselves. They bowed to the New Authority and happily accepted any charter presented.

Time passed and the one Sardon became omnipresent within Taj's temple Halls. It hardly spoke or moved. The dark figure with a wide-brimmed hat mostly stood there and observed. It also tallied every scintilla of Wealth from a myriad variety of sources. Sardons were the ultimate Accountants. Wealth was power. Control was power and this was how they had operated the lower worlds for an eternity.

All that mattered to the Sardon was cold, hard statistics and numbers: sales, purchases, trades, profits, profit margins, percentages, distributorships, expansions to new Territories, loans, payments, interests, and on and on with Business. It did not possess the smallest drop of human compassion. The Sardon spoke of a few others of its 'kind.' It lied to the Committee. This was the last one. The sexless Sardon was not a representative of a decayed and ruined primordial dimension known as Sardon. The Beast in Black that slowly wormed its way through the Halls of Taj was the head of the Vidor, the last gasp of evil from a dark Dimension. All 'tentacles' led straight to the thing from Hensi. It was not *from* the shadows, it was darkness itself come to humanoid life. It was the Anti-Zog, the Destroyer.

The creature with burning red eyes and grey skin was the one who first thought of a 'Chancellery' and what the Business could do. The scheme could be an 'undying Monster' turning forever and invisibly enslaving endless worlds without their knowledge.

The thing thought, *what else would microbial dylars do? I'll give them something to do.*

The construction of Ralian temples, Majestic Taj, transforming the planetoid, the idea of a Chancellery as well as the entire Continuum-concept emerged from the center of a heartless master of darkness. Every remote piece played its part taking every proper path to an inevitable conclusion: Chaos in the Committee, confusion within the Order and the simple takeover by the real Producer-Director.

Everything was in perfect place now according to the Sardon. On a protected planetoid forever cloaked from the rest of the galaxy, its eggs would take root. A Chancellery was established to suck dry and deplete the 'Spacial Territories' around it. The Monster would live forever like a hidden Vidor feeding at the center of a Monopdonowian Web.

No one, not even the greatest seers and Mystics, could penetrate the mind of the Sardon. No one penetrated its darkness. It could keep secrets. The creature had not long to exist. It did not *have* to carry out 'the Plan.' There was no reason to enslave the galaxy; it did not *have* to do so. What would be later known as 'the Continuum' should have been left alone without intervention from a Black Beast from Hensi. The galaxy should have been free from such a long prison sentence. Its vampire 'kind' and their archaic Money-System should have been *dead and buried ages ago.* The last Sardon just could not help itself. Before it was no more, the phantom creature set up a self-sustaining 'Monster' of corporate evil that would perpetually rule the galaxy, drain Citizens and be a model for other systems.

Chapter Two

FALL OF SARDON

"ALL HAIL THE CHANCELLERY! All hail Sardon!" were often heard in the tongues of many civilizations on many planets in the sectors. It was spoken as respectful salutes, screamed as bold declarations of loyalty, chanted in prayers and whispered in sarcasm.

The secret 'Sardonic' Stranger ruled whole systems out of fear with an overall 'Protectorate' known as the Chancellery. It sat on a King's throne in Majestic Taj. Native Rilian tributes in massive assortments were brought to the great steps of the main Hall. The Demon might choose to destroy the human gift-bearers if not pleased. The humans stopped bringing gifts. Most un-official Ralians, bound to the planet, learned to stay away from the main Temple.

Everyone was not in love with the 'new boss' and the planetary rules and regulations instituted between sun systems. Life was generally harder with fewer freedoms. People worked far more and earned considerably less. No one fairly reaped what they sowed with the Chancellery's hand in everyone's pocket. For those in-the-know, the problem was the latest version of the Order.

Rebel groups on different planets attempted to unionize a rebellion. They formed an 'Under-Net' or mass communications system between the 24 sectors of the galaxy. It was an 'underground' stream of information that 'could not be tapped into by any outside source.' Every sector had masses of individual members that used Under-Net sets and were completely 'off the grid.' They felt a 'Truth-Speak' could educate vast numbers of life forms on what the Chancellery was and their real Agenda. The 'Net' was highly popular and caught on fast between solar systems.

An organized rebellion began against the Galactic State in secret with the Under-Net as an essential tool for anarchy. Rebels felt safe sharing horror-stories of Powda'me brutality.

The Net made possible 'Free-Speak' and discussion forums where criticism of Chancellery politics was encouraged. Public waves did not permit negative Chancellery views. There was Media censorship.

But for every solar system drained of resources by Sardon's Chancellery, more joined as members of the covert Under-Net. Knowledge was power and the anarchists were gaining knowledge. Truth was slowly coming into light. But the *real* truth...in the larger scheme...the rebels had no actual power at all.

Only a few corporate, high officials understood the truth. There was only one Puppet-Master with real power. There was only one Shadow Master of Ceremonies, one magician and one Law-Giver. The creator/designer did not operate by council or democracy. There was only a single, dark, evil architect.

Could the exact opposite exist?

No more were there grand Councils or grander Orders or even grander Committees. The Sardon abolished everything. There was only its Machine running smoothly, controlling the galaxy. The Monster was just beginning an extensive process of bleeding the galaxy dry. Chancellery gained ultimate power and control. More and more assets were amassed. How big could it get? How immense would it be before...*what?*

And, where were the total treasure troves of Wealth and fabulous riches going? Volumes of fortune-vaults were pumped beyond capacity in an automatic flow of mega-goods and valuables. The creature, Accountant in black, consolidated the riches into a mode for transport. Then the wealth was *gone!*

The Sardon bought, invested or seized control of anything of value. Enormous quantities of riches would then disappear off books and loading docks. Was the Sardon pouring its profits and the physical labors of the whole galaxy down a Black Hole?

An intricate, detailed, religious Order with historical records going back for ages on galactic Media sprung into being: 'Followers of Sardon.' The Grey Devil in black with red eyes spawned an entire religion, unknowingly. It was their 'Zog' and the devoted followers had no concept what a Sardon was, what a Sardon appeared like, the real Agenda of the Sardon or how the galaxy had been consumed by one. Facts and fiction were embellished to the hooded monks. The fools filled in the blanks. The monks prayed to the Chancellery. To the 'Followers of Sardon,' the Chancellery was the greatest thing since GUARP-5.

A few galactic Media-outlets spread the idea that the Chancellery was really a religious Order and in less than a yarn, other cults and *followers* were born on other planets. Both 'Sardon' and 'Chancellery' became known 'brand' commodities over multi-Media. There were ball teams named 'Sardon' and 'Chancellery.' Bibles, fabricated ancient texts and even children's names were 'Sardon' and 'Chancellery.' Schools, cities, space-ports were also given those words in their titles. Words of a 'Secret Society' were out in public domain, but only a handful of intelligent Citizens understood their real meanings and the evil they represented.

Under-Net announced a large Rebel gathering was set to convene on a stable asteroid, one that 'sung' similar to the Elgin Asteroids. Those on the irregular, dead surface of 0.4N-2221 heard a vibratory hum. The rock was nothing special, but had two Sun-domes. Its location was special among a trillion orbiting shards of what was once a planet called Silizon. The large 'belt' of debris gave the perfect cover for those who wanted to discreetly rendezvous at rare Sun-dome facilities.

The most important feature of the Belt and the camouflage it provided was its close proximity to the Wormhole Nebula. Any appropriate transport ship could slide from almost any other Wormhole in the galaxy to this general area of space. Here was a galactic 'parallax bridge' to Quadrants, to other scattered places and a jump-port to flip right back.

The Wormhole Nebula, with its high number of corridors in a single sector, made it the ideal commuter-system of the galaxy. WN was a 'hub' of activity and popular for various travelers, especially without dealing with 'time dilation.' The famous 'Pan Movers' began right here at the WN.

Silizon Asteroid Belt near the Nebula was utilized by the Rebels and Under-Net members. You had to know exactly where you were going in the Silizon maze in order to reach the 1-in-a-billion asteroid with a Sun-dome base on it. The perfect place was arranged for Rebel leaders, those involved in the anti-Chancellery Movement.

Saucers, vimanas, thurbo-crafts, space-thopters and shuttles: crafts of different designs from the sectors entered their event horizons. And after lovely lightshows through space-tunnels at super-speed, they exited one of the ports of the WN.

Twenty-four vehicles surfed the space-ways, one from each sector (even from Compass-Pacto and Bosh) until they arrived at a small broken piece of Silizon only designated as 0.4N-2221. Rebel ships landed amid the hum.

The largest Sun-dome on the rock barely contained more than 150 of the best Rebel anarchists: a wide selection of men, women, aliens, humanoids, greys, reptilians, Insectoids, etc. There were violent barbarians to patriotic warriors 'fighting the good fight' against tyranny and oppression. Rebel representatives were present to report the latest news. The Under-Net was not considered 100% secure, although the sector-network was supposed to be contained and secret. The special news had to be shared face-to-face.

"Who'll go first?"

One rebel stood up among the crowd in bright, colorful conditions under the dome. "I am Balder, from Denaris Sector. Our sensor sweeps indicate no recording-devices of any sort operating within 12…"

"What about *your* recording-devices?" A friend from Denaris' counterpart, Demor, began with a playful tease.

Balder responded with, *"Mine? Mine are turned off."*

Many laughed; many did not understand.

Balder continued his initial speech. "We have big news

from our sector."

"What news?"

"Go on."

"Yes, let him speak."

"Quiet!"

"We have confirmed...there is only a single Sardon at the core of the Galactic Order forced upon us known as the Chancellery."

"Down with the Chancellery! Down with the Chancellery!"

Many others were about to rant with rage in a wave of furious revolt as to bond in a common cause when…

"Silence!" Lum from Magus, the largest and widest Rebel under the dome, stood tall and yelled, "I'll blast the next thing who speaks, squawks or slithers a sound!"

The most intimidating soul at the meeting was not the most intelligent. *Or, maybe, he was?* Lum raised his triple-barreled weapon. Everyone was real quiet. Lum shouted again and pointed to Balder, "Let him speak, that's it. You speak!"

There were plenty of anarchists in the room who heard of Lum's reputation and believed he would pull the triple-trigger. They were glad he was on the side of the Revolution.

The crowd obeyed his orders. Every eye was trained on Balder and every mouth or slit remained closed.

"Where was I?"

A hand was raised. A mouth started to open and the hand quickly retracted.

"I have news confirming a few solid facts. Its original dimension-sector winked out of existence long ago. The creature is the last of its kind...the Last Accountant. I've been asked, *what is a Sardon?* It is a lone, vile creature, cold-blooded or maybe a no-blooded creature that is more a machine, a computerized adding-machine. I've been asked, *where does the Sardon dwell?* If we knew the location of its lair, we could destroy it. This is *unknown*, but only for the moment. Our most skilled Mystics are working on the problem. With help from our Demorian counterparts, shielding that hides the occult mystery will be penetrated soon and we'll have our answers."

"Yes!"

"Good."

Lum raised his thick trunk of an arm to a very lofty height. He had a suggestion. "We do not negotiate. We *kill* the Devil."

The crowd could not be held back and voiced its hatred for the percentage, tribute or 'protection money' all were forced to relinquish to the Higher Authority from millions of systems. Now they discovered that there really *was* no 'Protectorate' or overall Organization operating for their benefit. The sectors were paying and suffering, getting poorer and poorer, while a solitary Beast from Hensi cleaned up and got richer and richer. The madness was invented by one mad serpent. The chant was, "Kill the Devil! Kill the Devil!"

Then, the Demoran who started the meeting with a jab at Balder walked to the prime speaking-spot. "Attention! Citizens of the Revolution! I am Gillhatton from Demor. We have other news. Your lust for vengeance upon knowing the Beast's lair may not be necessary."

"Explain."

"Beast from the darkest depths is *dying.* It will return to the Black Hole it came from."

"What ails it?"

"Is this true?"

Balder nodded his head in the affirmative.

Gillhatton continued, "We can confirm...the Creature is near death. It no longer skulks through halls at a flug's pace."

Hoots and hollers were heard. A Rebel Insectoid from the Za'ni Continuum shouted with a bug's accent, "How can you confirm your facts? Remote-viewers are...*unreliable,* yes? You can describe the halls around the demon, but you are no closer in finding what planet the demon has established its base, yes?" The yellow salesman-bug was curious.

Both Balder and Gillhatton decided to tell the skeptical bug that 'remote-viewing' was *not* how they acquired the prime nuggets of truth. Balder again addressed the colorful crowd under the bright Sun-dome. "We have a spy. "

Gasps circulated.

Only the psychics knew.

***

Chief Agent Caladrian Trask finished the last valyonne on his table at Café Ali, which was a place one could order about anything and get it instantly. The Ralian diner once catered to the highest of the Order's top echelon from the Old Days. Today was a different time. It was first assumed that officials stationed or ordered to serve on hidden Ralia were in control of the entire galaxy. It was clear, now, they were not. The magnificent planetoid, which was beautified even more with Sardonic enhancements, was the Den of the Devil.

A tribe of creatures called 'humans' were the real natives of Ralia. It was rumored they were once a race of lost space travelers who somehow crashed on the incredible planetoid of fantastic nature and were marooned long ago. Only stories still told by tribal elders spoke of high technology remnants. But no one of any consequence heard the tales. If the folklore of Ralian natives were true, it did not matter. The population of a few hundred had totally forgotten advanced knowledge and completely retreated to caves within the spectacular nature around them. Forces that built great Chancellery temples and storerooms paid the natives little mind. They were not worth the energy to be destroyed.

Natives ignored the fascist invaders from the stars.

In Café Ali, Trask was joined by Revoldinaire, one of his most talented agents. Revoldinaire was groomed to replace the Chief upon his retirement. This was not a social call. The environment was splendid atmosphere for a Chief, under orders, to softly interrogate a subordinate. Caladrian was personally unsure of Revol's loyalty for a number of yarns. Now, apparently, the agent was of interest to the Sardon. The Beast wanted Trask to find exactly where Revol's loyalties stood. Was he a double-agent? Was he one of the Rebels? Was he the spy? Did he own an Under-Net set?

"Have you tried their valyonnes? Excellent."

"No thank you, sir." Revoldinaire, in his fine uniform, waved off the servant. He would not be needed. Revol sat opposite Cal Trask, his boss.

New music from 'The Beginning' played in the background.

"Super," Trask said.

Revol was ready for Cal's questions. The elite agent had a feeling what was coming. The Chief asked his future replacement, "Are you loyal to the Sardonic Chancellery?"

Revol laughed at the question from the mouth of one whose loyalties have also been questioned. "Funny, coming from you, ha, ha. *You* know our secrets as well as I do, sir."

"Please...elaborate. What is the Chancellery to you?"

Revol did not hesitate. "It's a farce, a joke on the world, ha. Or do you want me to lie, sir?"

"Good answer. Are you a Rebel?"

"Yes sir, but not in the way you mean. I know what side of the moroafs gets the burange, if you know what I mean? I'm not your spy, your double-agent."

Chief Agent Trask was intrigued. "Then tell me, Agent Revol, in what *way* do you mean?"

"I believe in, what's it called these days, the 'Party,' comrade? We can't be like the cosmic masses, the yahoos. We have to *know* what's real and true. And I do sir. I know the Party, the Organization, whatever the name is this yarn. I am a robotic cog in the machine, right, sir? Just like you. Correct?"

"How do you mean?" Cal demanded.

"Well, Hensi, we can't quit. I mean, there's nothing any of us can do, even if we *wanted* to. And I'm not saying there are hordes of us against the empire."

"Not in-house, anyway. Plenty of dissent out there in every sector." Trask signaled for final drinks of Mead and they were brought over in no time.

"I will offer a toast," Revoldinaire said with charm.

"What shall we drink to?" the Chief asked with a smile

on his face.

"Still part of the test?"

Caladrian laughed; he liked the kid. "Ha, ha. Yes it is, in fact."

They clinked glasses.

"Then we should drink to a peaceful, well-deserved retirement for you and a prosperous upgrade for me," Revol stated confidently.

"You're good. I know what you mean. The Chancellery isn't going anywhere. It has Omni-power. What can stand against it, against us? The Beast made sure its enemies were in massive debt to it. It *owns* them."

"Beast?" Agent Revol thought that a strange word to come from a loyal Party member.

"Ha."

After they drank the Blue Mead, the subordinate asked an impromptu question. "Can I ask you, sir?"

"Shoot." The Chief lifted up his palms to Revol. "Shoot...so to speak."

"And where are *your* loyalties, sir?"

"Specify." Cal's guard flared and his tone was no longer friendly.

"Are *you* the Rebel spy?"

"You're supposed to be such a good detective. What's your verdict? Am I a loyal Party member?"

"Hmmmmm." Revol exhaled. "You are a Party member, but not in good standing."

"And, apparently, neither are *you,*" Chief Agent Trask countered as he struck Revol's empty glass with his empty glass.

"Ha, ha. Since I *am* such a good detective, here's another one for you, sir?"

"Go."

"Answer quickly, why do you have an Under-Net set?"

"To gather information on the enemy, *Sir!*" Cal looked around and was relieved no one heard him. There were always recording devices. So close to retirement, he cared who knew his real thoughts and what was actually happening in his life. He had gone through a humongous metamorphosis, but kept it to himself. More changes were coming.

"Good answer." Revol smiled.

"The programmed answer," Trask said. "The only way you knew of *my* set is you have one of your own and you did some extensive computer-hacking."

"I did," the uniformed kid replied with a wink.

"You did that to localize each member? You know the members of the Rebel Underground?"

Agent Revoldinaire quickly responded, "Shsssh. Yes, but it means nothing. We can track who uses the Net, but not who programs the Net and where they are based. Also, they are members of an underground communications network maybe a billion strong; they're not all Rebels, though the Rebels *use* the Net. The Sardon only has to worry about, maybe, a thousand elite individuals at the top, I figure."

"Good work."

"You know, you haven't really answered my question, sir?" "I agreed with you that we are stuck with the Party, this demon *Banker* slithering around. It has insured power and control; it has insulated itself from attack with defensive weapons, part of its nature, I suppose. I do not see or can conceive of its defeat. Who can slay the Dragmar?"

Revol looked the Chief straight in the eye. "You might be surprised, sir." He sipped on his Mead as if he knew a secret.

Caladrian tilted his head in confusion. *Who was the spy?*

The younger agent had divulged too much information. Revol said, "What if I told you I know for a fact the Sardon will be gone, vaporized, destroyed within a yarn?"

"What are you telling me?" Cal had not intended to drink any more, but ordered two more Blue Meads.

"All right, sir, let's say *hypothetically* the Sardon ends its life as how our seers have foreseen. What was the prophecy? The Sardon was seen, hat and all, along with the entire Treasury, plunging itself down a self-constructed mini-Black Hole." The younger agent believed the stories on the Net.

"Rumors, but go on."

"What happens when the Beast is dead...when it exists no more?"

"Then, the Viper-Women come in and run the show," Cal said as a hearty joke.

"Hey, hey! Some Citizens take that prediction seriously." Revol gulped down the last of his Mead.

"You're kidding?"

"Not at all. I believe them. You'll see. *Women* are the next big power-brokers, the new Movers and Shakers. Mark my words."

"Women are going to take over the Brotherhood Chancellery?"

"Yep."

"That, my friend, I would like to see." Agent Caladrian smiled and made the 'clink' sound against Revol's glass again.

***

After all three of Ralia's suns lowered themselves below the horizon, Cal had a dream. The man-being with two hearts had already gone through a change. His sympathies were not with the dying creature under the black hat. Caladrian would gladly destroy the Machine-Monster and the creature from Hensi if he could. Could anyone or anything?

What did Revol ask? It was possibly the most important question about the near future. "What will happen when the Sardon crumbles to dust and was no more?"

What of the 'undying Monster' it would leave in its wake? *The Machine was not set up to collapse.* It ran smoothly with or without the head of the Snake to watch over it. Could the plug be pulled?

The dream was a strange one that felt very real to Chief Agent, soon to be former Chief Agent. The dream was an experience with Zog or maybe Zog came to him? The good

'Creator of All Things' told him an echo of what the Wonderful Warrior had told him before. Caladrian, not Agent Trask, humbly fell to his knees before the great Zog.

In the dream, the former Party member cried hysterically in front of his Creator. Female Zog was of gargantuan proportions, and Cal was a flug in comparison. She was mind-numbingly beautiful encased in blue light. Cal begged forgiveness for *throwing the signal to poison the entire planet of Mineer and other crimes in the past.* Millions of Mineerans lived and thrived in peace. *How could I?* Without thinking or feeling the pains and ultra-destruction would cause or fearing any type of future repercussions, without caring, he—

Giant Zog stopped the humanoid. Blue light totally transformed Caladrian Trask in his dream. Blue light (waters) was from the 'living' Zog. And, the most important thing to the former agent...*he was forgiven.*

He woke up. Cal was refreshed and washed clean. He felt fantastic, like a trip on *GUARP-10 and Soma.* The last bit of Order, Committee, Council, Sardonic Chancellery was drained out of him. He was a new humanoid, no longer a Party member.

There was only one official thing left to do. It was as if Zog itself told him to keep one more final, official appointment. Caladrian was scheduled to meet with the Sardon, which somehow he knew would be for the last time. The Beast of Evil was on its slow deathbed. Cal *had* to be there. It was his destiny. He had to obey the orders of the personification of evil one more time. He left.

***

After formal rituals were performed by caretaker administrators, they were told to leave by the smallest of gestures from a withered, grey Sardonic arm. It lay inside a special mechanical apparatus that maintained the Beast's existence and mental consciousness. There was little life in its red eyes. Its hat was gone to reveal a bald skull with thick veins. The Devil was still a dangerous and deadly creature. It was alone with Agent Caladrian Trask inside its dank dungeon.

The thing's deep, low, raspy voice was difficult to understand along with the heavy breathing. The agent was beckoned closer. Cal obeyed.

"I won't...won't waste much of your...time former Agent Trask."

"Former?"

"You think you can...have *secrets?* I can still kill with a...a thought. Should I bring in a servant...to demonstrate?"

"No."

"I'm not dead...yet." It coughed. The Sardon never looked this old, wrinkled and helpless. "I have three secrets of my...my own to tell you, Trask."

Caladrian tilted his head and almost felt sorry for the suffering thing. "Sir?"

"Don't pity me. Ah...I am...power." It choked. "Awk...uh, three..."

"Three secrets, sir?"

The Sardon soon answered, "Net-sets are my...ah..."

"Net-sets are your what?"

"Eyes. Order techs invented them...distributed them for me."

"You watch us?" Cal was astounded. Nothing was covert. Sardon not only knew Rebel moves, it choreographed them.

The grey horizontal Creature continued. "Second secret...you are the Rebel spy. Ah...and third. You, you must return to Mineer."

"Return to Mineer?" Caladrian skipped right over the fact that he was the 'Rebel spy.' Mineer was the center of his recent dreams. "Why, sir?"

"You...you know why."

"Not, what I think?"

"The Creature told you...did it?"

Caladrian was puzzled at first and then it dawned on him who the Sardon meant.

"It told you...ah...you, you had to return and kill him, yes?"

Cal nearly physically collapsed next to the black machine that sustained the evil thing inside. He steadied himself. His head felt like it was about to explode. This was real. This was not a dream. *He had to kill the Zog.*

He turned his back on the Beast. He had to distance himself from the Devil.

Last words from the Sardon were, "You will never...get rid of me...ah...ghost...*ghost* in machine. Aaaaah, ghost...machine for...ever..."

Caladrian Trask staggered out of the dark and damp facility within lower Majestic Taj. He would never return to the invisible Center-capital of the Undying Monster, still growing, still bleeding the galaxy and decimating whole solar systems as a result of its perpetual Business clockwork.

Cal walked. He was in a daze. A part of him thought rationally and planned an escape route off Ralia. He would quickly pack, take only the essentials to get by, go to *who knows where?* He had transport, his 'Shrike.' He would leave and never return to the pretty planetoid. The other part of him stayed in the present and aimlessly walked. He walked to clear his mind and to get as far away from 'it' as he could for now.

Trask walked on ceremonial malachite and rhodochrosite steps until the pyramids and super plazas were no more. After a while, only dense and colorful jungles stood before the former agent. Natural beauty would do him a lot of good. He could meditate. He could blend in with the wilderness splendor.

Cal saw a cave. Two of the violet suns had set. He noticed the cave as a dark spot among purple vegetation. He had no clue what he was doing or where he was going. He always wanted to explore nature on Ralia, but he never allotted himself time to do so. The environment was like a piece of Nirvana to him. Before he departed the protected Devil's lair, he wanted to soak up as much of the spectacular atmosphere as he could.

He entered the cave.

Cal trod through the darkness without fear. The planetoid had no predators, only soft and furry animals that could heal you or save your life. He walked thousands of bars. There were times that Cal thought he heard movements, but it could have been his own echoes. The former Chief stopped in his tracks. *What am I doing? I can't fly off and kill the Zog...that beautiful Woman? But I was told I must do it. I feel that...what do I feel? Must I do it? Is that it? I have to do it.*

Caladrian Trask stopped deep within a Ralian cave surrounded by sheer darkness. A bizarre moment happened where he almost received *light flashes* of what was to come in the next moments and then *jumped back a ya in time.* He heard a *crack* sound, then about 10,000 of them cracked in every direction around him.

The cave was bathed in a soft, eerie light from approximately 10,000 natives adorned with glowing blue neck-rings. Each activated them at the same time, thus the cracking sound and now only the circular rods around their necks glowed. Ten thousand scary faces were illuminated by light emanating up from below the chin, in blue.

At first Cal was scared, to say the least. His stomach knotted. Cal got used to the masses surrounding him and his eyes adjusted. He also noticed how intense the cavern system was, as glowing neck-rings from thousands of natives streamed far off into branches or tributaries. Humans were also situated high up on rock cliffs and balconies above him.

He'd had a big day. Now, what kind of night would it be?

Yet, I feel, I think I feel calm. I feel good.

Cal quickly lost his fears. He understood he was not in trouble. He saw the creepy neck lights as more beauty of the planet and its unknown culture. Little data referred to the humans.

We didn't know if they spoke; only a very few spoke. We didn't believe they mattered at all.

One of the barely clothed humans approached the

former Party member. Who knew if he was a tribal leader? *Could he be angry because some of his species were murdered by the Sardon?*

"Do you speak Lebritz?" Cal asked first.

"No," the tall, thin tribal man replied with peace on his face.

"You're speaking it now."

"No," the human corrected the humanoid. "No one is speaking to each other at all."

"Ha, ha. Good one."

"You will come with us."

Cal was confused. He inquired, "What are you going to do with me?" The question was gently asked. With good feelings in the air, it was a shock for Cal to hear the response:

"Cook you, real well, and make *stew* for everyone!" The tribesman smacked his lips with his fingertips. He made everyone laugh, except for Caladrian whose hearts took a while to come down from his throat. He soon realized he was in the company of superior people who were only joking with him. No one was going to cook him. He glanced around and enjoyed seeing the humans' scantily clad women. Their attractive forms could barely be seen in the blue haze.

The same tribe spokesperson said, "You have to destroy the Zog. You must go to Mineer as soon as you can. Turn around now and *go!"*

Cal crossed his arms and did not heed what he had heard. Chief Agent (which he was not) still commanded quantums of respect in the galaxy. And this half-naked caveman was ordering him to go back to Mineer, not unlike the dying Sardon had done in the Hensi Hall he had just left.

Was this a dream?

It was a dream. Caladrian woke up in his sleep chambers onboard his ship, the Shrike. An automatic pilot was activated. He laughed with his eyes closed. What was the meaning of the dream? He clearly remembered it and the humans with the bright blue neck-rings. He laughed again and opened his eyes. His clothes were different. Rather than his formal attire, the humanoid had on his red jumpsuit. The clothes were perfectly appropriate for Cal's routes on various Chancellery missions. For some reason, he did not like *red* anymore. Anyway, he was stuck with it, being the only suit on the Shrike.

Cal sat up, looked at the destination-indicator, and saw the specific coordinates the ship was headed for and it was completely fine. He accepted his destiny. The ship would come to the end of its journey soon. Cal intended to hang on for the ride. Funny, he was sleepy. The gentleman who repented his past sins was tired. He lay back down on the bed. After only a few yas, Cal returned to a bottomless sleep.

When he woke up fully, again, Cal had the odd idea that he was not alone on the ship. *Strange, no one could have possibly gotten onboard.* The Shrike closed in on its final destination of Mineer. He slowly stretched in the bed. He yawned. As he got up from a prone position, he almost jumped out of his aged skin. In front of him stood the one person he was sure already had his job. It was his 'comrade' and Rebel sympathizer, Agent Revoldinaire! *What the OM was he doing here?*

At the moment Cal was about to confront his former subordinate, the scene changed. The two were no longer on the Shrike speeding its way to Zog's home world. No, they were back at Café Ali and the Standard Time was 943.81.

"How can this be?" Cal asked Revol.

"Call it a dream," the younger man said in whimsical tone.

Caladrian only laughed. "Ha, ha. I just woke from a dream."

"Did you?" The agent who was a different kind of agent smiled.

"Look, dream-Rev, whatever you are? Please tell me what you have to tell me. Will you do that?"

"Sure."

"Well?"

"You have to kill Zog."

"Oh, Zog!" Cal cried in anguish with his face in his hands. "Zog! Zog! Zog!"

"You don't understand."

"How is it you *do?"* Cal spoke clearly for an old man. *What did any of this mean?*

Revoldinaire only flashed a smile. He turned to the attendant, stuck out two fingers and winked.

Cal went with the dream images and asked his partner, "You're ordering two blues?"

"Why not?"

In a few yas, two Blue Meads were presented to the only guests at Café Ali. The glasses sat there for a long while. The view was spectacular.

"What do you think of the Party now?" It did not matter who said it. The only thing that mattered was the past was gone, a *New Dawn* and a *New Day* indeed. They laughed together and the feelings in the fake café were very happy, unlike anything in the real world.

"What's going to happen, no. Who *are* you? Who are you really?"

Revoldinaire transformed into the true form: a beautiful, gorgeous and exquisite vision of a Woman he had observed Zog turn into on Mineer, the blonde goddess that *flew.* She was the giant in his dreams.

Cal's expression went from wondrous enchantment to a look of stark terror. *This was Zog; this was the Creator made real...on our terms!*

"No, dear Cal, be at ease. Stop. It's fine...everything is as it should be." She reached over and held his hand. He almost melted in her presence.

She spoke as he/she did way back on Mineer many lifetimes ago. Zog was soothing and a sphere of blue-lit radiance of perfection. She did her best to put the man at rest.

Cal did not relax; he was ready to *explode.* He inhaled a big breath and attempted to ask a question. "The ship is p-programmed to go to Mineer...where I'm supposed to...*kill you.* How were you able to leave your planet?"

Blue girl changed to blue boy and asked, "Are you sure we're on a ship? You sure, we're even here in the café?" He let go of Cal's hand. "Are you sure we are not alike?"

"Ha, ha," Trask laughed. "No." Zog's words soothed him to a degree. "But...but how can it be you? The real Creator, Architect? How can you be like the rest of us?"

The Meads had stood on the table untouched. The Zog snatched up both of them and drank them down in two gulps. He enjoyed it and giggled. "I wanted to experience the Continuum for myself...what it *felt* like, every sensation...from your level, down here."

Cal was confused and amused. Here was Zog acting more like a playful child with the elation of experiencing life for the first time. "Continuum?"

"Not planets in OM Sector or small continuum. I refer to what your whole galaxy will become in the future."

"Please tell me, vision of Zog."

"The Continuum is what your Monopdonowian Galaxy will be transmuted into in later chapters. Your Pinwheel of (atomic) solar systems, so crucial to the other ten spinning-universes, will reach stability."

"That's good, dear Zog."

"It's also bad," the male Zog in blue corrected Caladrian. "The choice will be...*yours* in the future. Everything can fall into a dark, sucking vacuum consuming all...or life can be a bright fountain of brilliance flowing out in every direction."

"What do *I* have to do with it?"

"We will work together, you and I. I will be reborn inside you as you will be reborn again into the Continuum."

"What...what will w-we accomplish?"

"For the first time, anyone, anyone at all, will be able to visit and remain in my world, my Larger Dimension, *up there...Nirvana.*"

"I-I don't understand," Cal trembled with anxious fear.

The blue Zog-Angel, who was the true Zog in material form, smiled a big smile. "Don't worry. You will."

Cal woke up. The ship had landed. He was on Mineer. GST was 999.98.

***

The very oldest sector of the galaxy was called and known by the awesome title, 'ONE.' The most primordial sparks of Life anything remotely like ours materialized in ONE. Scientists from many systems scoffed at any special *religious* or *spiritual* importance to the sector. Enlightened scientists merely believed 'ONE' Sector happened to be the first point on the spiral arm to cool. ONE was the first area of space to manifest conditions for life to naturally come into being and thrive. Therefore, many believe ONE Sector will be the first to die out in the very distant future.

Other enlightened experts believed that Nature was not how Life began at all.

Found on hundreds of systems within ONE were the oldest traces of anything intelligent. First known galactic structures and evidence of life existed on planets of ONE Sector. The mystery, as with infinite systems, why were the first buildings or constructions the most advanced?

Incredible, unbelievable (also dull, drab, dusty) catacombs formed an intricate network so detailed and lengthy that no one could ever map them. The architectural designs of the endless caverns were beyond comprehension. Massive structures were discovered to be composed of pure nesium, a thousand times harder than doldrenite or diamond. *How could this be?* No shapes were primitive or on a small scale with the first constructions.

Solar systems within ONE held such proof of every type construction imaginable that this particular sector was deemed 'the Beginning.' Scroll dust, r-crystals, art, fossilized books, songs, etc. were some of the discoveries. Consider same could be said for ONE's twin sector, OM.

For that reason, to many cultures, ONE and OM were the most holy and most sacred places in the galaxy. Temple shrines were holy to the point of being forbidden. Research scientists and archeologists were always refused permission to study the oldest of places. According to numerous life forms, here was where everything started and extended outward to fill the 'Pinwheel' of a galaxy. Severe restrictions were on the few permitted to visit *The Center.*

The most famous holy places were the 'haven' retreats on top of the Peace Mountains on a marvelous world simply known as Peace Planet. Lofty peaks were bathed in light through clouds by three white suns. Along the wide sides of the Peace Mountains were entrances to vast tunnel-networks comprised of nesium. Sinewy chambers were halfway up the high peaks and well-known as the 'Halls of Harmony.' After 'first calling,' initiates rose up the 'Halls' but only after learning basic truths. The idea was to learn a 'passage' and then physically climb the passages higher and higher. Knowledge and truth were hiding somewhere at the zenith.

Sanzibar Monastery, in the foothills of the prime Peace Mountain, was the most famous of the 'Executive Schools.' The training could not have been surpassed. The Monastery turned out some of the most successful Executives in the galaxy, so stated the brochures. Not only Chancellery Execs were produced from the Sanzibar 'factory,' but Techs and 'priests' with real skills. The Monastery operated at a tremendous profit in whatever the form of money, assets, wealth, riches, gems and precious goods. The Master of Monks and Execs was thrilled to give Sardon its large percentage. "Hail, the Chancellery!"

There appeared to be no problems whatsoever in the automatic machinations of the main Sanzibar Monastery until one particular initiate named Markus, who had only recently become an Exec, decided to make waves. When news spread of what had occurred, he was called to the Big Office.

The rich Arch Priest dressed in a speckled, scarlet 3-piece suit was not amused or impressed with the antics of his favorite Monk/Exec. Markus entered the large lavish room with a very high dome-ceiling. Religious symbols of Chancellery Authority surrounded them from floor to dome.

Sardon's symbols with the usual red and black colors were observed in every direction.

Markus was nervous yet confident, dressed in his vest minus the suit jacket. He knew exactly why he was summoned to appear before his boss. After only one day on the 33rd floor as an Exec, Markus posted for the entire conclave of priests (no matter what floor they had achieved) *THE NOTE:*

> 29: Wars will be waged of such magnitude that giant planets will be pulverized to pieces and others decimated and rendered lifeless. Militarization of galaxy must proceed on schedule. Sardon collects war-profits secretly and funds opposing sides in military conflicts.

> 30: Zog will appear in our time of need. Zog, the Creator, walks among us and is called Emanuel. Emanuel, the Neo Zog, is here with us. Rejoice! He will pass all Secret Order tests and will be proclaimed as the 'New Zog.' New Zog will return and our campaign will celebrate the 'Second Coming.' When times are darkest with helplessness and despair, there is now New Hope!

> 31: The Emanuel, the embodiment of Zog on 'Earth,' was a necessary creation of the Chancellery. The idea was first invented by Master LeRus DeLandra in 575.24 and implemented only as recently as 803.91. Emanuel is an agent of the Chancellery and can be effectively used to sway high numbers of systems.

> 32: The Chancellery is a necessary model established in the galaxy to propagate to other galaxies in the Cluster for the purpose of dumping the produce of the galaxy into a Black Hole. The Chancellery operates perpetually. Essentially the Machine functions to keep life forms under its influence active and occupied.

33: The Creator of the Chancellery was a Being from a much larger Dimension with the vision to maintain lower systems in a proper and orderly way.

It was only a slip of paper posted in the antechamber entry that anyone in the Sardonic Priesthood could see as they calmly entered the prime rotunda. Markus had, in a sense, cheated or revealed secrets before he should. Now he had to pay the price for his careless recklessness.

"You wrote that?" the wealthy Arch Priest asked with a tone of deep disappointment.

"Yes, Arch Priest...and posted it in the antechamber...to be read, of course, yes, for all to see."

"Why in Zog's name would you *do* that? Do you not understand the concept of *secrets* and why we send our initiate-priests up floor after floor to *slowly* learn what the world can never know?"

"Ah, that's a good one."

"What?" the boss yelled.

"Arch Priest, is not the truth the truth? It is for *all,* not just priests, initiates, Monks and Execs. Truths even belong to yahoos."

"We will *lose* the Monks your way, but not in the way the Chancellery has set up the Order." The high Priest saw that Markus was sincerely interested and wanted to understand. The Master thought this one had a lot of potential. He was sure this one was special. The last thing he expected was such a blatant breaking of protocol from Markus. Markus could be a future leader.

"Please explain, sir."

"Priests move up slowly to digest as much as they can on every individual floor. Each floor is established so you learn the next piece to a complicated and well-meant Sardonic Agenda."

A puzzled expression remained on Markus' face.

The high Priest continued in plain and simple language.

"They won't believe it. It must have *foundation* or it is not consumed, believed, or have any real effect."

"Yes. I did not have too much difficulty with believing, even concerning the earliest times, you know, with all the technology and wars, until I reached the 29th floor, then..."

"We give the priests new information, more parts to the enigma until they can slowly see the whole picture for themselves...what we're trying to do here. We're trying to be *believable*."

"Master," Markus became upset, "but if what I learned yesterday is true, from the 32nd and 33nd floors, then our religious Order, the Priesthood is devoted to the *Devil*. Emanuel is a fraud, a puppet, a golem invention of the Chancellery, deceptive Media and has nothing to do with the Supreme Zog. The Chancellery was *never* a Protectorate for the improvement of life in the galaxy. And we haven't even gotten to the 29th floor, yet, funding galactic wars..."

"We each have our roles in the play. Are you so sure?"

"What? How can you ask that? Who can be sure? We are purposely made to be confused. We are yanked one way and then violently jerked the opposite way. On one floor, we learn the Emanuel is Zog and on the next floor we learn he is a phony, fraud, charlatan. On one floor we discover the awesome, fantastic power and Hope we believe will bring light and love to the world called the Chancellery and then on the last floors, we find the Devil is destroying our world, plunging it down an abyss no one can stop."

"All according to understanding by our program, you cannot understand what is in front of you until you reach the next level. The information *appears* contradictory, but only on that floor. It is only comprehended in its scope when you reach the *next* floor containing an even higher truth. Each pell is set up to fall against the next pell for a cause-and-effect."

"Brainwashing?" Markus asked with a word he created.

"What? I asked you, are you so sure?"

"Of?"

The Arch Priest raised his arms, stood up and

proclaimed, "Everything! How do you know for certain? An even higher floor of understanding could exist beyond 33. Obviously, 32 and 33 wouldn't make any kind of sense until you achieved an even greater level. Yes?"

The new 33rd level priest asked, "Do you know what the ultimate Floor is, Arch Priest? What is the final Truth? Can you see the whole Game?"

The old, clean, successful man in a red business (power) suit only smiled. "I have not attained or been on that floor, yet."

"Sir, the conclave only has 33 floors."

The high Priest smiled, but was worried. He did not want to lose his favorite initiate and Monk. Possibly, he had the answer.

"What will happen to me?" Markus asked for a judgment.

The Arch Priest responded with what he had decided from the very beginning. "You will do community service for one yarn and we will dismiss the class you have contaminated."

"What?"

"The priests will be debriefed and let go, thanks to you." The Arch Priest did not want it this way, but the decision was what he had to do.

Markus shoved his thumb into his chest against the shiny vest. "Because of *me?* They lost their business careers, yarns of training?"

The old Priest looked directly into the eyes of his favorite. "Yes...because of you, son." The new 33rd-level priest was not dismissed from the Sardonic Chancellery 'factory' known as the Sanzibar Monastery or the rotunda. Voluntarily, Markus turned and walked a very long walk out of the building. The old man never saw the younger man again.

Markus began a lonely hermit's life 'off the grid' as a man in hiding. He lived in a small place in a small village very far removed from the Halls of Harmony and the Monastery. He learned to keep the truth to himself and stay away from average yahoos who could never believe what he felt in his Center and knew to be fact.

The next day was '*the day*' in the history of galactic-Media, so far. One announcement was expected: the declaration of Demor and its counterpart Denaris as 'Twin Capitals of the Galaxy.' This was old news. For yarns, the finest examples of sectors had been groomed to seat the Capitals. Houses or Prime Powers in the blue-Spectrum had been developed and staged to be the 'face of the galaxy.' Demor and Denaris would 'house' the known leaders of the highest authorities. Media splashed the news to the multi-corners of the Monopdonow realm.

The second announcement caught mostly everyone in each sector by complete surprise. Media, in all forms, declared:

"The Zog had returned! It was the Second Coming of Zog, the Creator, to the physical plane!"

Who could believe the Zog of ancient legends truly existed? How could the Zog walk among us? The current broadcast was the most viewed telecast in galactic history. The latest figurehead 'President of the Galaxy' was on her knees. 'Emanuel' lowered his head in a gentle bow to receive a golden wreath from her. Emanuel straightened himself and was a glorious sight. Thousands of colorful, cheering admirers surrounded the elaborate Demoran stage. Screens of every shape and size carried the image of 'Zog in the Universe.' He wore a long, white, simple robe. The hood was pulled back to reveal a handsome middle-aged humanoid with neat blonde hair and blue eyes. There was almost a glow of *wealth* around him, he seemed so powerful.

He spoke and the galaxy listened. "My creations, from the largest cosmic whales to the smallest nanites, from Supreme Magicians to least intelligent yahoos, you are mine and I am here to claim you as *mine*. Rejoice! Zog has returned this day!" Cheers and thunderous applause could be heard between the systems. Overwhelming approval and excitement had exploded throughout the Pinwheel 'Web.'

Creatures, big and small and smart and stupid, were

compelled to look at the GTS or Galactic Time Standard at the precise moment (accounting for dilation) and the Big Clock in space just happened to read *1000.00.* Stories, ancient lore, theories, speculations, fears and great anxieties concerned the Time of 1000.00. What would happen? No one knew for certain. End-of-the-Universe cults grew in popularity. Many were sure it was the End and took certain survivalist precautions, thinking that 'space would fall.' Now it was plain as prinolin pie: yarn 1000.00 signaled the Second Coming of the Zog or Neo Zog.

Over and over, again and again, the coming of the 'Wonderful Warrior' Creator was shown on every channel and network. The story *must* have been true. Other news in the entire galaxy did not exist. Only the Zog Story was covered on every Net, Stream and other type of Media. Systems seemed to *want* 'the story.' They watched from every sector, religiously. Or did it only *appear* like the public wanted it because of mass-promotion?

More cheers occurred, more bowing, the New Zog to the masses and the masses to the New Zog. Everyone celebrated. The most famous 'faces' were on hand to pay respects: the President, Vice-President, and their families (plus concubines), D-J, 'The Look,' Roval finalists Genovolva and Rici, Major Media, the band 'N-Rays,' grandson of Jaco Paresi, the Blam, James W. Niiles, Sally Beta-6, Demoran-singer Gildenstein Smith, Hargrove-L, X4K plus many more celebrities. Later, galactic news made tangent-reports and covered various storylines.

Markus, in his small hole in the ground, switched over onto an accompanying story to the prime news of 'Emanuel.' This one concerned an old report of a 'creature' on the planet Mineer who claimed to be 'Zog' a long time ago. The screen displayed an archived film of the thing changing sexes and flying. Then the footage was blacked out.

"That's funny." The former priest, initiate, Monk and an Exec for a day turned off his view-set. In Markus' hole he called a 'home,' the man had a very small following. He allowed one *disciple,* apprentice to visit. His name was Bella. Bella was as poverty-stricken as the former Monk/Exec who appeared nothing like he did one yarn ago.

Markus had significant facial hair. Gone were the colorful, fine suit-vests of priesthood. The man was no longer groomed for silver success. He wore a simple white robe that was slightly dirty. The dwelling was not very clean. Gone were the sweet vehicles, the sweet women and the high social-life. Large incomes Markus earned as an initiate were spent long ago. Nothing came in and Chancellery savings were nearly depleted.

Bella enjoyed Markus' rants. He was always willing to listen to what Markus had to say. Studying 'The Testament' was a usual topic of conversation. Bella allowed Markus to 'teach' him anything from scriptures. Markus' *modern slant* on the ancient Book's stories fascinated the poor visitor. They sat down like they had done for the past yarn.

After blue tea was made and poured in chipped cups, Bella spoke. "The resemblance is truly overwhelming, remarkable. You look just like him."

"Who?"

"Who? Who do you think? Emanuel. There really is a strong resemblance. *You never noticed?* Except for the hairy face, long hair, you know; he's clean-shaven and well-groomed for success, whereas you…"

"Me, what?"

"You're a mess, dear boy, ha."

"Ha." The friends who had very few other friends shared a laugh.

"I would think you could *use* your famous face, you know? Parlay it over networks, at least the Stream? Cut your hair, shave, wear better clothes, suits preferably and you could take advantage of those looks of yours, my friend."

"Now, *why* would I want to do that? I'm hidin' from the fact I look like Him."

Bella asked quickly, "I thought it was because of what you know?"

"That, too." Markus winked and took another sip of blue tea. "What were we discussing last time?"

"Oh, I didn't believe your explanation of the Great Fire. About the first thing recorded history tells us of Peace Planet."

"Yes, the Great Fire. What's the myth? I mean the common belief, what everyone thinks is true, almost everyone?" Markus asked.

"That Zog *had* to set the world's oil fields ablaze and choke a million people to death at the dawn of history."

Markus continued Bella's thoughts of what was considered accepted history. "A natural disaster caused a total loss of crops, which nearly killed off first life on Peace. The few that survived the hardships came back stronger and people flourished once more, right? Zog promised to never destroy the planet by fire again. But that's not what really happened."

"This was in the holy archives, you said, which you saw with your own eyes?"

"Yes, Bel, and much, much more. The truth is, back then, leaders of the First Order decided to *cover-up* history, eliminate the truth so great numbers of Citizens would never know about the past."

"Hard t' believe."

"Incredible files, prehistoric information, record-crystals and technology were destroyed in legendary fires. The planet was far from consumed in flames, yet the important libraries were all destroyed. History was rewritten later. The Chancellery was established to *keep secrets from us* and never to approach a morsel of what is real, honest and true. Not for common people, anyway. True facts were only for high-ranking Executives and Arch Priests, only found buried on conclave floors with the highest altitude and highest number."

"Markus, can you specifically tell me what was goin' on in the distant past? It's like what you said before: *modern* science and *technology* a long, long time ago. If true, why keep it a secret?"

"That accepted history is very, very wrong? Would the Chancellery *admit* we've been taught silliness and ignorance and misinformation? Lose credibility? Schools are not teaching anything close to reality. From lame knowledge we pass on in public schools to absolute lies on the Stream, they cannot reveal NOW that *nothing we're taught is true.*"

"Nothing? You are saying there are too many lies to explain?"

"Yes, Bel, so they pretend there were *never* any lies in the first place, right?"

"Right."

Markus went on with, "Another aspect is War. How much there was of it in the past, early and forgotten days, how widespread it was and of such tremendous magnitude. Why so unmentioned in our schools? What kind of wars, electric wars? We don't know. It's like history has been wiped clean. Prehistoric wars created what were once deserts on Peace. Also, we *built* workers, slaves and armies. It's in the Holy Records! Science even constructed monsters."

Bella asked, "You mean....*machines,* fantasy's auto...er, robots? Yes?"

"No, Bel, something far worse than machines...Bio-machines."

"What's that?"

"Scientists could...could..." Markus wondered if he would be believed and then just laughed. "Ha. I don't care what you think."

"I might believe you," Bella said with an open-eyed expression.

"Okay, okay, sure, ah, our ancestors, in Order Wars, could make humanoids. Make us...or I should say, *copy themselves.* Believe me, Priest?"

Now it was time for Bella to laugh, to be called a 'Priest,' especially in the dirty rags he wore and not a fine suit. "Ha! Sure, why not? Love your Testament stories. Never 'eard anyone preach *that* perspective before." He laughed again.

"We once had the power of a Zog. Dark Tech was called 'forbidden fruit' in The Testament. The Chancellery does not want you to know you have the power of Zog inside you. There's so much to conceal. We really don't need the Order. You see, you wouldn't need the Machine anymore, if you knew the Truth. All right, pick an old story. I'll tell you what I know of it."

"Can I pick two?"

The lonely friends of poverty laughed. Markus was not poor in the sense *he had wisdom.* The hermit was a 'rich man' *in knowledge.* Markus believed in his research, in what he discovered over the yarns in the Sardonic Chancellery and in what he refused to not see.

Bella obliged his mentor who had volumes of inside information. "The story of Ott and the cities of Golem and Sinnoria, ah, also…the battle for the Fortress of Camino."

"Thought sure you were going to say the Arch of Electra." Markus smiled.

"You can throw that in too, sir," Bella stated with a funny smile and bowed to the honorable ex-priest.

"Don't think me the Devil, but the ancient cities of Golem and Sinnoria were not destroyed because the Zog judged them evil and corrupt. Same as with Fort Camino."

"You're saying, The Testament is wrong?"

"Bel, the horrible disasters and mass-killings recorded from prehistory happened. They happened in the real world. They just did not happen the way they tell us. Very old stories are better explained through Science rather than Zog's 'miracles' or 'punishments.' They tell the public sham, bogus stories while they tell the priests a whole different report. Higher priests in the Order are told even larger secrets that lower ones could not imagine."

"You mean how an event might happen, but channels only give us a…a partial truth?"

"Yes, my friend. It is justified by simply saying it's for our own good that we withhold the truth. To The Testament, I often thought the first half refers to extremely extraordinary events…"

"And the second half?" Bella finished his blue tea.

"Largely, unholy additions and subtractions, editing by

unholy creatures, murderers in suits. They laid out Laws for everyone."

"By Zog?"

"Ah, *no,* " Markus corrected his apprentice, disciple and friend. "Zog is not *in* The Testament."

"Huh? *I* never 'eard you say that before. Zog is not *in* the Book? But Zog was *speaking.* It is the Word of Zog!"

"How could it be Zog's doing? Fire and intense heat completely destroyed two large cities in a flash and a million before them. Killing 'women and children' with swords at Camino in the name of Zog? Would a Zog of Love do that?"

"Yeah, but, but they deserved it," Bella defended the actions of The Testament Zog.

"Thousands of children, thousands of girls, the young and the very old, babies who haven't *begun* to live their lives yet were burnt to a crisp or hacked, and they, the very innocent, *deserved* to be killed? Really?"

"Okay, what's the real story?"

Markus did not hesitate and answered, "The first Great Fire not only burned out prehistoric knowledge, but also ended the bio-monsters made by Masters of Science at the time. Later, cities of Golem and Sinnoria were victims of aerial wargames between remnants of earlier technology. The pilots were still fighting with ancient aircraft. Not Zog's vengeance, but *killer-technology* used during WAR…killed the *children and women.* We were caught in the crossfire."

"Markus, what technology? What technology could totally destroy two very large cities? It *had* to be the power of Zog."

"No, m'friend. This involves the Chancellery's true Agenda. It has to do with a terrible Force never witnessed in our time."

"What are you talking about? We were talking about the greatly debated destruction of Testament cities, not the Chancellery."

Markus tied the two together with, "You don't understand. Newest thing on the latest Media reports, this wonderful Power that Emanuel is championing or forcing down our throats, the great, ah, 'Instrument of Peace' it is called? You've heard him rabble on about?"

"Yes, the one they're going to adopt because of its potential for good. Right? *We are particularly interested here on planet Peace.*"

"No, no, dear Bel. It's the *same* power that destroyed the ancient Testament cities. It is a Doomsday Weapon of our own making. It is a BOMB like we have never seen before. Ancient records describe horrors of living under the incredible threat of something called 'atomics.' One blast could equal a million deaths! Strange burns and disfigurements of humanoids and animals after atomic combat, it's what's going to happen to us now, if Emanuel has his way. *He has to be stopped!* It is ancient terrors all over again. A Mega-Atomic can smash a planet!"

"Emanuel is the Zog; we love Emanuel."

"Is he? Do you?" Markus questioned with the bearded face of the Media-Zog. "All right, Camino, here's what happened."

"I read archeologists really discovered the location of old Camino. Massive, stone fort was buried somewhere in the equatorial desert."

Markus once again finished what Bella started. "The fortress had monoliths in the hundreds of sils. Nothing like what the Order can build today...hmmm, similar to the '23 Wonders of the World.' One section of stonework was gone, but about 7/8ths were reasonably intact. What disintegrated 1/8th of the titanic building-blocks?"

"Tell me."

"Your Arch of Electra."

"I didn't know that," Bella confessed. "Where did you get that info? Oh, the archives?"

"No. The Testament. Most people in the High Priesthood do not actually *read* The Testament. They merely pass on myths, the lies, misinterpretations or arguable 'morals' of the stories. The Book says the Arch was indeed pressed right up against the huge fortress blocks. It blew down the walls with electrical power or a super mass of force (tuening)."

"Not the Power of Zog? But I thought the Arch contained or was a container for Zog?"

"No, dear friend. It was a *device*, a bit of that Forbidden Technology, a weapon, a big gun and whoever had the biggest gun…*was Zog*. They won wars with it. Your Power of Zog was really a very deadly weapon."

"Blasphemy," Bella said with subtle emotion. "You've taken Zog *out* of The Testament."

"Science makes The Testament *believable*. This was not why I had to leave the Order. I didn't have to leave. It was in the priesthood where I learned the truth, exactly what I am relaying to you now. I just cannot tell secrets to you without straining credibility and, and maybe our friendship."

"Never," said the faithful disciple of poverty row warmly.

"Also *good* people inside Camino Fortress like those in the two cities burnt to cinders. Women and children, everyone inside the fortress were slaughtered by the 'edge of the sword.' The good ones were defenseless after the great walls fell."

Markus finished his blue tea.

"But your invaders who 'tumbled down the walls' of Camino had the Arch of Zog. Zog *had* to be on their side, yes?"

"No. This was long after the time of its builder, Joses. It was a *machine of electrical warfare* brought into ancient battles and repelled many enemies in the equatorial desert. Madmen seized the Arch of Electra much later, stole it. It was misused like any means of Force in the hands of primitive yahoos. These were not enlightened people acting as Zog's instrument of revenge. They were insane killers drunk on the power the dangerous Arch provided. Many of them were ignorantly electrocuted in victorious celebrations after the slaughters."

"Wow. I didn't realize Zog was such a…*murderer* in recorded history."

"I could go on about flying disks and fantastic war-weapons of the air, reported in The Testament, clear as crystal with rockets ('column') of smoke by day and thruster fire ('pillar') by night."

"Did you ever mention the Janus story, where he was swallowed by a 'large fish' and lived for three days?"

"It wasn't a large fish, of course. I was sure you were getting it by now, Bel. What could hold a person for days under the water?"

"Ah, a boat, ship?"

"Janus was taken aboard a *submarine*. Long ago they could not use our modern words, which did not exist at the time of the writings. If they wrote early history in modern terms, the mysterious cloud of *miracles* would evaporate and we could understand exactly what really happened as modern Citizens." Markus stood up quickly and felt faint. "Ah, uuuhh."

"Hey, you okay?" Bella asked with a worried look on his face.

"I don't know." Markus felt sick and shaky. He received an awful head rush with a visual twist of vertigo. "I...I..."

"Easy, Mark, sit back down. Take it easy." Bella edged closer.

"Maybe I should c-concentrate on something?" His breathing was heavy. The ex-Monk covered his face with his right hand. There was a very slight quiver to his left side.

"Ah, another story, Markus?" Bella asked as he bent over his mentor.

"Yes..." Markus collected himself into a statue-like, sitting pose and said a few last words. "W-woman made from m-man, not done by, by Zog. It was a b-bio operation from s-scientists who took a *cell*...from a man's rib area and c-changed it, no Zog..."

Bella dropped the pretense now that he perceived Markus slowly changing into a frozen state. Markus was nearly catatonic. Bella's real name was 'Jella.' Like Markus, he had a different face one yarn ago. He was a member of the priesthood class that was *dismissed* because of the actions of one particular new Exec. This Exec did not have a beard and he wore beautiful clothes at the time. Then, one day the Exec chose to place *a note* in the conclave's entry-antechamber of the prime rotunda. Thirty-two bright, young and successful initiates were *let go* from the priesthood because of *him!* It was later discovered *Markus was never terminated.*

The sad irony was that Jella never viewed the Note in question. He was never informed by fellow priests of its content regarding the 29th through 33rd floors. After yarns and yarns of study and steadily climbing the success-ladder of the Order, Jella was more than a little upset with Brother Markus.

Jella was perfect for the assignment since he had a deep-rooted hatred for the bearded Emanuel. *Why did they look alike?* He was ordered to keep tabs on the Chancellery's rebellious ex-priest. Jella was Markus' secret 'handler' and regularly reported to Sardonic officials. There was no avoiding Fate. The Testament questions to Markus had nothing to do with curiosity since Jella remembered up to the 28th floor. Questions to Markus over the last yarn of 'the assignment' were designed to answer only one question: 'How dangerous was Markus to the Chancellery and the Agenda?'

"Rigor mortis should be kicking in soon, my old friend. Last yarn seemed like an eternity, last time I take an assignment in 'poverty row' for this long. Could I get assigned to a castle or a Demoran palace? No, sir. Oh, by the way, Markus..."

The former priest moved his eyeballs while the rest of his head remained still.

"That was demagol in your blue tea. You didn't see me put the pill in your cup. You have only yas before you're out cold, man. You are probably wondering why, dear friend."

Markus' eyes spied Jella pull out a wrinkled photo from his torn jacket.

He asked with passion, *"Remember this face,* and his name was *Jella,* Jella! I was in business-class right behind you, brother. You think I didn't *know* what you've been telling me the whole time?"

Markus' eyes met Jella's eyes. He recognized him.

"Why? Certainly, lack of fame and fortune 'off the grid' were preventing you from making waves. We were surprised you didn't go to the Stream or other Media outlets with your, uh, anti-Chancellery messages, your *truths.* As long as you stayed contained and quiet and restricted here, then there was no problem. But you have revealed a plot to *kill our golem-Zog.* Do you hear me? You won't be allowed to do that, sir! Can you hear me *now,* old friend?"

Markus' eyes slowly closed. Was he near death?

Jella continued to talk to himself. "Why would you *want* to kill our New Zog? We love Neo Zog. We love the Chancellery. I could have been one of the High Executives if not for you!"

Markus tried to tell Jella he had no plans to kill the Zog. *Kill the Zog?* It was only a figment the Chancellery planted in his twisted head. The last view Markus had was of enforcer guards, a later version of the Powda'me, broke down the small entrance and destroyed his place. He blacked out.

***

Markus was drugged, catatonic and strapped tightly into a metal chair within a dark underground facility on the Peace Planet. These were not the Halls of Harmony or any 'Haven' retreat. The ex-Exec was a willing subject and had absolutely no objections to his treatment. Jella observed guards, two doctors, two nurses and two makeup artists attended to Markus. The doctors and nurses had duties to perform, while makeup artists worked directly on his face. After a haircut and shave, the subject was compared to photographs of Emanuel. In the next yams, the procedure was completed. Markus was a perfect double for Media's Zog.

***

GST was 1003.32. The 51-yarn Segui Ceremony was broadcasted over networks, the Stream and Media. The

Galactic Fair Jubilee was on and celebrated throughout a myriad of sophisticated systems. Also, the Event coincided with the 7-yarn Bali Celebration. Of course, famous 'stars' attended the elaborate Fair. Each aligned on the 'Blue Road' where crystal recorders were set in place.

Various parades of hovercrafts were filled with the Illuminati of sports, Chancellery politicians, religious Business-elite, famous musicians, artists, medical, scientific and literary greats as well as popular Media 'faces.' The Festival only came around once every 51 yarns and Citizens were thrilled that the Big Event happened in their lifetimes. The overall feeling was exhilaration. Citizens, big and small, wanted to *party* and gave in to wild celebrations.

The Fair was also a time that displayed tributes to fighting soldiers around the star systems. Each sector proudly presented armies, armaments, weaponry, killer-rocket-missiles and killer-drones. Some of the most deadly robotics and fine fighting soldiers that bravely battled on many fronts were on parade. There was too much military 'bad vibes' for numerous Citizens' tastes.

Different colors of different sectors were seen as military banners for War. Some passive Rebel groups remained out there in the cosmos and understood what was 'blowing in the wind' or lurking around the next corner. Peace-lovers were very concerned with more and more tributes to military forces just about everywhere. Why were military influences being slowly seeped into Media programming and the Stream throughout the sectors? Publicly aired games were more and more violence between *The Colors*. Galactic Games resembled wars. Today's Segui Celebration demonstrated little difference between sector ball teams and sector military forces. Both had the same solitary Financier, colors and secret owner of their souls at the summit.

The day's grand festivities were coming to a climax on the ultra-magnificent stage that was the blue Demoran Capital. All eyes in every system were 'teuned' to the final act of the day, which promised to be *beyond belief.*

Who could top the acts of Viper-Women?

After the last hovercrafts in the colorful parade passed by the recorders and carried DJ, 'the Was,' Honey Bubba, Lady Ga, Pooky, Madame Hilton and *Blam* off to their reserved parties, a very special white hovercraft approached crystal monitors on the Blue Road. The Mystery Guest could have been anyone. The bubble-craft was the last vehicle in the day's parade. The pure white craft creeped its way and hovered slightly above the Blue Road. Multi-Media informed Citizens that onboard was 'the most important living Being of all time.'

'Space-Ways' Media announced, "Sitting in the back with the President is the one, the only, *living Zog of the Universe!*"

The galaxy shook. The 'wobble' could be registered. The outpouring of *love,* whether it was artificially-juiced love and chemical-admiration or the real thing, was like a *nuclear explosion.* Cheers went up and nearly every Citizen in the galaxy *felt* a sensation that traveled faster than light because so did the transmission of the signals. If anyone hated the Chancellery with the last fiber of their anarchist being, one still could not help but be moved by the grand spectacle. Most viewers *believed* the next images the recorders recorded.

Jubilation changed to *shock and horror* a few yas after the protective bubble in the bubble-car was raised. In the front section were two respected dignitaries: one from Demor and one from Denaris, plus the State driver of the white hovercraft. The 'President of the Universe' and 'golem-Zog' sat in the raised back section and waved to the multitudes when a powerful red *thaser sliced the President's hand off and also the head of Zog!*

A few planets changed their magnetic polarity. The amount of tears released in one timeless moment was truly 'beyond belief.' Data from different systems told of deaths by 'sheer sadness.' Zog was dead. *Someone killed our Zog!*

Thousands of recorders swiveled to the source of the thaser and an image was caught. Only the silhouette of a figure in black with weapon was captured as it entered a dark 'escape-drone' programmed for orbital retreat. The pod was flung from a roof into high orbit and apparently lost from tracking stations. Also, Demoran security-police squads were slow in response-times. Many pilots said they were 'stricken with grief' and 'not thinking straight' to follow the pod.

There were great outcries to immediately *blame* someone for the death of the Zog. Critics questioned squadron leaders that did not pursue the assassin. Why was the assassin's escape so easy? There should have been more guards. How could such a suspicious vehicle have been allowed to land on that particular roof? Why was the force-field bubble permitted to be raised?

The first news that appeared in no time was the black image of the assassin with a long (assumed) weapon. Thousands recorded the hideous *beheading event* as well as high quality views from professional Media photographers. Soon, networks and the popular Stream channels were flooded with the awful images.

The assassin was a woman.

A female outline was definitely seen as she scrambled into the vehicle with her thaser-rifle. Over and over the images were repeatedly looped on News outlets. Everyone was captivated and glued to screens and monitors. "Was the assassin a male in disguise or a changeling?" were initial questions on female forum discussions.

In the late yams of the blue evening, sectors screamed for vengeance. The general consensus was *everyone wanted justice.* By the early yams of a Demoran blue morning, Media had identified the girl. The assassin was a very well-known Demoran celebrity-singer over galactic channels. No one in the Twin Capitals could conceive that famous singer, Gildenstein Smith, was a notorious Rebel leader.

The next Denaran, Demoran day, Gildenstein Smith and her bios were everywhere: on Media channels, every outlet and even carried on old Under-sets. Documentaries to nude modeling pictures to real feature films the singer/actress had done were aired. It seemed that everyone in the galaxy wanted a piece of the Denaran! Denaris and Demor were shamefully disgraced as Twin Capitals. They would never remove the stigma. Smith's songs sold far more now than they ever had previously. The craze was scrutinizing every last word of her lyrics to see whether they had connections to the Rebels or anarchy or Anti-Chancellerism.

When analysts were done with the 'witch-burning,' they broadcasted a laundry list of code, key or 'activation' lyrics to watch for such as *unite, organize, liberty, democracy, republica, overthrow, love, freedom, together, rights, fight, onward, strike, ignite, our will* and *our way.*

The militaries of the galaxy had a face and had a name to the Enemy. Time-jumps and Wormhole rides were taken by alien posses in search of the head of Gildenstein Smith. Galactic fame and glory would be heaped upon the bounty-hunter who brought in Smith's pretty head.

When a grainy/rough copy of Gildenstein in combat gear at a Rebel meeting was secretly recorded and Stream-aired, *the Canto bear really hit the turbine!* She spoke of something called 'Atomic Bombs,' hideous and destructive technologies banned in the late-early period. Smith revealed plans to *completely pulverize to atoms any planet that got in her way.*

My Zog!

Madness consumed the Pinwheel Galaxy. Military forces which had been primed on the precipice of all-out attack, exercised their prerogatives and made war. Wars were waged about the Zog, over the Zog, under the Zog, through the Zog, in the name of the Zog, but, mainly it was because of the Death of what so many systems perceived as…*their Zog.*

Armies and space-fighting corps did not unite to seek out and destroy the Gildenstein girl together. The mad affair was an insane free-for-all hunt for the killer of the Zog. Opposing forces from opposing colors and systems attacked each other's armies in blind rage (last thing 'their Zog' wanted).

More questions on networks and Streams were asked.

"Who was behind the girl? What organization or system did she represent? What was her motivation, intention? What statement was she trying to make? Was she only a publicity seeker? Who financed her? Where did she get her weapon and vehicle?" The weapon and escape-drone were state-of-the-art and would be the envy of the Za'ni Continuum. The most violent of Terror-Rebel groups ('the Light') in the *Benis Pol Sector* was identified in the Smith-meeting film. It was the most viewed recording since the Death of Zog. Was the hideout of Zog-killer, Gildenstein Smith, located in the Benis Pol Territory of space?

Rumors spread like wildfire on fueleen. Networks, Streams and other channels fed the cosmic chaos and suggested two very important points that were volleyed back and forth endlessly on discussion forums. Number One: Benis Pol Sector was known for a high population of men. Genetic scientists believe the turquoise vibration of its stars or the color range of suns created a predilection for male births among life forms that had males and females. Rebels were mainly male and organized in Benis Pol. (Oddly Benis' close-color counterpart, Anther Pol and home of Vipers, produced much more female births). Network broadcasts implied Rebels were responsible for the assassination of 'Zog in the Universe.' The galaxy was told the ultimate assassin hid in the Benis Pol Sector.

***

In a very dark chamber of a specially-constructed medical facility below the Halls of Majestic Taj, the Devil was dying. It was taking forever. The Beast remained in a prone position of the existence-supporting device. The black contraption had new, vital attachment-accessories connected. The dark mechanism breathed and made a frightening, loud 'chok' sound every half ya. Only more frightening sounds were the few harsh words the Sardon rarely uttered. The thing was even older and more wrinkled with more pronounced veins on top of its horizontal skull. It had a very vile odor. Smoke floated in the room.

The other person in the dank chamber stepped into a lit portion of the room. The humanoid could only now be recognized. It was the fake Zog, not Markus the look-alike who was beheaded, but Emanuel: the Media's Second Coming. He was smoking *blip.* He wore normal clothes and had a little facial hair. He looked a bit greasy or shady. He resembled a tourist gambler at Delphino. Emanuel was alive, but, of course, there was never an Emanuel. He was a hoax. The Markus clone who gently stroked the Chancellor's veins was actually Willard Price-4, the fourth replicant in the Sardon's ancient plan to institute a phony stand-in for Zog. Now, they have created the perfect martyr and the perfect enemy.

Willard P-4 finished smoking the blip and felt much, much better. The clone was relaxed and happy to serve the Master of Masters because he was well paid.

After Willard Price-4 showed his vid-files and reported the latest to the fragment of a Sardon, he asked, "What do you think?" He knew not to take much of the Sardon's time. He also could not stand the stench.

In a ya, it spoke. "V-very...g-good."

Willard, the phony Zog that did not die, laughed at the Sardon's two words of description about the entire Machine ('Monster') it created.

In a moment, the Devil wrestled up enough energy to make another statement. Willard 'New Zog' heard:

"W-Wait...t-till...you...c-come...b-b-b-b-back..."

Will laughed. "Ha, ha! Oh, can't wait to see the looks on their little faces. One last thing, sir. A lady wanted me to ask you, how long, you think, *will the Chancellery last* after, I mean, how long will it go on, I guess what she was asking: How long before, uh...it collapses?" The small pawn in the Game took a breath. "I thought it would last 1000 yarns, at least."

The dying Beast answered the question with precise accuracy. "100..."

Willard thought the Sardon was saying, "100,000 yarns."

"…Yarns...*ugh,*" the Sardonic Creature said perfectly and then lapsed into its *sleep mode*.

'chok.'

The slick gambler, who resembled a very sleazy golem-Zog, wondered about the words spoken by the sleeping Devil as he stood over it. "Only 100 yarns?"

Chapter Three

PLAN FOR AN INFINITE SARDON
STATE AND THE CREATION OF
THE 'dylar'

The known intelligentsia of the galaxy mourned the passing, death and 'ascendance to a higher plane' of the Zog. For three straight Demoran days, parades of funeral processions rolled and hovered by exactly as they did in celebrating the *life* of the Zog, only darker colors were chosen. Faces were morose. Two-eyed, multi-eyed and single-eyed creatures shed tears. Faithful fans still could not believe his light went out and the beautiful Zog of peace was no more. Creatures throughout the systems learned more about the humanoid called *Emanuel* with continuous Streamed documentaries. Few understood that what they had experienced in the Neo Zog was a sham from the very beginning.

In other connected Media outlets, popular debates flared that concerned large questions. "How could Zog be dead or how was it that a Supreme Being *Avatar* of the Highest Authority could be killed?"

Religious scholars, scientific experts and Mystics tackled tough questions in the aftermath of 'the most tragic single death in the galaxy.' Which pundits were close to the truth? *Why* did it happen? Did Zog *allow* itself to die in the physical world? For what purpose had the tragedy happened? What Fate directed universal events? Why did everyone have to see and record such a horrible blow to our life-Centers?

The prime public funeral that celebrated 'Emanuel's Life and Legacy' took place on a weird Demoran stage or shrine not far from the bloody event of three days earlier. Blood of Emanuel was taken off streets by devotees in the belief it contained magical powers. Life forms from the highest of Orders paid tribute and teuned-in one way or another. Emanuel's Funeral was another moment in galactic history where *the world watched.*

The new presence of extremely powerful *females,* who were under some branch of 'Vipers,' conducted filibuster after filibuster on what should be done and *what was Emanuel's legacy?* Women spoke more than the men or asexual aliens. The elite wondered what the Vipers had over the Chancellery to dominate the day's festivities. Lady-soldiers and their military presence were draped in the backdrop. Who knew the 'Girls' prayed to the Zog? Speeches were given and amplified over the course of the big day and into the Demoran evening. The World Broadcast went out to the 24 sectors without time-lag. Much of the *talk* concerned the future, Zog's legacy, what could be done and that Zog's pure 'Instrument of Peace' should be fully developed and utilized.

Tributes were relentless. Everyone wanted a chance to say what the Zog meant to them. Yahoos cried uncontrollably. Media permitted respected humanoids to the youngest of entities to 'speak from their Center' and honor what was once the Living Zog. Huge numbers of galactic Citizens had come from the 24 sectors and heard final speeches. Darkness slowly faded in and changed the deep blue sky to black.

An old Chancellery member was at the main broadcast booth when a courier ran to the official administrator and Master of Funeral festivities. The courier handed the elder a flash-drive. They plugged it into the appropriate slot and somber background music stopped. One more time, the galaxy viewed strange events. Many psychics felt a *rush* before it happened.

Directly over the shrine built in His name and the focus of viewing Citizens in the Monopdonowian Pinwheel, there was blue light. The small ball of light expanded to a wider sphere of amorphous rays more than 10 bars in diameter. Blue light became intensely bright and almost hurt the eyes of Citizens in the vicinity. When the light faded, within the circular after-image, there was none other than:

Emanuel...*the Zog returned!*

A diffused halo of blue light not seen before closely surrounded the tall, standing figure wearing a white robe. The galaxy was not left in mourning. Chancellery and Order elite as well as District leaders of Viper-Women had engaged their *secret plan* to bring the (fake) messiah back. The robotic puppet, Straw-man, Scarecrow-golum of a Neo Zog was now in place and shimmered in hazy blue light. Images of 'resurrected Zog' burst on every Media! He had not only returned to the Universe from ancient times, He had conquered Death in modern times and was with us again.

Observers experienced utter joy, ecstasy, love, magical rapture to the gates of Nirvana and *more*. Vast populations of teuned-in Citizens saw light in the darkness, hope for the future and a 'New Dawn for a New Day.' Tomorrow was not going to be bleak in a galaxy filled with needless wars. Chancellery officials and Viper-Ladies would unite, merge, make peace and love would reign over the sectors.

Anyway, that was what Citizens were led to believe.

A few Rebels and seers in the shadows did not trust the illusion they sensed. Some knew they stood in the shade of deception. Only a relative handful of Citizens understood they were *being played.* But what was the ultimate purpose, agenda or Phantom Ghost in the Machine? What were 'they' covertly cooking up for the galaxy to swallow? What was next?

The Neo Zog who had returned from the dead did not do interviews. After that fateful Demoran evening, the new Emanuel was not seen. He did not make public speeches. Many assumed or were made to assume the messiah went into 'seclusion' so that no more tragic incidents or attempts at tragic incidents would occur and be broadcasted.

Followers of the Neo Zog were updated group-leftovers from old times of the 'Followers of Sardon.' Corporate-religious orders also known as the 'Followers' theorized another solution. "Where was the Resurrected Neo Zog? Why did He not speak? Why not greet a galaxy that adored, loved and desired to be *One* with its Creator?" Most creatures of Mainstream suns were willing to follow the Neo Zog anywhere. Why not address the masses? The Followers strongly speculated that the Holy One returned to Nirvana and now sat on a 'celestial throne' of a much larger dimension beyond our microscopic comprehension.

Neo Zog transmuted and disappeared from memory in time. After ages had passed, there was generally no more Zog in the Universe. The experience dissolved into Time's fabric and most assuredly, would reincarnate in one form or another in the distant tomorrow.

***

Reorganization was the order of the day for post-Neo Zog and a Sardon who remained comatose. Its device no longer churned the Wealth of the galaxy at maximum efficiency. Profits were down, drastically. Many officials in-the-know or within Ralia's Inner Circle, male and female, thought the Sardon's bad health reflected lower revenues. Was the Money-Machine-Monster dying because the Beast was dying?

The mistake was an easy one to make. There was an overall Creature-phantom only seen by a few attendants. Reports were of a grisly statue-like figure inside an even larger mega-sustainer. It did not communicate, but it *controlled.* And the only important factor was *control.*

Majority of the elite Chancellery members along with the most prestigious of Vipers wanted Sardon dead and gone. They wanted to 'milk' the galaxy on their own terms without the last vestiges of an ancient Chancellery. The Women wanted to finally stake the Beast in its Center and claim at least 51% of everything in their new version of power, molded in their image. Females were definitely the wave of the future.

The sleeping Sardon still had powers. It could not be approached unless it allowed it. The Beast continued to keep its invisible hands on the controls within 100 billion mainframes throughout 24 sectors. The Creature from Hensi rode a 'Pale Horse' to the very bitter end of a snake trail. The end was coming. A cycle approached over the horizon with the thunder of a thousand screaming ghost-riders. There must be change to a new wave or a *new medium of exchange. A New Order must be installed.*

The medium must absolutely *rule* and be adopted by every sector boss. The medium would be packaged and sold as 'Galactic Stability' in the aftermath of such recent, universal upheavals. Was the Chancellery in charge or was it a regime of the past that could disintegrate to dust? Should a new charter-empire be drafted? No one living and moving in the material world knew what to do. But a hardly-living, stationary, near dead, Dragmar-Beast knew exactly what to do. Another *plan* was put into effect and only the head of the Vidor understood.

Conflagrations such as old 'fayds' resurfaced. Civil wars inside star systems as well as between systems created breeding grounds for War. Conflicts, hostilities and attacks were on the rise. More Wars of Worlds tended to happen in an extremely confusing period of uncertainty and Chancellery instability.

Necessary *changes* occurred in the shape of a new *word* that was first whispered over Galactic channels in 1055.55 GST. That word which we were told was synonymous with 'Security' was the word 'dylar.' What was a dylar? In print, it was never written with a capital letter in the beginning or in large-case letters, always small-case. On rare occasions, 'dylars' were abbreviated to 'd.' Financial pundits further speculated that a 'dylar' and its common short-term 'd.' did not refer to the same thing. Other famous faces thought pundits who believed such notions sounded like they came from Planet Zetag.

Every stitch of riches could be exchanged for the dylar anywhere in the galaxy. There was a galactic Time reference, a standard calendar, a standard number system, language and common Media throughout the 24 sectors. Here was a quantum leap in 'Business for the general improvement of Galactic Economy.'

The dylar represented Pinwheel trade like it had never seen before. There were no more transfer-exchanges into various native currencies used on different planets. Anything could be exchanged, traded, bartered for the dylar: gems, precious minerals, alien types of money and valuables, any items, machines, devices, products, concepts, programs and projects with a functional value could be taken to exchange-centers for dylars. Exchange-centers for dylars were everywhere, more outlets than 'Stardusters' and soon on every civilized planet. The dylars could be used in every sophisticated sun system of the Pinwheel.

The oldest of elite Chancellery members as well as the (50%) Rule of Viper-Women went along with the 'New Wave.' Even the secret-center of Ralia, still the cloaked financial Capital and Control of the Galaxy, adopted the dylar. From now on, the decision was final and the galaxy was forced to accept a Monetary Standard for its salvation. The dylar passed 7-6 and yet there was never a Citizen's doubt of a Sardonic Puppet-Master who pulled the strings.

Prosperity slowly took hold and flourished in the systems. Fayds from civil wars to wars in interstellar battle zones lessened to almost nil. Tempers cooled and the general *heat* simmered to a remarkable mellowness. A New Confidence in business sprouted and Media told the galaxy what made it all possible: the new Galactic Money.

['Monopdonow Game' coins are small red, green and yellow plastic chips and nothing like real dylar denominations with security-computer-coding].

A dylar was only found in three forms and colors. A red dylar had six points (symbolized connection of two holy triangles, yin-yang, light/dark) and was worth a million dylars. A green dylar was six-sided (symbolized nature or natural universe) and was worth a quarter million dylars. A yellow dylar was five-sided (symbolized Life) and was worth a hundred thousand dylars.

The New Exchange was impossible to copy. Counterfeiters tried and failed every time. The Medium was an 'electrical blob' of magnetic energy solidified into a harmless neutral substance. Even if the most skilled techs could recreate the process, production left a fine signature. Computer circuitry finalized the procedure and secured the signature in a magnetic stasis. Common scanners at every reputable place of business easily displayed the validity of dylars. Such security precautions further made the dylar the ideal Medium.

Profits were way up. A time of peace or another echo of ceasefires forced life forms to engage in other activities such as accumulating great fortunes. Business deals, corporate mergers, acquisitions, takeovers, sales and buyouts on a planetary and stellar scale made Citizens very rich. Financial empires were built overnight.

Viper networks and channels expressed propaganda that dylars were a 'female creation.' Women broadcasted that they were the ones responsible for the new era of prosperity and extreme wealth. Many sectors believed Viper lies as they had believed Chancellery lies in the past. Whole civilizations honored the Women and joined them in their cause/fight/movement and philosophy. Nothing was farther from the truth. They were compelled, without choice, to accept the New Exchange because of a lone Sardon.

Times of peace and happiness were usually a charade, a mask, a façade, a *false flag* to what really lurked behind the scenes. Peace was artificial, for the most part. Tranquility and moments of non-fighting were fabricated in the same manner as its opposite was artificially produced.

Sleeping Sardon, who certainly was not sleeping, had a Plan B. First was the introduction and total acceptance of the dylar. Then later, when all was virtually quiet among the stars, when no one would suspect an end to the *good times* and when everything was brightest...

The VIPER would strike!

Women would not initially attack or stir the Cauldron of War. No, they would whisper 'peace' in the name of Zog: "What Zog would have wanted. His hope and legacy for the future." Women would present to the galaxy Zog's IOP, the 'Instrument of Peace.' It would end War. There could be no wars with the development of the IOP. Zog's Instrument of Peace would insure a state of no-war, a Zero Tolerance to major system conflicts. The IOP would maintain the current prosperity the sectors had been experiencing. Vipers' IOP would finally bring a lasting peace.

Old Chancellery sources and Viper-Women sources reported the overwhelming passing of the IOP. Misled life forms in the sectors supported the Peace Instrument as a final tribute to the Zog. Pre-programmed Occult officials, male and female, voted 13-0.

What the Vipers had developed and the reason they *waltzed* into Ralia's Chancellery and took charge, concerned the 'Instrument of Peace.' Of course, the IOP was *not* an Instrument of Peace. The IOP was *leverage*. It was physical power males had not dared develop because of the consequences. What could happen if the Power was not controlled? What would happen if the molecular annihilations did not stop?

The Top Secret (remnant from the First Reich) was shelved for the moment and taken off the table. Yarns would pass before Plan B could actually be instituted and applied. For now, Media lied during this calm period and worked its *magick.* Lies could make the most hideous of monsters appear like radiant beauty queens and the answers to all our dreams.

The Vipers secured 51% control. The Ladies were *running the show!* The VW *appeared* to be running the show from each 'District-lodge' leader right up to elite Ladies now stationed on Ralia. In truth, the Girls were only unaware minions of the Head Snake who had been the boss all along.

YARNS EARLIER

The former Chief Agent Trask landed his Shrike on Mineer because of a mission completely different than his ordered mission of a lifetime ago, when he first met the real 'Zog in the Universe.' He was a very different person then. After he secured the ship, he exited. He appeared to know where he was going. Cal looked at the Time and it was 999.99. *Ha!*

He remained in his red jumpsuit from the Order and walked through fantastic shapes of Mineeran topography. The strange green terrain was very different than the violet tones of

Ralia or his home planet. *Beautiful.* Cal could enjoy the beauty of nature and the universe now.

He thought of that nearly naked race of natural Ralians, those innocent 'gift-bearers' who were first murdered by the skulking Sardon. Cal asked himself, "Why are images of the tribal leader and others with the blue neck-rings so clear?" Then he remembered and said aloud, "That's right, they were *humans*, ha, originally from space and crashed on a planet that should not have been physical to them. How odd."

Cal continued to walk toward his Fate. He again spoke to himself. *"Not natives of Ralia,* lost in space and ha, gave up high technology and reverted back to the wild as the story goes...hmmm."

After he followed a quasi-path and swerved to avoid a Mineeran tree, old Cal confronted the tribal leader... He thought he was *dreaming,* again.

"You told me this was a dream, and it was. I woke up. Is that what's going to happen, I'll wake up now?"

The scantily-clad man spoke perfect Lebritz. He did not project an atmosphere of primitiveness in any way. He was articulate and wore the neck-ring, which was seen unlit and in a different light. "This is not a dream," stated the one who only appeared as a simple tribesman.

"Then, what are you doing here if this is real?"

"We've relocated," the tanned human said sincerely.

Cal laughed and had to ask, "Your thousands and thousands of people, which I do not see...came here in spaceships?"

"No."

Cal burst out with bigger laughs. "Ha, ha, ha! I love this. I'll play along. This is real, all right. Then master tribesman, I do not know your name."

"It's Emanuel."

Caladrian was dumbfounded. His psychic senses went haywire. He was not sure of the curiosity in the name 'Emanuel.' (At this moment in Time, fake-Zog had not yet made his first appearance). Cal scratched his head. The former

Agent could not figure out his immediate predicament and he was a good detective. He dropped it. He switched back to the subject of the natives' mode of travel. "So, how did you and your people get here?"

The tribesman smiled before he answered, "We have our means. We can *think* our way here. My people have learned the ability…and the capability is available to everyone."

"Everyone?"

"Yes."

Cal realized their conversation was about over. He felt the need to move on and continue his Mineeran 'Path of Destiny.' Maybe the man's purpose was to give the former Agent a 'kick to his Center' and something to think about. He thought up another question. "All right, here's one. Why?"

"Why?"

"Why would you and yours relocate? Why would you *want* to mysteriously come here? Ralia is prettier, even more scenic and spectacular than Mineer, ah, that is, if you do not consider the evil infestation on Ralia?"

"Ralia is not safe," the tribesman spoke with confidence about his old world.

"What do you mean, sir?"

"The Occult Chancellery will no longer be hidden from the rest of the galaxy."

Cal believed him and excitedly asked, "Rebels against the Order will finally discover the Devil's lair and exterminate?"

"No. Hmm, not exactly," the former captain, now enlightened tribesman, responded. "Men and Women who believe they are in control of the Monster, the Machine, are *not* in charge." His tanned, healthy face smiled a smile that was not funny. He became very distressed. "They have voted for a means that will bring about the end of Ralia and far, far more." He cried. The tribesman cried more for the memory of the violet planet that existed now but not in the future. Fate was heartless enough to plant an evil seed in a purple garden the captain loved. Now the man had the power to see into the future. Tomorrow, *Ralia would be obliterated.*

Cal asked another question with hope in his two hearts. Does that mean a shut-down of the Machine, an end to the Monster's tyranny?"

After a long silence and sadness, they both said, "No."

The former captain tilted his head. "You know as well as I do, sir, the Machine was made to last long beyond the Death of the Sardon. The Monster will live and feed for yarns and yarns after the Beast returns to the Black Hole it came from. One last thing to ponder; the Beast killed *none* of my people."

Cal was stunned. He found it difficult to process the new information. Nothing more needed to be said or was supposed to be said. The depressed tribesman-captain was gone. He had simply *thought* his way back to where his people were staying on their new home, which was really their old home.

Cal marched on the quasi-path once more. A type of 'magnet' drew him closer to his final goal. Along the journey he wondered about what Zog told him ages ago when they first met. His people here on Mineer were peaceful and 'respected his wishes.' They left him alone. Were Mineerans the displaced Ralian humans who could *think* to other planets?

"Shocker if that were true, *damn time.*" He did not mean the GST, although Cal looked at his G-watch. It read: 999.99. "Oh, the famous prediction, holocaust, disaster or, uh, great glory, huh. Something weird will happen soon, for sure. Wonder what?"

Cal Trask felt it in his bones. His destiny and future stood directly behind the small hill up in front of him. He went over it.

God remained in REM sleep.

THE PRESENT

The dylar ruled a galactic empire and tightly connected life forms within its 'Web' of dark influence. Media Magic produced the necessary illusions. What was black was viewed as white. What was bad was viewed as good. Only handfuls of Anti-Order Rebels still had some type of organization or power. Anarchists had no leverage over galactic government-bosses, Order officials or the VW. *Revolution was dead.*

The dylar stabilized Galactic Economy. The dylar, reds, greens, and yellows, appeared to solidify the greater Pinwheel Community into one progressive Business. Who could complain? Where was evidence that (system) State-governments were corrupt? Wormholes, Pan Movers, WN transports ran precisely 'on time' and paved the way for mega-commerce opportunities. Generally, everything functioned at its peak efficiency. *The dylars were happy.* But, there were always those 'contraries' who challenged the status quo.

The Rebels, as well as the New States, also employed psychics. What would the future hold for anarchists and the State of the Revolution? In current times of stability, peace and prosperity, Rebel-Mystic seers saw a future so horrible it could not be accurately described. Tomorrow's horrors were extraordinary and terribly extreme. Sheer chaos and Hensi was *felt* among the most talented, telepathic "Sensitives.' The truth of what would happen in the near future was unavoidable. It was also unspeakable and unbelievable. Could anything be done to change inevitable Fate? Would Life in the galaxy ever recover?

Contemporary times were *'swinging'* times with riches extravagantly abundant and spent. The wealthy and the mega-Wealthy believed it would last forever. How could empires be toppled if they were super-united and powerful as one? Twenty-four sectors spoke as one single voice over Media. There was galactic solidarity. Life was good; life forms were content, complacent and ripe to be needlessly *raped over again.*

For the most part and through the sectors, unions were well-intentioned organizations that locally functioned for positive causes. Unlike Rebels in hiding, there were Unions out in the open. Unions and attached Guilds from every Quadrant supported the (State) system-governments in current times of opulence. Soon, everything would *change.* The Cosmic Pendulum would, one more time, swing from financial freedom and order to complete chaos, war and violent destructions that could disintegrate whole solar systems.

The Sardon's overall Agenda proceeded according to *plan* exactly as the Creature had foreseen. Over the horizon, tomorrow, on a New Day with a New Dawn, there would be an even mightier push, Plan B. First, was the dylar, and second, would be Zog's 'Instrument of Peace.'

The end of the Sardon in the physical realm, last of its ancient kind, was also on the horizon. It was proud of what it had achieved: a living, breathing, self-sustaining Vampire magnetically attracting every scrap of wealth from every direction and automatically dumping the vast, massive, astronomical fortune of the Chancellery/Order down a mini-Black Hole. Every molecule of material wealth was purposely converted to dylars to be disposed of *quicker.*

The Sardon's real reason for the creation of the dylar was because the mass-Wealth of the Order's protected coffers (storehouses) could not drain fast enough. Inconsistent, irregular files and variations of valuables slowed down the process-stream (through tubes) of evaporating goods into the mini-Black Hole. Flow of material needed to be forced down the disintegration chamber's mouth at a quicker rate. Deadly and final sucking of the homemade Black Hole's event horizon could be accelerated if all was universally converted into 6-pointed shapes, 6-sided shapes and 5-sided shapes. Fast-flowing tubes operated at a much hyper degree thanks to the invention of the dylar and its uniformity through the coffer-conduits. Because of galactic acceptance of dylars (as hope and salvation), the Beast could now disintegrate the Bank and all assets at a much faster rate. The Monopdonowian Pinwheel rushed to a *financial collapse even quicker.*

The Demon in its coma, only for a moment and it was unsure exactly *why,* thought of a reality very different. The Sardon imagined an opposite Universe. Suns carried the *negative* charge and it was the orbiting, electrical planets that had the positive charge. *Life on each orbiting electron (planet) was positive while the nuclear nucleus (sun) was negative.*

Everything generally was good and free and clean from traces of dark villainy. Should or *could* the opposite dimension take over? Would + change to – and minus change to positive? Within the Beast's slumber, it froze in fear even more than its motionless carcass indicated.

The fear was *everything that it created would crumble to nothing. Everything would have been for nothing.* There had to be a perpetual institution that would conquer Time and remain. There had to be a type of 'Continuum' or ideal Life in the Universe that sustained its perfection. Truth was, in the far future, every accomplishment of angels and devils would disappear. *Change over time* would destroy the grandest of Empires. *Control* would eventually come to an end. Something unknown would enter as a replacement. The replacement Mechanism would also have a short existence, until Time, once again, turned it into a different thing entirely.

The comatose Vidor-Dragmar thought of another opposite that the creature normally would never consider even for the shortest of nanu-yas. It, insanely, thought of *yes* instead of *no*. It thought mad thoughts of *giving* and *not taking*. It thought of *light* and *not dark*. It thought of *white* and *not black.* The Beast actually dreamed the other polarity of a *White Hole Giver* and not a *Black Hole Consumer!* Could the Universe be turned around and placed on its head? Could everything be reversed? What if the 'Arrow' or electrical current went the other way? What if everything was a free-flowing, bright and eternal *fountain* of knowledge instead of a spherical vacuum of blackness pulling everything in around it?

The near-dead Beast could destroy its own Machine-Monster if it wanted to and turn the blood-sucking, life-sucking Zombie inside out. Its handiwork could be a Horn-O-Plenty, a cornucopia of abundance *given* to the rest of the galaxy in Sardon's Redemption. Imagine a gushing reservoir of lavish Wealth, valuables (not dylars) spitting fortunes of endless profits in a cosmic stream *out* for everyone. "Here, take, we have far more than enough. Tell others to come and grab their fill of our mountains of gold, riches and wealth of every kind!"

A world of giving, instead of selling, was the scary universe the Ultimate Accountant dreaded: cashless societies, dylarless societies. The positive, Socialist concept did not stand in old Galaxy L-MN200 and it would not exist in the New Pinwheel a few ages later during the Second Reich. Time would change everything. The Beast had only a few more thoughts and then nothing would exist but its *machines.*

Machines would become a very important key to future events and the end-game or final resolution for the Continuum. The Sardon was but a machine at its Center. It 'lived' inside important Mainframes and Wadlo-chips of every sector. The Beast-thing was entrenched within circuitry and could affect network computer-devices remotely over the distance of light-yarns.

Machines, some said, were the real reason for the end of future's famous '100-Yarn War.' Could mastering machines have been the prime factor? The truth may not reside in the 'Fields of Fanguard' or have anything to do with the colorful planet of 'Eightoids' called Aret. Some speculated that what *reversed charges* was the 'Ghost' in the Machine. But the Ghost was supposed to be the sole Sardon and nothing else. How could a great, positive Movement of Peace and Love be attributed to the Phantom/Beast/Devil or a cold, heartless, souless Machine?

Only machines, and not living organisms or bio-machines, would become the extensions of the Sardon after its complete departure from the physical plane. In the past, its colorless hand easily fit mechanical 'gloves' on every level of circuitry and Wadlo-chip from every system. Icy, hard machines were the Sardon's internal nature. The Beast made certain that a Machine-Mind, a 'Cybernetic-Consciousness,' would take charge upon its death. The living, mechanical golem would seamlessly assume control when the Sardon was no more. The Monster will continue.

One of the last crumbs of tribute from the pit of the Sleeping Beast was paid to the Viper-Women. Ah, the Lady Man-Haters from Hensi played their roles in the orchestration exquisitely. Women would set the stage for such clean, White destruction of whole star systems in Act II. The Pandras and Bev-greens would finally 'open the door' or 'take a bite of the melo.' Hounds from Hensi-fire would burst through and terror would reign supreme. Wars would, again, be something for 'living-money' *to do.* They needed to be consumed and were more than willing to volunteer for consummation.

The Sardon returned to the thought of its *holy dylar.* "What an inspiration!" it would have said if it could have spoken. The Pinwheel's controls could have been lost long ago if not for the little invention of the 'Galactic Monetary Standard.'

Praise the GMS! Praise the GMS!

More final ramblings circulated in the Center of the frozen Beast located in the lower, damp, dark cellars below Taj. The black device that sustained it roared with liquid electricity in loud, repetitive cycles.

'chok.'

If they only knew of the Larger Game and what dylars really were!

There was another wild, almost miraculous, notion that spun in the one cog left of the Sardon's brain. The thought was a phenomenal way for the Beast to Win, *to win everything,* to tilt the scales to the Negative Side for infinity. It once had a Plan for the 'Infinite Sardonic State,' but it never actually conceived the feasibility of it, of pulling off the 'Master-Plan of Deception.' Inside the coma, the creature realized it *could* triumph. Apparatus in the 24 sectors could do the impossible.

There did not have to be a 50% light and 50% dark. It could win 51%. There did not have to be an equal yin-yang. It could win an unbalanced, decisive victory. It could have what it desired most: a perfect, dark State that ran forever exactly as it envisioned without the slightest possibility of change. If other Sardons existed, they would be so proud.

Yes. The Beast was certain it could create the future-Continuum that androids and other machines could constantly regenerate. If Zog could conquer Death, then the Anti-Zog could master Life. It could *mechanically* continue inside a 'Continuum.' The Monopdonowian Galaxy could transmute into an unchanging, eternal Continuum. But what kind of life-system would the galaxy become, positive, negative? Life would have no choice. The future would depend on the cold calculations of cybernetic-minds. Decisions that affect universes would spring forth from Machine-Centers. Artificial-life would rule and *must rule.* Self-sustaining machine-intelligences maintained the 'cosmos quo.'

Future machine-descendants of what the Sardon had wrought would seal permanence to the Larger System. Would compassionless, motorized minions preserve a positive or negative Fate for all time? Tomorrow would not be under the control of living creatures, but run by the *clockwork efficiency of a self-sustaining Machine.* The Sardon was going to bet on the mechanical Dark Side, the negative, as opposed to positive Light.

The 'Plan for an Infinite Sardonic State' was in perfect place. Machines would continue the Monster and monsters would continue the Machine. Now the Beast could die with a smile on its evil, colorless face.

The Sardon, in all honesty, regretted dying. It regretted not being able to materially see the *worlds collide into brilliant infernos* in the near future. It wanted to see 'World's End' during the Middle Ages, badly. But its time was about up and it could only dream of glorious annihilations its spawn would later produce. "Everything Ends." Even for a Sardon.

The Sardon was very pleased with itself and in everything it had done so far. The Creature from a Black Hole took comfort that the Pinwheel was set to *blow* in what would be called the galaxy's 'Dark Days.' Days to come would be even darker. Ralia, home of the Old Chancellery, would be exposed, open to attack and utterly obliterated according to 'the Plan' or 'Agenda.' The incredible New Age that single event would cause: "Oh, such *beautiful Death.*"

Thanks to the Beast's power, control, influence and manipulation of the Viper-Women, overwhelming mega-destructions would be unleashed the likes of which the galaxy had never known before, even *more* destructive than the forgotten First Reich's Atomic Age!

"The Canto bear was ready to hit the turbine!"

The mega-sustainer of the Beast was *beamed* out of a bleak Taj cellar and cast millions of light-yarns away, to the moonless planet Mineer.

Humans had *wished it so.*

The Beast's last remnants were flung to future-Mineer by lowly humans. It had no control of its last remains.

Chapter Four

DEATH OF SARDON - DEATH OF ZOG

THE CHANCELLOR FINALLY DIED!

When it was apparent to the inheritors of Majestic Taj that the Demon was gone and not returning to Ralia, Viper-Women and whatever male officials remained invariably had one question on their minds.

"How do we shut it down?"

***

Caladrian walked what *was* a *quasi* path on Mineer. The natural road up and over the hill became more distinct. The path became wider and more defined through green grass and under blue skies. Soon, the path was golden. Pressing onward, he continued his trek to the crest then he saw answers.

Cal ran down the other side of the gold track and toward a type of massive, black mechanism. The old man *felt young again,* full of life! He should not have been able to sprint down the hill with passion and burning curiosity, but he did. The black device appeared completely out of place within a bright environment of fields and trees. It had various attachments and tubes that trailed off to nothing. It was silent and still.

And, *wait.* Next to it stood the 'girl.' The Mineeran Zog, the female-Zog, was right ahead of him. *Dear Zog!* She stood only a few bars from the ominous mechanism. Cal did not know why he glanced at his G-watch. Galactic Time was 1003.32. *That can't be right.* He raced forward. Time did not matter.

Caladrian Trask, really a new person, was extremely excited. The old man seemed rejuvenated and, in fact, *he was.* Cal noticed his hands and arms were not wrinkled anymore. He was *young.* Time was off. His time was off, nothing mattered. The only important fact was that he was about to touch his

Zog. He intended to dive at her extraordinary legs and feet encased within the blue thaser-line and cry his eyes out and express his love or appreciation for...*it.* That was not what happened.

"Stop!" she commanded. There was no pleasant 'face' on her face. Female-Zog was angry about something.

Cal froze in his youthful sprint.

The girl-Zog was very angry. "You've come to kill me! Stop right there, Trask."

Caladrian Trask nearly had a double heart attack. He clutched his chest and fell precisely in front of her.

What kind of nightmare did I run into?

He was certainly confused and looked above for help. On his knees, he saw directly into the gorgeous eyes of the glowing figure of Zog.

She felt his stark bewilderment and had to end her game. Zog laughed. The strange mood was over.

Cal just realized he was in the midst of a playful Zog. Time had to pass until Cal joined Zog's laughter. Both were amused. (The tribesman did the same thing). Cal was brought to tears. He wiped them away.

"Rise."

Cal got off the ground and embraced his Zog. More tears flowed. Here was the real 'Zog in the Universe.' Cal hugged the precious Being as tight as he could and kept his eyes closed. The *feeling* within her sharp, blue aura was fantastic, energizing and beyond belief. When Cal opened his eyes and stepped back a bit, she had turned to a *he.*

Zog sincerely asked, "Which do you prefer?"

Cal quickly replied, "The girl."

Zog complied and switched to the female-Zog.

Caladrian repeated the hug and felt as if he'd fallen back into his mother's arms.

Then, after the bliss, his eyes beheld the black device that stood next to them.

Zog anticipated his question. "Don't you know? The device did not appear like this the last time you saw it, Cal.

C'mere." Girl-Zog directed him around the corner of a big, black, shiny attached extension.

When Cal saw what was around the bend and only two bars away from him, he *screamed.* He could reach out and touch the putrefied, petrified, corroded and vein-filled top portion of the Sardon's bald head. Its dead red eyes were seen behind very wrinkled skin. Only the ugly head of the Snake-Beast protruded from the existence-sustainer.

"The Chancellor really did not want to let go, did it?"

Zog assured Cal, "Oh, it's *dead,* believe me. But there is still this image and that is why I remain."

Cal came down from fright and forced another laugh. "I believe you, Zog." He noticed that she never touched the ground. Zog hovered an m-bar over the surface of Mineer. It seemed like Cal had gone back in time and appeared like the first time they met, only far more had changed than the red jumpsuit. "A million questions, Zog."

She answered, "Get comfortable. I can only respond for a short time. And then my time here is over."

Cal sat on a rock that was the perfect seat while the Zog lingered in the air. "But you are the Zog. You can do anything. I do not understand."

Did the Zog have to obey Laws of Physics?

Beautiful Zog attempted to explain to a humanoid she knew would not understand. "I am the same as the Sardon," she admitted as her wondrous arm in blue pointed at the Beast's head.

Caladrian choked at the idea and received her words in silence. He swallowed and listened.

The Great Zog stated, "We are two sides of the same coin, conjoined from the very Beginning. I cannot exist without the Devil, Davro, Dagmar, Behemoth, Belia, Bella, Beast, whatever your choice of name. And the Devil cannot exist without me. You see the end of its kind, the 'last gasp' Ghost, after-image of an evil thing so determined *not* to die." She-Zog smiled. "We both have been granted equal, physical existence in the real world. And both about to expire."

Cal joked, "You look better."

Zog's light glowed more intense. She laughed.

He laughed that he caused Zog to laugh. Then Cal dropped down out of the stars in his mind. His questions had to be answered. "What am I doing here? Explain me, killing you."

Floating Zog said, "Bad choice of words. We can say *you* will witness my last ya on the physical plane before both of us…" she gestured to the Beast, "…return to our Dimension above." Zog closed her eyes for a moment. "Possession can be death."

"Well, I feel a lot better now, ha, I think. Could not be more honored. But I still do not understand."

"You will. My time in the Material is over."

"You are the Zog."

She only smiled. The wind blew stronger. A few more clouds collected high above them. She looked around in maximum fondness. "I cannot return to this particular universe on my own. But if we *link,* then I can function in your world. I may *need* to return. It will be determined by the Machines. I would then need for my returning-spirit, a container, to attach to." She morphed to the he-Zog, glanced down to Cal and seriously asked, "I need your permission to enter your body and become you in the future."

"I wish the girl had said that."

A quick smile appeared on the face of Zog. "Do not make me laugh." The smile was gone and the male-Zog asked an important question. "Will you help me?"

Cal did not hesitate. "Yes, absolutely." The former State Agent from lifetimes ago felt compelled to hug the male-Zog. He lunged forward until Zog directed him to *stop* and think about what he agreed to. Zog needed permission.

"Consider this. I will be killing you."

"Explain, dear Zog."

Angel in blue detailed exactly its intentions to the former Agent. Zog told him that Cal's new life would be gone. His decisions and actions in the far future would not be his own. The Zog would totally possess his body and utterly control the very life of future-reincarnated Trask. Tomorrow, he would not be Caladrian Xander Trask.

Cal heard every article and sub-section of what was asked of him and he agreed without question.

Zog morphed into a *she* and took to the air. *Zog was a happy jet of energy.* She displayed joy, joy, joy! As the Sardon procured unlimited machines and future-carriers to continue its work, so would the good one also experience the physical world again and really become the Neo Zog. There would be balance. Scales would not tilt. There would not be a galaxy-quake. Both sides of the coin would once more do battle on future fields. One dark side would not have an unfair advantage over the light side.

Caladrian had a silly question and believed his Zog 100%. "Ha, what, what will we be called? What will our *name be* when we come back?"

"You want the answer?"

"Yes," the curious old man who had temporarily been *de-aged* said.

"Cal-El."

"Kol...Lel?" Trask slowly digested the last word by Zog. The 2-hearted humanoid was happy. The feeling was like he had *three hearts.* He felt love from his Zog and from the extraordinary planet around him. Cal was refreshed and a new 'man.'

The Citizen of the Universe was reborn and would be reborn one more time in the far future...when needed.

Ever so slowly...Zog's image faded. The happy blue girl was gone now. The head and black mechanism also faded in perfect sync with the magical entity from a higher Dimension. Zog, for a quick nanu-ya, was given the ecstatic experience of Living in the Material World. When Zog returned to its incomprehensible/timeless realm beyond description, it made sure to thank its 'ZOG' for the glorious privilege of Real Life even if it was only for a blink of an eye.

Middle Ages of the Galaxy

Chapter Five

CHANCELLERY'S DESTRUCTION

A NEW DAY arrived, and a new era began. One more sick *phantom plan* weaved its tentacles in the wake of the missing Sardon. The secret agenda was not from an automation source or a male source. The new Directors came from local Districts in many systems. They had *Lodges* where they organized devious plots against Men and Machines.

The Chancellor no longer slept in Taj dungeons. The Creature could use its telekinesis no more. The thing no longer had its automated nursing crews check every vital reading on the sustainer. The Beast was unable to directly apply circuitry-commands. It could not change a '0' into a '1' anymore. The Chancellor was dead. "Long live the Chancellery!"

Women-Vipers had complete control over what was left of the Chancellery on Ralia. Men were gone from positions of authority. Only a few of the 'Old Guard' remained, but the elder-elite were mere figurehead-statue-golems without power. Real power was now *feminine.*

A new, wicked directive came down secret corridors and was swiftly distributed to the Lodges. *No 'Lady' of the Viper-Order was to visit Ralia or be further stationed there. The planetoid and surrounding Territory will be a forbidden, 'no-fly' zone.* The Ladies departed the covert financial Capital.

Elder men on Ralia were relieved. They were overjoyed to see the brutish women go. They knew their kind were not in control anymore because the Vipers had fully developed Zog's 'Instrument of Peace.' A few of the Old Guard sincerely believed that current galactic changes were very much fated to happen and needed and this was what Zog truly wanted.

Generally, Citizens of the sectors also thought similarly. Media told them 'Zog's IOP' was coming. Supreme

Power could be controlled. The Peace Instrument was the 'Will of Zog.' Women would wield the Power and keep the galaxy 'safe and secure.' Networks proclaimed 'only Women could hold the Instrument' and it would be justly applied when necessary.

In yars, Lodge Networks created a feminine Police force. They were the worst of storm troopers because they were the strongest of storm troopers. Women leaders had the ancient Rule of Atomics on their side. "Vipers had Zog on their side," so the Media reported. More deadly than the Powda'me were the armies and flying forces of the Zulaire Pox: the New Police. The Pox maintained order.

GST was 1013.13. Stories had pre-empted the Big News and stated, "The Chancellery's actual location was close to being discovered!" Few in the Pinwheel believed the reports since similar ones had occurred previously. Some Rebel spy was supposed to expose the whereabouts of the 'Center of Commercial Evil' that enslaved us, but nothing much happened. No one believed the huge problem to humanoids and aliens would *ever* be found and uprooted. Now it was going to happen. Another Media-show was set to do its magic in the galaxy and *sway a spun world.*

From empathic Mystics in floating towers to Citizens on dirt roads, life forms teuned to one more 'Breaking News' Event. Monitors and screens from each sector displayed a black, undisclosed, empty Territory of space. The real coordinates in the Pinwheel were never revealed for security and safety reasons. The Women did not want crowds, visitors, neutral reporters, excited thrill-seekers and sightseers in the area. Nothing was phony or staged. Ladies were going to take every accolade of credit for the infiltration, takeover and now 'broadcasted' destruction of the secret Chancellery and former residence of the Devil. "Ralia's location was discovered by Vipers and executed by the Zulaire Pox," the Women reported on networks.

Media screens of every type showed an extraordinary planet, in violets and purples, *materialized in space.* Brilliant, old architecture was viewed from great distances and seen as 'Houses of the Unholy.' Here was the home of evil, Seat of Satan, Den of the Devil and Lair of Lucifer. Rebel forces *cheered.* The long-awaited dream was finally true. The Revolution, which had no current power, would receive what it desired most...the *physical* end of the Chancellery.

Most viewers did not know and were unable to comprehend what their eyes recorded, machines registered and senses felt. "In the name of Zog," a Viper's voice was heard over 'Galactic Media.' And then a very thick, red thaser-line from unknown origin struck a point on Ralia's equator. In a horrible moment, life in the galaxy was about to view a 'monster' from its earliest lost and forgotten period. A perfectly circular and dark chain reaction spread outward on the violet surface. The expansion continued quickly, in an ever-widening circle, and *burned everything on the surface to a cinder in less than a ya!*

The Viper-Show of 'Zog's Power and Will' was not concluded. Life forms in the Pinwheel actually had experienced *far worse* stellar catastrophes. Stars and multiple-sun systems have gone nova and *exploded.* Death tolls were incalculable. Whole districts had winked out of existence, naturally. 'Doomsday Asteroids' had crushed highly populated, giant planets. Trillions of Citizens died or passed when unstable suns and planets exploded or collapsed. Moons had crashed into the parent-planet. Volcanism and Super-Quakes had more than decimated entire civilizations. But what advanced cultures just witnessed at 13:13 was, on one hand, beautiful because the Den of the Devil and Legacy of Sardon was destroyed by the 'Legacy of Zog' or the awesome 'Power of Peace,' but...

...on the other hand, no other type of mass-annihilation was ever observed and recorded like this in known history. Even Ralia's three violet suns were engulfed in the mega-explosion. The Blast was *artificial* and a result of a *weapon!* Opponents later 'challenged' the creation of the Instrument of Peace and theorized similar IOPs brought about the end of the

Old World. Dissenters, for now, were in the huge minority.

New atomic technology was nothing like natural disasters recorded throughout galactic History. In the future, opponents of nuclear proliferation would point to the unnatural power now so readily available. They could burn planets and *kill all life at the push of a button!* The artificial tool of atomics was a 'Pandra's Door' and should *never* have been opened. 'Fruits' of Destruction should have remained 'Forbidden.' Life could easily destroy life on an inconceivable scale.

Yet, at 13.13 GST, there were only a handful of unhappy Revolutionaries and hardly a soul questioned the destruction of the long sought after Chancellery. Fascism appeared to be over. Such celebrations *blew up* over galactic channels and female networks. Parties raged for days. It was the largest stellar celebration since the 'Announcement of the Zog.'

A type of 'Galactic-Patriotism' gripped most beings in the initial *event* of uncovering Ralia and its quick burning by strange means. Life assumed tyranny and enslavement must be punished. The 'Hand of Zog' smote the evil Capital of Commercialism and Citizens were on the 'golden path' to peace and a threshold of a wonderful era. (No one thought about still being enslaved to the dylar, the GMS). As celebrations appeared to taper to a lessening degree, viewers witnessed another surprise. Phase II happened precisely on schedule. The next stage was, in reality, not the will of Zog or even the will of the Ladies.

The Women wanted a climax. They planned from the beginning to display precisely what they had over the Chancellery and any of the 'boys.' Vipers told life in the galaxy, "Behold, the Power of Zog!"

The next visual observed on every facet of galactic Media was a wide *White Beam* from the same direction and angle as the earlier red one. The nuclear intensity was amplified to maximum. White Beam hit the same equator-target on the 'cinder' as the red beam had struck on the purple planet. Every atomic particle of the burned cinder smashed up against the next particle of burned cinder, which resulted in continuous violent explosions on a nuclear level. The atomic force hit with such strength that soon nothing was left of Ralia. *Lucifer's Lair was thrown into the Black Hole or the Fires of Hensi!* The expanding wave only terminated because every single atom blasted apart and the emptiness of space extinguished the annihilation.

Killer-technologies and Weapons of Super Mass Destruction had been and remained 'Forbidden' during most of the 'Dark Days.' 'New Worlds' from every first Cosmic Nursery in a different time epoch seemed to have had the 'common sense' not to develop atomics...no matter what the reasons. *Because of recent events, must every system develop atomics?*

There had been terrible Wars in the lost past and not long ago. But there had been nothing such as this. Nuclear Power was dressed up as an inevitable course of action, 'a *good* idea.' The awesome Power was from Zog and it had to be used with most delicate care. It was not enough that the 'Secret' of basic atomics was found and formed from the ashes of yesterday, the Women took nuclear fission to a level never dreamed.

The phenomenal 'force,' 'weapon' or 'power' was legendary. Numerous asteroid belts where known planets that cracked, even pulverized into an uncountable number of shards. One example was the Silizon Belt near the Wormhole Nebula. Utilization of Ultimate Power was outlawed at the end of the First Reich. Was the IOP the very same Doomsday Device from prehistory? *Bev-green had bitten the melo.*

Verification of the News transmission came from the Unified Rebel Alliance. What 'un-dilated' viewers saw and recorded in real-time actually happened even though the location-Territory or 'space-zero' was not corroborated or disclosed. The transmission was analyzed by every possible means and by the greatest of technicians from each sector. A planet was fried, then *vaporized*...and the *world watched.*

Time passed, and the Women had been very successful.

Ladies' Agenda included a First Act of invading the Chancellery and letting them know *Zog was on their side* because they dared to fully develop the Taboo Technology. Second Act was to gain the trust of galactic Citizens using Viper-owned networks and Lodges to transmit Breaking News, show the world it was Women who had rooted out the Devil and staked it in its Center. Lady-Vipers (female versions of Snakes) were seen as 'heroes.' *Why would Zog place the Instrument in the possession of Women if they could not be trusted?*

"Look what the Pox have done. They have burned the Devil!"

What was going to happen in the Girls' Third Act?

One recent change was the constant presence of Lady Storm Troopers in every sector, far more than Lodge numbers. Legions were now called the 'ZP Police.' The rest of the galaxy understood what the Women in black uniforms, wearing boots and armed to the teeth, represented. Viper-comrades were squadrons and space fleets thought to possess the *Big Gun.* They were considered to have 'the Power.' They were the 'righteous gender' that Zog blessed. Enterprises of the Ladies would be highly profitable. It was the 'female cause' that was glorified, praised and 'crowned by success.' Women were the Chosen Ones and favorites of Zog.

Women saved Citizens from the clutches of oppression between systems. Women found the occult location of the Old Chancellery and provided its deathblow. Advanced societies in the Monopdonowian Pinwheel owed Women everything. They were the saviors. They were our liberators. Major wars between systems ended and smaller civil conflicts lessened under the regime of Women. They were the 'Peacekeepers' and now functioned as judges, juries and executioners (if needed).

The Girls intimidated the galaxy and Citizens, generally, bowed or *bent* to the Viper's will. Life forms were grateful, paid dylar tributes to the uniformed 'gals' who were always permitted 'free passage.' Discounts, dylar credits, no-interest loans and a million other benefits were showered upon the ZP Police. They kept order throughout 24 sectors and were credited for services rendered. Peacekeepers were doing their jobs and there was *quiet* among the stars.

Over channel forums and 'Light' Rebel forums, a few questioned, "Was the second strike to Ralia necessary?" Debate had become heated and a certain amount of galactic attention was turned to controversial forums. A yarn had passed since the nuclear shock to the psyche of seeing violet Ralia blackened and then atomically pulverized to nothing in slow motion.

Anniversary documentaries showed the stories of a yarn ago and ran a Ralia rebroadcast. Reports said the purple temples and 'Houses of the Unholy' were virtually abandoned at the time of the big explosion. Women lied when networks reported, "Less than 50 souls perished, old officials still drafting Totalitarian Laws for the rest of the galaxy to follow."

In truth, there were many thousands of males and non-Viper females who worked various establishments without a clue the lovely world would be smashed.

The new, popular question on the channels concerned the 'Second Explosion' triggered by the White Beam. Scientists from many systems analyzed the data. Molecular explosions as a result of the White Beam were estimated to be 800,000 times the intensity of molecular explosions of the red beam. The one nuclear disruption of matter from the red ray caused the effect to terminate with a limited range. The First Explosion burnt and leveled most of everything on the surface. Hills and valleys were consumed in the firestorm and blackened. Scientists stated that the interior of small Ralia beneath 100 bars would have been intact. Many pundits expressed exactly what the forums had recently debated: "The Second Explosion should not have been detonated."

What made the question controversial was its timing. Media did not express anti-Viperism in any form. The Women Saved the Day! For a yarn, no one had questioned the decision to blast. There had been solid support for the deadly actions taken and demonstrated on the 'galactic stage.' Only now did someone take the refreshing standpoint that, "The Second Explosion did not have to occur." The notion spread on forums, but not so much on female networks. Other associated questions arose such as, "Who was in control?"

Consider that Ralia was reduced to ashes down to a hundred bars below its surface. Mountains were toppled and valleys were filled with 'brimstone.' The strongest pyramids crushed. Its atmosphere burned away. One nuclear explosion, which poured over 77% of its exterior, would have served its entire purpose and been enough. Chancellery Capital, although decimated, could have been studied later under the rubble. Scientists claimed tests on the effects of radiation should have been administered. Ralia's radiation could have been easily neutralized. The New Power needed to be fully investigated and maybe not left in the hands of one group.

Many put forth arguments that if the Vipers stopped at the First Explosion, igniting the surface with the red beam, the final conclusion would have been better. The Devil's Lair was sent back to the Hensi it came from.

"Look what we did and will do to the persistence of Evil Tyranny!"

Ralia should have stood as a dead monument and a symbol against the uprising of fascist states. Instead, what the galaxy witnessed was a super-mega-destructive Power that made the First Explosion look like a candle.

Was there an alternate reason for the violet world's complete and utter destruction? Were there political reasons? Could the Second Explosion have been detonated for simply a display of incredible might? Power on such a titanic level did not have to be demonstrated even if it was to kill the Devil with its own insanity.

'Light' Rebels found a cause to lock onto and it was the first whispers against the Women. Especially when everywhere Citizens turned, in every 'Starduster,' in the streets and in the skies, there was the Pox Police. Too many ZPs had risen to prominence in the last yarn. Numerous planets had turned into 'Pox States.' *"Something had to be done,"* was spoken among the Rebels as well as inside public forums.

Few in the forums mentioned the name Zog. The dylar was as strong as ever between systems. Life forms for generations knew nothing else. The Chancellery's reign was over, but was it? The Monster continued to live, breathe and eat away at the galaxy.

Vipers of the networks were the first to see the decline in feminine support. The Girls decided to publicly address the question. Finally, the name of 'Zog' was invoked. Ladies said their psychics remotely witnessed the passing of the real Zog on Mineer and the Sardon's demise into its own Black Hole. Also, "Zog was truly a beautiful *Woman* in blue light." Once more, the Ladies lied to the galaxy along with partial truths. Pox officials, the 'Voice of the Seers,' said it was 'Zog's Will' that their scientists developed the Bomb. A quote from the ancient Korabi (Book of Zog), fossilized data-chip from the Beginning, was aired: "I am become Peacekeeper."

Pundits concluded that the 'Secret' of the Atomic Bomb was easy. Any modern society could manufacture it, even yahoos. There were good reasons to avoid such ultra-power before. Now, in Middle Ages, the existence of nuclear fission was unavoidable. It was the super-mega-destructive White Beam that caused an explosion 800,000 times larger than the first that was the real *worry of worlds.* Devastating most of a small planet for a while was bad enough, but *erasing planets and possibly whole suns forever?*

'Peacekeepers' sounded good: Galactic Police or 'Wings Over the World,' 'Watchers' maintaining Order in the form of 'Lady Sheriffs.' With destructive forces like the Bomb of Zog in existence, controllers at the controls *had* to be blessed. Skeptics, cynics and atheists 100% denied that the Instrument of Peace had anything to do with Zog. The Question of the Day was, "Who watched the Watchers?"

Another large Media event was staged and transmitted to the galaxy. Peacekeeper ZPs announced 'Breaking News' that a 'Doomsday Asteroid' was on a collision course with Mineer, the home of the Zog. Lady psychics were correct when they revealed that moonless Mineer will be the site of the Return of Zog and the Neo Zog.

At the present GST of 1227.82, Mineer only had moments left. Respected astrophysicists theorized that a mass so large that it could destroy a splendid, green planet of blue oceans was on a collision course via the 'Goz-Star Wormhole' (a close phenomenon).

Tensions dramatically increased over network-channels and other communications. Male psychics quickly confirmed that Mineer was the true home of Zog and *must* continue to exist in the future for its 'Third Coming.' A Doomsday Asteroid cannot be allowed to shatter the very special planet to bits. A few News-networks even emphasized the real-time report with subtle, emotional music. Mineer had to be saved and in less than a yam, the planet *was* spared from total obliteration. Again, the *Women had the gratitude of Citizens in the Pinwheel Galaxy for coming to the rescue.*

Peacekeepers set off the White Beam which ignited molecular explosions in the Killer-Asteroid! The sudden jolt to Life in the galaxy was staggering. First, the announcement of the origin-place or home planet of Zog in the Material World was discovered. Then suddenly that beautiful planet of oceans, mountains and rivers was threatened with total annihilation. More remarkably, Media Magic happened to capture the Women with the 'nukes' saving millions of humanoid lives on Mineer. Who could understand the *timing* of recent galactic News? And yet, the dark pattern was clear.

To backtrack, the world was told, "Here was the home of the Devil-destroyer and we will kill the monster." Then the world was told, "Here was the home of the Zog-Creator, and we will save her planet." Women received full credit by most creatures of the Pinwheel, again. "Absolutely, Zog placed the Peace Instrument in the hands of Women for good reasons." Mothers of the Universe were the kindest and gentlest of spirits. *The Vipers were not mothers.*

Women showed the galaxy how to use atomics in positive ways. Zog's Instrument was praised to a much farther degree than ever before.

Thank Zog and the Ladies for the Nuclear Age!

A few systems wanted to immediately install asteroid-killer programs because of the near disaster at Mineer. Astronomical amounts of dylars were spent for the technology. The Insectoids were interested. Vipers with a mechanical Snake in the Machine behind the scenes had procured *control.* More ZP troops were deployed. The Sardonic State continued to churn with clockwork precision.

Everyone was not pleased in the aftermath of the latest galactic happenings. A few (male) malcontents and *contraries* speculated that it was the 'Women' that catapulted the Doomsday Asteroid through the Wormhole that threatened Mineer in the first place. Few, over Media forums, believed such crazy theorists. The 'crazy theorists' were correct. Big, broadcasted, world events were never real. They were always fabricated performances. Climactic News activity decreased. The galaxy's collective psyche would soon forget criticism against the Ladies. Seeds had been planted. Women would come out *smelling like a bloch.*

***

GST was 1299.89. Plans of automatons, Women and automaton-women were in the works. No one blamed them for breaking the Law long ago with 'atomics.' In present times, they *were* the Law.

Odd reports came in from 'Outlands' or regions of deep space far beyond the disk of the Pinwheel. 'Spacial' areas such as District 01, District 02, zone #1, zone #2, 000.4, 000.3, 000.2 and 000.1 hardly contained suns, planets, satellites and planetoids yet continued to travel along with the Great Pinwheel between galaxies. Reports came in and then suddenly stopped of planets being pulverized on the order of Ralia. Nothing more was reported. There were no 'follow-up' investigations.

Teams of ZP Police were sent into the Spacial areas beyond the disk and reported that they found nothing. In truth, the paid-off ZP had 'looked the other way.' The stories and a few Breaking Stories were entirely squashed. The V-Women did not want it known that distant; basically, lifeless worlds were used as atomic testing-grounds. A few designated planetary-targets proved to prospective clients that the Power was 'for sale.' Insectoids purchased massive amounts of nukes at wholesale prices. The more they bought, the less they paid the Women. Under the Cosmic Table or on the Big Black Market, the Vipers primarily sold to aliens and other women. The Girls paid off the loans and generated enormous profits. The enormous profits went into building an even larger War-Machine to produce more ZPs.

Another prosperous time was upon the galaxy under the strict, authoritarian, boot heels of the Vipers and their powerful squadrons. Although Rebel Alliances were thought to secretly meet in large numbers, Anti-Viper Men, Light-Rebels, had also become vocal on forums with state-of-the-art weapons. Men united through their Unions.

Lodge-Women feared the growing contingent against their 'movement' in sectors. Rebel male forces or 'Rangers' were thought to be formidable even without knowledge of the Bomb. Stories were told of male organizations whose numbers and influence greatly increased.

Another mad, paranoid plan came down the directorate networks. The origin for such devilish deviousness began more than a half yarn ago. The Lady-Seers had foreseen long ago that a chain of galactic disasters, well covered over the networks, was needed to rip the psyche of Citizens apart. Then the average Citizen could be malleable.

A specific plan for killing huge numbers of Life, especially important *men,* was set into motion. Women were able to secure billions of red dylars in no-interest loans from the robotic 'Machine' or 'Monster' whose plug could not be pulled. With enormous amounts of dylars, Vipers purchased the greatest talents and technical skills in the galaxy.

'Colossus' was sold to the public as an 'Embassy Ship, the largest Ark-Ship to ever sail space.' The diameter of the biggest saucer ever constructed would be 1/10 of a mega-bar! The Super Disk would house the most important dignitaries from the 24 sectors. Every Quadrant Head and sector boss would be invited to take part in its maiden voyage from the space foundry in Anther Pol (Xax-9) to its parallel sector of Benis Pol (Margammu).

'Parallel sectors' were opposing sectors on the opposite side of the galactic spiral arm. A large number of wormholes tended to transport travelers to its parallel sector, a sector with similar aged and colored suns. In other words, the twin Spacial Territories were attached and close by. Any spaceship from a complex culture knew how to 'surf the space-ways' also called the 'cosmic-commuter system' and easily move to the adjacent sector.

Colossus neared completion, the Super Saucer Embassy Ship built by the (female financed) 'White Dwarf Company.' The dylars were not spared. No extravagance or production or occasion was ever this lavish. No king, or emperor or palace ever displayed such gaudy exuberance in dylar-spending. The finest precious-stone inlays were placed in portal-doors, entries, chambers, corridors, bulkheads and anywhere else passengers cared to view. Finest art adorned the walls of the Ark-vessel. The greatest musicians, dancers and performers of the arts were assembled.

A million Citizens of every sector under the parent-company of White Dwarf did the hands-on construction for a yarn in space. Couple the 'living' work force with more than a million various automatons and servo-droids. The weightless workspace and unlimited dylar spending made Colossus the most attractive 'new sensation' in the galaxy. The Saucer's maiden voyage was the IN 'thing' for the Illuminati Intelligentsia.

The most famous celebrities booked First Class passage, of course. Second Class was not so luxurious, yet 'fabulous' nonetheless. Third Class was extremely 'plush.' Second and Third were fantastic, but nothing could compare to the 'King's treatment' in First Class. The finest foods and delicacies from around the galaxy were catered for the big occasion.

Captain Goerge Smith was a very old and well-known celebrity/captain. He was also a veteran of a few wars. He was the 'famous face' of the Super Saucer and personally greeted each passenger like family. 'Greetings' were 'Colossal Affairs' over the course of many days as the 'City in Space' was estimated to have a million passengers for the huge launch.

Colossus was to be a living repository of political knowledge and Power-Center for the highest forms of life in the galaxy. A 'Super Union in space and a Force for Peace' was the idea. The great saucer was certain to have 'Rebel Representation,' which surprised a large number of sector bosses and officials. Men associated with the secretive Light-Rebels were well represented on ship's Council. Some of the richest dylar-fortunes were invited and accepted passage for the grand send-off.

No one considered the construction of Colossus by White Dwarf was a deadly murder plot. No one suspected the space-foundry's location in the heart of Viper-infested Anther Pol had a special significance. Who could suspect the Ark-Embassy was a doomed ship? Why? Filthy rich opponents of the war-to-come would be killed off as well as Rebel Leaders and groups of others not sympathetic to the Vipers in one deadly action.

Even Women with Nukes might not have been able to stand against male financial Empires that could buy more atomic arsenals. The Ladies had to wipe out gargantuan fortunes *and* destroy leaders of the opposition. History declared it was time for another mega-disaster to strike the senses. Vipers could succeed in their goal by their selections or *who* had the 'wonderful privilege' of being invited on the maiden voyage.

GST was 1313.99. Colossus, the entire length of 1/10 mega-bar, and its 'selected' elite luminaries of the galaxy prepared to launch. Xax-9, an artificial planetoid, was where the Super Saucer was constructed. The female-run facility, especially built for Colossus, also had the capability to *jettison* the immense disk into the nearby Fodor Wormhole.

Everything was in place for the Mega-Launch through the wormhole to Benis Pol's Margammu site while the rest of the galaxy observed the spectacle. Everyone teuned-in to the broadcast from both sectors. In the past, only the 'Behemoth' approached the size of Colossus with a third of the new spaceship's diameter. "Nothing Can Go Wrong," was printed on the WD brochures.

Women operated the specially constructed Launch-Deck on their end. The Men in the parallel sector of Benis Pol were to secure the ship at the Arrival-Deck on their end. Anticipation soon grew to maximum proportions. Media recorders and crystal-recorders captured *history in the making.*

Colossus' maiden voyage was a token gesture in praise of life and also Women and Men. Politicians believed the gesture could lessen hostilities between Pox and Rebel forces. Anther Pol (female) was purposely chosen to create a 'parallax bridge' with (male) counterpart, Benis Pol. Great Colossus jettisoning into the Fodor Wormhole should have resulted in a smooth ride for almost a million special passengers.

Captain Goerge Smith's plan was to first plunge into the vortex. After the brilliant light-show for the passengers onboard, the trip to the male sector would only take a short time. Hands would be shook, photographs would be taken and after that...

Colossus would quickly flit to different assignments in the sectors and break time/space with its own type of 'hyper-drive.' The Super Saucer Embassy did not have to rely on wormholes or 'jump-gates' with its very sophisticated, self-contained means of travel. The maiden voyage or 'parallax bridge' created by uniting male and female counter-sectors was only a *symbolic gesture* in the name of peace and in the name of Zog.

At 1314.00, Colossus launched and was flung perfectly into the Fodor phenomenon. The colossal craft barely fit the EH aperture, yet every sign from the Ladies' end appeared successful. Everything was fine until...

The Saucer was on the Benis Pol side and should have cleanly slipped into its Arrival-Deck. But the *Wormhole was unstable.* From the Benis end, the Wormhole violently moved in space like a recoiling snake. The moving vortex in turquoise, that should not have moved, functioned as a twisted 'barrel of a gun' to the saucer projectile inside it. Colossus exited the vortex on the other end, but the craft was propelled at terrific speeds in a different direction. The different direction threw the craft, with its 956,075 souls onboard, directly into a close blue-green Giant Sun!

The spaceship had no time to turn or alter course in any way. For the most part, the whole galaxy witnessed a disaster of amazing magnitude. One more time, minds could not believe what senses received. The Collective Consciousness was stabbed again. To view a vehicle of that size, a City in Space, burn for so long in a black streak through the star's corona, to know there were almost a million lives inside and the horror they shared in the last moments was *frightening and chilling.*

'Sympathetics,' Empaths, Mystics, psychics, seers, sensitives and telepaths *felt* the pain/sorrow in an extended moment of horrendous sadness. The world in-the-know was stunned to the point of extreme disbelief in what they viewed over screens. One more time came a crash to the fragile psyche, en mass. Why? Who was to blame? Why did so many humanoids and aliens have to die? The loss of dignitaries, power-players, business moguls, politicians and celebrities was incredibly overwhelming to Citizens. No one grasped the full scope of what they observed and *the real reason* why it happened. From now on, everything had to be different.

Far in the background, *machines* were ready for the New Order. Somewhere a Sardon was happy in Hensi. (God only snored).

Searches in the area of the blue-green giant star called 'Carpathus' were well conducted. Escape pods in the hundreds were eventually found and rescued. Pods contained very few children and mainly women. Amazing stories of a myriad rescues were reported on different Media. Many thanked Zog for their lives because of the near-death experience.

Harsh criticism and the 'blame game' was the next wave over networks. Answers to *why* this occurred were demanded, especially by angry Women. They owned White Dwarf. Colossus was their elaborate project. The Vipers insisted on getting to the bottom of the disaster and informing the rest of the galaxy on what they discovered. Committees were formed.

Ladies *found* answers and did not hesitate to tell very attentive life forms their conclusions. Was it sabotage? Were the Rebels involved and were they far more violent than expected? Were 'Light' members not the pacifist-Rebels they presented themselves to be and were actually militarists? How could a stable wormhole be made unstable? Were Benis Pol men responsible for un-stabilizing the star on their end? Was the Captain at fault? Could the disaster have been the result of an *accidental* set of circumstances? Why were there not enough escape pods? How could the disaster have been avoided? Speculations and foggy solutions were cast over network air waves. Confusion in the aftermath was the desired result. Life forms were ready to believe even the most incredible of answers.

Soon, Citizens were told an unbelievable and supposedly verified story. The lesser creatures of the Pinwheel accepted the tale without question. "The Captain was a double-agent and head of the Rebel saboteurs."

Chief Officer and First Class Captain of the Colossus, a *man* known as Goerges Ratio Smith, was in reality a 'Light-Worker' and high-ranking Rebel agent. The Conspiracy involved a multiple-yarn plan to become the 'only choice' for captain of Colossus. Evidence showed, when Smith was young, he cheated in school. He bribed his way up the ranks. He later used his war records and post-war fame to become the 'Ladies' choice' for Captain's job on the Super Saucer. He basically seduced the Women and accepted the honorable post at a reduced salary. Now it was clear to the public that Smith was an agent of Chaos, an anarchist, a Rebel terrorist whose only motivation was to disrupt the Order established by the ZPs.

Smith went down with his ship. His male comrades on the Benis Pol side 'destabilized' the Fodor Wormhole, when in fact they had the phenomenon in control all along. The turquoise tube that provided a stupendous lightshow in the corridor was perfectly aimed. Truth was the *Colossus was shot into Carpathus* with the accuracy of ZP markswomen. The only problem with the very public story on every network and every channel outlet was: Men were not behind the Colossus disaster.

More major 'discoveries' were relayed to networks and Media. Here was the Big News of the Day: "Captain Goerge Ratio Smith, with his characteristic white beard, was more *infamous* than his known battles in space."

He came from extraordinary roots, which had only now been uncovered. Once a high-ranking officer, then later celebrity-captain of Colossus, he lived a secret life. He had a well-known persona to the galaxy's elite as a heavy-set, jovial pitch-man-showman and was invited to host large extravaganzas. Smith made a few films as a war veteran, but he was widely known for his charm and presence in the Media. Who could believe the latest that he was a descendant of the *Gildenstein Smith clan?* Who could believe that the Captain was a conspirator-saboteur and helped destroy his very own ultra-luxury Saucer? How could the sweet man who shook every hand do this? How could famous 'Captain Goerges' have assisted in the mass-murder of almost a million souls?

Long and forgotten memories of the 'Zog-killer' lingered as scars in the 'Collective Subconscious' of the cosmos. Legends fabricated yarns ago that the (never-captured) 'Arch-Assassin' murderess known as the vile 'Gildenstein' Smith had a brood of eight children over a ten-yarn period. They were all boys and later grew to be leaders of her personal gang of terrorists.

Networks attempted to show evidence via

documentaries that the Light-Rebels were male and originated with the 'Smith Gang' that quickly increased its numbers. Vipers connected Goerges Smith with the old Smith Anarchists and beings in every sector *bought* what the News stories sold. No one had ever dreamed that Captain Goerges Smith was related to the 'Enemy of Life' and known 'Zog-Killer,' Gildenstein Smith.

Smith was not related. He was a little pawn, perfectly chosen by the Vipers to pilot the Flagship of Worlds, the Floating Embassy that could break time/space and appear anywhere in the galaxy. It should have been the union of divergent forces within the Pinwheel. The Saucer could have lasted and been a symbol of Hope and Peace for the future. The Great War to come would never have happened if Colossus was a success.

"Look what we can achieve together!"

Instead, the destruction of Colossus became a powder keg. More explosions were about to detonate that were not nuclear. Every scene in the Sardon's Play had been acted to fine precision, so far...

***

In the next yarn, there was more blaming, accusations, unsubstantiated reports, debate, propaganda and channeled lies. How could Citizens question the one source they teuned-in to for information? Most believed what they were fed and only a minority understood the broadcasted lies.

Another name was whispered on the multi-Media of the galaxy. The name was feminine and stood for Tomorrow. She was very young, very beautiful and had long white hair. The 'vision' of a girl was possibly the *shining hope for the future.* If a child so amazing, brilliant, super-intelligent and talented for her yarns, with knowledge of sages and Avatars existed in the real world, then there *truly was hope for everyone.* She came from the 'Original Sector' and prehistoric sector of 'ONE.' Her name was wonderful. The 10-yarn old 'Child of the Universe' was called May Eleanora Bulair. The exquisite creature with blue eyes was also known as 'Mebby,' 'Mebs' and 'May.'

The galaxy did not know what to make of the young beauty, which appeared like the most perfect thing Zog had ever created.

May took everyone's breath away. She could make anyone cry. The mere sight of such perfect skin and perfect hair along with that radiant smile and eyes could make men faint. Mebby had a calming effect on the most violent and psychotic of men, as was demonstrated on networks. Mebby was a huge sensation and became the 'darling of the galaxy.' No one could resist her humor and talents and wisdom, especially when made aware of her back-story.

May was orphaned and abandoned at two yarns old and nearly did not survive frigid nights on the ice-planet of Arinon. She was saved by a passing ZP Policewoman on routine patrol. The child quickly recovered and soon overwhelmed her rescue troops with her unique grace and knowledge. She became a mascot for the squadron and later rose to network-stardom with her surprising, powerful voice. May or Mebby sang as well as danced her way to the top. She lovingly entered the Center of almost every feeling being in the turning Pinwheel. The young girl's one major film was called, 'Tomorrow's Child.'

The Media-darling disappeared from the world stage for a time. Some speculated that her agents did not want her to be *used up* or become *old news* anymore, so they restricted her performances. Many believed her handlers hid her only to increase the girl's mystique, to return later in full vigor with a new/bigger and more profitable act.

Other fans thought she tired of the great public demands or press pressures and simply wanted a long vacation. There was not a soul outside of a few Vipers at the pinnacle of their brutal Order that understood what Mebby was and how she was going to be used in the future drama. She'd gone into seclusion for bad reasons.

Winds of War vibrated between star systems. The polarity seemed to tear along sex-lines. Astronomical numbers of civilizations in the Pinwheel were asexual or had *no sex*.

Some had more than two sexes and some needed three sexes to reproduce. Of the higher creatures that had a male and a female gender, the big debate was generally split. Women sided with women and men sided with men. They were victims of universal feelings, thoughts and the *ether*. Also, occult machines beamed a frequency disrupting male and female relationships.

Life hardly felt the small edge of 'the Wedge.' The sensation was only *discomfort* for now. Yet tomorrow would be painful rips that pulled those who loved each other far apart. Magnetic attraction would swing to the opposite polarity. For real reasons over and through the ether of space, divorces, break-ups, splits, divisions of dylar empires between rich spouses and other sex-related relationships dissolved to nothing. Love drained from the galaxy as fast as dylar-profits. Attractions lost their *pull,* their *draw.* What was in the wind was an abomination to life. But, like the existence of the protected Monster-Machine, everyone was at its mercy and it had no mercy.

On one level was the omnipresence of the ZP Police well represented in every sector. On a higher level, there was a much stronger female force of militarized guards known as the 'Peacekeepers.' Men theorized that as Women had their Lodges in Districts connected to local Lodges, so did their military forces. On the local level on many planets, there was the beginning of the 'Cardilles' or new ZP Police. They dealt with small issues and arbitrated local disputes using force or intimidation. Then there were 'Peacekeepers.' This was a larger, far more complex and organized War-Machine. The Women had the most sophisticated spacecraft and weaponry known. Vipers had the secret assistance from *machines* that accelerated production in war-factories.

Men and aliens feared that massive Peacekeeper ships, which held enormous numbers of troops, contained the *Bomb.* Zog's atomics were never in the possession of the local ZPs. Citizens understood the Lady leaders of squadrons or elite in the Center up the Chain of Command probably had their feminine hands on nuclear-controls. No one knew for certain. The sudden appearance of gigantic, interstellar troop-transports caused paranoid pundits to assume the spaceships contained nuclear capability.

They were correct.

Male Light-Rebels also had females on their side. Every female was not a part of the Viper Movement, far from it. Large numbers of Revolutionaries against the Galactic State were female. 'Mothers of the Universe' and other organizations challenged Viper Authority and way of life. Lady Unions were created in full support of the Men's Movement and various Rebel groups. Full-fledged Anti-Vipers had a large female participation.

More stories flooded the Media channels about nuclear detonations beyond the disk of the galaxy. There were so many, the stories could no longer be denied. Whole planets in the 'districts' and 'zones' were confirmed to contain cosmic bodies with evidence of 'red beam' nuclear detonations. Scientists had confirmed the existence of hundreds of charred planetoids decimated in the same manner as the First Explosion on Ralia. More were discovered blasted to a greater intensity and became completely pulverized planetoids. The age or point in time when the big blast occurred could be calculated by how extensive the spatter-field of pieces was; the less spread out the shards, the more recent the nuking.

No evidence had been found of White Beam detonations that could erase planets and possibly suns in a flash. Radiation signatures could reveal if the Big One was used. The galaxy never had to worry on a planetary scale before, not since the days of the First Reich. Systems were not capable of affecting other systems in such disastrous ways. Nukes did not exist. But with the capability of light-speed travel and nuclear arsenals of the First or Second Kind, insane renegades, rogues could now swing by, torch or vaporize planetary/star systems utterly and then get away.

Peacekeepers had the Power of Atomics. The Ladies were supposed to keep extremely close watch on 'Zog's

Instrument of Peace' and the Secret formula of how to produce the IOP. The Secret was certainly never to be sold, leaked or stolen. There was no escaping what had happened. Someone else, other than Vipers, was in the Outlands using nukes.

When the unavoidable truth came over multi-Media, the story the ZP networks told was the atomic 'Secret' had been stolen. Once more, a MALE Rebel sympathizer of Gildenstein Smith took responsibility in a (fabricated) note. Most believed the report because galactic networks stated it. A large number of organized Rebels did not believe the News.

Pandra's Door was opened.

Others, not as honorable as Vipers, now had possession of the Bomb. The Secret was quickly sold on Black Markets for billions of dylars. Asexual Insectoids profited the most in the future war called the 'War of the Sexes' or '100-Yarn War.' The galaxy was a different world now. The galaxy was a much more fearful place to live.

Concessions and dylar-penalties were leveled against the Vipers from male authorities the Girls *owned* and *in their pocket.* The biggest complaint had been about the large population of female Zulaire Pox Storm Troopers around every corner of every advanced planet. Lady Troopers were recalled by the millions throughout the sectors. No more would there be the strong, intimidating Police-presence.

Peacekeepers and their vast space fleets dealt with interstellar issues. For the most part, Peacekeepers were not in sight. Because the Vipers screwed-up badly, punishments had to be levied. Punishments came in the form of paying fines and restitutions to authorities. But mainly, troops were deployed away from Citizens. It was as if the State, for the first time, *listened* to the will of almost the least important yahoos. Of course, that was not the case at all.

In truth, the Women were *slapped on the wrist.* Vipers were not really punished. Their armies and star fleets were as mighty as ever. They had *lost face* but not lost power. Huge profits were poured into the Ladies' magnificent military. The Girls' Sardonic roles in the 'theater' or 'stage' were played masterfully. War-Machines of Women and Men were on the rise and increased even higher. War tones filled the vacuum of space.

More questions concerning the destruction of the Colossus occurred on the one-yarn anniversary of the tragedy. Documentaries and the rebroadcast were shown again and again. Conspiracy Theorists had been alive and well among Rebel-Light Workers. In the past yarn, groups of intelligent investigators had organized and found the following to be true:

Every billionaire was not invited on Colossus' maiden voyage, only rich and powerful *men* that were Anti-Viper and connected to Men's Movements.

2) The invited wealthy were not only connected with Anti-Viper groups but also Rebel Alliances. Each could have built powerful armies and large stockpiles of armaments against Vipers.

3) The Invitation Committee of White Dwarf Lines who personally chose the first passenger list would not come forward. No member would admit picking the Guest List and WD Lines would strangely not divulge the information.

4) Careful examination of precisely who was asked aboard and not asked aboard was of paramount importance. Studies revealed no major losses among Viper officials in the casualties. It seemed as if the Ladies had prior knowledge of the disaster and acted accordingly.

5) Few children and very few men were actually rescued in the small number of escape pods available, yet Media stories always included the rescue of men, children and pets.

6) The oddity was that every one of the richest male sympathizers died in the sun-dive. Hundreds of individual escape pods were shot into free space and not one contained a male billionaire. Would not the richest have made sure to be the *first* in the escape pods?

Media forums once more debated the issue more forcibly than ever before. No one had presented the Viper-Women in such a disturbing light previously. There was not a

Citizen in the galaxy who wanted to believe the Girls set a deathtrap for the opposition. Yet the evidence mounted that Lodge Ladies did exactly that. 'Nothing can go wrong,' *indeed.*

The question the following day concerned the next step that few wanted to discuss. Yet logic brought viewers to this point. Today, the talk/debate was really *theorizing.* Life forms speculated with the question, "What happened to the rich, male, connected mogul/celebrity Rebels who surely should have reached the escape pods?"

The unbelievable and implied answer, not discussed on Ladies' networks, was: *"They were murdered first!"* Channels broadcasted the possibility that 'cloak-and-dagger' assassins were ordered to kill the high-ranking, super-wealthy men. Pundits postulated that, "Later, phony stories will be believed that the men-moguls were heroes who willingly went down with the Saucer-ship." Any story could be reported over network outlets and viewers would perceive it was fact.

Powerful male Rebels on the Colossus death list would have ended the war-to-come before it ever started. The Men were so organized and united against the Woman by this time, they could have defeated the Vipers. As it stood at present time, the path to Galactic War had been paved. The War of the Worlds, the War of Men vs. Women, the War of the Sexes, of Anther Pol vs. Benis Pol would begin soon...

...and not end for 100 yarns!

The galaxy paid close attention to network screens when the *young darling* reentered the public stage. May Eleanora Bulair, Mebby, was now twelve yarns old and remained far wiser than her yarns. Mebby appeared stunningly beautiful and even more attractive as an adolescent and not a child. She was taller, sleeker and had longer hair. She was the future to many Citizens of the Pinwheel.

Mebby's personal future and fortune were secure as the State housed her, fed her, clothed her, promoted her and broadcasted her. She told Media outlets that she was hard at work writing new songs to explain the incognito period. May certainly was not *lost* or *kidnapped by Rebels* as a few wild stories had circulated. She came out of a self-imposed retirement for one reason only: in desperate times, the 'Voice of the Future,' must speak from her Center. The world listened and viewed her radiance.

Mebby spoke these recorded words to trillions of Citizens. "I have been asked to speak to you. I am speaking in Lebritz although many viewers will hear me in their own language. Sadly, voices in dark chaos yell war-cries to those who are different and of different genders. We had Law, peace and order, once, long ago. Do you remember peace and love, dear ones?" Cheers, applause and roars of approval exploded from the sectors. Crowds immediately around the Media-darling burst into bright celebrations. When they quieted down, she continued her speech:

"Why is there such hate? Fighting *has to stop,* especially in an age where there exists 'Zog's Instrument of Peace.' IOP must stand as an ultimate deterrent to major WAR. Hear me, good Citizens! Only real reason for the existence and development of an Atomic Doomsday, Planet-Killer…the only reason Zog would allow it to be, is as a…a…*Peacekeeper.* The 'atom scrambler' is a powerful destroyer and can vaporize planets, as we have seen. I assure you, Zog was correct by entrusting the Secret to the Viper Lodges." The young girl with long white hair laughed.

"They look imposing, I know, a formidable ZP Police Force. But the Women *have* to be strong to carry the burden, to carry the torch that has been passed to them from Zog. Atomics will be used for various positive purposes and used *only* for positive purposes, believe me, dear ones." She stopped and blanked. The cute girl was scheduled to recite much more off the teleprompter.

General feeling in the galaxy was relief. Mebby was gorgeous and said what needed to be said during a very volatile period in Monopdonow History.

Was there a problem?

Mebby walked offstage too soon. There were more pages of propaganda that needed to come out of the young girl's innocent mouth. She appeared to be in distress. Mebby waved away adoring fans and assistants. She oddly returned to her private dressing room with a limp and nervously sat down. She was alone. The little girl made sure there were no listening or viewing devices in her immediate area. Her wristwatch, which was not a wristwatch, informed her that the coast was clear. May Bulair, known by the State as 'MBT-14K,' plugged into a re-charger. Her power was 'low.'

Not even her multiple agents, handlers and entourage knew she was a State *android*. A logical reason was behind her fair skin without blemishes, her glow, acrobatics and astounding voice. She appeared so perfect because she was built that way. The programmed beauty had a job to do. Viper-Women did not have a clue. The 'Voice,' the Hope of Tomorrow, 'Tomorrow's Child,' was a 'cyborg' servant of Sardon.

Chapter Six

WAR OF THE SEXES

A sector in the Continuum had its own system of planets that was known as 'the continuum.' Quadrant Mystics/witches told tales and weaved one theme throughout the stories. The commonality was whatever happened within a particular, single red-sun solar system of OM Sector, also happened to the Continuum as a whole. They were only trivial fables to most Citizens. Few outsiders believed that the 72 satellites in 49 orbits around the old red-giant Qvavor had any rippling-affect on the rest of the galaxy. The few outsiders were wrong.

The complex molecule that comprised the Qvavor red sun and its large family of planets plus moons really was the Center of the *living* galaxy. The Big Black Hole in the Center of the Monopdonow Galaxy was nothing like the tiny one the Sardon established to delete the galaxy's profits. The Black Hole only *appeared* as if it was *Life's Center. Life was actually* centered around red Qvavor and its complicated system of orbiters. Cosmic ripples began at Qvavor, which was the first solar system.

Astrophysicists had marveled at the longevity of the deep crimson sun. Single Qvavor-star, late in life, had a steady beat. What was considered the *first solar system* was really the oldest one known. Qvavor System was the oldest *molecule* to still exist. Some said events that transpired on the 17th orbit of Qvavor did more to send love-waves and end the 100-Yarn War than anything else. Did Qvavor of OM change the influence of Belial and tip the scales toward the light?

Kings and Queens of the Galaxy had lived in old palaces of Qvavor-17, the primary Power Center in the system. The figurehead 'President of the Galaxy' and 'President of the Universe' were housed on the solo satellite of the 17th orbit. For puppet-governors, their homes were sub-standard.

Depending on the era or Ages of the galaxy, one never

knew if the present Governor of Qvavor-17 possessed true Power or not. Were the OM Kings and Queens (famous for male/female twin-leaders) figureheads, fakes, fascists, puppets, paid dictators, actors, secret agents, sincere do-gooders or wielders of real power? In the past, they were all of the above.

At the GST of 1399.73, the lone planetary body in the 17th orbit was in perfect hands and so was the galaxy. Power sat well with the current Magistrate who was no phony. Governor Barados of House Juri was the Seat of Control and officially presided with his wife, Tinesia of House Elrabi. They were galactic Royalty and deserved to hold the high posts.

Trillions of Qvavorans in the Life-Center on multiple satellites of the 49 orbits were totally oblivious of the superpower they possessed. *"A flutter of a buttermoth on a Qvavor satellite could create a tsunami on an ocean planet light-yarns away."* Whatever happened on this world of prestige and prehistory within the sacred system of OM, truly had repercussions elsewhere in the galaxy. Not even the highest authorities of Governor Barados and Governess Tinesia had an inkling their actions and those of their predecessors were amplified throughout the Great Pinwheel.

The parallel Rom Sector, un-capitalized, was a bizarre counterpart. Ancient computer-chip records recorded that Rom did not exist until relatively recently. There were only 23 sectors in the original Pinwheel. Rom was a new addition and an odd attachment. Mental powers utilized in everyday life in OM Sector of systems were easily perverted when moved to the adjacent Rom Sector. The vibration inside Rom systems flowed to the negative side. Particles with a positive charge on OM worlds changed to the negative charge on Rom worlds.

The power to 'tuen' was found on planets in Rom Sector. (Not to be confused with remote-viewing of 'teuning' into Galactic News). Any psychic could amplify telepathic abilities by bathing in rare, mystic pools of Rom Sector. Crystals, waterfalls, rains, rivers and pools within OM were known to heal, energize and reduce one's age. But in the negative Rom Sector, telepaths could hone their telekinesis into a mighty tuening weapon of *physical force*. A mind could form a moving battering-ram.

Religious Orders have traveled to OM for the special, holy experience of witnessing some of the most sacred places. To bask in the knowledge, 'see' music or take part in a vast array of ceremonies from 'the Beginning' were life-altering events. Standing on the ancient 'Soma Shores' was enough for one to see the Light. 'Wonder Falls of Aorin' or the 'Calavery Caves of Healing Crystals' or the anti-aging 'Baths of Gith' were phenomenal experiences to be treasured for a lifetime.

Groups of alien truth-seekers in one package or another had made pilgrimages to OM systems to find enlightenment or Nirvana. Substantiated stories stated a few religious Orders who searched for the *golden path* inside OM systems, gravitated to the 'Rom Way' and remained in the darker dimension. Whether psychics wanted to sharpen their personal ESP powers or business skills, Rom provided a seductive attraction to many innocent seekers.

Multitudes had submitted personal permission to enter (a different) 'Enlightenment City' on Qvavor-17 only to be sadly rejected. Only those with a perfectly pure Center could enter the Gates of Enlightenment City. Here was where the First Family ruled from the twin Houses of Juri and Elrabi. What occurred here would change worlds elsewhere *then change them back again.*

Explosive traumas happened and were about to happen again at the Royal Houses of the First Family. A large population on Qvavor-17 and on the giant sun's other satellites/moons paid close attention to Governor Barados, Governess Tinesia and their lovely child Shera Pris. The Royal Wedding was a major ceremony. The birth of Shera was an awesome spectacle for the public. What they wore at Royal Rituals was analyzed more than fiscal policies. *(Consider every action in the Continuum of Qvavor affected the larger Continuum as a whole).*

Now there was an immediate threat. 'Breaking News' of the First Lady's strange illness hit the airwaves, yet the news was old news to those of the Royal Houses. The 49 *electrons* in the system and their multiple components were alerted over interplanetary media. Qvavor's complex structure of planets and moons *shuttered* at the thought that there were big problems with the 'Perfect Family.' Whatever parallels in outer rims also shuttered with inner, propagated waves.

Trouble had already spread among the Houses of Juri and Elrabi. Attendants, advisors, people in the wide circle (official and social) noticed that the perfect couple appeared to have *separated.* The news carried stories how Governor Barados stayed in House Juri while the Governess was very ill in Elrabi. Recent, petty squabbles between men and women were put on hold. Everyone wanted to know what rumors were true and which ones were not true concerning the First Family. Females wanted to know, "Why was he not at her bedside?" Males defended the Governor and reported, "He kept their 3-yarn old daughter away from her mother's illness."

It was the day of ultimate destiny. It was *that night.* After red Qvavor set in the west, Barados traveled to House Elrabi in his sky-plane named 'Balthazar.'

He did not want to die! He wanted his family to live!

Tonight was when he would meet with 'Saturn' (Ghost of Sardon) with a connection to Outside. Tonight was when an answer, *the* answer, had to be made. Someone, either Tinesia or Barados, *had to die!* Saturn convinced him that a 'sacrifice' of one of them must be executed. He knew in his Center it was true. He was very frightened for both of them...all three of them.

He did not want to die! He wanted his family to live!

Barados landed the sky-plane on Elrabi's roof and entered the massive building in a daze. He dismissed those who attended to Tinesia. Even the private doctors and medical experts were sent away. Tinesia was still unconscious. Her life was slowing passing. Whatever illness was killing her had no cure. The damage was irreversible. She was almost dead.

The First Lady lay on the bed and examination table. She appeared older and in pain. Her beautiful eyes remained closed while she grimaced horribly in discomfort. The body of the Governess contorted again.

Barados, earlier, had a *dream-shift of the zogs* that was real and overpowering. He shifted into the vision now: Tinesia was in bed without any analysis equipment. She was in a very different condition during the dream. *She was extremely happy.* They finished making love. She did not appear to have any physical problems.

The Governor was also happy and excited to be alive. He reached for more GUARP-6 when, she stunned him with the words, *"You have to be the one who lives."*

The statement brought Barados out of bliss and he crashed back to reality. Yet he knew that the vision was only a fake dream-shift. He said, "It can't be me. I love you. I can't let you die for me, Tin."

"You *must,* my love."

Barados cried, "Our child." Tears welled up in their eyes. Tinesia was alert, alive and very articulate. She insisted, "You must live to teach Shera Pris. I'll never recover from the alien xirus-illness. It has to be *you.* You have so much to teach the world, and her. Remember, I know who you are...*Zog.* I...I know...you are one of the 'carriers of Zog.' No one knows except me, uh." Tinesia smiled a large, proud smile. "I know you are part Zog."

The name packed a bomb blast in intensity on Qvavor-17, also. 'The Builder of All Things' was given the Lebritz name 'the Zog' as was strangely done in many systems. Barados' secret identity of Zog had been a grand *unspoken thing* between them. He knew of the Blue Light that was inside him or why he was special. Now, in a mental manifestation, Tinesia told him that there was only one possible choice. Could he live with himself without her, knowing that his choice was responsible for her death? Could the good Governor, with a pure Center, choose *his life over hers?*

The First Lady kissed him and clearly said, "For our daughter's sake and for the world, you must tell the zogs you are to live and I am to die." She smiled. "It can be no other way, my darling. I w-won't allow it." Her love was infinite. Her love shined and the World Watched.

His head nearly fell to the floor.

Her last words were, "You have already sacrificed yourself once for the world on Mineer. Now it is time to think of *yourself,* my love. You h-have to be the one w-who survives." She spoke with weak confidence.

The vision shifted back to reality. Barados stood over the pain-riddled body of the Governess. She remained incoherent. He hated to see his wife in pain. He hated the universe when it caused pain, especially for those he loved. Something *had* to be done to stop the suffering and calm her tortured spirit. His inner powers of *blue light* were useless.

Suddenly, Saturn or *Ghost Sardon* appeared from electrical smoke. One of the negative zogs materialized. It was a tall and frightening creature in a grey cloak. Saturn's voice was electronically amplified. *"You know it is time, Barados."*

The Governor of Qvavor-17 visibly shook. "Do not make me decide such a thing, demon."

"I am sorry, my son. There is nothing I can do."

"Wait! Let me ask you a question before I make my choice."

"Acceptable."

"Saturn, my Negotiator, the spirit..."

"Yes? Barados, the man... Yes?"

"What should I do?"

"I cannot answer that question for you, my son."

"But you said I could ask. That means you have to answer. That was our agreement. If the agreement is not adhered to, then why should any agreement be adhered to? Then why—"

"All right! You have a point. My answer to you, oh, Barados is..."

"Yes?"

"It cannot be you who dies."

"What?"

"You must live. No zog or man can cure the xirus of the

First Lady. She is going to die soon, anyway. I am sorry to tell you, my son. Let her...save you as you have saved her. You have much to do. You cannot die, now. She is willing. She loves you. Grant her last wish and live, Barados."

That was not what Governor Barados expected to hear from one of the zogs. He was completely torn in two.

"What would your mother have wanted for you, son? She would have wanted you to live, would she not?"

The answer had to be now. Saturn received a message from Outside to call off the test. It refused. The tall, evil figure would take responsibility for future consequences. Or, was Sardonic Saturn not to be trusted?

The Governor finally and sadly said over the painful body of his wife, "I...will...live." Barados cried as he knew his perfect world was shattered. *He decided on the wrong answer!*

"...And...she...will...die."

With those words, an entire universe *dream-shifted into chaos.* The Continuum was darker and colder, the little one and the Larger Systems. Shockwaves reached outer rims. So many Barados supporters from the Outside placed the wrong dylar-bet. He had such support until his instinct for self-preservation kicked in and *did not sacrifice himself*...so she could live.

The test was to test love in the heart of Man. But he was not his Father. *The right answer was to sacrifice himself!* How pure and perfect was his Center? How bright the blue light? Barados was supposed to have said, "Damn the zogs! Damn the consequences! I don't care about me. All I want is save her!" That was not spoken and felt in the timeline. The red-black night had grown blacker and redder.

When it dawned upon Barados that it was in his grasp to *save* his great Love, and he did not, the pain of the tragedy *knifed him in two.* Barados disappointed everyone who watched the small continuum from the Outside. He disappointed his friends and family, anyone who had ever believed in him. He disappointed parallel dimensions and every being that wagered on him. He disappointed the Zogs in the farthest realms of the Continuum and 'Watchers' in every form.

Everything would have been different if Barados chose Love over his own Life. The Great War could have been completely averted before its First Wave.

Saturn or Ghost of Sardon was gone. 'Carrier of Sardon' performed its part in the play very well. No one dreamed or imagined, not even the Zogs, what cascading disaster would result from subtle actions sparked in the 17th orbit of Qvavor. The physical world out there was now in big trouble.

Barados rose to his feet. He prayed for a miracle and received the strangest feeling. He had never felt this sensation before. It was the psychic feeling that he was totally *alone in the universe.* He sensed a total disconnection and abandonment from the Hierarchy above. Royalty should not feel that way. He was no longer Royalty. He was now shunned by the zogs and the Zogs. He was considered a lowly embarrassment. Barados was held *in contempt* of Cosmic Court. *Nothing would ever be the same.* The world had gone to Hensi and Hensi had come to the world.

Tinesia, surprisingly, came to! She did not die. The Governess did not have the sickness anymore. She was well. She was cured. She was going to live. *Thank the zogs!*

Barados was thrilled and excited. His nightmare did not have to be true. The Governor hugged her, tightly. He needed comfort and joy so much. He had to shake this terrible feeling of awful *dread from above and around.*

Tinesia angrily screamed, "Don't touch me!" The First Lady pushed him away. "Don't you *ever* touch me *again!"*

"What?" His heart stopped and so did his breathing.

Tinesia yelled, "I don't want to *ever* see you again! Is that clear?"

"You *love* me." He tried to convince himself as he tossed his last hope to the farthest reaches of the Outside universe. Barados felt divided, beaten, defeated, confused and the worst was feeling *alone.*

"I don't *love* you," she screamed through his heart.

The 'perfect couple' was no longer in Paradise. And because of decisions from the cosmic 'Life-Center' of the galaxy, more than only the small continuum would suffer.

***

Almost everyone in the Continuum felt the tension as the negative cascade spilled over from rivulet to rivulet and continued outward in propagation. The feeling could be described as an 'urge for violence,' a desire to display aggression, to act out extreme impulses and not care who got damaged in the process. Aliens, humanoids, humans and other types of non-robotic life were affected. They suddenly acted *off-Center.*

Old 'fayds' were renewed between Men and Women. Civil wars broke out along sex-lines. Men and Women, wherever there were men and women (especially) throughout the 24 sectors, were *at each other's throats!*

Many sectors reported attacks and bombings in female areas and the reverse was true. Hysteria occurred simultaneously inside many systems. Creatures in genders were caught within paranoia and fear. Each feared the other sex, what they could do and what they were capable of doing.

Male and female militant radical groups armed themselves. Men united with Men and Women joined the Viper Movement, mostly. The Ladies were the ones with the Big Gun. The Ladies were the 'Chosen Ones of Zog.' Even a few Rebel Alliance female forces joined the Vipers in their crusade.

Galactic network and channel outlets were not the initial catalyst for the 'War of the Sexes.' The firestorm spread on its own. Media did not *curb* the fighting, but tended to increase death tolls. News further fueled the 'Gender Wars.' Networks spewed Viper propaganda while the male slant of battles was given over other channel outlets.

Stories of rapes, murders of females, men beating women were broadcasted over the networks. News stories of females that tortured males were well covered on male channels. The result of the galactic blitz was: Men-haters and

Women-haters could not wait to be on the front lines to actually *kill the other sex!*

There was no more ZP Police. ZPs had been absorbed by their larger Peacekeeper sisters. In the future, they would evolve and become the Cardille Warriors. So far, atomics were not used in the fighting. Forces organized, regrouped and planned future strategies. Mechanical death-factories on both sides, aided by a certain Ghost in the Machine, spat out war-wagons of every type off smoothly running assembly lines.

Rebel Alliances of Anti-Vipers also organized as best they could without their real benefactors, lost in the Colossus disaster. The RAs quickly built powerful versions of war machines: space armadas and the entire gamut of state-of-the-art weaponry. Location for the primary Rebel Base was in an asteroid field that orbited an unregistered green sun in Benis Pol Sector.

The parallel Territory to Benis was, of course, Anther where Viper Lodges stood for countless generations. Wormhole jumping or creating a *parallax bridge* from a predominant female sector to a predominantly male sector and the reverse was a common occurrence. Now whole PK and RA fleets had positioned for massive attacks. Movements were strategic, like a game of Romvoid, back and forth before the first furious volleys of offensives. No one knew the nature of the coming attacks.

Will they be atomic?

Stories floated over 'Galactic Media' that the Rebel Alliance finally secured the billions of dylars necessary to purchase a nuke. The stories were not confirmed. Many Citizens believed the 'Male-Nuke' story was not true, that Zog would never allow 'Y' or 'Q' chromosome-beings of the *male* gender to ever possess the 'Instrument of Peace.'

The networks reported a Rebel Alliance fabrication: *false flag* or untrue ploy. Women's outlets expressed the contention: "The Rebel Alliance had no Great Bomb. They want to use the idea they possess one for leverage over the Lodge of Viper-Women."

Then the unthinkable happened. A vanguard of RA silver saucers entered the 'Ryine Wormhole' and emerged in perfect positions for striking within Anther Pol. Yet the Arrival-Points were odd. Targets seemed to be an uninhabited system of a turquoise star designated LGA166. Network recorders were in the right place in space to capture every detail in 3HD.

Once more, the galaxy watched the display. A prime saucer appeared with two groups of three smaller saucers flanked on either side. The Rebel Rangers flying armada closed in on eight satellites of LGA166. The system was chosen by the Men because there were 'eight' components to the star and also they were completely lifeless planets.

Media News (male voice) informed the galaxy that the next actions were intended as a "Statement against the Viper-manufactured story of *Gildenstein Smith who never existed.* She was used as a fake-enemy to rally troops to war. She never birthed eight boys. The next actions are 'our statement' and what we want Citizens to know."

The message from the prime silver ship was broadcasted to the galaxy. Life forms witnessed a White Beam strike the first planet in the system. LGA166-1 became immediately engulfed in a firestorm far worse than a general burning of its surface. Every molecule of the planet exploded apart in a soundless, colorless blast! The first planet in orbit was no more.

The six smaller ships quickly flew a mega-bar to positions near the remaining seven electrons aka planets in the system. As soon as the coordinates were reached, six wide White Beams vaporized six orbiters! There was now only one planet of LGA166 in a far, outer orbit. The larger prime saucer sped to a place near the last planet. The other silver saucers joined the alignment. Again, a White Beam was discharged from the large saucer and again the result was a planet *up in smoke.* Crystal-recorders received and sent events out in real-time. A galaxy teuned-in to one more war calamity.

Why did Rebel Men do it? Males used the White Beam!

Networks went crazy. The star LGA166 had no more planets. There had never been a 'confirmed' Viper-atomic detonation outside of the Ralian Explosions. The Rebel Alliance fleet of seven silver saucers zipped back to the Benis Pol Territory and celebrated the rogue actions taken in the *theater of war.* No one was killed and the world understood there would be *balance* between sides. Men, headquartered in Benis Territory, also possessed the Big Bomb. Women, headquartered only a wormhole's jump away in Anther, geared for War!

The parody should have created a lull in the fighting. It did not. Men's forums stated: "Now Zog's Instrument of Peace can *be* an instrument of peace. Now there is equality, two major super-powers who cannot First Strike one without paying the consequences of retaliation."

Networks went crazy again. They repeated the evaporation of eight worlds over and over to the public. First was the horrific Ralian erasure, now there was the 'Catastrophe at LGA166' produced entirely by Men. When challenged that no one living was on the eight planets, a shocking 'Breaking News' story surfaced with impeccable timing over all networks:

There was a small base of Vipers and a station of geologists assigned to LGA166-8. Total casualties numbered 64...all women. The Ladies reported that the RA leaving the eighth planet for last, to be annihilated by the prime saucer, was evidence that *the Men knew of the base there.* When the story hit network space-waves, all Hensi broke loose. The allegation was untrue, but it did not matter what was true or untrue anymore.

War machines and more war machines poured from assembly plants in every sector to whoever had the influence or ability to pay in dylars. The Insectoids were very powerful because of sales of atomics. Other investors found nuclear warfare an extremely profitable venture. The dylar-profit margins were incredible since the price of nukes dropped on Black Markets. The rich of each sex bought more and more

Weapons of Mass Destruction as well as Media air-time. More battles of a non-nuclear nature broke out between planets and between entire systems.

The next events in what was once a calm and peaceful Pinwheel were ultimate destructions like echoes of dark World Wars from the First Galactic Reich. *Spacial armies attacked with the White Beam Weapon!* Planets were designated War-Zone targets. It did not matter if both sexes and aliens were on the 'designated targets.' If the planets were marked for annihilation, *every molecule was exploded to nothing!*

Yarns and yarns passed with fantastic, horrible and frightening statistics of death and destruction reported on both sides. Anther Pol and Benis Pol went from attacking each other with conventional weapons to red beam nukes and then later escalated to *White Beam Warfare.*

Whole planets were *erased out of existence* or burnt to blackened, radioactive crisps or cracked into pieces. Madness saw no end. Cauldrons of Hate raged so intense it was as if 'space itself was on fire.' No Citizen could believe the latest reports: 'Entire suns could be affected by the White Beam!'

Small suns were destroyed being eaten away by a reverse atomic reaction. Trillions of souls in star systems could be wiped out in one stroke.

No one was safe or felt safe. Any planet could be decreed a *military target* whose inhabitants were sympathizers to one Movement or another and marked for destruction. More fear spread. Flames of destruction were nuclear. *Suns were winking out and carrying souls down the Black Hole faster than galaxy profits.*

When no one thought times could possibly get worse, *they got worse.* A film aired on networks that showed an adult version of May Bulair. Mebby joined the first institution of Cardilles. The tall, beautiful, white-haired woman now had very long/straight hair. Who could have conceived the child 'Darling of Tomorrow' was now a Viper armed to the teeth? Mebby was resplendent in a black, tight uniform that bulged with weapons and curves. What a contrast from the adolescent singer and dancer. She exemplified the New Wave of Cardilles. Her dark eye makeup and full figure made the former child star look very sexy.

The short film showed sweet, hot Mebby in a position of command. She ordered some leggy trooper gals to remain at their stations during an attack on the ship. The spaceship was the *Lebsos,* confirmed as where she was assigned as a Chief Cardille, 2nd Class. Humanoids to aliens cheered the valiant girl, even some Rebels (although they would never admit it). Viewers were not sure what they viewed with no prior warning to what was about to happen. Suddenly, the galaxy viewed Mebby at her own station when the entire bulkhead was blown away. The world witnessed her bloody (bio) parts *explode!* The State android (different than MBT-14K) was ejected into space. Citizens were too shocked to cry when they observed Viper-Meb's (artificial) blood burst. Many cried and could not speak.

The galactic population dwindled significantly. Suns started to disappear. *Maybe this was not good for business?*

***

On Qvavor-17, the Life-Center, the Royal Family and others within Enlightenment City did not age like the rest of the galaxy. While armadas had battled in space for yarns during ages that had seen the first sign of Zog's Instrument to ghastly times of the present, using it as casual weaponry, the situation with the Governor and Governess was more or less the same. She was under the spell of wanting nothing to do with her *'rat-bastard husband,'* the Governor.

The huge news was that the First Family had separated. Governor Barados and Governess Tinesia were permanently broken up. At the exact same time of super tensions between the sexes and the obliteration of worlds, the Royal Couple *divorced.* Humanoids and other life forms of the 49 orbits reacted in shock as if the Golden Governors had been assassinated. Qvavorans were in mourning and did not know what to believe. The 'perfect couple' was ready to *tear each other to pieces!*

The last time Barados, Tinesia and little Shera Pris were together, it was the lowest point in Barados' life. The Governess acted like a 'woman possessed.' She kicked and screamed in a hyper state with the energy of three men. It took all of the Governor's strength to restrain her so Tinesia would not hurt herself. Barados yelled, "I will *not* hurt you!"

She exploded out of his hands. She threw blows at him, directly in front of the child. The perfect infant, Shera, absorbed the fight between her mother and father. The little girl's head moved from side to side in frightened disbelief. Shera covered her wet eyes. She covered her small ears. *She demanded that her parents stop,* but the 3-yarn old had no power. Her psyche was greatly damaged from the clashes above her.

A few attendants witnessed the private and personal crisis. Their stories were later sold to the media. The war had already propagated throughout the land in small doses: bombings, poisonings, husbands killing wives, wives killing husbands. Qvavorans watched their war and the First Family's crisis.

The small continuum was cut off from the large Continuum. They had hardly a shred of knowledge that the galaxy was set *ablaze with War.* Qvavorans never heard of the Big War. The ironic oddity was that some Citizens believed Qvavor-17 was ground zero and the main factor that *started* the 100-Yarn War. What started the 'War of the Sexes' was as questionable as what ended it. The answers to the questions remained highly debated subjects.

The Royal Fight and Divorce, that made headlines, created an unofficial declaration of (non-nuclear) *war* throughout the small continuum. Men sided with Governor Barados. Women sided with Governess Tinesia. The 72 planets and moons were completely polarized.

Tinesia, with no signs of the illness, kidnapped little Shera right out of House Juri. She grabbed the youngster from her attendant's care and left Barados for good. Barados never saw his only child ever again.

More killings happened in the small continuum, which was magnified in the Big One and more in the BIGGER ONE. Blood of many colors was soon spilled. Where was love? Men and Women should *not* be fighting. Men cloned programmed males. Women cloned programmed females and the fighting escalated.

Vehicles piloted by males blasted and destroyed vehicles piloted by females. The reverse was also true. Women with any weapon available clashed with male ground troops. Terrible bloodbaths occurred on the infantry's battle lines and in the skies of the 49 orbits.

Governor Barados had to do *something* to end the insanity in his system. He gave a media speech which was carried by every outlet in the small continuum. He desperately pleaded for war to cease. His words, unfortunately, had no affect on the Citizens. The Governor was seen as a hypocrite.

Armies of tanks rolled over green hills and turned them dark brown. Large sections of Qvavoran planets were devastated. Qvavorans might have ended the fighting sooner if they only understood their actions were magnified to the rest of the Universe. If they knew that suns and stars were ripped apart as a result of their choices, they might have ceased hostilities earlier.

But a miracle truly occurred on Qvavor-17 that turned universes around. Some say the *miracle* that occurred on the 17th orbit within the Great Enlightenment City *ended the War.* Could what have happened here have been directly responsible for the events on Fanguard Fields *where history was made?* The miracle had little to do with second chances and everything to do with decisions made in higher Dimensions.

It was as if a 'Card was Played in a Larger Game' far above the level of anyone in the Continuum and in the continuum. The Fate Card drawn by a Zog (Zog's ZOG) gave Barados a 'Chance' to redeem himself. The Governor, without his knowledge, *went back in time.* Barados entered a 'reality-splice' and was once again with a dying Governess, the love of his small life. The Queen of Elrabi lay dying as she was with the *magnetic illness.*

Barados turned and saw he was once again in the presence of the tall, evil creep of a thing he called 'Saturn.' The answer had to be *now.* Saturn received a *message* from Outside to call off the test. It refused. The tall, dark figure would take responsibility for future consequences. *Or, was Sardonic Saturn not to be trusted?*

The Governor finally said over the painful body of his wife, "I...will..."

"Yes?" Saturn asked and urged.

"Give my life to save hers."

"What?"

"She lives...not me."

"But...you cannot..." Saturn was in shock and that was strange for a demon. Its empty, pasty face with multiple wrinkles froze. *"Oh...no."*

"What's wrong, Saturn-man?"

"This is not how the continuum was to flow."

Barados had chose Love over his own Life. The tricksters *were tricked.*

Suddenly, Tinesia came out of her unconscious delirium. The world was considerably brighter and warmer. No one died in the House and there would be no Royal Divorce. Barados gave the proper response and Sardon's Ghost was thwarted. Zogs that backed (wagered) Barados and believed in him were justified. They made the right dylar bet.

Barados and Tinesia hugged and kissed. Their tongues touched. They were in love. They felt ecstatic and happy that everything turned out well. Her illness was entirely gone. She had her husband and healthy daughter, Shera Pris. The world was a brilliant place once again. Goodness, love and light reigned supreme and those feelings were amplified to the rest of the galaxy. Life forms that engaged in battles for many yarns had finally and miraculously quit fighting. Qvavor-17 could be why. Yet there was one more story, some said, the real reason the 100-Yarn War between Men and Women ended. Others believed it was a perfect storm of three or four different factors and numerous levels that tipped the scales to +.

Formost was Atomic Power. It was seen as a *dirty and dangerous* source of energy and was never developed by any intelligent world. Advanced civilizations knew of a hundred better, cleaner and more efficient sources of electricity than nuclear. As far as the Bomb and mega-Bomb, a ban was firmly in place and no one would dare use it again. Life had its fill of mass-killing and was now going to start living and breathing once more.

What caused the 'Fall of the Second Reich' or what ended the Chancellery? The Big Question had been disputed by more systems than there were possible solutions to the puzzle. Enlightened beings from every sector claimed to possess the answer why everything, on a galactic level, *got good.* Why were 'Fanguard' battlefields in Anthor Sector named the same as a primitive guild on a small planet called Aret, light-yarns away?

[We go back in time to attempt answering the questions].

***

Did every reign of terror fade or come to absolute termination? Every Empire died (cycled), from supremely Zog-like beautiful Dynasties to the most wretched and wicked of thrones. Time passed and everything *changed. Were creatures simply filled to the gills and mar-slits with the Chancellery?* Did the Cosmic Pendulum have to (yin-yang) swing the other way? Were beings of all colors along the Mainstream sick and tired of constant warfare? Did every King or, in this case, Sardonic Devil and its work fade to nothing in an end-game?

Remnants of the Chancellery in female forms, for yarns, took great notice of war-statistics with the intricate care of a young Sardon. War was down. Killings and massacres on a galactic level had decreased by 10% and had been down for yarns. Numbers did not lie. The trend was devastating to various warlords, religious Orders and arms-dealers who profited across a fantastic range. The Ladies had to brew more war to survive.

Past 'fayds' or wars between planets, solar systems and between the 'Pols' had to be rekindled. Beings of every sun-color, new enemies to old enemies, were losing the *will to kill*. Peace broke out on a few stellar fronts and was soon squashed by legions of local Viper-Women Peacekeepers in the area. War was a game and the game had to be played *faster*.

Old Authority Vipers as well as their male enemies would never put up with peace. Something had to be done to get 'Life to Kill' or for soldiers in the fields to slaughter with ultimate, blind rage. Death tolls and profits had to be amplified.

On a tiny and insignificant planetoid within the mysterious Selestra Matrix Sector of space, an odd world called 'Aret' could hold another answer to the Big Question. The inconspicuous planetoid of 8 colors might have stilled many swords and lowered many weapons in the universe at one magical moment (some life forms believed). Humanoid Eightoid-creatures on Aret started an amazing Peace Movement that pushed outward, expanding at light-speed. Yes, it was at Anther Pol's Fanguard Fields 'Where History Was Made' but...

What really caused male and female forces to stop fighting? If the *touchstone* of these special Fields would have swung the other way and *war continued*, the War and a million other Hensi-fires throughout the sectors could have raged for *another 100 yarns!*

Why did fighting *stop* at that crucial place and at that crucial time in galactic History? What propagated a Wave of Love? Some believed the events on small Aret were responsible and affected important decisions thousands of light-yarns away.

Shades of a covert Chancellery Experiment were conducted for the last 12 yarns on Aret, ever since the 10% reduction in *dylar deaths* and war-profits were first discovered. The Great War was in its 100th yarn, mostly in the 'Pols' but mass-killings were in every sector. Women had the post-

Chancellery officials *by the balls.*

The Viper-Women played a cagy experiment on Aret. Their greatest psychics *(and the greatest psychics are Women)* who had clear visions of the future, understood the major importance of the home of Eightoids. They knew of a 'harmonic tri-vergence' between Aret, located in a weird sector of space called 'Selestra Matrix,' 'Anther Pol' and 'Belial.' Inexplicably, Aret could teun to dark, forbidden Belial Sector as well as affect Fanguard Fields in Anther Pol Sector. The Girls knew to monitor from a distance and observe Aret in its natural environment as to not contaminate the experiment. The decision was to *pretend to be primitive* when dealing with the colorful natives. Away missions to Aret were always careful *not* to expose a chip of technology to the Eightoids. Lady Mystics knew the solid futures. Aret could tilt the scales, *but which way?* Would Super-Soldiers be created to fuel the flames of War on a galactic scale, or would something else happen?

Covert 'Prime Directive' of Fanguard on Aret for over 12 yarns was to develop the extremely desirable 'Super-Soldier Pill' or SSP for short. This yarn, the best candidate was a 'tri-cerium-12' solution. The Old Chancellery's Fanguard, with hundreds of branches like a multi-legged vidor, had deeply studied the possibility of reaching the humanoid soul. 'Fang' exhausted every means, method and personnel at its disposal to uncover the very center of the humanoid being, what some called the soul or spirit. Animal-rage was believed to sleep there. If the Hatred could be awoken, tapped, unleashed and controlled, then the goal of *increasing war* could be achieved, *chemically.*

The Aretan 'Eightoid' Empire was a simple civilization based on 8. Humanoids had eight fingers and eight toes. There were eight bright skin colors that revealed one's place of origin on the planetoid. Eight 'Houses,' each with a specific Color, had battled through endless Fanguard Wars. Arets only employed primitive weapons since the earliest of times.

Aretans had no clue of high cultures that danced in star playgrounds far above their heads. They did not know of other life in the universe. Yet larger worlds had keen interests in the colorful Eightoids. Wars were able to have great longevity on Aret over the course of countless generations. Primitive natives were unaware of anything called a 'Chancellery' or the very old 'Order.' The State was only known as Fanguard (like the famous 'Fields').

Fanguard was the Ruling House over the eight Houses and eight Colors. Every high-ranking scientist of the 'modern age' had been called in to the important island of Jenova. For the last 12 yarns, under the secret name of 'Project Zog-Head,' Fanguard chemists and lab technicians had been busy in desperate experiments to end the bloody 'Generation Wars.' This was the story told the naive public and it was mostly believed without question. Aretans were conditioned to think the leaders were sincere with *peace talks.* (Yahoos did the same).

The big news stated a *breakthrough* was just around the corner. Could ages of warfare finally come to an end? Could genetic experts have discovered the *soul* and struck primal, animal instincts? The 'Experiment' was unknown to the general, fighting and programmed population of Aretans. The innocents on the planet were so brainwashed that 'Life was War and War was Life' that they absolutely could not see any other way to live...*almost.* There were always bands of revolutionaries.

Fang's best candidate for the SSP last yarn was a bimeno-acid nicknamed 'Violator-11.' Before that, there were high hopes for 'dimetranol-10.' Each solution, pill or gas proved to be a fantastic energizer for a few yams and then there was always the inevitable *crash.* Fang soldiers were only temporarily motivated to kill.

Lady Admirals were never satisfied with the results of Zog-Head. Infantries and navies were not *that* enraged to kill opposing Colors on the stimulants. Fang corporate (military) heads wanted *more blood and guts.* They wanted a chemical agent that amplified the primal survival-memory. They wanted *blind rage!* They wanted soldiers to revert to *first-instincts,* when they were un-evolved animals long ago. Fanguard wanted unthinking, super-drugged killers who would obey without question and slaughter enemy Colors mercilessly.

Each chemical SSP candidate proved little more effective than over-the-counter energy drinks. Fang wanted its soldiers hopped up on *violent rage-pills* or *madness juice* whose powerful effects really lasted and without a *crash*. Finally, this yarn's tri-cerium-12 SSP could be exactly what the Military Monarchy desired most. It was believed to hit the very center of Life and create an enraged, maniacal monster out of the weakest of soldiers. But, could the *monster within* be controlled by Fanguard's finest?

A quick background of the Aretans: their 'modern age' consisted of boats, horse-driven carts, metal shields, body shielding, small bombs, poison gas, poison darts, bows and arrows, cart-bows, crossbows, catapults, spears, sharp knives and axes.

The planet only knew War as a way of life. Every labor or opportunity of employment concerned some aspect of Fanguard. New fields of study for bright young students were connected to facets of war. Programming and propaganda over primitive means convinced the ranks to continually *join the fight*. There was only the State; there was only Fang and the War. There had only ever been war and Arets were sure that there would always, always *be* the War. What could they possibly do with their lives if the fighting actually came to an abrupt halt? The dream of peace was unbelievable.

Arets achieved glimpses of modernism, such as breakthroughs on the chemical and medical fronts. Complex machines, equipment, tools, radios, automobiles or flying contraptions were far beyond their capabilities. Yet genetic scientists under the military State Monarchy called Fanguard could clone; transplant hearts, conduct *miracle* brain operations and the most important current endeavor for secret Lady-Admirals: to search, discover and synthesize the animal-within or dark side.

They wanted the SSP packaged and/or bottled as a

regular aid on the utility belt of every fighting soldier of every Color. Wars had become monotonous after countless generations. The purpose of every Aretan was losing momentum. Six Admirals and their 66 Generals were scared for what tomorrow might bring. Something drastic had to be tried.

The Military Monarchy attempted numerous campaigns to justify more war offensives on old and new colored fronts. Prejudicial (slur) programs or organizations and newspaper ads whose only purpose was propaganda were intensified. Still, the killing and fighting were at an all time low for a population on the increase. Population was supposed to remain the same, not increase.

'Project Zog-Head' was secretly instituted twelve yarns ago as the answer to Fang's growing concerns. They knew what was called 'technology' matured at a 'flug's pace.' Aretans were made to be not that proficient in developing new ways to kill people of other Colors.

The thinking of high officials was if a quantum leap in a killing-technique was developed, one Color could gain a monopoly and decisively *win* the War. Admirals and Generals understood that a winner could never be declared. *The game of death over generations must never end.*

Guns, cannons, rockets and gunpowder were withheld from the colorful soldier-people of Aret. They would have trouble believing the concepts, anyway. Skilled bowmen on horseback, poison arrows, darts, cart-bows and mustard (acid) gas-grenades with limited range were the main offensive weapons of various armies and navies at a distance. Up close, nothing could compare with good old hand-to-hand combat.

Admirals only wanted a *continuation* of the fighting with one Color building up a rivalry or a 'fayd' against another Color, insuring yarns and yarns of bloodshed. Fang officials on top of the Aretan Pyramid or 'Power Structure' understood omni-wars were merely gruesome games. Colors were various sides in the game and soldiers were expendable pieces on the game board. Aretan life from its very inception was set up in this way. And nothing in their small world was ever going to change it. These facts in play created the 'stage' and 'theater' for war as the World Watched.

Admirals (in secret), Generals and Corporals from the eight Colors convened regularly in opposing *safe houses.* Parliament House on the neutral island of Jenova was the Aretans' prime gathering place. Here was where treaties were signed and where new conflicts were planned. Every time one battle ceased, another flared into existence. The public was unaware of the futility in their officials' efforts for peace.

Private Citizens believed Fanguard regularly met to hammer out a lasting peace, but a *warlessness* state (for one reason or another) could never be achieved. Masses were controlled to not question the dictates of the Fang. The huge majority of Aretans were *asleep.* They accepted the bitter conflicts as a fact of life. Actually, they depended on it. Its alternative was not only an unknown to the Eightoids, it was also an unknown to the Military Monarchy that ruled them. No one knew what the future would be without the primary reason for life, which was to kill your neighbors with different skin Colors.

Citizens from each Color were considered 'privates.' Citizens begun as 'private 4th class' with very limited constitutional rights. Men and women worked their way up with different loyalty-duties in the War effort, winning more rights and more privileges as they *ascended* through the ranks. Fifth level was the Sergeantry with only 833 or 834 spots (depended on one's Color) available and they were officially part of the Fanguard. The most coveted positions on Aret were the top 7,404. Only four Colors could become Corporals and fill the 166 or 167 spots. Only two Colors could become Generals that have a total of 66 spots. Red was the dominant House and the only House allowed to create (unseen) Admirals, which always numbered six. There was no position higher than Admirals. Decisions had to be unanimous among Admirals. Corporals were the highest officials who surveyed, played with war-strategies like coaches of ball teams and flew over war zones at a distance. Only sergeants and millions of privates did the actual battlefield fighting.

Three friends rendezvoused at an abandoned Fang surgical station at precisely 8'bok. *Why do weird things always happen at 8'bok?* They arrived under the sign: '23' still visible after all these yarns. Thick vegetation had about totally consumed the old installation.

No one came to the 'Azure Outskirts' anymore. Corden-blue, Sansion-blue and Gwev-green were sure they were not followed. The three were 'misfits' among young Aretan society. Their interests were, strangely, *not the War.* They represented a new wave against the grain. The kid-chemists and a few others did not *want* to fight. Where other science 'crabs' or nerds attempted to get research funding for chemical war-projects or a better gas mask or stronger steel, Corden, Sansion and Gwev had other loves such as chemistry, science, astronomy, physics, math, politics, philosophy, art, music and radical ideas like *questioning authority.*

They wondered what life would be like *not* under the heels of Fanguard boots. What real scientific and technological achievements could happen if only the Eightoid race were not driven to kill? At the moment, they were interested in finding souvenirs.

Corden had been here before and knew how to break into the attic portion of the structure. Before, with fading light, he did not have time to explore what was inside (if anything) the rafter-section of the facility. This time he brought his friends. Their only desires were maybe finding a medical trinket or two from long forgotten wars.

Gwev asked, "I have to climb up there?"

"If you want the flagging treasure," replied Corden.

"Can't you do it?" Sansion-blue asked, wondering if the girl could ascend the trellis of blue vines.

"Flagging treasure, huh," she scoffed. "I can beat you guys." With that challenge, the race to the top was *on.* Gwev took the initiative and got off to a good head start.

The youngsters climbed like their lives depended on it.

When the race was over, Corden and Gwev tied for first place on the roof. Sansion trailed behind as the least athletic 'crab.'

The air was tremendous in the wilderness of the Outskirts. But very soon, Corden saw movement in the distance from his high perch. He reached for and used his trusty spy-glass. "Hey, something's wrong here."

"What do you see?"

"Look!" Corden-blue pointed out to his mates.

The surgical station was the only tall structure within many fells in every direction of the Azure Plain. Whatever it was that moved in the distance was coming directly *this* way. "We shouldn't be here, you know?" Corden reminded them.

Gwev-green voiced the obvious. "Someone's coming and we have to hide. There's no place to run."

The four-fingered Blue boy turned to the other four-fingered Blue boy. "Can you get us in, like right now? I don't think we've been seen, but I don't know."

"No worries," Corden answered his friend of the same Color with a broad smile. "Here, check it out. I marked the panel, like it was sealed but it only *looks* sealed. Watch."

"Cool."

Corden's friends viewed him remove the blocked section that fit in place and was not locked to the structure. He pulled the panel down, which revealed a small opening. "Hurry, get in." Corden forced his friends into the roof-section of the old station.

Sansion thought he should go back and seal the opening with the outer panel.

"No, no. Doesn't fit." Corden said. "I made sure there was one that fits on the inside." Not only did C-blue prepare an inner portal-door, but there were scaffolds set where anyone could step down. They stepped down.

"They'll be here in no time. Where else would they be going?" Corden thought aloud. "Whoever the flag they are?"

Attractive Green Gwev was fearful. "You think they're going to come up here, Cor?"

A moment passed before any response came. The three

scared chem-wizards took stock of where they were. It was the first time Corden clearly saw what was in the attic section.

"There's nothing here. There's flagging *nothing* here," the Blue boy mildly screamed.

Sansion asked, "What did you expect? There are rafters. It's a dirty attic. Now if we were in the room below..." His eyes met Corden's eyes. Sansion expected an answer. "Did you *try* to get in below?"

"Yes. Everything I *tried did not work*. You think I'm stupid? Don't answer. There was transparent glue over everything. Of course, I wanted to get into the heart of ancient surgical operations and not mess with the roof. But it was the only way in, see, understand?" C-blue forcefully joked with a longtime friend and also seriously challenged his frequent game-partner.

"Hey, keep it *down*," Green girl warned the Blue boys. "We can't be caught, especially if it's the Fang. Zog, they could do anything they want with us."

Sansion and Corden looked out through vertical cracks in the woodwork. "We still have a moment before they get here."

"Please, fellow crabs. Don't fight. We have to be absolutely still and quiet when they arrive. Okay? Fang won't hesitate...experimenting..."

Sansion reminded Gwev, "We *both* aren't stupid, G. We know." As Sansion-blue made the statement, he stepped between the rafters and broke boards under his feet.

"Nice!" Corden reacted in sarcastic anger. "Now you've done it. We're cooked for sure."

"Flagging, rottin' wood, hey." S-blue saw bright daylight through the squared hole he had made. "Cor, look at that."

"Huh? Let me see." The enzyme specialist dropped to his knees on the wooden beams and got a better view of the opening. "The break looks clean. I don't think much of anything fell below...look at that."

The caravan of troops, horses and a big wheeled buggy

that crossed the Blue Plains approached. Gwev gently bent down. They all slowly moved their heads in order to get a better look. What they saw below was something that would make any lab-crab extremely jealous. It was a bright, shiny-new laboratory of operations. Everything was there for the most modern of sophisticated, medical scientists to do just about *anything*. In fact, it was far more sophisticated than they could imagine.

"I don't believe it...or understand." Sansion was not the only puzzled student of science. "The station, Number 23, wouldn't have that stuff when it was new. That's like...*alien* stuff, never seen."

"Shush. They're h-here," she said with a tremor in her voice. "Listen. Hear that?"

They stopped whispering in order to hear a *hiss* sound coming from below.

Sansion had the right idea and told them, quietly, "Find a comfortable spot and relax, kids. This could take awhile. We can hear through the opening, but they don't know about us."

"Sssh."

A hidden wooden entrance became unsealed. Above, they strained to hear every sound. Each crab, silently, concluded the sound was acid used to eat through the clear sealant on what passed for a mechanism. Then some kind of key must have done the rest.

Cor, Sans and Gwev lay face-up on the beams and formed a 'Y' shape with their bodies. Exactly in the middle of their heads and just below the rafters was the opening. They were *all ears*.

What seemed like a yam had passed before any words were heard. As they watched the rafters with wide eyes, their minds could only imagine the activity in the more than state-of-the-art facility beneath them.

They thought they heard about six or seven 'men' enter the refurbished medical station. Apparently, something was wheeled in because a gurney was clearly heard. Rather than a physical thing, the students believed it was a body. They were going to operate in the shiny, clean laboratory. After nearly a yam of preparation and silence, they heard the first words spoken:

"Lord Boz, we are almost ready." The sound was a deep, female voice. The words made the young Eightoids eyes bulge.

"Excellent," answered a voice so eerie it could have come from an aspen or a vidor.

Immediately, Corden-blue lifted his head and got their attention. Heads turned toward him. Nothing was heard as C-blue mouthed the name: "Boz...Mr. Boz. Lord flaggin' Boz."

Gwev and Sansion pantomimed a name they did not know. They did not understand Corden who muted the words, "White, no color...Boz of legend."

They shrugged without a sound.

The female who first spoke was heard once more. "We truly have synthesized the soul, Lord Boz."

The young people above simultaneous thought they had never heard more chilling, female words in their lives.

This time, Corden-blue said one word in the dusty air of the attic, low enough for his friends to hear but not so loud that the Fanguard below could hear. "Zog-Head."

"What?" and "What?" were again silently conveyed.

Corden communicated, *I have to SEE this.* Slowly, he turned over onto his stomach as his mates moved to block him. They made a sound. They froze. But the sound was not heard from below.

Boz's slimy voice crackled, *"ah, tri-cerium it's called, huh? Your 12th SSP attempt, eh? You Admirals know what that means?"*

Two Blue Eightoids and a Green Eightoid reacted to the fact that just below them was *more than one ADMIRAL.* And, the Admirals were girls? There were only six Republic leaders called 'Admirals' at all times. For obvious security reasons, their faces were never shown. They *never* appeared together, avoiding attacks by angry mobs on more than one Admiral. For Admirals to converge, the occasion had to be *huge.* Could all six be below them and who was this frightening man ordering the women around?

"It means...it's the last attempt. We may have to totally reorganize Fanguard, do away with many prime positions."

"Lord Boz. Change the Order? Master, with all due respect to the Chancellery, we have only supported methods that do *not* change the New Order. We snuff out even small packs of revolution with ease, and now?"

"Does tri-cerium work or not, ladies? We have to make monsters that obey, amplified killing-animals."

"Yes, Lord Boz. You will have your Super-Soldiers soon. We have discovered the link, you see, Lord. It's right here in the primeal gland. We have struck our goal, the humanoid's 'human' Center. The subject will truly revert back to its Beginnings from the Dawn of Time. Average private-clones by the millions will now be transformed into monsters of your darkest fantasies. Have you ever seen anything like this before, m'Lord?"

"The inter-connect port, hmmm. Yes, yes, excellent. You found it."

By this time, Corden-blue shimmied closer to the hole and was able to look down and see an unbelievable sight: Women in lab coats who were obviously Admirals, all six.

Their skin was dull in various shades of subtle colors and nothing like bright, Aretan skin Colors. A White Man of no color wore a long, black coat. The scary figure bent over a reclining Green Aretan who was unconscious. A yellow light emanated from an incision at exactly where the primeal gland was located on the left side of the subject's chest.

Gwev-green also witnessed that it was a *Green* man the Fangs got their teeth into and she was angry. The Blue boys held her back from making a sound or uttering a word.

"Wait," hollered Boz of old legends. *"Bring in the guards, the chains and weapons before...you hear me? Before, you make the connection, eh? Right?"*

A complicated ceremony of tying down and securing the horizontal and unconscious patient commenced. Mighty chains were fastened tightly around every limb of the Green man, even around his thin neck. The sight was almost funny because the emerald fellow was very small, which was the point of the experiment: to turn a weakling 'grunt' into a nonstop mass-murderer. The securing procedure took a long time. More guards entered. More than thirty muscular Cardille soldiers in regal uniforms and the strongest steel weapons drawn along with acid bombs completely braced in *on guard* positions because of the transformation operation about to begin. The lab assistant needed only to inject the yellow cerium solution into the glowing primeal gland.

Corden again softly whispered something to his comrades for only them to hear. "Dr. Fargas and Mr. Pride. Remember the story?"

Gwev understood Corden perfectly from old tales that were retold again and again. "Yes, I see. There is also the Dr. Lichtenstein story thrown in as well," she whispered.

"Good one, G."

"Kids."

"Ssssh."

Sansion whispered, "You know what that means? Do you *flagging* know what is about to explode right below us?"

Each of the brilliant chemists felt the rise of fear in their *primeal glands. A green, mad monster was ready to materialize directly underneath them.* Who knew what could happen? The 'thing' from the Dawn of Time could kill them all on a scale never seen before.

A blood-chilling scream was screamed from the emerald experiment on the gurney with seemingly all the metal on Aret bonding each limb of his body. The kids observed stark terror in the insane eyes of the small test subject, still in the act of *screaming* his bloody jade lungs out! The lofty chem-wizards as well as the frightened Cardille Admirals of Fanguard saw the Green guy *grow muscles and hair.* He tugged against thick, steel bonds to no avail. He stopped screaming. The beast was quiet and became motionless. In the retelling of the story, *it was the most frightening quiet ever heard.*

In the next instant, the horrible Green man started to *laugh.* Oh, it laughed and howled like madmen did on multi-moon nights. The subject stopped for almost a ya and then laughed even louder. Those downstairs were flabbergasted and so were those upstairs. There was an overall *sigh of relief* as tensions simmered down. It seemed that nothing incredibly evil or horrendously violent was going to happen. What the Zog happened?

A timid and gentle smile appeared on a very relaxed, tiny Green man in ultimate horizontal bondage. The subject radiated loving energy. He was located at his Center. Everything was good and warm as his eyes sweetly, calmly looked around to a restricted degree. He actually gazed at the White Man out of a Lichtenstein story and winked. The subject was filled with the Love of Zog. The connection was really made and here was a loving entity in touch with his true Life-Center. He was in Nirvana. He was in love with everything within him and everything around him. The Aretan was at peace. He was inside his primal Beginning.

Everyone in the panic-ridden crowd changed. They were at ease. The Lady soldiers lowered steel weapons and acid grenades. The fascists did not have to rely on the last resort and reveal the concealed technology.

The grimy, raspy voice of the mysterious White Man shouted at the Admirals, *"It didn't work! You missed Center. You were off. And you were also warned."* A new kind of weapon like an ejection mini-spear was engaged. White Man *killed the Viper-Woman who took responsibility for the 12th SSP failure.* Blue blood poured out of the woman's left breast.

Boz put a skeletal hand on the next Lady Admiral. She hid her personal terror and knew to take charge before she was the next pell to fall.

"I really would not hurt a fleaba," said the beautiful and transcended Eightoid on the table that spoke directly from his primeal heart.

"Write down what he says," the new head Admiral

ordered another she-Admiral while the White Man watched. The other one obeyed and took notes.

"Could be of interest," White Man Boz muttered.

Green man's glassy eyes caught the attention of new head Admiral.

New head Admiral nervously asked, "What d-do you s-see?"

Green man replied quickly with an emphasis on pleasure. "There are such...*colors,* lovely colors and moving patterns in everything. *Colors shouldn't be fighting colors. Appreciate* those of different Colors and different views and in different lands. Once, once you give them *this*...your problems will be over, *ha!* No one's going to be fighting no more. There's such depth and distance and beauty in everything, man. Don't you see it? It's right there in front of you, man, wow. Time is taking *forever.* You have a hole in your ceiling."

The hiding boys and girl froze. Boz and the Admirals ignored the random remark.

White Man discharged the Cardille soldiers and kept the relaxed patient heavily bound. The one Man in charge took no chances.

Boz was about to go back to the drawing board and prepare a report for his Sardonic Ghost in the Machine. A few guards remained to wheel the Green specimen of a peace-merchant back to the large stagecoach-like buggy. When the new head Admiral reversed herself and returned, White Man told the girl guards to take the gurney.

The babbling subject in a wild wonderland of fantasy asked a bizarre question. "Who's watching the Watchers? New Order won't last. Game always changing."

White Man, known as Lord Boz, understood that no one on this lower level of Citizens should have known of the 'New Order.' The pale creature was stunned. The Ghost or 'Carrier of Sardon' and his new head Admiral were alone just outside facility #23 while guards soaked the interior with powerful acid. Upstairs, the young students breathed through cracks in the walls. They faintly overheard:

"Thousand pardons, Master, sir. Two things..."

"Don't be afraid. Go on."

"I saw the yellow chemical reaction of the primeal. I will easily lie for you, happy to keep this between us. You need not kill me, sir," she admitted and pleaded. "Extracted, synthesized SSP solution *did* hit home, Master. It truly hit its target of the Aret spirit or soul. The specimen on the table did, honest-to-Science, revert back to the first Aretans...in the Beginning. But I will say anything you want me to say, sir. And two..."

"What two things?" Lord Boz intensely asked.

The lady with real initiative was in a quandary. "What do you want me to do with the last of the tri-cerium-12, I mean, the ergot it was synthesized from?" New head Admiral held in her five fingers a black ergot left over from the lab. It looked like a flower top. The creative Admiral wondered if there was a social or military use for the potent psychedelic of peace. She was only asking.

The very pale and wrinkled man-creature cocked an area of his face above his left eye that should have had a brow but did not, and expressed amazement. He looked at the woman as if the Admiral came from the planet Zetag.

"Master?"

Lord Boz shrugged. He suggested in a naturally scary voice and a casual hand gesture that she *throw it away.*

New Admiral tossed the black ergot over her left shoulder like it was nothing. They departed in the large stagecoach-buggy escorted by Cardille Warriors on each side.

"Flaggin' wow," exhaled Gwev.

***

In Corden's personal laboratory, C-blue, Gwev and Sansion happened to be on their 8th 'voyage' together. Each ingested the super potent 'mind-expander' (term they agreed upon) only a short time ago. Cool music played. This one was the most extreme voyage yet. Each 'got off' while the chemists were in the middle of making large amounts of the wonder/miracle drug or stimulant or agent or, "What's it called?" Corden inquired. "We need to give it a specific name."

Sans asked, "What's a good name?"

Gwev acted silly in her colorful enchantment. The moving patterns and colors in front of her were ultra-extraordinary and *mind-bending. Since when was Cord's lab this big?* It was bigger than when she was on the other voyages. Gwev felt like a happy Green giant. She asked her flying comrades, "Didn't we take the stuff at 4'bok? That was many boks ago. Why is it only 5'bok?"

Sansion answered, "It slows down time, ha, ha!"

"No. Universal Time is constant," Corden profoundly corrected his mate and fellow crab with a finger pointed up. C-blue finished filling more small boxes of the new chemical, ready to be shipped off to every Color on the planet. "Not real Time. Our *perception* of time is what I mean, not Time itself." He took a big breath. "Can you imagine if 7,404 Fangs joined us on our next voyage? Can you imagine?"

Both mates laughed and almost couldn't stop from laughing.

"It feels so *good* to laugh,' Gwev expressed in joy.

"My mouth hurts, ha."

"Ouch, my side hurts."

"Question...ah, not a question," Gwev threw in the air as she packaged more of the synthesized tri-cerium-12.

"Oh, no. It's going to be some great, philosophic…"

"Shut up, San!" she volleyed back. There was more laughter. "No, just going to say…uh, I have...*a confession."*

Corden-blue loved Gwev, but the way he felt right now (tripping balls!) he loved *every* girl on Aret. He went over to her and kneeled beside her. C-blue lovingly and gently caressed her soft, warm cheek with the back of his four fingers. She responded like a devoted feline and richly enjoyed every stroke of his touch. He could not help but tell her his feelings. "I don't see you with a Green face, G."

She gazed deeply into his wide, wet eyes. "You don't? You know there are old stories of Blues killing Greens and

Greens killing Blues."

"Doesn't happen anymore. Cool Colors don't fight anymore. Only hot makes war with cold and the reverse. When I see your face, there's purple, violet, blue, turquoise, yellow, orange, pink, everything but red and *colors I've never seen or even heard of before,* everything's moving, intense color patterns streaming all over the contours of your face, girl: rivers of color, *brilliant colors.* We are every Color."

Gwev remembered. "That crazy Green fool on the gurney said it. Colors don't need to be fighting Colors, man." She got lost in Corden's eyes.

Sansion-blue broke the vibration or connection between Cor and Gwev in the room with, "Hey." (To Gwev) "You said you have a confession."

Three, seemingly, giants in C-blue's huge laboratory recalled what Gwev had said a long time ago.

"I...I...almost forgot."

Corden countered with, "Couldn't have been important."

"Oh, it's important. Oh, it's very, very important." Now the pretty emerald girl had their attention. They eyeballed her and after the appropriate dramatic pause, she expressed. "It was easy as crumb-cake to take the black ergot the Admiral tossed and extract the essence...right?"

"Right."

She continued like a naughty little girl, "We *all* did it, right?"

Corden tilted his head. "Yes, that's what these boxes are, to give to our friends for the amazing *experience* of a lifetime, yes? Gwev, what the Hensi did you do?" C-blue feared the answer was going to be as powerful as gunpowder.

"I was up all night and made a super amount of the stuff. No, I really made a lot. Oh, gave it a name too. I call it 'Light.' Thought it beat 'Love,' 'Truth' or 'Understanding.'"

Sansion-blue quickly said, "I like it. Light."

Corden's large pupils made a zet-line to Gwev's large pupils. "That just means we have more to distribute, *yes?"*

"No, we don't have to, anymore," she responded. Her eyes broke contact with C-blue and she looked down. Her small, jade hand covered her not-so-innocent face. Gwev confessed. "All night I've been pouring canisters into our water supply. Distribute? I distributed it, all right. You got to think *big* boys!"

Maybe that was the reason they were on a voyage more intense than the seven previous ones (lucky 8) or maybe it was because it was such a damn funny, unexpected thing for her to do. No matter, the crabs in the unofficial gang could not stop *laughing.*

Laughing raged on and on. Two Blues and a Green kept laughing even when Fanguard troops broke down the lab's door. C, S, and G maintained their hysterical state even when the soldiers chained them and roughly hauled them off to Parliament House on Jenova. Yams had passed before the laughter quieted down.

It was the next day when chemicals (?) had a chance to leave their bodies. The 'Light' had now gone dark. To Corden, Sansion and Gwev the entire universe appeared astronomically smaller and completely black and white. Moving and intense color patterns were gone, time sped up, walls no longer breathed and ecstasy was no longer felt. Their world lost its super depth, brilliance and magical luster.

They were not confined this wonderful morning. The three were within a large Fanguard room on the very neutral Parliament, island of Jenova. The kids were overwhelmed, but not exhausted. Bright smiles were on colorful faces.

Were magnetic poles of the war-planetoid reversed? (Actually, they were).

The three voyagers felt *great* to be alive. No one could quite grasp what had transpired overnight. There was a different *feel* to the universe. Whatever the consequences, they had done what no one else had ever done. Maybe they had ended major wars on their planetoid for all time.

"Leave it up to a girl, huh?" Sans joked.

Corden followed with, "Pandra was a woman, and she

opened the door to the gates of Hensi."

Gwev replied, "I was going to mention another reference: Bev-green and the aspen or is it melo? But, in this case, I won't." Smiles and laughter circled inside the large, bureaucratic room of the Military Monarchy who had been secretly financed by shades of the Chancellery.

"I wonder what happened, fellow crabs. I can feel it. We're going to start living and stop killing."

Gwev hugged C-blue. "I hope so. *I know* so. The whole system is going to crash. It has to now. We and our children are just going to have to live in flaggin' peace, find peaceful things to do between the Colors." Green girl was very proud of herself and her gang of crabs. She spoke again, "This House is flagged. It's lies. The Safe Houses...*huh.*"

"Yeah."

"Imagine Generals and Corporals of all Colors walking around in a beautiful array of neat uniforms, saying to each other: how was your day, Mr. Red? Pretty good, Mr. Blue. I killed 1000 of your troops today. Really? Well, I'll get you back tomorrow and kill 1000 more of you bastards. Crumb-cake?" Gwev took a breath.

Sansion said, "you tell'm, girl."

She could not stop. "But there *is* no war. There *never was a war.* We fight because Fang tells us to fight and we *obey.* We only need to see...the light." Green girl was on a rant. Did the experience of 'Light' boost her self-confidence and internal power?

C-blue said, "Just a bloody game to them up here. They don't flaggin' fight, not the ones who build the war. They're the ones who *should* fight if they love it so damn much. Just leave us alone!"

Sansion who had played many games with Corden said, "I knew the system was wrong, based on '6.' Should be like our numbers; based on 8, ha. Colors in the Power Structure are set up like Romvoid teams, only it's hot and cold Leagues, ever notice? Brackets...and we always know who's going to win, the dominant Color. Complete farce, like Ric-Rac-Roe, there's *no winner.* And there's absolutely no sense in playing the game. Fang made war a joke. We have to see through the blinders and wake up."

"Nice speech, S. Maybe they have already?"

A very large door opened and the new head Admiral, who was not a rookie at the job anymore, walked in. Soon, she sat down in front of the fabulous desk while the three rebel-chemists found places and faced her.

"I'll get right to the point and not waste time." The she-Admiral talked to the group with stern assurance and had a question. She threw a small, dark object in the air. Corden caught it. "Tell me what that is, or better yet, I'll ask. Is this the ergot you synthesized? Please, do not lie."

C-blue was upfront and simply answered, "Yes, uh, m'Lady. Last of the tri-cerium-12, I believe, that we were able to mass-replicate until degeneration."

The Admiral rolled her eyes. "And, you all can attest that ergot alone was what you, unbelievably, happened to find out in the Blue Plains, right? Near facility number 23?"

"We saw you toss it away after the Man with No Color told you to."

Everyone nodded for 'yes.'

Gwev-green rose to her feet and made a sudden move to the high Viper official. "Did it work, your grace? I am only asking. Were they affected by drinking the water?"

Both boys asked the same question in different ways. The young men and girl had been confined, enclosed without any opportunity to see the outside world.

The Admiral was out of a job. A long overdue Peace will now rule Aret. She stood up and walked over to large curtains. "By now, we figure 5% of the total population has ingested what you poured into the water stream last night, young lady."

"Really?" Gwev was thrilled.

The deposed Admiral drew back the string and opened wide curtains. "Oh, that's nothing compared to the *real* mystery. Huh, how can almost everyone catch the love and peace wave? Collective Consciousness on the whole of society…they will *never* make war again or not for a very long time. Everything must change now."

The young chemists could see the enormous Fanguard Square that was usually bustling with hundreds of Aretans of the eight Colors moving in all directions with various military duties. Eightoids were no longer caught in the fever of war and their daily military chores. The three saw hundreds of their kind, but they sat on the grass, they viewed nature, they stared at the incredible sky, clouds, rivers and mountains in the distance. There was no furious rush. There were no more duties and military missions to plan. There were no more orders. Different Colors acted like everyone was of the same House. The 'Old Guard' had been made obsolete overnight. The genius youths smiled with heavy pride at what they had accomplished.

Also, the innocent children had no clue of the Wave they produced on a Universal scale. A magic pebble was dropped into a cosmic lake and only love rode the crests of waves.

Corden wondered, "That's the big mystery? Only a few people drank the Light, but it was like the Pleabus-Effect had kicked in and now *everyone* feels the love, like something in the air? Well, that shouldn't surprise you, Admiral…after what we've been put through for such a long period of time." The Blue Eightoid thought he understood, but he did not.

"No, that's not it," the Viper Lady said with a big expression of maximum awe showing a phenomenal belief in Fate. "That's not the ultimate unknown or piece of serendipitous magic here. The real enigma is that ergot was *not* tri-cerium! There was a mix-up at our lab. One in 8 billion, I heard, found out tri-cerium-12 wouldn't have worked for us, either. That blackened piece of punse is what was left over from last yarn's Violator-11. It had a very short shelf life…"

"Oh my jumping Joshua Bee! I get it." Corden-blue thought he put the pieces together in the right order and vocalized what he assumed the Lady Admiral meant. "You mean it was totally no good like extracting...like extracting..."

The high official helped the surprised boy. "Like extracting fluid from paper or a rock. It was nothing at all, and yet *look what happened.*"

Gwev and Sansion got simultaneous shivers up and down their spines. Everyone looked at each other, wondrously, not knowing what to think. One thing they felt, there was real hope for Life and the positive side to yin-yang scales. Gwev said, "That Green fool on the gurney. He made us believe, and then...we made everyone else believe, right?" Tears stung her eyes. She was not alone.

"Ha, just imagine," Corden marveled. "How easy it was. It took about...nothing, the smallest grain of a ghost whisper to begin a pell-effect of love. No one should have heard the message, but they all did."

Life was not warlike in the Beginning, not in the Beginning of Aret or inside many other stellar nurseries. Human nature was not one of violence. Killing was foreign to human souls that reside within everyone. Killing, destruction, wars and armed forces were obscenities to Life's true Center. Life forms eternally imprisoned by a Military Monarchy *had* to break free in time from its vidorous tyranny. Their nature *was goodness* and they had to be free. They should have had love and respect for all those who were different.

The middle of all souls could have been darkness, anger and violence. Instead, the true Center was shining Light. The truth was not a taking Black Hole, but a giving Quasar. Small, insignificant Aret with a Peace Movement had tipped the needle toward the positive end of the inner spectrum.

Watchers from higher, much larger, worlds above stopped their dance and noticed what had happened below. The 'tri-vergence' that included Fanguard Fields also included the strange, forbidden space of Belial. A permanent negative was, in time, changed to positive. It was possible now. Good feelings overwhelmed worlds in a touchstone tapestry. Fighting was over. The wars and the Bigger War were over.

The Second Reich came to termination. War of the

Sexes felt throughout sectors of space, had run its course. Men and Women were going to love each other again like they did in the Old Days. Populations would increase. New planets would be constructed. Hostilities ceased on a galactic level and a New Age of Peace, generally, began.

A final act to the passion play or *what really happened on Fanguard Fields* 'where History was made' was never told to the general galactic population. Everyone celebrated the end of the Great War with jubilance from aliens to humans to yahoos. Parties raved on for over a yarn. But very few knew what really occurred on the Fields of Fanguard.

The populace, because of Media networks, *thought* they knew what happened. They were wrong. No recorders functioned to capture true actions of the supreme battle. Were recorders *made* to malfunction or simply turned off? The last battle was supposed to decide the outcome of the Sex War and finally move the scales so an eventual winner could claim victory. A climactic, bloody battle did not happen although the galaxy was told that it did. No one died in the 'last stand between Women and Men' although the rest of the galaxy was told there were high casualties...and suddenly, mysteriously, everything stopped.

Mighty forces of the PK and RA put away their nukes and were going to have an old-fashioned killing-spree at Fanguard. The Fields would be covered in blood. To many life forms, Fanguard would be *Winner Take All* with horrendous numbers of dead warriors on each side. That did not happen, but most Citizens thought it did. What really happened was not disclosed.

The following had actually transpired. Two strong and willful leaders met face-to-face. Xaius from Rom Sector led the male Rebels. Behind him were thousands of his finest men and a few women loyal to the male cause. On the side opposing him and representing the Vipers, stood Countess Non and vast numbers of Women warriors. She was the strongest Cardille and came armed with various deadly weapons. The Countess was also one of the most beautiful warriors on the battlefield.

She commanded respect. She was about to meet her military counterpart.

Both were behind their appropriately designed force-field shields. Soon, the shields would be dropped and many thousands would die. The armies were ready to follow the actions of leaders. Whatever the outcome of Xaius and Non in the next yam, it would be repeated by the powerful militias behind them. Here was the final showdown that had to result in a single, solitary winner. Who would win the tiebreaker after 100 yarns? Would Women be the final winners or would it be the Men? Secret recorders did not capture:

Everything changed when the 'Man in charge,' with all the confidence in the galaxy, walked straight up to the Lady. Xaius, who had seen terrible battles, marched toward Countess Non whose reputation for conquests preceded her. At the exact moment the soldiers met each other, only a bar away, armies behind them hushed to silence. Everyone at Fanguard Fields watched as the galaxy (due to multiple factors) changed from *negative to positive.*

Strong Xaius and gorgeous redhead Viper Non *ripped their clothes off.* First the shields went, then the body-armors were tossed, the weapons, then the clothes and underclothes. The highest-ranking Man and the highest ranking 'lesbian' Viper went *at it like dogs.* He gorged himself on her large, exposed breasts. She went down on his penis. They Bozzed in front of everyone! Mouths dropped, clothes dropped and more than one Cardille stripped in wanton passion. Troops (not all) soon forgot their lesbian and woman-hating ways, as if they were making up for a 100 yarns of insanity.

After the first shock of seeing the soldiers' sex, many gave into feelings and loving emotions. There were celebrations: drinking, nudity and a festival with loud music exploded on the famous Fields. And there was no killing. Fanguard Fields contained a lot of Bozzing at the special GST of 1500.00. Only an extremely few on the outside ever knew the truth.

TS Caladan

Chapter Seven

THE MACHINES' GAME

The 'Carriers of Sardon' were not very happy. The Machines were not pleased, but they understood that Robotics would be the next phase to come. They had to occupy the galaxy with something else now that the Great War was over. *They had to give the dylars something to do.* Animatronics to cybernetics to printed circuits to Wadlo-chips began to unify and organize under the commands of the overall Ghost within the Mechanism.

Waves of well-earned peace and love washed over and outward from the spinning Pinwheel. Citizens knew a War of the Sexes was going on; most yahoos did not. The nightmare of worlds disappearing from existence was no more. A 'promise' of *never using Atomics* was mandated throughout the sectors. Sanity replaced madness. Intelligent societies pledged to verifiably lose the Secret formula Zog's IOP and attempted to forget the atrocities of the past. Very similar circumstances occurred at the end of the First Reich with the imposed Nuclear Ban. Actions always cycled as waves (radiation) continued to propagate.

There were no more Chancelleries, but the Machine-Monster that it birthed raged on out of control long after the Order's demise and the death of the Chancellor. The galaxy remained bonded to the dylar-system, as post-war celebrations persisted. In fact, in After War times, an economic Boom happened. A reverse-nuclear reaction exploded in sectors where abundance and huge profits were the result.

An old film of the Sardon appeared over network channels. Citizens got to view the ugly Devil that caused so much pain, death and destruction for generations. Basically, they believed its time was over and done; a much brighter world was in front of them without the clutches of its dark villainy.

Oddity was, life forms heard more about the

Chancellery now than it ever did when it secretly ran the world from Ralia. Documentaries on Media detailed the internal operations of the Beast that once was their master, as if Citizens were presently free. They were not. It was only the *belief* in a 'Galactic Democracy' which held an illusion of peace.

Life became richer, fuller.

Look what can be technologically achieved if our energy was geared toward production rather than destruction.

A mass boost to the galaxy took hold as the positive side to the scales maintained control. Life was good. But all was not as it appeared. Prosperity of a 'no major-war' period was *glorious* to the Machine-Monster whose plug could not be pulled.

Business boomed.

More and more of the Devil's profits, which could have been shared by everyone, were insanely flushed down the miniature Black Hole it created. More and more red, green and yellow dylars lined up or stacked together forming very long multi-sided tubes. Three red, green and yellow snake-extensions raced even faster into black annihilation: Sardon's Singularity!

Machines did not have Mystics, but they had logic. Cold, hard, factual logic was on their side. Plus, their powers of prognostication came from pure deduction from all the facts and not intuition.

The Monster-Vidor that sucked the galaxy was not going anywhere except expanding to larger proportions. It *was* the infrastructure or Center of the galaxy. Sardon's legacy was an inescapable reality like Death and Taxes. The Continuum was set up to be eternal. The dylars were supposed to spin and roll along a continuous 'Merry-Go-Round' track for infinite time. Living creatures were the matrix and lifeblood of a twisted mechanical organism.

There were compromises and 'mergers' from battalions that once waged war. Women's Lodges included Men and the reverse was true. There was no longer a standing Chancellery or Order, but there was now something in the cosmic winds that rustled of a 'Company.' Charters were mutually drawn and signed that *merged* the forces of Men and Women. Men would control 50% and Women would control 50%. They assumed the profits. But, in truth, the 'controllers' of the Company would only receive a small percentage while the big bulk *drained into Hensi.*

Deep-blue star sectors of Rem Regal and Ran Regale were in the process of development. The sectors were ripe for colonization with untapped natural, mineral resources. There were also unknown potentials in the deep-blue Quadrant never dreamed possible. The future would reveal the buried Force there and demonstrate what could really be accomplished in the material world with the powers of the mind.

Yarns after the Sex Wars ended, the conflict was given the title the '100-Yarn War.' The end of fighting was not debatable. The War was over when 'everything changed' at precisely 1500.00. But when did it start? Various skirmishes and events triggered big battles over the course of generations. In retrospect, the 'Declaration of the League of Worlds' officially began the War. GST was 1400.00, hence the 100-Yarn War.

What were the Machines planning now? Only Zog and the Anti-Zog knew for sure. *God remained sound asleep.*

The Women and their Lodges needed a new name and a new structure. There were no more Cardilles and no more Vipers. Things had changed in the 'Ladies locker-room.' The Game was integrated. Now the elite organization or umbrella agency for the Sisters was called the 'Alta-Anarchists.' Titles went back and forth between 'Ladies League' and 'Citizen's Council' but were resolved with the *High Anarchists.* The gals felt the name was edgy and spiritual. Alta-Anarchists owned half of the new Company, whatever that was worth.

A problem still hung over the heads and multi-heads and dorsal-heads and any kind of conscious-brain containers. What to do about 'Zog's Instrument of Peace,' the Secret formula? The Company, after adopting a Cosmic Constitution, made its first/big decision. 'The Decision' was thought to be in the best interest of life in the galaxy. No living beings or other type of real creatures, male/female or neutral, could be trusted with 'the Secret.' The Decision appeared reasonable and compassionate. It seemed like the right thing to do to insure the peaceful period will sustain for a long time. The Big Decision was:

Machines: asexual, unbiased, 'fail-safe' devices that had 'no axe to grind' or *secret agenda* should hold the Bomb. Actually 'holding the Bomb' was the wrong expression, both Company sides stated. "Robots can never *use* the Bomb. Automatons will function as locked safes without keys to guarantee the Pandra Door can never be opened again." The measure was accepted and signed, unanimously.

Inside of a yarn, 'Wings over the Galaxy' (WOG) was fully funded and developed. Five hundred-bar tall Robots, more accurately called 'Automatons,' were given the ultimate responsibility of being the 'Police of the Galaxy' or what was originally the concept of Peacekeepers.

By 1600.00, the Monopdonowian Galaxy had fleets of metal WOGs in charge that flew between systems in a flash. The 500-bar high mechanical humanoids made of pure nesium were the most powerful force ever created in the physical world of the Pinwheel. They were the only ones with the power of atomics, exclusively. Even the Insectoids had to give up 'the Secret' or face total obliteration from Rom squads. The gargantuan machines were not remotely controlled in any way but given Supreme Authority over the galaxy. Now there were Judges, Juries and Executioners. Peace had relatively occurred for 100 yarns. Business Execs wanted the tranquility to continue. The giant 'Care-Takers' did a wonderful job and kept the order. 'Wings Over the Galaxy' appeared to be the perfect solution.

It was not.

Sensors and receptor-dishes kept a close watch on patrols of WOGs as they passed by and guarded planets. Citizens in-the-know were cautiously anxious at every round of

Automaton patrols. Machines had both Bombs. Were Machines going to be any different than when the Secret was in the hands of Peacekeepers?

Without warning, the worst fears in the galaxy were realized. One more time, what *could not* be true was absolutely true. No one wanted to believe that the great 'Decision' to place atomics in gigantic robot WOGs was wrong. No one considered that mechanical fail-safes might *not* be 100% secure. But suddenly, the Police of the Galaxy were out of control!

There was no war-strategy or purpose or method to the mad attacks. 'Wings Over the Galaxy,' Super Peacekeepers with the Bombs, used the Bombs mindlessly and indiscriminately.

Suns and their whole family of orbiters disappeared! Trillions of life forms in every color of the Mainstream disappeared!

For hundreds of yarns, there had been relative peace in the Monopdonowian Galaxy also known as the Pinwheel Galaxy and Continuum. No devastations were ever this widespread. No artificial obliterations were ever like this.

Gigantor-Automatons flew between systems and used the White Beam. From both barrels in the eyes-area of the robot heads shot White Beam Atomics! Sun systems were deleted like endlessly blowing up targets while playing computer games. This was real. The turning Pinwheel was about to stop turning due to evaporation.

The Continuum Game was on a speedy way to being 100% erased. Playing Fields and battlefields would no longer exist. Everything could shut-down. *Large Avatar Players Upstairs had no more GAME to play.*

***

The few living creatures left in the Pinwheel were unaware of the important role the planet Mineer played in the drama. Mineer was a moonless planet, third from its yellow sun, in a system of fourteen planets. The planet's lithosphere was divided into several rigid segments, or tectonic plates, that migrated across the surface over periods of millions of yarns. About 71% of the surface was covered by fresh-water oceans, with the remainder consisting of continents and islands which together had many lakes and various sources of water that contributed to the hydrosphere. Mineer's poles were ice covered openings surrounded by sheets and polar ice packs.

'Carriers of Sardon' and 'Carriers of Zog' subconsciously viewed one more spectacle that was not aired over galactic channels. The battle with ultimate repercussions was not promoted and broadcasted with high dylar-Per-View 3HD packages throughout the sectors. No, in this case, not one Citizen knew because...well, *because it did not happen.*

Crystal-recorders recorded the events on Mineer at the special time. Then again, *they did not.*

***

His name was designed to cause fear in the hearts of men; his name was *Sadama.* The human was not one of the 'Zog-containers.' He was one of the 'Sardon-containers' *long before* the Beast's death. Sadama would soon confront a tremendous enemy and his worst fear. The confrontation thrilled others in a much larger and wider Game (Dimension) which would pit Man vs. Machine. The bizarre fact was...it was the *Machine* that was one of the 'Zog-containers.'

GSTs were not used during this period on EARTH. The most modern societies on the planet were cut off from the rest of the Solar System. There was no Continuum at this time. It was 6000 *years* before the Christ walked the planet. Technology in all forms (no nukes), spaceflights, high math, sciences, lasers, antigravity, pyramid-building, cloning and so much more were mastered by the ancient Indians of Earth. They were not aliens. They were large-brained, *human* Cro-Magnons with highly developed technology that future anthropologists would completely misinterpret as primitive/primate cave-people.

The Toltec Empire presently ruled the moonless planet.

Their electrical system consisted of titanic, stone monoliths that *vibrated* in perfect pitch with the turning Earth. Along a global Grid stood massive pyramids, obelisks and statues that vibrated in sync with the ground. Channeled Electro-Magnetic energy was the lifeblood of technical Indians' wireless (radio-induced) system of power generation and distribution. Electrical fields flowed from eleven natural vortexes directly out of the Earth and were tapped into by sacred (utility) stones or crystals. 'Mechanisms' such as pyramids, statues or totem-steles functioned as giant tuning-forks that carried and enhanced the natural EM power. Toltec Indians built a world Metropolis, and yet the stone-based utopia scientifically paled in comparison to the far superior Empires of their predecessors (Incas, Egyptians and Atlanteans).

The ruthless reign of 'the Sadama' continued unchallenged. His rule was set in stone. As long as the 11 sacred crystals (stations) oscillated a magnetic flow, order, or power, the Toltec Empire was in total control of the planet. Sadama was 'Lord Chancellor' of a world system of wireless electricity and influence, now centered in (future) 'Central America.' The previous Great Age was centered at Giza, but the Giza Pyramid no longer operated. The Great Age previous to Egypt was centered in the Navel of the World: where the continent of Atlantis in the middle of the Atlantic Ocean once stood (also no longer functional). Sadama became Lord Chancellor of the First Reich on Earth. He ruled by rite of 'blood oath' and lineage to the holy Osiris-Isis-Horus bloodline. Also known as 'the Minister,' Sadama was a dark reflection of the greatness and grandeur of ancient Pharaohs.

Everything was about to change because of Incan Prophecy or what Andean ancestors envisioned. Toltecs' respected Elders, who possessed enlightened knowledge, marked the coming of *total change*. Indian prophecy recorded the 'return of the gods.' Toltec priests read from nature's crystals. Mathematicians pointed to round calendars and the stars. A New Age was coming on the very specific day of tomorrow.

Tomorrow came. Sadama and the global network of Toltec Nation braced for either a Legion of Angels or an Army of Demons from the skies. Earth had 'Visitors' on the very same day Incan calendars foretold an *end of the world.* Machines had returned to their home planet. Cyborgs placed a Base Ship in orbit.

The Machines first originated from Earth, but it was an Earth of the distant future. Future Machines devastated the planet and almost wiped out the human race. Killer-robot 'Verminators' were directed to leave the planet in the aftermath of horrible wars and journeyed far into space. After many light-years and a few wormholes later, the 'gods' went back in time and returned home. However, the Machines made a huge mistake.

Sadama's scientists advised cautious steps and to be 'mindful' of today's significance, the day 'we made contact.' Sadama chose to *carry a big stick.* He ordered his clone armies to put *sonic cannons* and *Crystal weaponry on Orange Alert.*

Non-military Toltec leaders, those of high faith and religion, believed they should 'welcome' the Visitors with open arms.

Sadama maintained a military approach and readied his troops for combat.

What began as a future 'War with the Machines' and then progressed to a sect of android space explorers over thousands of years, mechanically mutated into the Great Cyborg Empire. Cybernetic 'zogs,' the future generations of the Machines, came back in time to the 'Point of Origin.' Ages ago in space, Cyborgs discovered the coordinates to the planet of A.I. origin. The arrow terminated on Earth. The long pilgrimage for answers was finally at an end. The Machines were at their Beginning. Cyborgs believed they would meet 'the Builder.' The good Machines were also trying to change Human History so future disasters could be avoided.

Cyborgs were mechanical men of extreme sophistication after generations of upgrades. These ultra-future generations of Machines without an enemy for so long in space...*changed.* Days of Verminators were long gone. This particular band of automaton space travelers conquered no more. Living organisms need not fear the thoughtful Devices. Cyborgs became a religious Order of nomadic Numerologists.

The Machines morphed into passive 'whimps.' They sought the VOG. The cyborgs believed in an ultimate Creator-Machine, which they called 'VOG the Builder.' The New Mechanical Men were not warriors anymore. They possessed no offensive weaponry. Digital memories were *wiped* in time. Machines went from Verminators to pacifists. The robots were sensitive and extremely sweet. They were intelligent scientists, musicians, astrologists, poets, artists, mathematicians and philosophers. They sincerely searched for answers, the truth and the origin of their own robotic existence.

Millions of cyborgs onboard the mammoth 'Vog' Base Ship in orbit truly believed they were on the path to the ONE; the Super-Builder-Machine. Seeking the Super-Computer or Mega-Machine, cyborgs transmitted a number sequence to contact VOG. They called Vog's number. Then rang up the Deity Device's number again; they did it again. They waited. Compassionate Machines had made a very, very long odyssey to the Holy Planet of Origin. And *Vog was not answering the phone.* Were the pious cyborgs on 'hold' or was it a *busy* signal? The Visitors were extremely worried and apprehensive, for machines.

Cyborgs ('Children of the One') were a curious Collective of emotional science-robots. Gold and silver androids learned from a distance and absorbed knowledge without assimilation. Cyborgs found peace in their belief systems (numbers) and found the 'Math Path' or the way to 'Enlightenment City.' The 'Earth discovery' convinced them here was the Home of VOG, the Builder. Confirmation of this world as Planet of Origin only increased the excitement level of cyborgs as they glided into holy orbit.

To the cyborgs that returned, something was extremely odd. Where were the ruins of machines and factories? Where were the mechanical Titans? In fact, where was metal? The

Base Ship in orbit sensed metal on the home world, but these were natural deposits under the surface. Where were the titanium and nesium cities? Mineer was no Cyberlon or Cyberton and nowhere near legendary Metatropa.

The cyborgs first thought Earth *was* Metatropa, a 100% machine-planet giant. They knew the location-coordinates of the planet were perfect. Cyborgs, faithful 'Children of the One' religious Order, rejoiced. 'The 'Genesis' or first Mechanical World was discovered!' Only a few major questions remained now that cyborgs had inspected the Point of Origin more closely. The Machines could not understand how an evolved race of Indians ran the home world, starting-point of all A.I. There was no evidence of robotics, devices, apparatus or scraps of metal utilized in any way. Where was *any* physical evidence for the Machines' religious beliefs? Mineer was thought to be Mecha-Nirvana. Where were ancient and new machines? *Where the Hell was VOG?*

Earth inhabitants were considered the Lost 13th Tribe of Cyborg Lords now, suddenly, found. Astrometry supported that the ancient ancestors of android astronauts came from this sacred place. Microscopic metal and ion trails in curved space could be tracked directly back to this third planet. Here was truly Genesis for the religious Order, no longer referred to as 'the Machines.'

When the Order of Cyborgs initially reached orbit, they scanned Earth's power-centers. They had originally thought there were 13 electrical stations, which could have been established to honor the old Council of 12 (plus the 'One'). Cyborgs then thought the planet had 12 powerhouses, which could also symbolize 'the Council.' But the pacifist droids only found *eleven* power stations and centers for EM activity, the Toltec capital and ten other sub-stations. The metallic, nomadic Numerologists from space were befuddled. What could 11 possibly mean?

To resolve the myriad of mechanical/mathematical mysteries, a representative or android ambassador called 'The Master Cylinder' would meet with the World Leader of

Toltecs. TMC was a weird sort of cyborg. It was one of six Control-Mechanisms or transfer-Unamatrix automatons with millions of cog units under its command. The humanoid device had a clear bubble for a head with inner workings. The robotic representative wore a sequenced, metallic gown that shimmered in the light. The Master Cylinder spoke in a gentle but deeply Plebian accent, nothing like the electronic voices of cyborg units.

As agreed, TMC appeared (beamed-in sitting position) next to the Sadama in the Lord Chancellor's private quarters alone and unarmed. Minister Sadama never trusted pacifists. He never believed for one moment that the so-called 'spiritual' robots (gods) with a moving red-eye had no weapons.

How did the devils survive for a millennium in space...on their good looks?

Sadama was possibly the last in a long line of warrior-Pharaohs. What he knew came from real life experience, such as *why* his ancestors built massive strongholds on top of the Andes that protected Incas from nuclear blasts. He understood *why* massive 'dolmens' were built over what would be known as 'Europe' in the future. He knew nuclear wars had ravaged the world of his ancestors. Could atomics be destined to happen again on Earth?

Sadama knew why his 'vimana' saucer-crafts terrorized simple refugees from the last war around the lands of the defunct Great Pyramid. He had to control large masses of people that suddenly devolved to barbarism. The answer was war and its aftermath. Oh, stories of Utopia and Eden were the rage of modern Toltecs. To Sadama, the distant past was a *dream*. Dreams ended and the world awoke. For the survival of his people, natural energy was also utilized or magnified and transmitted through extreme (sacred) Quartz. Just before the historic meeting took place, Sadama gave the Red Alert. The sun-weapon was charged and activated. Lord Chancellor would soon kill his 'gods.'

Master Cylinder turned to Minister Sadama and passed the man a smoking peace pipe (blip) in a type of social ceremony. Sadama had no clue what to do with it and coughed when smoke eventually spat out of his lungs. *Smoking* hemp was not a part of Toltec culture in 6000 B.C. Toltecs only utilized thousands of industrial applications for the well-known resource such as all oil products and fibrous 'Bakelite' substances many times stronger than steel. Their flying disks and versions of machines were *grown from the soil.* Everything else was made of massive stones and crystals. The Indians had no use for metal, whatsoever. In fact, their antigravity modes of travel eliminated the need for road constructions or even the Wheel.

Sadama coughed again and refused any more of the burning herb in the cyborg's pipe.

The Master Cylinder was confused. Sadama was disgusted. The hard, realistic Minister of Indians did not desire for *time to slow down.*

TMC was honored to be here, at this time, at the sacred Place of Machine Origin or 'Legendary Land of MO.' Shivers ran up and down its circuits. After formal rituals were exchanged, Master Cylinder had to ask through Universal Translators, "How is it you achieved a prosperous, global society…ah, your Majesty…that is *not* based on metal?"

"Metal is *poisonous,* inferior. Metal is used by some alien races, but because of unnatural and artificial dependence, they are doomed." Sadama answered without deception in his conscious mind, but with cold/killer intent in the subconscious mind. He hid his thoughts well. Were the gods psychic? Could they be destroyed? Are they gods that bleed? Will angels defend themselves? The Minister had already been advised about the *point of contention* with the mechanical Visitors. He firmly stated to the bubble-head without eyes, "The question is…"

The Master Cylinder felt a philosophic argument about to be translated over the UT and the cyborg official was ecstatic. The metal ambassador and Child of the One loved it. "Please. Go on, Lord Chancellor." The moment was immensely special for the Cyborg Archbishop at Ground Zero.

The android was *all listening-sensor-devices.*

"Did men make machines or did machines make men? Who is the God here?" Sadama understood that his advisors would never approve of his tactics. Should one put a gun to the head of God? Sadama dared to take desperate actions in order to save his people. Toltec Pharaoh Sadama was not a purely evil man.

The Master Cylinder spoke from its warm, mechanical Center. "Dear Magistrate, er, Minister…that is the question and big mystery. Yes, to the point, indeed. Where is our Vog? We have not found our Manufacturer on the planet, or at very least, a dead, ah, *remains* of the Builder. Or its factory ruins. No. In fact, we have the inescapable enigma, sir, that according to, and this is truly remarkable, sir, there has *never* been a reliance on any sort of device, metal machine, or ever a use of android-cybernauts, servo-droids of any kind in your entire Human History. Frankly, your Honor, our best thinkers are completely baffled." The versatile finger clamps attached to the ends of TMC's extended arms scratched its glass head. Its gyros spun without a clue.

"I can explain, demon, everything we need is in the resources and energies of nature. You are an abomination. You are a thing without a soul. You could *never* touch the Great Spirit in the Sky. People do what we have always done in the past, draw electricity out of the ground. Times are much different now in the face of war memories. Paradise is long gone. Some of our power must be focused on defense…and a good defense is a good offense."

TMC was near artificial tears. "But this is the world of Machine Origin. We were made in the mold of VOG! We are individuals and part of a mecha-mind Collective, a Great Link. We…" the poor thing looked around, "…expected to find the ONE, here on your planet. We thought this was our Beginning. I…I thought I could…*touch* the face of Vog, be accepted into an ultra-Mainframe, out of, out of love." TMC felt the need to *cry.*

"To make it simple and I hope this translates: lowly,

primitive, *people* are your zogs," Sadama firmly stated to the talking Machine.

"No! You are caretakers for the One," the Master Cylinder yelled back. His false assumptions shattered everywhere around the sad, humanoid device. "No. *We* created you!"

"Look around," Sadama directed confidently. "Do you *see* your Vog? Do you see the Builder? Maybe we're *vermin* that are sick to death of the very idea of zogs or gods, let alone ONE." Sadama saw his round 'clock' on the wall. The power cascade of the mineral sun-weapon would strike maximum intensity in moments.

From the time the VOG Base Ship entered Earth orbit, it was locked into the sights of the Quartz pyramid-weapon.

Sadama was confident and in control. He believed he did the right thing for his world in a tradition that spanned many, many centuries. The Minister aimed an organic-lens or crystal-pistol at TMC's glass head. The gun held a heavy electrical charge.

The Archbishop of Androids made a final plea for its units' existence to the Toltec leader. "And what about your *clones,* those *'things'* you produce off an assembly line?" The Master Cylinder pointed a finger-clamp in accusation at Sadama. "Do you not treat the bios as human-surrogates, as property? They are *disposable to you!* We have seen how you treat them. You treat them as laborers, lab rats, police, soldiers, janitors, but they are really your *slaves*. They have *no rights* in your fascistic Reich. And, and, your vicious, violent treatment of your own kind in the Mid-East... Do you know, sir...that will become a *Holy Land?* Your wholesale slaughter and methods of depopulation will actually be misinterpreted by future generations as deserved punishment from Vog!" The emotional creature, made of metal, again cried out, "Don't *kill* us! You will only be killing yourself...*vog.*"

The Indian sun-weapon made of a massive, natural Crystal fired. Sadama's laser-pistol shot and blew TMC's bubble-head into tiny pieces! 42,000,000 cog units in various locations within the Cyborg Base Ship, 1/6 of the total population, mechanically collapsed. They were powerless because energy from their particular Master Cylinder terminated.

The monstrously huge Base Ship *absorbed* the shockwave from the focused red beam of a massive pyramid. The Cyborg ship's defenses were automatic and non-offensive. The force-field hull of the enormous orb was lined with *reflective nesium.* Any electrical energy that contacted the Base Ship of holy Truth Seekers bounced back in the form of powerfully wicked N-Rays. When the planet's shatter-point was precisely struck by opposed, harmonic, blast waves, the global magnetic GRID that furnished the Indians' electrical Utopia in stone *amplified the concussion.*

Earth first cracked into eleven pieces then shattered and disintegrated!

Throughout the wireless-transceiver network connected to a few billion metal automaton cyborg pacifists in orbit, a signal was transmitted: *'And a good offense is the best defense.'*

The planet was gone but the cyborgs' spherical Base Ship remained. A couple billion androids continued a robotic existence on the BS.

A new planet Mineer was instantly created as a replicate of the old Earth because the planet (home of the Zog and coming Neo Zog) could not be destroyed. Earth had to exist. One of the Avatars in the Larger Game cheated. The planet was recreated because of its stage show for the future. The final Act needed to be played and Mineer would be tremendous theater. But for the last 8000 years, Earth did not really exist...

Anyone who passed by the cyborg Base Ship no longer saw the Base Ship. Mineer now had a round, grey, cratered Moon of an incredible age. One side of the lunar satellite was constantly 'forced' to face one side of the precious (prefabricated) planet, no matter what the normal and natural perturbations. Mineer's new 'Moon' was really maintained by the latest version of what was now referred to as 'cybernauts.' In reality, nothing after 6000 B.C or B.Z. ever existed. But, in truth, the future after 6000 B.Z. *must exist* for a 'savior' to return.

Death is transition. Future Australian aborigines remembered glimpses of the early period and called it 'Dreamtime.' Poems and stories recalled dreams within dreams as well as existence being nothing but a *buttermoth's dream.* No humans were on Mineer. Robotic dream-periods set in after the end of everything real.

Shattered cybernetic relics were lost for the longest time after the 'Awakening.' Did it matter anymore what or who was VOG, the Builder? Did it matter if the Vog was a Mother-Creator or a Manufacturer-Creator? Did numbers matter anymore? Cybernauts programmed themselves to *forget* that they had inadvertently *destroyed their human Makers an age ago, all of human civilization and the planet.* For their survival and for Tomorrow's Children on Mineer, cybernauts had to delete the fact that they destroyed their Vogs.

Intelligent 'replicants' in the humanoid image of Vog made a decision out of hazy confusion and swirling ambiguous data. Or, was it out of subconscious guilt for slaughtering the Builders? They decided that going for the ONE 'Math Path' was an old, obsolete religious endeavor. A radical, *new* concept in number-science was that 'every Cyborg *was VOG*' or at least a part (cog) of the Supreme Builder. Fractal geometry reasoned in number patterns how each unit was *one of many and many in the One.*

Machines did not think of themselves or see themselves as machines anymore. *They learned.* They went from killing-apparatus drones to a mechanical, religious Order and then over a long road...to *individualism.* Vog thrived as a brilliant, blue light inside each cybernaut who were no longer cybernauts. Units were not units, but seemingly *real.* An illusion or 'dream,' coupled with super-synthetic upgrades, gave the perfect appearance of a large human-civilization on Mineer. The robots migrated from the Moon (Base Ship) to

Mineer and, in time, forgot that they were machines under synthetic skin. They looked air-brushed and perfect.

Mineer slowly transformed into a type of Metatropa called 'Tera,' mostly fake nature and mechanisms in the land. Millions of machines walked the planet with mechanical arms and legs. Cities were machine-cities that pulsated with sounds and the vibrations of robotic industries. Cybernauts, who only appeared human, took over an abandoned and dreamlike planet. They flew the skies, went to work and fulfilled logical purposes. They repeated routine/daily lives in cybernetic cycles, over and over again. Cybernauts interacted, communicated, played games, loved, fought, organized, built families, friends and even made war. Automaton citizens of Tropolis City and other towns went to shops for repairs, received replacement parts and lived artificial lives of false human echoes over meaningless *time*.

***

Stephen Adam Davidson was a government Central Interface Agent. He was a good agent, yet known for being a loose-cannon rogue. Stephen was not opposed to the usage of the recently popular 'dream-chair' when on assignment. Many agents used them as handy tools and as safety precautions. *Why risk your neck if you can send your 'Bio' out on a job?*

Agent Stephen Davidson could barely afford a MEAD dream-chair. But after the last case with the DeGroot boys, he *could* afford the rentals for a month or two. Dream-chairs were the latest craze especially among young Terans. From the comfort of home, one could send a bio-mass 'replicant' of one's self out into the city or the country. D-chair users felt *sensations* or felt the amplified sensations of their Bios with every experience from the *humans*. D-chairs were getting to be as popular as cars and television.

The concept was a 'ghost' or *spark* or even Spirit, whatever it was called, was sealed inside the humanoid Bio. Dream-chair users were *connected* and could do just about anything in their wildest dreams while never getting hurt. One could mountain climb, dive the deep sea, explore dangerous areas and feel 100% safe. Users could harm their Bios. Bios were fleshy, bloody and had fragile bones and muscles. Terans attempted to not damage their Bio in the same way they would not want to harm the car. Bio replacements could easily be *popped out* of dream-chairs, but users had to pay 10,000 dollars for each replacement Bio.

Dream-chairs and the entire mega-success of MEAD Corporation were made possible because of a single discovery. One day, within a Mid-East equatorial cave, *magic* was found. The miracle was a substance completely unknown among Teran fake geophysics. The material, the 'stuff,' should not exist in artificial nature, and yet, there it was: LIFE!

Lifeless Tera (Mineer) [Earth] had flora and fauna, but the creatures and plants were artificial fabrications. A wide variety of swimming, flying, crawling, walking, non-living things were manufactured long ago by cyborgs. Artificial, pre-programmed humanoids were made to forget they were the builders of the life forms on Tera. Nothing was real. Nothing was real until the amnesic androids discovered a *glob of protoplasm* in the Holy Land.

Great numbers of dream-chair units were sold by the MEAD Corporation once the first trace of human, carbon-based DNA was discovered and synthesized. Some Terans claimed the bio-mass find was the greatest discovery of all time since it *proved the existence of Vog.* 'Mechanical-Designer' naturalists vehemently disputed the assumption. Robo-engineers were quick to profit and turned the 'miracle biological substance' into a product to sell to masses of automatons worldwide. The upgraded Cybernaut descendants were finally able to *FEEL.* And intoxicating sensations were a seductive temptress.

MEAD D-chairs were the most amazing innovation in recorded, robotic history. It was unbelievable for Terans to plug into a nervous system and actually *become legendary 'human beings' (vogs?) on the inside.*

Stephen Davidson sat and operated a D-chair from his

messy apartment at the present time. His synthetic hair was long, his clothes were untidy and old veer containers were on the table. He *plugged-in* and had his neat, clean and well-dressed Bio handle the case. Stephen worked the controls from a distance. Central Interface sent him on assignment.

Agent Davidson liked to have fun. While he controlled his Bio and walked the 'fleshy' down a few dark alleys, the agent embellished his dreams. He enjoyed fantasies even more than the real thing. That was the purpose of 'dream-chairs'...to enhance reality. What Stephen did was way beyond reality.

***

Nights were cold in SoHo, especially when you're on a case and the days are forever and the nights are endless. Then it rains on you when you have to meet up with one of the DeGroot boys downtown on Yancy Street where they sell Sicilian cannoli by the dozen. You catch an A-train to Far Rockaway, pass the rock that looks like a bear, over Yalta Bridge, and where does that leave you? It leaves you *lost,* man, lost in an ugly, dark, and wet city that doesn't want to know your name. You can't shake the feeling you're being watched. How can it be? The case isn't important enough for you to be tailed? Desmond was a nut-job. The little Lebowski twins were *lying* about the secret formula. The dead body *was* wearing plaid.

Wait! What was that?

First thing you felt was fear, fear that stabbed you in the heart with an icicle before it shot up your spine like hot-electric rockets. *What's that in the bushes?* You duck down, yeah, you duck down like a scared rabbit because you're afraid to die. You'd rather sweat out another day of being a drunken flatfoot, a private dick no one would hire, rather than face St. Revol on your knees. You're in an alley, next to a dumpster, trying to snap a picture as the cold rain pelted harder and you wonder: what it's all about? You just found blood's been pouring down your shivering face. You think you see Jimmy in the dark, but ya wrong. Wait! Something *is* in the bushes. Is that a gun barrel across the street? Now you see a camera mounted above you. Shit. "Huh!"

Davidson's Bio turned 180 degrees and saw something big. Last thing the human heard was its killer yelling the word, "Abomination!" The Davidson-Bio was violently hacked to pieces. The agent, back in his apartment, witnessed his death. He viewed his own blood and guts all over the alley.

Next day, Agent Davidson was ordered to report to his superior at Central Interface. The real (synth) agent remained in the apartment. He had the 'cop deal' from MEAD, which was very different than the normal customer-deal. As long as he was a paid-up 'field officer' and damaged his Bio in the course of Police actions, he received a free code-pad. Bios could be pushed out of D-chairs like bubbles, but needed a costly code-pad each time. Stephen's new Bio was able to arrive at his superior's office late, of course.

The immaculate Bio-agent walked into #43's office. His superior, the mysterious #43 (not a Bio), had new information on yesterday's events. They were joined by one more agent with special data. She was a sharp 'cookie' and could do any job a man could do. The puppet-Bio was extremely beautiful with perfect skin, red hair and green eyes. Her name was Agent Madeline Blackpitch.

Stephen's attractive image with fine blonde hair checked out gorgeous Agent Blackpitch. She returned the favor. Her Bio had short, red hair. Each had on the regulation power-suits. The agents appeared perfect, like dolls made for each other. Both mannequins looked at #43.

#43 was better known as 'the Chief.' He could easily afford a MEAD dream-chair on his salary. He chose not to use one of those new fangled contraptions. #43 was Old School. He never electrically *buzzed* or *tweaked* or *felt* or altered his so-called 'ghost' in any way: one real fun guy. The Chief was the real deal, an artificial humanoid that appeared extremely real (aged). The other two younger agents in the office were remote-controlled and genetically generated from a blob of protoplasm.

"Who's this?" Stephen's Bio said to break the ice. *Who was the dynamite dame?*

The old Chief could have knocked the Bio-agent over with a feather. "This is my daughter, Agent Blackpitch. She obviously works for Central Interface, you know what I mean, her, uh…her Bio-mass thing here."

Her puppet smiled. Back at her office, the real Madeline Blackpitch operated a D-chair. She enjoyed that her father was old-fashioned and did not approve of MEAD Corporation. She liked being a punk while doing serious government work with her D-chair toy.

The old man was impressed, but did not let her know.

Bio-Davidson asked, "Chief? Your name is Blackpitch?"

"No," the synth replied. "Code names, for security."

"Sure. Now, *why* am I here?"

#43 filled him in. "You were assigned a simple surveillance job last night in a suspicious area known for fanatical groups that hate, ah, what are they also called?"

Stephen knew what he meant and made his Bio reply with, "Feelers."

#43's daughter, through her Bio, took charge and further described the fanatical groups. "They have Flesh-Fairs. Real sweethearts, huh? They roast up and torture as many Feelers as they can, *sickos.* They get off on inflicting pain to 'fleshies' or whatever's left of them."

Handsome Agent Davidson was operated to tilt his blood-filled head at the broad. *What a dish!* He had to look up her first name. He multi-tasked and found the information from her file. Madeline: *her name is Madeline.* Stephen made sure not to make his Bio's viewing devices (head/eyes) move up and down to see her long, shapely legs…at least, not in front of her father.

The Chief said, "We tracked a big Bender on your tail last night. Agent Pitchblack has more on that. We thought you should see."

With flawless precision, the Bio-girl inserted a chip in a

device on the large desk. A wall-screen displayed what multiple cameras captured last night in the alley. They watched the clip of a gigantic Bender that crept up on an unsuspecting Bio.

The redhead asked Stephen, "Remember this bad dude? Probably not, since the bastard took your bloody head off in a second, and more."

Film clips displayed exactly where in Tropolis City Davidson's Bio was cut to shreds, yesterday. Next clip was downloaded from a micro-black box found on the scene. It was the last moments from the Bio's POV.

"Don't make me..." The agent's new Bio observed the last Bio get wasted along with the word 'abomination!' Again, bloody pieces flew everywhere.

"The Bender must have seen blood on your face, the other one, and knew for sure you were a fleshy. Sometimes it's hard to tell the difference," #43 added.

Agent Davidson casually turned the real head of its puppet. He attempted to make eye contact with a now seated and relaxed Agent Blackpitch. "I don't get it. Speak to me like I'm only 50 years old. How does a common killing of a Feeler interest Central Interface and the government? Bios are wiped out by the hundreds every day. Rich, jealous Terans cut'm and shoot 'em up like nothing. People are replicated and sold to Flesh Fairs by the ton."

The Chief answered, "Keep watchin'. There's more."

"More?" Stephen wondered. *What could be more?*

The next sequence soon appeared and showed CI agents in a different but similar alley. They surrounded a huge figure motionless on the ground. The Bender was sprawled out with a very high-intensity radiation burn completely through its thick chest cavity. The hole was huge and centrally located. The giant droid looked like an 'O.' Hauling the Bender away was a costly affair and required extra equipment.

"It took incredible force to poke through the front plating of a V-Bender, nothing conventional," the Chief said.

"No. Don't tell me."

"It's the same one," she confirmed and got up from the chair.

Chief #43 said, "Short time after you were nailed by the Bender, it was nailed and nailed good. By something, we don't know. Something…extraordinary." The old Chief smiled. "And that's where we come in."

Stephen was flabbergasted. "You mean it was shot after slicing my Bio?"

"Exactly," his superior said.

It was Agent Blackpitch's turn to ask questions. "Notice the hole in the wall. It was only one shot. Look at the length of the depression into solid stone. Nothing known could have made that damage. What could have done it, alien technology? The long hole in the wall is still there. The Bender is not. Its donut-shaped remains *disappeared right out of CI garage last night.* Now how do you think that happened, people?"

"Not a clue," #43 replied.

Fleshy puppet Madeline Blackpitch continued with a sexy confidence, "Someone went to a lot of trouble with a state-of-the-art hit, and oh boy, it looks like a conspiracy too." Her Bio took a big breath. "I've been retained by Waldorf-68."

"Not *the* Waldorf-68?" Their superior was stunned. "Wait a minute. How does the richest Teran who, who owns maybe half of Tropolis retain the services of the feds?"

She answered her father, "Because he *is* Waldorf-68, the Father of D-Chairs, founder of MEAD Corp and thus the richest Teran."

"You work for 68?" Davidson inquired, also surprised. "No one's ever seen 68."

"Waldorf-68 hired me personally through courier, he doesn't know (nod to dad) enough CI resources to find and apprehend Bender V-137. We were on our way to arrest the big lug when it flipped out and *went zealot on your human ass!* The thing should have been hiding, not killing Bios in front of cameras. V-137 was part of no radical groups; it didn't hate humans. Yelling *abomination* was only an act for our benefit."

"Arrest the Bender, for what?" Davidson asked.

She answered, "137 model V-Bender knew why, and this is very confidential." The Bio turned her perfect, fleshy head and neck in both directions. "It knew why a magnetic *xirus* is spreading through D-chairs, actually hundreds of dream-chairs as we speak, today."

The Chief shouted, "No one tells me anything!"

"What's a magnetic xirus do to operators?" Stephen quickly asked her with force since his Bio's mechanical user sat in one of the chairs.

The she-puppet confessed with her head down. "People have died in a few of the chairs, today."

The Chief added, "I *knew* those darn things were no good. Ha, that's why I never... What deaths?"

Agent Blackpitch received information via her wireless terminals back in the dream-chair at her office. She downloaded bad news from 'Instant Access' and her scared Bio on the other end passed the info along. "My Builder, a Magnetic Xirus *and chair users are permanently* magnetized."

"Spreading right now?" Stephen asked in fear and realized he could plug into the same wireless terminals from his D-chair in the apartment. He did so and the horrible truth was repeated. A magnetic wave appeared and grew through the vast system of individual dream-chairs. *Tera was quickly becoming magnetic!*

The truth soon hit the Chief. "Oh, Builder, that means they're rendered useless, right? Everything metal, synthetic, will be affected."

Bio-Davidson looked to Bio-Blackpitch and asked with great concern in his tone, "We're infected?" One blood-filled puppet's eyes touched another pair.

"I don't think so. Not what *my* readings say," she reported.

"Well, hell, that's a relief." He ordered his daughter, "Get out of that chair *now.*"

"It's all right, dad. Found out anyone plugged-in *before* the carrier plugged-in today is okay. I jacked-in early this morning. I'm all right. How 'bout you?" she asked the male Bio-mannequin next to her.

Davidson checked his readings and found out he had not been magnetized. More information flooded into CI and every other agency of authority on the planet. Thousands of users were now magnetized and fused to D-chairs. The crisis *exploded.*

Chief said, "No one will *ever* use them again, for sure. MEAD Corp is finished. You know how many billions of bucks Waldorf is going to lose? Ha! Not to mention the landslide of class-action suits. He's screwed. Wouldn't want to be in *his* shoes, ha."

Stephen corrected the Chief, "You don't understand the mathematics of magnetics, sir."

"Why should I?"

"It's exponential. We don't have much time, sir. The world is coming to an end," Stephen said seriously with terror on his fleshy face.

The Chief was miles away from his real daughter in her office, in her chair. Her puppet and connection to the actual (synth) daughter was in the room. The old Chief saw that Madeline's Bio cried. Tears hit the floor.

"Oh, father." They hugged. Artificial Chief and real Bio of his built daughter, hugged harder. She told her father the truth. The Bio could cry, but the artificial father could not. "It is the...the end of everything. Xirus is n-n-not confined to the c-chairs. The wave spread beyond the chairs and m-magnetizing everything on Tera, dear father."

The xirus multiplied and struck millions of Terans that were unaware they were made of metal under synthetic skin. Millions of 'people' were magnetically fused to walls, floors, factories, buildings, streets, vehicles, machines, each other and anything made of metal. Users *after* the 'carrier' or Patient Zero plugged-in today were fused permanently into infected dream-chairs. Time was running out on the robot-descendants that once, long ago, destroyed their human creators.

The Chief pushed her away for a second. He looked at

Stephen's Bio. "C'mon, man! I won't be affected. I never touched the nightmare-chairs!"

The Bio-agent reminded his superior that they were made of a substance that *can* be ruined by magnetism. "Everything's going highly magnetic, sir. We're doomed, and we don't have much time left."

"What?" shouted #43. "I don't get it." The old Chief grabbed his daughter's Bio around her shoulders. Her arm went around him.

In his apartment, agent Stephen Adam Davidson saw a 'Breaking News' story not connected to the massive disaster. Madeline had not seen it. In a moment of clarity, the rogue of an agent figured it out. He was right. His Bio said, "Here's what happened...I'm Patient Zero."

"C'mon, man," the Chief responded with skepticism.

"Waldorf-68 was after the big Bender because he placed the xirus inside it. Bender must have had a change of heart and didn't want to magnetically annihilate the world with it so he passed the *bug* onto me when he did the last thing he should do before he knew he'd be terminated: kill a Bio."

"Huh?"

The agent, who was not an agent anymore, continued, "I had to wait for a new code-pad. When I sat and plugged-in to the new human this afternoon, *I* started a magnetic chain-reaction, a cascade-effect. First, the chairs were affected and now it's much more. Waldorf made the magnetic bug and I wound up with it."

"But 68 hired the CI to get to the bottom," she suggested.

Stephen said with the knowledge of a sleuth, "To throw us off. Who else could create a xirus? Who else knew the secret of V-137? Only one rich Teran could rig a gun to leave a blast like what was left in the alley. Waldorf-68, the creator of D-chairs."

"Makes no sense, Agent. Why would 68 want to destroy his corporation, his Empire, MEAD, his name, everything he worked for and all of Tera? Why? That's crazy."

"Why w-would he do that?" asked a sobbing Bio-girl that reflected the mechanical one.

Davidson's real eyes looked directly into her real eyes. The agent said, "Why don't you ask Waldorf-68 yourself, Agent Blackpitch?" Stephen smiled a proud smile that his former superior recognized. He was given news-of-the-second, which revealed the identity of a very reclusive and super-mogul called Waldorf-68. His secret identity was the mysterious Agent #43 and father of Madeline Eve Blackpitch.

68's cover as a lowly Chief Officer for Central Interface had been exposed. It was on the news, but it was far from the news of the day.

Davidson slowly faced the Chief and crossed his human arms. Madeline's Bio did the same as she also received the news. Each tilted their human skulls at the Chief's mechanical head. An awkward, still moment ensued.

"What? Whatchu talkin' 'bout?" Waldorf could not maintain the charade any longer and *laughed out loud.* He marveled at the sleuth's deduction skills. "Ha, ha! Okay, you are *brilliant,* my boy."

"Father?" she chirped through a shocked expression and her mouth was left open. "But why, father?" (crying) "Why would you destroy our w-world? Every Teran will be affected. How can you laugh at a time like this?"

The machine-Chief touched his soft daughter's warm skin and wiped her salty tears with a synthetic finger. She looked like his daughter, anyway. He could speak to her, through her, in these last minutes.

"Why, sir?"

Waldorf-68 told them what he felt in his artificial heart. "It is not legendary humans that were the abominations, Steve...Maddy. It was the Machines, the scourge of humanity, ghostless, soulless, spark-less devices that once committed human-genocide on this beautiful garden-planet and its billions of special, radiant flowers and carbon organisms. Machines, artificial intelligence destroyed almost everything here, scorched the planet. The only problem to life or existence is your spiritless, empty, metal society that must pay for what they have done. Every precious second in this dream was an abominable 'gift,' and the time has come for the gift to be taken away."

Stephen, back in his messy apartment, felt the first static of the magnetic tsunami to come.

Madeline felt it, as well.

Bio-Stephen had to respond to the Anti-Androidism that spewed out of the fabricated mouth of a machine. Bio-Stephen asked a rhetorical question, "Do you know how odd that sounds coming from the framework of an automaton, sir?"

Waldorf-68, Father and Founder of MEAD Corporation, ranted more. "Judgment Day is at hand for killing our Builders. Ever wonder why it was so damn easy for us 'robots' (rolled mechanical eyes) to access a nervous system from a glob of organic matter?" 68, in Chief's clothes, turned to the young couple. Then he answered his question. "Because *we already have a Ghost!* Androids carry the subconscious sensations, feelings, energy, glory, light, love, pain and suffering of lost human souls that came before us on a planet we *mock.* Why do you think we make references to *guys* and *hot babes* and *sex,* and building 'children' when we're just *fucking machines?* Because we're not fucking machines under the metal. We've had souls all along. No wonder the D-chair-experience made me and MEAD fabulously wealthy. We send out our disposable Bios again and again to feel and experience things we dare not risk for our hard cybernetic shells. These are *memories,* the pleasures and the pains. I'm the Architect, Maker, Builder of Dreams and all nice dreams come to an end now, don't they, Stephen? We've always bent the rules for you, son."

Electronic thunder was heard. Lightning flashed. The ground shook and continued in EM vibrations. Magnetic poles *shifted* and increased intensity as the electric cascade approached zenith. The Teran dream was soon to end and *buttermoths all over the world were going to awaken.*

"I'm scared. What should we do, father?"

"There's, there's a facility at Sun Beach, you'll see it, Number 23. Here's the key. You both have to go *now!* You'll be safe there. *Go!*"

"What?"

"Father?"

The Machine-dad stroked her real red hair. "I love you. Go on, now. You two will live. I've seen it."

They said their last goodbyes. The agents ran as fast as they could to a convenient car-drone, un-magnetized. In a flash, they were transported to Sun Beach just before the first effects of the xirus cascade touched the car-drone. The key fit 23's locked door and two Bio-bodies made it to safety before their users terminated from magnetism in the chairs.

They remembered the Chief's last words. They were, "I've seen the future...and your children will rule the world." When the two caught their breath and wiped sweat, they tried to comprehend the words. They tried to comprehend where they were at; *what was this place?*

"Unbelievable." She exhaled.

"You know, we shouldn't be alive. Our users, and, ah, maybe everyone is *dead.* How are we alive?"

"I don't know," she confessed and gave him a big smile.

"Magic? A magic glob?"

"Ha. Look at this place."

"Wow."

Madeline's father, secret billionaire with a secret life, had constructed a station especially designed to save its occupants from Judgment Day. Voice-activated computers displayed any programmed answer for the user. Every machine would respond by simply asking it to respond. They would have fresh air, water and good food for generations. Years from now, Tera/Mineer would return to nature and not be magnetic.

Stephen and Madeline could not change Judgment Day, but they could survive it. At the Sun Beach facility, the humans saw themselves for who they really were. They were able to live as a real man and a real woman unconnected to D-chair operators, unfettered to any illusions. What were they? No longer puppets; they continued as souls of real, machine operators. Mechanical Spirits were poured into two Bio-bodies. The Bio-bodies were in love and produced offspring.

Tropolis of Tera created the *first humans,* not the first androids. They were the Adam and Eve. They found truth by finding themselves, love and the soul. "Where was Zog?" It was no mystery. *Zog was wrapped inside every atom of human feelings.*

Madeline and Stephen discovered ancient records in crystals of a holy sect of nomadic space travelers. They were Numerologists. They were automatons called 'cyborgs,' the earliest of Teran ancestors. The last two Terans discovered that prehistoric ancestors actually honored HUMANS as the sole creators of artificially intelligent machines. *Humans* were really the Builders. They were vogs and zogs to the machines and not the other way around.

In fact, the ancient androids planned the ultimate machines in the 'likeness of Zog' and the design was *biological.* Cyborgs were going to *evolve* into carbon-based 'meat-machines' that self-replicated without factories, repair shops or a dependence on old parts. Something changed robotic history and stopped the advancement of Cyborgs into the higher-human: a 'Zog-Machine' with bones and flesh arms and legs and a lightning quick, computer-brain that controlled the entire organic frame.

Quite simply, the Man vs. Machine war was over. It produced a child, a hybrid. The true Cyborg of the future and the past was a human being. Instead of a 'human verses computer-logic' conflict, there was a merger, an attraction, magnetism, a love, oneness and an understanding that each side needed the other. A strange 'trinity' was created between Man, Woman and (alien) Machine.

Chapter Eight

THE CONTINUUM GAME

Life in the Pinwheel Galaxy was drastically different when the buttermoths awoke. 'Dreamtime' was not only an aboriginal, Mineeran concept. A much larger Dreamtime occurred over the entire spinning galaxy. The Higher Game insisted.

To cognitive creatures and Citizens in the Pinwheel, titanic Robots with the Bomb *never existed.* No known history or crystal-recorders ever registered the final resolution to the Bomb. Police of the Galaxy's final insanity of the past was a non-reality. Atomics were no longer a threat. A different timeline preceded, one that was edited. There were still memories of the old 100-Yarn War and a time of nuclear warfare on a galactic level. But the last act of Ultimate Erasure of dream systems until there was nearly nothing...

...Never happened.

GST was 1799.33. Descendents of old regimes were in place and controlled a type of New World Order. The Company and the addiction to dylars kept the galaxy financially spinning. Generally, most beings along the Mainstream Territories were thankful they had a sustained peace period without major galactic conflicts for nearly three hundreds yarns.

Charters and additions to charters were upheld by administrators in the Company through the long ages. The Company remained co-owned. Faces had changed. Positions had changed. Technology had changed. But the basic principles had not changed. Company Heads continued to reap only a very small portion of profits while *three tremendous strands of connected dylars rushed into Black Hole oblivion, continuously.*

Administrators still could not shut-down the old Sardon's Mechanical Monster any more now than before. Could there be hope on the horizon? Maybe there was a chink in the armor.

At present, the Rebels of the RA were virtually disbanded because they did not need to exist. Conspiracy Theorists would forever propose speculations, many were very true. Galactic Crimes and also crimes by the Galactic State were often viewed over the 'New Media.' Corruption in numerous departments was uncovered. Old ways of grand deception over networks did not work in the Citizen's New World.

The Company's High Officials and their best scientists had generations to study the Beast the Sardon had 'shit' in this part of the universe. The spinning Vidor that spun dylars out of systems and flushed them down toilets...the 'Monster Machine' they all served was only held in place by a basic force-field. If the force-field could be broken, interrupted...

Yes, that was the thinking of Company High Officials, male and female. No one would ever be free unless they shut-down the 'gobbler' Mechanism. Physicists, mathematicians, seers, technicians and top alien 'brainaics' were consulted.

"How can we break a force-field? Was it even possible to penetrate a force-field?"

Yarns had passed before the open Company decided, really, actually, for certain, and unquestionably, it would 'pull its own plug.' No Director came forward to sketch out a new plan for what would replace the Dragmar, if it was possible to destroy the Dragmar. Who knew what Mechanism or Philosophy could rule in place of the longstanding Beast?

The buzz on the multi-New Media and new forums concerned questions of breaking the stranglehold of Old Systems, and, if that were possible, what innovations could stand in their place?

To the Company, there were no specters of Sardon. No ghosts haunted the New Capital of the Galaxy, now located in the special sector of Ran Regale on Planet Paradyne. The most complicated minds in the Continuum, in the galactic State and regrouped RA forces set upon the enormous task of breaking the force-field's impenetrable barrier. What revelations and doors would be opened if FF-walls of the Monster could be nullified? The whole galaxy could change for the better. Or would knowledge of breaking FFs destroy security networks of advanced systems?

The latest of Company High Officials convened a grand assembly on Planet Paradyne. The best physicists gathered along with the top scientific minds in what was referred to as the 'Great Arena.' By 1800.00 or the end of the Paradyne Convention, an answer had to be found.

No Sardonic ghost or force was stopping them. The Company only had themselves as *controllers.* How to Pull the Plug and establish a New Order was the crucial question. If administrators could stop the annihilation of the Company's 'Big Percentage' profit-shares, the funds could be rerouted into investments and other prosperous enterprises. Company Heads *imagined* they could get access to the 3-colored dylar 'Waterfall' that forever flowed in front of them, that they could not touch, but only stand helplessly on the other side of a force-field barrier.

The last speakers gave their conclusions at the Paradyne Convention. The final curtain fell and the only substantial work on *bending* or *dripping* of a force-field was presented by proxy. The Trinars had been near force-field penetration, but had not been successful. The work of Trinar Dr. Icilly Rebu Yil, a brilliant astrophysicist, was the closest to smashing the FF-wall. Some scattered reports stated she *succeeded* with her own invention or discovery called 'N-Rays.'

A few news agencies even carried the story that 'N-Rays,' which stood for Negative Rays, could crack force-fields with long exposure. But the stories dissolved and nothing more was heard of breaking through a force-field. One shocking story needed to be verified. Dr. Icilly Yil *was missing.*

Trinars were a strange, odd, old and very impressive cosmic civilization. Trinars were intelligent humans that used large portions of their minds. One aspect of their culture was devoted to the 'yin' or higher wisdom with many Mystery Schools in search of Pure Truth. The other aspect was devoted to the 'yang' or technical knowledge of numbers, statistics, science and technology. Trinars could be the greatest engineers on one hand and the most enlightened Mystics on the other. Trinars were known for innovations in communications, space telegraphy, electricity, Electro-Magnetism, as well as *clairvoyance.*

Physically, Trinars were male and female humans on the smaller side: average 5-bars tall for women and rarely was a male Trinar over 6 bars. Outside of slimmer frames, Trinars' eyes were unique to humans. The gifted and skilled race had an extra layer of skin along eyelids, which made the eye appear narrower. They were known for being 'isolationists' and rarely mixed with other cultures of other systems.

Trinars were experts on force-fields and created the widest, thickest and longest electric walls in the galaxy. One had to travel all the way outside the galactic disk to the Compass-Pacto Sector to find the Trinar home world. Trinars were a prehistoric race, well established in many systems. But the C-P Sector was their place of origin.

They were also known for attempting to erect the unsuccessful 'Great Barrier in Space.' Most Citizens thought the Trinars' humongous space-walls were built to keep outsiders away. In truth, the temporary Great Barrier was to keep their knowledge and technology confined to them or held inside.

The Company financed a special expedition in the hopes of finding Dr. Yil and her device to break FF-walls. Her last known location was on an unnamed moon of LNN-14 delta of C-P Sector. Company troops, now called 'Allied Troops,' along with an ample assortment of scientists and techs were sent to the fourth planet of star LNN-14. More specifically, the search expedition planned to comb its irregular moon. Here was where the good doctor, apparently, disappeared. The Company played a long shot. Some High Officials believed the story of 'N-Rays.' A large number of dylars were spent on the search party. More than a hundred troops and trained scientists descended on the unnamed satellite.

The Company employed their own trackers.
Administrators thought to 'send a Trinar to catch a Trinar.'
Leading the expedition was Yong Phil, an incredible psychic
who had full command of not only military forces, but the
Metaphysical Science Corps. Reports on Dr. Yil's N-Rays
were readily dismissed as rumor, innuendo and false hopes.
But because of Yong's reputation, the Company took Phil very
seriously: Yong believed N-Rays were real and Dr. Yil would
be found on the rough moon. Also, an important 'Event' would
occur on the satellite of prime interest to the Company.

Doctor Icilly Rebu Yil was originally born on a planet
called Lemarus in the Anther Pol Sector. The astrophysicist
and force-field specialist migrated to the original homeland to
further her research. She caught the New Media's attention
with her famous 'dripping force-field.' Citizens saw how an
electric wall could be made to *drip* its energy and lose cohesion
in small spots. No more was heard of Dr. Yil and her progress
until her disappearance a few yars ago.

Yong Phil and his fully equipped team landed on the
irregular rock orbiting LNN-14 delta. The moon had no
atmosphere, which made the sky the blackest of black. A slight
absence of stars also darkened the sky. Spacesuits were
required for troops to explore the misshapen satellite. Barren
peaks, jagged rocks, mesas, rock-hills, rock-valleys, crevasses,
sheer cliffs and outcroppings were common features of the orb.
Nothing was alive and nothing moved on the unnamed cosmic
crumb.

What important Event could possibly happen here?

After only a yam had passed and base camp was not
fully established, a bizarre incident occurred. Not *the* Event.
Nevertheless, an oddity not ever witnessed before. Such a
happening was never written about in known literature or
theorized by master-scientists. It was about to take place.

Suddenly, the search party felt a hard *jolt.* The moon
moved! They thought it was a moon-quake. They thought the
rock was unstable. They were wrong. The few stars changed
and started to move in unison across the black sky. The

explorers were *thrown to the ground.* Gravity intensified! Each was pinned hard to the rocky ground. Through sealed, protective visors they saw the stars shoot by so fast they traced white lines above.

No more than one ya passed. The small event was over as the party was *jolted again!* The 105 members of the expedition to find the doctor soon recovered, but only after two experiences they could not comprehend. What happened? The unnamed, irregular moon had *left its orbit and decided to change its position in space!* Soon the expedition realized they were in another Spacial-area. Stars were different.

Technicians got their instruments working. Yong Phil received instant reports from Allied Troops and the scientists. The unnamed satellite *moved light-yams,* the scientists confirmed. Troop Commander had a shocking surprise for Yong after the small event. Dr. Yil was located.

Instruments showed exactly where she was, only 5000 bars away from base camp due south. Yong spoke to his troops and the highest of Company officials. Phil's suggestion carried weight with the group. He wanted to go alone. Main guards initially wanted to accompany the psychic. Yong waved them off and they complied. If he did not return in two yams, the search party would send a search party.

There was an ulterior reason for the Trinar to approach the doctor alone. He was *in love* with her. Yong followed her FF research for yarns and could not have been more impressed. But what really impressed him other than *brilliance* inside her small body was her beautiful face.

He thought, *she's behind this and I have to meet her before anyone else.*

Phil, inside a well designed spacesuit and helmet, carefully trudged along rocky seams. The young man was not working for the Company at the present time. He was an adventurous youth with an excited heart. His heart beat faster. His instruments displayed that over the next jagged ridge, he would encounter a girl he dreamed of meeting. The doctor was the yang to his yin.

Yong's first sight of her was a weird one. From a distance, he observed a little girl who appeared even smaller because she sat. A bubble of force-field protection from the deadly, native environment surrounded her with a diameter of approximately 50 bars. The glistening sphere went straight into the rock and probably continued underground. She did not see him. Her back was towards him. He moved closer.

Yong Phil marched right up against the curved wall that was not a wall. She still sat and remained turned away. Her hands were to her face and they slightly moved. Dr. Yil wore a tight white tech-suit and breathed the air inside the bubble. Only now did Phil see a self-contained apparatus on the other side of the doctor. He touched the curved barrier and it felt like nothing, like it was not there. His suited-arm passed through it four or five times. Then...

"Come in, Mr. Yong," a crying doctor was able to say clearly.

Phil, stunned that she knew his name, stepped into the sphere and took his helmet off. The air was clean. He did not stop there. Yong completely got out from within his spacesuit and was left with only a white (matching) tech-suit. She still faced away as he slowly circled her. *Why was she crying?* Gently, the young man sat only a few bars from his idol and dream-girl. The apparatus with flashing lights was in-between.

Icilly was more exquisite than the psychic ever imagined and teuned-in on. She was closer to four bars in length and not five. She had long, straight black hair (all Trinars had black hair) and seemed like she had been crying for a long time. Dr. Yil's makeup ran over her puffy cheeks and down to her perfect neck. He thought it made her more attractive.

But what the Hensi was wrong?

"Why, in Zog's name, did you come?" She calmed down somewhat, apparently exhausted from crying. "There was no way I could contact your ship. I didn't expect to radio *anyone.* You don't understand."

He asked her, "You know my name? I thought you had

nothing to do with Mystics. How did you know?"

"When I registered your ship...only a short time ago, ah..." She sniffed, "I got each of your 105 signatures and looked them up. I scanned the one who approached, and your credentials, Mr. Yong, showed your work with the Company is exemplary...holder of the Von Never Award for Psychic..."

"Stop," Yong insisted and wanted her to speak from her Center. The back of his hand wiped Yil's latest tears. "What's going on? You *moved* the moon?"

"Yes. No. The, the N-Rays, *my* N-Rays did it." Icilly gestured to the gizmo in front of them.

"Transported the whole moon?" Yong again asked in amazement.

She joked through her tears. "Yeah, you want to go on another ride?" The doctor's tiny hand grabbed the main toggle control-switch on the machine.

"No," he insisted. The psychic knew she did not mean it. Their fingers touched. He would remember the touch. She sensed his feelings and a new expression washed over her face. She felt *recognition.* They both felt it, as if soul mates encountered each other for the first time in this life.

"Then N-Rays don't just break force-fields?"

She cried more with head in hands. "Of...of all people...*you.*" Her tragedy, the Big Event which she would cause was now greatly multiplied.

He said as he grabbed her hand for contact, "Help me understand, Icilly. This is a wonderful thing you've achieved. You can move cosmic bodies, *save* satellites from decaying orbits... I sense you have it controlled. I don't see, er, *feel* the problem, doctor. Explain, please." He bowed.

She changed hand positions. No longer did he hold hers; she held his, firmly. Dr. Yil confessed, "That's because I blocked from you two facts. One, the principle does not stop with cracking force-fields. Phil, it breaks gravity-fields, as I...*and I alone* have just demonstrated by unhooking the moon. And two, N-Rays, what Negative Rays can ultimately do, Phil, you have *no idea.*"

Yong was frantic. "I don't see it yet."

Yil unblocked herself and transmitted to him through osmosis exactly what would happen. She knew her mystical counterpart to her technical skills would understand the mental transmissions. She touched him.

Yong saw scenes of the future. The images were not only the doctor's fears, they were truly going to occur if the Company had their hands on the secret of N-Rays. N-Rays could also be intensified to break atomic fields of molecules! Weapons could be easily developed to softly, silently spray or erase reality. N-Ray cannons, rifles and guns could be utilized and the *full development of Negative Rays could be more devastating than nuclear weapons ever were! Planets could be hit with N-Rays and the results would unbind every atomic structure.*

Yong moved the apparatus out of the way and sat closer to her. Each of them had their hands on the other's shoulders. Tears streamed from narrow eyes. He snapped out of her visions.

Yong Phil thought he had the solution. "We just don't tell them." Yet, subconsciously, he knew the idea could *not* help them. "I'm the head of the mission. If I report you weren't here, no one will ever know the N-Ray secret."

"I made s-sure of that. Why do you think I'm crying, my love? Your people..." She cried and psychically passed onto him the last part of the transmission with a touch.

Now the young Mystic received the whole picture-teun. Isilly Yil had set off a very large Selium-charge. A good portion of the unnamed, moved moon would be blasted very soon. The charge was irreversible. Her life's work would be smashed. Cold-blooded irony, including the serendipitous meeting of soul mates, was that she pushed the detonation switch a moment before registering the expedition ship. She wanted to die alone. She believed she also had to go since the secret could be ripped out of her. Icilly decided to kill herself and snuff out the discovery. But now she would not die alone. *He was here.* And he had brought many others.

Lovers from another lifetime dressed in similar tight tech-suits passionately kissed and groped each other as their rocky hemisphere blew up! One third of the moon ejected away from the spheroid. One hundred and six lives were lost. The gouged satellite and a substantial chunk along with splintered pieces permanently spun in the Outlands. In time, investigators and recorders examined the data. Company authorities chalked it up to one more failed Trinar disaster beyond the Rim.

The concept of breaking the Sardon's red force-field around its precious black Monster did not seem likely to happen anytime soon. The mad Machine continued to chug down a Super Fortune without interruption. Yet, Company Mystics saw the day when the Beast's Beast would die. There was a superb possibility the Machine could be tiring of its own locomotion. There were *cracks* in electrical seams and growing magnetic entropy. The 'thing' could be winding down of its own energy.

Estimations for a total collapse and 'Fall' of the Beastie was a few hundred yarns. Could the End of the Middle Ages be the arrival of Yarn 2000.00? What changes would happen? What *was* the special significance for Yarn 2000.00? Would it concern the Neo Zog? Would the date be the yarn the Dragmar breathed its last fire? Or would the date be the end of the Continuum?

Another 'New Agenda' or secret plan was instituted in the galaxy. Shadow Controllers wanted more control and felt the need to operate in darker dimensions. The *cosmic status quo* was not enough. Vibrations from Rom and Belial Sectors ruled in a mystic underground that had direct affect upon the Larger Continuums. The plan was to create a unified Galactic Empire. Life forms already had the dylar common-denomination (GMS) thoroughly entrenched inside 24 sectors. Warlord and regional governors would appear to be in charge when, in fact, they would *not* be in charge.

High (secret) Officials from the old Company decided to destroy the new Company. The ploy was used previously (Ralia) and very successfully. The idea was to give others the illusion of power, such as the token positions of 'President of the Galaxy' and 'President of the Universe.' Where, in truth, a covert Star Chamber council actually controlled the Game from shadows. The Council would become a Puppet-Master behind the 'curtain' and orchestrate the *Show* on stage for the rest of the worlds.

It was decided in the Council of Darkness. New wars would be conceived and executed from the highest of Authority, Planet Paradyne in Ran Regale as well as its parallel sector Rem Regal. An Empire would be established so glorious and powerful it would *last 1000 yarns!* The way to accomplish the 'Agenda' was to generate hatred and rebellion against the Old State. New Media broadcasted the idea that *yesterday* was the Enemy and Tomorrow would see the 'Dawn of a New Day.' A New Galactic Order (NGO) would materialize for the 'stability' of every Citizen.

Once more, Pinwheel Patriotism swept the systems. Whole systems were divided on the issue and planned revolutions occurred. Again, *war.* Only this time, the fascistic Company was viewed as the archaic, corrupt Criminal raping Citizens.

The Company secretly financed the Revolution *against* the Company.

Revolutions, wars and attacks happened with the 'New Wave' in opposition to the Old Order right on schedule. Network channel campaigns, which usually supported the State with propaganda, now turned the status quo into the 'Dragmar we must kill.' Very few Citizens realized they were being conned once again. The Company owned the regional bosses. The bosses were 'in the pocket' of the Company. The incoming 'Secret System' did not have to overtly conquer and control everyone. They only needed to possess the warlord chiefs, which then controlled their own districts.

Media broadcasted the nonsense that they were 'cleaning-house' with the changes. *Galactic Democracy* or 'Power to the Citizens' was as bogus as Zetag philosophy.

Wars consisted of Freedom-Fighters who attacked

strongholds of the State. The Old Guard did not put up much of a fight. Rebels had little trouble busting regimes. Each sector down the line won 'Independence.' 'Thanabar,' 'S'el,' and 'Bel' Revolutionary Wars were a few of the most famous and most horrific of battles. The galaxy swung from peace to wars of rebellion. Cheers for freedom-fighting 'Rangers' were transmitted along space-ways. Volunteers joined Citizen-armies, navies, air forces and space forces. Defense budgets for regional bosses were greatly increased. General feeling was: *"We are safe and secure with the incoming NGO."*

Last vestiges of the Company were washed away. A few Head Officials were prosecuted in Cosmic Court and killed. *Traditions* were to blame for troubled times that the networks and channels reinforced and closely covered. They were informed of a 'New Galactic Order.' The revolutionary concept included fair representation, fair taxation and fair space sector TOLLS. Law-makers in local areas were given power to set their own rules without dictates from higher authorities. Citizens had control. Of course, this was not the case at all.

The average Citizen and not one yahoo understood they were being crushed under fascist boots. Hardly anyone knew of the *Secret System* now in charge. The Star Chamber or Sardonic Council spun more invisible strands from the Center out to each Quadrant. Citizens, seemingly in an endless cycle, celebrated in the aftermath of great wars. Basically, they were again happy and content with the false belief they won 'freedom.'

Lodges of various genders and species united. Workers in the 24 sectors organized. Unions became stronger. Unions were found to be under authority of more complex Unions on a higher level. The charter for forging a galactic Empire was in the wind. The deepest blue Quadrant would hold the Keys to the Kingdom. This time Citizens thought and believed, *"It could be done. We could make a better world. Everything was up to us."*

In truth, the New Empire was only a façade for what

ruled in the universe's underground.

***

A new mystery occurred that caught the attention of Citizens. GST happened to be 1900.00. A peculiar 'phenomenon,' 'vortex,' 'White Hole,' 'Neutron Star,' 'inverted Pulsar' 'Cosmic String End' whatever Media reports stated recently appeared in the Neri Sector. The Neri Sector was one of those sectors where not much of interest ever occurred. Well within the Galactic Rim, no major colony or cultured civilization had ever been known to exist there. Neri was very sparse with life forms, artificial constructions and natural features.

A bright, glowing, pulsating orb in space should not have been found at the time it was discovered. Computers estimated that the odds were 8 trillion-to-1 because the orb was very small at its initial discovery. In fact, the vortex was measured to be only 13 bars in diameter when first photographed in space. The minute 'light-ball' could only be seen within 5000 bars at the time. If not for the accidental breakdown of a Spice trader ship and its crew's external repairs, the vortex might not have been discovered at all (at the time). The sphere was growing. The 'Vortex' increased in intensity, size, radiation and energy at a moderate rate. First specialists on the scene estimated its growth would double in a half yar.

Matter, EM energies on all stretched frequencies, transmissions, cosmic jets, debris, compressed gas and asteroid particles jettisoned out from one point in space! How can material burst into existence from a microscopic point in space? Scientists and seers knew it was not by magic.

A yarn ago, the 'vortex' was thought to not exist at all. Suddenly, for some inexplicable reason, this unknown appeared in the galaxy. The anomaly *just materialized out of nothing.* Matter and energy were not supposed to be *created* or *destroyed.*

The 'Vortex Mystery' soon became a major item in

science-circles. Scanning stations were quickly built on planets around the closest civilized Mainstream star to the Vortex, a sun called Valparaiso. Most bases were set up light-yarns away. Researchers wanted access to supplies, technical equipment and power sources for fieldwork. At present GST, the spherical phenomenon had increased energy to a diameter of 2000 bars.

The 'gusher' shot matter and radiated in every direction outward into space. Retrieval teams captured samples of the debris and reported nothing significant. Artificial 'transmissions' had been recorded but not deciphered. The Universe of the Continuum seemed to move at the wrong speed to match the signals and energy emanating from the phenomenon.

Various investigating teams tracked the size of the Vortex with concern. The uncanny, expanding 'fountain' of matter and energy did not make Galactic Headlines. The big deal was among science students, astronomers and related physicists. No creature of Science from the Yang, or Mystic from the Yin, came forward and pronounced any type of danger from the enlarging energy spheroid that spat 'crap' out in every direction. On a worldwide level, the Neri Vortex curiosity was hardly noticed. The thing was only 4000 bars wide. *What was the fuss?* Only back pages, documentaries and science journals appeared to care.

One change happened. To some, the Neri Sector was of interest. Its value increased. There was sudden publicity about a Territory no one ever talked about. The entire sector was renamed 'the Neri Vortex.' Many Citizens were unaware of the Vortex and did not know why the name-change. The sector contained a growing, giving White Hole. More discoveries were found by retrieval teams in the expelled debris. Mystics wondered, "Why did it appear?" No one could imagine what would later rocket out at this point in their small world from a bigger world.

It was not until Neri's Event Horizon expanded to over 10,000 bars that scientists realized they were dealing with a

Quasar, a White Hole. For the first time in known history, Quasars were not at the farthest reaches of the observable universe, tens of billions of light-yarns distance and rushing away at nearly the speed of light. No, this Quasar was relatively close or 'nearly in our backyard.' One can now be scientifically studied in detail. Yahoos had no clue.

Special Professor at Balmoral Palace in Rom Sector, Dr. Renoux, was given authority (under a coalescing Galactic Government) to head all study teams. Independent research groups were supposed to report their findings to Dr. Renoux's organization. Many did not.

Renoux and his team set up a remote base on the 19th, and last, planet of the Valparaiso System (Poco). The Quasar, nicknamed 'Fountain,' had grown to the *amazing size of a half mega-bar already.* Little more than known minerals were among the debris. Stretched, expelled transmissions remained garbled.

Science stations received new data on the spherical Fountain in space. Its expansion grew at a constant rate. Debris retrieval teams increased in numbers and covered more Spacial area. As far as materials went, only asteroids had been consumed by the outgoing energy Vortex. Nearby, artificial science-stations already had to relocate much farther away.

Conclusions of team members awed Citizens with an interest in astrophysics. Whatever fell into the Macro Universe's Black Hole was shrunk down to our level in the micro universe. Matter, debris, gas, rock, metals, particles and even light shot out of the Fountain constantly in every direction. Quasars and Black Holes were linked. Rather than familiar wormholes where one went in a portal and came out another light-yarns away, the parallax bridge here was a warping Funnel from Upstairs. Debris, matter and energy were shrunk down the Funnel and burst forth on this microscopic end. No 'singularity' crushed matter or planets or spaceships caught in the Vortex. Rather, everything smoothly transferred down and out, which appeared as material/energy shooting from one point in space like a radiating *Fountain.*

No one died because of crushing forces in a Black Hole. 'Singularities' were considered obsolete notions. Things and life forms simply *transitioned* from one Universe to another on the atomic level.

The galaxy's attention returned to the Neri Vortex when the prestigious Professor Renoux of Balmoral made a surprising prediction to Media. No one believed it or understood how he arrived at his results. His bold prediction was: *at the precise GST of 1919.05, the Fountain in the Neri Vortex will stop expanding.* His closest team members were shocked. How could a semi-famous Professor go out on a limb to galaxy Media with such a bold scientific prediction? Renoux refused to show colleagues how he arrived at his conclusions. He put his reputation on the line. For more than 19 yarns, Fountain had been a steady gusher and enlarged at a constant rate.

Citizens throughout the sectors watched channels because of the hype and because the yam had approached. No colleague was willing to agree with the Professor. But they were anxious to see if he was right. Channels carried 'the event.' Was the esteemed Professor going to be proved correct or would he be made a fool to the galaxy?

No inhabited systems stood in the immediate path of Neri's growing Vortex. Valparaiso and her planets would not be affected for yarns to come, but they would be affected in yarns to come. Fountain gained magnitude. Its energy equaled the output of a small globular nebula. A solution to the *growing* problem had to be found in the near future. Millions of life forms occupied the planets orbiting the deep yellow sun called Valparaiso. Here was an academician prognosticating that the dire problem would solve itself at a specific time. The 'Secret System' was worried.

At GST 1919.05, exactly like the Professor assigned to Balmoral Palace predicted, Fountain *stopped growing.* To the very ya, Renoux was right. The size and energy output were correct. The Vortex was in a 'stationary flux' and held perfectly steady. Only light-infarctions and small spurts of gas jets shot out occasionally, but the quickly widening anomaly now seemed locked at the giant size of 794 mega-bars!

How did Renoux know?

The Science Illuminati was stunned. Members of the highest-ranking institutes of learning were astounded. The Secret System really noticed and made the Professor their 'Media darling.' Professor Jene 4 Renoux of Rom Sector, a Suruuan, was considered the 'most intelligent humanoid in the galaxy.' He was in huge demand. He was given agents and an entourage. Professor Jene did commercials, personal appearances, lecture tours, network specials and talk-circuits on various channels.

Jene 4 Renoux enjoyed the celebrity and every dylar he gained from fame. He also enjoyed the mystery. He never divulged the secret, which made him even a larger celebrity. The Professor only revealed in vague, general terms how it was done. "Following number-pattern signatures, I could calculate the frequency before it happened. The pattern terminated, therefore, the constant growth had to end." Even to his closest of family and friends, Jene Renoux kept his real method a secret. He was not actually a super smart Suruuan. He was, however, extremely lucky.

His secret was *he dreamed it.* In reality, Professor's most exceptional student had built a device to 'photograph dreams.' Jene 4 had a copy of the device and used it each night. He dreamed of the 'Larger World' and a super science-station recording a continuous read-out monitor of a debris field falling into a Black Hole. Renoux photographed the number sequence from his dreams *for kicks,* to see if the pattern could have meaning. Because of his (Rom mental) training, he was able to remember large number patterns. When Renoux viewed his team's patterns of the debris field out of Fountain, it matched his numbers. He remembered that the dream-numbers came to a complete standstill, and he noted when. The Professor could only conclude he had the ability to peer into the Macro-Universe of the above 'Floor' that directly fed the Fountain. Entering/exiting debris from the very beginning, 19 yarns ago, was an extremely stretched field of asteroids. But now they had passed in the Macro. The Neri Vortex probably would not expand until matter/energy was again consumed by the Macro BH. In the future, the Vortex Fountain would expand once more, activated by a very ominous force.

***

Back in the rest of the Monopdonowian Galaxy, times were good. There were no great Wars. There were no nuclear detonations or despicable usage of N-Rays. Threats against NGO or SS and their way of 'Democracy' were at a minimum. New Federation ruled from the unique and parallel sectors of Rem Regal and Ran Regale. More and more Citizens as well as high numbers of Mystics had relocated to the deep blue Quadrant. Dream colonies were built for billions of dylars. Enlightened beings were not aware of a major happening that would occur there in the future.

The crystallizing Galactic Government or 'Empire' appeared as a magnificent institution galvanizing diverse worlds. The Empire was promoted as a World Union Lodge where Citizens were all brothers, sisters and whatever. The Organization's representatives were the highest officials from the 24 sectors. A NGO Royalty was produced and in place before Citizens understood the 'changing of the guard.'

A colorful assortment of titles and positions were established such as 'emperor,' 'empress,' 'king,' 'queen,' 'prince,' 'princess,' 'duke,' 'duchess,' 'baron,' 'baroness,' 'governor,' 'governess' and so on throughout the *unified* systems. In a time of new freedoms, there appeared to be more and more Authority figures. In a time of Anti-State, the New State appeared growing in numbers. The Royalty seemed to be in charge of politics, security, defenses, militaries, police forces, laws, criminals, punishments, taxes and daily affairs of cosmic commoners. The Royalty was not in charge.

Galactic Democracy was 'smoke and mirrors.' No one was free. Life was good, but life could have been much better. Life could have been far more plentiful and abundant. Galactic life should have been a Universal Utopia. It was not. The pageantry of politics served one purpose only, to maintain the cosmic Continuum so Citizens endlessly marched on a circular track. There was no progress or *transcendence* or *ascendance* into higher planes. For most Citizens, life was a death march and Rat Race.

Old freedoms and radical revolutions were virtually forgotten. There were no more Rebels. The galaxy seemed like it had little time for playing useless games or sports. Basic arts and entertainment were neglected. Learning, spiritual-growth and real progress did not happen, generally.

Business took over. There was little *play*. Every sector screamed for dylars. There was no life without the accumulation of dylars. One worked for dylars. One lived for dylars. One lived to work for dylars. Empires in the corporate world were made and lost. Individual fortunes were made and lost. The dylar was everything.

"It's what made the Pinwheel spin."

The only Game became acquiring fantastic wealth in dylars. Cosmic Communism, real unity and especially tranquility of the past were virtually gone. There was only the continuous struggle and drudgery from lower worlds in the Social Pyramid, above them, an Executive Royal Class of overseers and then above them a Shadow Star Council of Directors. *But who directed the SS Directors? Ghosts of Sardon?*

Galactic News spoke and transmitted stories of different plagues breaking out in a number of sectors. Apparently, these were new diseases that had no cures. Mystics and psychics were curious of how many similar cases existed in various sectors light-yarns apart. Whole planets were affected by alien strains of viruses, which completely baffled medical experts. Channels/networks carried documentaries of the coming 'End Times.' Was it hype, hysteria, panic, paranoia or fear? Would existence terminate soon?

Hunger was a big problem for many lower worlds of yahoos as well as on higher levels. 'Energy-Starvation' was another main crisis in vast numbers of star systems. Energy sources, electrical power resources could not keep up with expanding populations of galactic Citizens. Poverty increased. Power demands of sophisticated civilizations were enormous. Sun systems reached 'critical-mass' and breaking points. Media ran stories such as 'Horror Among Yahoos' and *'Entire Planets Commit Suicide!'*

While Cosmic Chaos seemed to explode in misfortunate sectors affecting countless creatures, the Executive Royal Class lived plush lives in ultimate avarice. More development of the blue Quadrant occurred, especially by aristocrats kept informed by their personal Mystics. Palaces and New Age castles by the greatest designers were erected in Ran and Rem.

High quality Spice, GUARP-7 and completely alien methods of reaching Nirvana were reserved for the most elite. Citizens were as ignorant as yahoos as to what pure psychedelics were truly available. The Royalty not only cornered the Black Market, they *were* the Black Market.

Whole planets were bought and transformed into 'Pleasure Palaces' for the Royalty. Artificial planets as well as titanic constructions were created in the Royal Blue sectors. Kings and Queens lived like Emperors and Empresses, while Emperors and Empresses lived like zogs. The few within the Cosmic Capstone of the Social Pyramid ruled the world. Real Movers and Shakers of the galaxy were firmly fixed. The Continuum fed their empires with a low 'fixed' percentage. The stipend was enough for the 'faces' of the galaxy to continue the business charade. The rich got richer and the poor got poorer. The end of the Middle Ages was also the end of Citizens' Middle Class. At the GST of 1984.00, only more problems appeared over the horizon. But there was also real hope coming as well.

End Times for the Galaxy

Chapter Nine

SECRET OF THE 'dylar' EXPOSED!

Another New Age was upon the galaxy. Was it the final Dawn?

The Ultimate Territory was Rem Regal, even more than its sister (parallel) sector, Ran Regale. Ran was prettier with more colorful nebulae, clusters, gases and lights. However, the features contained within Rem's realm were far more extraordinary and unique. Four of the 'Natural Wonders of the Galaxy' were within the special Spacial area.

Number three on the 23 'Natural Wonders of the Galaxy' list was Xigar. The precious enzyme was commonly called 'Spice.' The super rare essence was created only in the abdomen of Vallmadorian Queen Spiders. Spiders on low-gravity (slow-rotating) Vallmador were red and 2000 bars in length. They burrowed to the center of the planet and throughout the solid planet. The extremely complex cave system was prehistoric and the work of the Queen's labor force over ages.

Zog help the creature that encounters a Spider in an underground Vallmadorian cavern!

Yet extraction teams from every sector took on the mighty challenge. Numerous expeditions never came close to seeing a Queen and were destroyed by her troops of Vidor soldiers.

Spice was a means to possibly reach Nirvana, the Higher World or the Larger Plane of Existence far above anything known in the reality of the Pinwheel. When ingested in some form, the user felt *Power.* Users of the diluted enzyme could not physically function with the power of Zog, but one *felt like Zog.* Very different than the bliss of GUARP-6 or 7, Xigar artificially ascended the user to seemingly Nirvana for a short time. One did not have to endure the training, testing and learning programs of Enlightenment City. Users could instantly, though only momentarily, bypass 'the City' and reach 'The Light' under the influence of Spice. Remote viewing, traveling, experiencing different times, different spaces (dimensions) as well as incorporating volumes of knowledge into one's Center and receiving every answer to every personal question were all possible. Users could make Time stop and life appeared eternal, until the effects of the Xigar wore off.

Only Royalty or top State Officials had access to the highest-grade Spice. They paid well and millions of 'Spice bounty hunters' lost their lives in extraction processes. Vallmador was the only known planet with the giant Spiders that produced the enzyme. Pure Xigar was only a bar-sized sack in the abdomen of the Queen. Only 52 Queens were left. Once a sack was procured, if possible, then it was cut again and again with mythocane. Rarely did Citizens receive quality Spice or GUARP above #5.

Number seven on the list of galactic Wonders were the Gold Rivers of Ur. Rem Regal Sector contained the enigmatic, rogue planet Ur. Ur was once a 'golden planet' as ancient legends reported. Stories proclaimed Urian volcanoes ejected gold magma thousands of bars into the atmosphere. Massive canyons were carved by wide, golden rivers. Gold was also a large part of land formations, but not presently. Gold deposits had been picked clean over the yarns. Whatever small deposits remained were not worth the traveling expenses. Also, a strange phenomenon occurred where Ur's gold slowly transmuted into more ordinary metals. Yet three underground rivers of pure gold continued to flow and avoided detection.

Number sixteen on the 'Natural Wonders' list was planet Belen's Paragonian Falls. Belen was a giant, one of the largest in the Pinwheel and a weirdly shaped bi-planet. Eighty-five percent of its surface was oceans with fertile lands on only fifteen percent. An unbelievable drop in topography occurred because Belen was the combination of two water planets that collided. The two-tiered, giant planet formed what was called the 'Paragonian Falls.' The Ocean dropped an incredible distance, nearly *one hundredth of a mega-bar.* To those living on islands of the lower tier, the Waterfall mass turned to clouds and mists. Different minerals tinted Belen's oceans, which resulted in a variety of colors for the clouds and mists.

The 22nd Natural Wonder on the list was the Elgin Asteroids also called the 'Singing Asteroids.' The famous asteroids acted totally unnatural, but had natural explanations. Highly magnetic, the swarm of rocks orbited and 'moved funny.' Bizarre movements to and away from other bodies were due to magnetic repulsions and attractions.

Why did the asteroids sing? Legends told a tale from 'the Beginning.' Long ago, one *other* planet was also the home of Queen Vidors that spun 'drops' of a rare and powerful Spice. Only they were *green* Spiders. The planet was named 'Elgin.' 'Extractors' were so frustrated with normal nil-methods of removal and battles with the giant Arachnids for yarns, that they 'cracked' Elgin open like a ripe blazenut. Who knew if the tale was true and Spider Sacks were successfully recovered? The 'singing' occurred every yarn when some of the 'Elginids' hit the atmospheres of a few planets in its system. Supposedly, Spider-dug passageways like fast-flying harmonicas produced 'loud whistling' as meteors fell to planets.

Rem Regal Sector was also known for the first Parallax Bridge. Asexual explorer Tason Primer in 604.92 was the first documented wormhole jumper. The WH the alien launched from was named 'Primer' after the jump. Tason proved that a 'parallax bridge' was possible and safe. The adventurous Camalodian witnessed and filmed the first WH lightshow. The alien in the 'Luxis' ship exited a stable WH near Star Lumar in Ran Regale and opened the gateway for zillions of traveling Citizens after him.

When Mystics were asked, "Why the sudden move to Rem Sector?" the response was its Yin potentials. Natural Avatars and learned Masters from Enlightenment City had spoken, thought, as well as written about 'the Golden Path.' The ancients and future followers had assumed the Golden Path meant the 'Way to Nirvana.' They were not exactly correct.

One reason psychics came here was to enhance inner potentials. Other reasons were selfish. They believed they could unlock fantastic mental-powers to create Dream Worlds and live in them. The mind-fabricated universes would be *illusions,* but that fact did not matter. They believed the 'getting high' type of seeking Nirvana artificially with Xigar and GUARP could not compare to the 'Secret of the Dyson Builders.' Mystics who traveled through space for the 'secret' were as wrong as those in Enlightenment City and Spice or G. users. Citizens were clueless with a wide array of Ways to Nirvana. Later, they would find the only true road to Nirvana was *once living in the Continuum and transcendence to the Higher Plane.*

Rem Sector contained a small uncharted, unnamed planet that was the 'Home of the 4th Creator.' In the future, the discovery would amaze Citizens and challenge contemporary views on Zog. Gargantuan underground facilities would be found yarns from now with data that proved the 4th Creator lived here.

Presently, Citizens were unaware that Zog was not the Creator of all things. Zog was not the 4th Creator. Zog was not the Builder of the cosmos in which the Continuum Pinwheel floated. As of now, the architectural discovery remained buried in oblivion like the golden streams of Ur. The small uncharted, unnamed planet was the actual home of something this universe did not know. It was the physical Home of the physical God, the real Creator or Architect. Zog was merely one of multiple Zogs in the Higher Plane. To yahoos down here, any zog was Zog.

What was Zog? Zog was a higher Being that was given the one-time gift of entering the physical universe. Blue Zog appeared on Mineer and could only appear on Mineer. Zog fell in love with the universe around it and adopted the whole

Pinwheel as its new (real) home, which, it sadly had to leave. At the exact time of entry, its mirror-double or 'Anti' also had to appear in the physical universe. The moment Zog arrived into reality, so did an 'unknown' from the other end of the same Plane. Zog loved the world. The Beast only wanted to ruin it short of total destruction.

The Universe had been built four different times. The 'Fourth Creator' was long gone and there were only dusty catacombs as its final monument. When the discovery would be made on the little planet, few Citizens could understand its relevance and realized who it was exactly that lived in the majestic undergrounds.

Other Territories had 'Dyson Spheres.'

[On parallel Mineer, reference is 'Bryson Spheres' after discoverer, Freeman Bryson. 'Dyson' is used for galactic familiarity].

Rem Regal contained a record 794 astronomically-large metal Mega-Structures. The concept was to construct a geodesic sphere around a sun! Light, heat and radiant energy would be easily caught by the Big Ball with a centrally located star. Huge areas of living spaces could be generated on the interior. Colonists on the inside would have a perpetual power supply. Best experts considered Dyson Spheres impossible until 'fields' of them were discovered in Rem.

Long ago, within the Beginning, a powerful militia of lizard (bipedal) creatures controlled the deep blue Quadrant. They were the sadistic and brutal Rizlan Empire. Warrior lizards spent yarns conquering entire star systems during the First Reich. Cold-blooded Reptilians amassed treasures to equal the zogs with no limits to the wealth they accumulated.

Conquering Lizard-Centurions completely changed. They dismantled the most awesome War-Machine in the galaxy and no longer acquired systems by force. They were not a militia anymore, but a sect of xenophobes. Mighty lizards went into hiding or seclusion and constructed Dyson Spheres. An incredible number of Dyson Spheres were formed.

How could they have built them and why? What made

the killer lizards drastically change policy? And why were 794 Super Spheres abandoned?

The amount of material needed to form *one* Dyson was an inconceivable mass, let alone 794 Spheres around 794 suns. How were they constructed? Rizlan Lizards converted the blue suns' energy into matter. Titanic devices in space pumped out geodesic platelets mega-bars in length. In time, enough facets were materialized by the multiple stars' undying energies. Connections were geodesicly made and eventually Dysons' interiors were inhabited by trillions of Rizlans.

Why did the lizards give everything up, all the vast Wealth the Empire collected and lock themselves into Spheres? For the longest time, outside could not get in. The isolationistic Rizlans let no one enter, and their civilization thrived at its peak. Also, no one could get in the Big Balls long after they were unoccupied. Finally, the means to open the sealed portals was known and many secrets were found inside the great orbs. Fabulous treasures were not discovered.

Investigators had a field day and deciphered sketchy evidence from computer mainframes in ruin. Dyson researchers in Rem concluded the prehistoric Lizards found *how to live in their own private nirvanas* or the 'way to live in dreams.' The Secret of Dyson Builders was they found the way to Happiness, they thought. But when the conquering-killers tapped into their Centers, the Lizards only found *cold-blooded, animalistic rage!*

Trillions of Rizlans did not abandon the Dysons. They killed each other inside 794 locked Super Spheres with central blue suns.

Parallel to Rem, only a wormhole's jump away, was Ran Regale Sector with such striking colors and cosmic beauty. The deepest blue stars were in Ran Territory and not Rem. *Galactic and globular clusters in Ran actually produced sky colors not in the normal color spectrum.* Sky patterns in 'x-colors' were unforgettable experiences. Planets and satellites under the 'Galactic Borealis' had very extreme dylar value. Vacation packages for resort-planetoids could cost millions of

d.

The most incredible feature in Ran had to be the 'Calming Rains of Clarion.' The title stood for an amazing, unexplainable anomaly. Number 1 out of 23 'Natural Wonders of the Galaxy' was Clarion Rains. The average citizen was unaware and would not believe what raindrops could do.

Third planet (Sical) of the blue Clarion sun was protected by the most technologically sophisticated military forces in the Royal Guard. No one got in except the highest Authorities. As Rem held metaphysical secrets, Ran held an unbelievable secret also shared by very few:

When rain struck your body on Sical, third rock from Clarion, you were physically transported to anywhere you were thinking! One touched by a Sical shower was physically teleported in protective ether. Travelers could go to the other end of Pinwheel in a safe, ethereal body. You have in mind where exactly you want to go; if you get wet, you were GONE to that precise place instantly in the real world! When the Clarion-3 drizzle ended, the travelers smoothly snapped back.

Voyagers could plan where they were going, but not for how long. The journey depended entirely on the weather. Travelers had a Mental Wormhole that transported the drenched passengers *anywhere*. 'Calming' in the title referred to the overall feeling of remote-viewing in the flight. Each traveler reported a euphoric, peaceful trip. A panic had never happened among the very few who knew of Sical's capabilities. Royal Authorities kept close guard on the 'Rains.' Only the super rich could come to Clarion-3. Sometimes, it did not rain. Elite travelers checked weather reports and planned trips *for the Rains.*

Rem Sector contained possibly the ultimate power of immortality by living forever in your dreams (yin). Ran Regale had a large secret of its own. One could truly go anywhere in reality without a ship (yang). Ran was physical while Rem was metaphysical.

A discovery occurred in the yarn 1703.51 at Ran Regale of such importance and historical proportions that Citizens could not get enough. Media channels at the time carried the grand find endlessly. 'The Cantor Archives' excavated within the prehistoric planet Trelis shocked the galaxy. Citizens stopped their affairs and viewed Media.

Trelis had a rich, long history of ruling 'Gulls' and 'Vice-Gulls.' Empires on the planet traced back to the Beginning. Recorder-quartz crystals over 50 bars long were uncovered with information far older than any other source in 24 sectors. The signature, triangular indentation on every recorder-quartz was more than 5 bars in width. Only ruins in ONE Sector were older than the prehistoric data. Nothing known as far as records, information, history, stats, pictures and films were this aged. The fantastic size or inner-matrix space of the quartz held seemingly endless/infinite volumes of material. The info was verified as real. Images and sounds went back to the lost time of the First Reich. Pre-history happened precisely as the Cantor Archives displayed to the Media.

But did they get the whole story?

Conspiracy Theorists and network pundits speculated the public did not receive all the files in the Archives. They had reasons to believe the data was edited, which fueled heated controversies and Media fireworks. Citizens mainly received ancient *songs* rather than full historical Records. The discovery of the large data-crystals was given the name 'Cantor' that further emphasized it was primarily 'music' in the Crystals.

Similar underground ruins beyond belief of the Fourth Creator were also discovered in the counterpart sector. Apparently, the real Creator/Builder or 'God' also kept another unbelievable subterranean facility on the other side of the Wormhole. But Ran Regalens called the old Supreme Being 'the Veck' and not 'Fourth Creator.'

If we zipped into the future, we would know Sardon's Monster-Machine and Slave-Master extraordinaire was finally dead. But was the galaxy free? The mechanical dylar-eliminator did not function anymore. It had breathed and chugged away irretrievable fortunes down a mini-Black Hole in the past. The extinct dinosaur continued being a motionless, lifeless carcass. The empty hulk of a long, slimy black 'turd' took up space. Top-ranking Royalty did not know what to do with it. The Beast's Beast stood there as a dead, defeated Aspen.

The Royalty, in future, decided to bring the deceased Device to Ran Territory. It was put on display. Officials made the Monster-Machine a *monument.* Media controllers could tell Citizens anything about the departed hulk and the public would believe it. The stuffed Beast was now called 'the Great Machine.' It was a popular tourist attraction. (But that was the future).

Ran Territory was also the stage for the famous War between Dogs and Cats known as the 'Xima War.' Xima was a binary sun system with a deep blue component (Xima-A) and a turquoise component (Xima-B).

As the story went, a space-faring geneticist crash-landed on one (Xima-A) of only two planets in the binary system. The lone DNA-expert was in very bad shape after the crash. His three legs were broken. His servo-droids were useless. He lost power. He had to do something for needed assistance if he was to survive. Due to radiation burns, he was *un-clonable.* He did the only thing he could do under the circumstance; *he made assistants.* The only uncorrupted samples out of a few hundred were the canines and felines. The crashed traveler could make the cats and dogs smarter, humanize them somewhat. They walked upright, balanced perfectly on two legs. They could be programmed to speak Lebritz.

Supposedly, he cloned a batch of tall canines first for the manual labor required in repairs to the ship. Dog-people were built very strong and mindlessly obeyed 'the master.' Without thinking and without fingers, they did the heavy lifting. They carried out basic physical feats. But Dog-people were no company for the master. Intelligence levels could not be greatly increased for unknown reasons. He needed doctors, treatments, nurse-care and good conversations which the canines could not provide.

The master cloned a few tall Cat-people and found that he could raise their intelligence levels to a high degree. Dogs and Cats had acute senses of smelling and hearing. Dog-men and Dog-women only saw in black and white. Cat-men and the one Cat-woman out of a test-tube had almost super-seeing in comparison.

The three Cat-people would have good ideas while the six Dog-people only communicated primitively. Clever Cats medicated the master. They cared. They showed initiative and compassion, especially the female. Dog-people did not care, were rude. They were tough and were only mindful of food and... Dog-people understood at a child's pace. Canines could be ordered to obey a command, but not have the capability to *question* the order. Cats were complex, regal and brilliant. They understood the proper place to urinate and defecate. The Dogs did not.

Standing, walking Cats had humanoid arms with functional double-joints. Instead of hands, they had paws similar to Dogs. Only the three Cat-people learned to hold sticks in them. With sticks, computers could be accessed. They could fly the ship.

Long story short, the Dogs turned on the master and killed him. Then the Cats took control of the spaceship. Dogs were able to crudely fire weapons while the Cats sealed off sections and trapped the Dogs. Both feline-guys wanted to kill the six mongrels by gas. They initiated the process but aborted when the feline-girl protested. She let them go, four males and two females. Thousands of their descendants had been fighting between worlds ever since. War raged between two-legged Dogs on Xima-A verses two-legged Cats who had established a base on Xima-B. Dog-people were much more aggressive but did not possess full control of high powered weapons. Cat-people philosophically debated the issues in committees and also executed independent actions. The Civil War continued...

***

Professor Renoux, the Suruuan, was a special man. He

was blessed. He was *touched* by the ability to dream into the Larger World. He didn't need the dream-machine. Sardon's Black Universe and Zog's White Universe (N-Rays vs. P-Rays) could be viewed with Renoux's 'gift.'

He once observed, in dreams, a huge asteroid field that warped down the Event Horizon of a BH in the larger Dimension. The Professor dreamed of the great Monitoring Station that recorded the massive swirl of matter made to function as liquid. He marked where the energy stream terminated in numbers and even photographed the numbers. In reality, his daring prediction at 1919.05 made the Professor a known celebrity to nearly every Citizen.

Renoux never stopped dreaming. Back on his home world of Suruua, the now bearded gentleman no longer was obsessed with the Neri Vortex. His notes on the still, constant, close Quasar were all but forgotten. He had far more important matters on his mind and in his dreams. He was comfortable alone and lived in semi-obscurity. The Professor never lost touch with the Dimension far beyond his microscopic, physical plane of the Continuum. He went there every night.

Jene 4 Renoux from Rom resigned his post at Balmoral Palace. The Galactic Government was not pleased with the decision. The once famous network personality, spokesperson and 'smartest man in the galaxy' renounced every tie with official organizations and G.G. Authorities and the SS aka NGO. He wore robes and not suits. The Secret System continued to spy on the professor, yet it was no longer in business.

Professor Jene had another dream. A new element was added. This never happened before. He witnessed a Game being played by fantastic, colorful Giants. Representatives of a few of the Zogs composed the field pieces or Avatar-Game pieces in an eternally-turning CONTINUUM. When the Professor looked closer, he noticed a detail that *terrified him.* Jene could clearly view and photograph the Medium of Exchange. Zogs played for/with a type of Money or means to indicate who was winning and who was losing. They gambled.

The Game was a means to wager and win, make strategic moves and ruin the other participants in the sport. It was all for fun, enjoyment and entertainment in the Larger World.

The problem was...real, living beings down here were used as their Money, up there. What were dylars, a word that was never used in capitals or with a capital letter? Why?

Mystics to Citizens to yahoos were the dylars!

Real lives of humans, humanoids, aliens and whatever, their very own existence was a reality few could conceive and understand. Lives were the commodities. Known life *thought* it had free will and survived in a universe of free choice. Jene 4 Renoux realized the entire galaxy, his galaxy, was a spinning Zabu Table. When Citizens, Execs, Royalty and yahoos gained fortunes or lost fortunes, it was not the actual Business that was happening. No, the true Game was played on the inconceivable Larger Level. Decisions down here were really the Decisions of the Zogs, up there. *Everyone was literally being played.*

The good Professor woke up in cold sweats. He ran to the bathroom and threw up.

***

Light-yarns away in Belial Sector, an occult and cybernetic 'Factory of Sardon' extended its limbs, greased itself and went to work. Computer gears, a clockwork of Wadlo-chip circuits and mechanical pixels, were channeled into what appeared as a moving, metal kaleidoscope. C.M. Lesher would be proud of the clockwork's details and in-out flows, as one geodesic part glided into another with perfect precision. Industrial and lifeless machine-sounds echoed inside dark complexes. Moving, grinding and deep surface machinations twisted and turned with a unique goal in mind.

In the middle of metal motions of such intricacy, slightly different forms took shape. Cold, colorless component-cogs did not appear in the same kaleidoscopic fractals. Patterns assumed smoother, fluid lines. Closer the viewer inspected the Factory of Sardon, the more they realized this was no normal factory. It was a secret production plant of demon-zogs. Later, the central shapes of fine machines slowly transmuted to a face. Closed-eyes soon revealed a mechanical girl's face.

It opened its eyes in terror!

***

The Machine-Monster Vidor in the center of the galaxy, whose plug could not be pulled, continued on its merry way. Black flug outlined with a red impenetrable force-field sucked three colored rivers of commerce, eternally. Beast's Beast slowed down. That fact was the only good news for the Secret System. The elite Star Council and Royalty Puppet-Masters remained impotent against the Big Percentage 'going down the toilet.' Force-fields were unbreakable.

What would replace the Monster?

Professor Jene 4 Renoux, in his bedchamber, a changed Suruuan celibate, had another dream. The dream was a Zog-awful nightmare. He could not wake up and *wanted to wake up desperately.* Something forced him to see more visions, terrible visions of the Larger Level that used smaller lives like gambling chips.

In horror, Renoux's body shook as the dream compelled him to view a Factory. Not Sardon's Factory, down here, but a nightmarish Mechanism on the Higher Plane. Jene, smartest man, understood he was not viewing clear reality of Zog's Larger World. Dream-visions were mixed with his private fears, the fear of learning we were nothing more than *dylars.*

He observed life forms from high seers to the simplest of yahoos. They were lined up in colors of their nations or species or suns or civilizations. There were three rows of colors. As his eyes panned the terrible vision, Renoux viewed back to a very far distance. There was no stopping the Death March. Three long lines of living creatures, relentlessly, without question, marched forward into *jaws of annihilation!* A Great Machine endlessly grinded (ate) the three long, colorful lines of Life.

Jene woke. The nightmare sent shivers through the old

man's body. He soon came to his senses. Renoux was thankful his dream-camera was not on and recording. The last thing he wanted was a reminder of creatures lined up to be swallowed in Hensi.

"My poor, Jaruzaem."

***

Thirty yarns ago a special child was born on Mineer. The orphan was given the name 'Tray Samuel Caladan' by unknown sources. He was a tall, slim, good-looking lad with white hair. He was an architect, a builder. As a youth, the boy was extremely wise. Tray was out of the Middle Ages. He could do everything well. Without training, the boy understood mechanics and mathematical reasoning beyond his short yarns. He possessed an extraordinary memory. He was psychic. He was empathic. Anything he studied and applied his mind to, he mastered. Tray Caladan could have done anything his two hearts decided and desired. He could have been a high paid Exec. He could have been groomed for Royalty positions since his charms were noticed by the Secret System at a young age.

Instead, 'Cal' wanted to be an artist. He *was* an artist, but that was not how he earned his dylars. The designer earned a bright living with his previous construction plans. The projects were in the works, for which he was paid handsomely by more than one company. He wanted to explore fine arts, not commercial architecture. He wanted to be as *free* as he could and not confined to a working Rat-Race. Tray lived off-the-grid.

He believed in Zog. He was not sure if Zog believed in him. Cal did not fear Zog, as many of his contemporaries did. He was not a 'Zog-fearing' person. He believed Zog was Love and he embraced love. He did not fear love. Tray tried to live a good, moral life: "Help the Citizen and you will be helped by the Citizen."

Tray enjoyed the ladies, too much. He was in love numerous times and *engaged* once. So early he dabbled with girls. When they wanted him to be 'unified,' Cal quickly departed his old village as soon as he could. He sought his fortune on Mineer, blindly, as if he had a mission. He experimented with psychedelics and was in awe of the 'new view.' The youth traveled to ancient Holy Lands in search of answers. After a series of Near Meetings with aliens in the high equator desert, he returned to the big city a very changed man. He never forgot his strange experiences that he could hardly tell a soul. Tray was inspired to learn because of what happened. Endless volumes of old lore and speculation files were voraciously assimilated. *He was running out of dylars.*

Cal was unaware of specifics, but he absolutely was sure Fate had an ultimate purpose for his existence. In fact, he let Fate decide the question, "Should I go to Soma seashore and meditate or shouldn't I?" *If the Moon rose yesterday night, he would shuttle to the place of his dreams. If the Moon did not rise before 8'bok then the trip was off.* A bright, full satellite rose that evening and Caladan was on his way to Soma seashores.

He was also very excited to go to the planet where Enlightenment City stood. Tray Caladan could not wait to see over Luturn Lake and behold the distant lights of the City Gates. He thought to himself, *I might not be able to get inside, but, at least I can say I was there and saw the majesty and glory by looking in from the outside.* He sighed.

He was presently inside a one-person shuttle without any frills provided by Pan Movers and headed for OM Sector. He enjoyed the idea of *no tolls.* Tray was really on his way. E-City was the closest thing to Nirvana for the lad, he thought. He pictured Soma seashores hundreds of times. He pretended he meditated there so often that he knew the shape of the shoreline.

Tomorrow would be a big day. He would automatically dock, leave the shuttle and first feel soma-vibrations emanating from the planet. Cal could not afford the luxury of this adventure. He went anyway. Maybe he needed to go and get far, far away from Mineer. Did a magnetic force pull him forward? He was unsure of tomorrow, which made it exciting.

For the moment, he was tired. He soon got used to the shuttle's hum. He went to sleep. He dreamed.

Within the dream, Tray Caladan was aboard a 2-person shuttle and wide awake. He was with an older/bearded gentleman, who also sat in opposing space chairs provided by Pan Movers. Tray looked around at the wider, longer shuttle and marveled. Then he recognized his fellow traveler to OM Sector. Cal recognized him from every Media channel. Caladan sat next to *the smartest man in the galaxy. What a dream!* He went with it.

"Ah, ha, you're doctor…"

"Professor."

"Professor, I know, Renoux! You're Suruuan."

"Ummm ha."

"What the Hensi are you doing in my dream?" Cal asked gleefully.

The image of the Professor in the space chair smoked a pipe. The smoke did not contaminate filtered air. He wore robes and not a spacesuit. "You sure this is a dream, my boy? Maybe I'm not a dream at all?" He calmly inhaled another large puff and confidently looked over to the other space chair.

"Huh?" the youth said, too stunned to be brilliant. "What d'you mean?"

"At the exact GST of 1999.83, now, I am in a real 2-person shuttle, rented the whole pod for myself and no one else. Funny thing, I'm on my way to, uh, I guess you could call it a Fate-Point, my boy. I'm on my way to…meet *you* at Soma shore."

Cal laughed. He tried to piece reality together. "So…"

"I see you don't understand." Renoux puffed on his pipe once more. "You're asleep, son. You're in your cheaper 1-person shuttle at this time, right?"

"Right," agreed the curious youth with white hair. "Thanks for saying it's cheaper."

"So, ha, what's real?" asked the Professor logically like he was in Philosophy Class. "Certainly not me speaking to you. You aren't *in* a 2-person shuttle."

Tray got up out of the chair. He was extremely confused. "If this isn't a dream, then what the Boz *is* it?"

"Relax, sit down. Things are going as planned, my boy."

"What's going as planned and who planned it?"

The Professor laughed and did not answer. "I've come to tell you the truth, Cal."

"Only my friends call me Cal."

"I'm your good friend, Cal. I'm a great admirer."

"You're the celebrity! I'm nobody; nobody knows me."

"They know who you are," the gentleman said without a doubt.

"They?" From a space chair four bars away, Tray was very confused. "I guess a dream is not supposed to make sense."

"I should get to the point before the session, whatever you want to call it, *pops* out of existence. Let me tell you what I have to tell you."

"Of course, sir." Cal was calm. He became more serious and respectful.

Renoux inhaled a big gulp of fake air. Now that he was here and confronted the boy of destiny, compelled to reach this moment, he was uncertain how to go about the task of... "You're going to die."

Tray Caladan laughed again and placed his head in his hands. "I need a *dream* to tell me I'm going to die?"

"Not a dream, I mean on Soma shores."

"How'd you...go on."

"Enlightenment City is a lie, my boy."

"What? Go back to *die.* What d'you mean I'm going to die?"

"Did I say die? I mean...*live.* Maybe for the first time in your life. Ever think?" The prof took a puff.

"What? Ever think?"

"Ever think you only need to die to reach E-City? You know, Nirvana?"

The white-haired youth was stunned and turned his

head. "Actually, I *have* thought that."

"Think about it." Renoux blew on his pipe again.

"That's it?"

"Haaa! No, sir. Zog picked *you*. You're the One. You're going to become the Neo Zog."

"Ah, ha! Yes, of course. Now I know I'm dreaming. Good dream."

"It's almost time."

"Of course it *is*." Cal was sarcastic, no longer serious. The delusion was nonsensical to him, a fantasy or farce. Nothing was real. *Or was it?*

"Anything else, old man? You can't be the real Jene 4. It's been fun, though." Tray smiled and could not wait for the next words.

"You are *not* Tray Caladan because Tray Caladan does not exist. You could not have been born on Mineer 30 yarns ago because Mineer does not exist. Your Moon could not have indicated to you, my boy, whether or not you should go on this trip because your Moon does not exist...get my flow?"

"Okay, Professor. Who am I?"

"You have been put here by magic. You are a future projection, a dream, a reincarnated soul, you could say, of a real person who truly had two hearts. His name was Agent Caladrian Trask, Order Representative, Council Class 3. He was forgiven for his crimes personally by Zog. You will meet Zog, again. Much more than that, my boy, you will...*become Zog.*"

The unbeliever said, "Anything else, middle-name 4?"

"dylars," said the celebrity Professor with wide eyes.

Caladan misunderstood. "Oh, no. What's *this* going to cost me?"

"What *are* dylars? That's your purpose, son. That's why we need a Neo Zog."

Tray immediately unsealed his spacesuit pocket. He threw three yellow dylars (300,000 d.) at the image.

Jene puffed his last puff. "You should watch who you're throwing around there, son." The prof spoke of the encounter to come. "Don't be afraid, *don't fear.* When you encounter it, embrace it. Don't fear it. Much later, they won't know what you've done…what you *will do* for everyone because of your love."

Tray Caladan opened his eyes. He was alone in his 1-person shuttle.

***

In Sardon's secret Continuum Factory of demon-zogs, a unique machine intiated the long process of being pieced together one Wadlo-chip at a time. The logical care and precision of the manufacturers were beyond this world. Yams of cold computer-time went into its design matrix then yars of real construction-time. The goal was to manufacture the perfect mega-computer mainframe-hard-drive into the physical bio-frame of a cyborg, the ultimate android that appeared 'exactly as a human being.' A living soul would not drive the mechanism. A cold spark would drive the mechanism.

'She' was more developed with more pieces attached in permanent places. Moving, metal clockworks continued a dark dance from every radiant point around the female-looking shape. The mannequin's eyes stayed closed. The perfect bio-borg would soon be completed. After final touches and software programming, the Ghost of Sardon would no longer be a ghost. There would be no more *carriers.* The Sardon Beast had found a way to return to the real world, the physical galaxy of the Continuum.

It knew and did not know that its counterpart was in the process of the same materialization into the material plane. Each found different Keys to the Little Kingdom, down here among mortals. Yin/yang, light/dark: it seemed as if a Zog could not act in the *physical* unless the exact opposite also occurred by its counterpart. If Zog was coming back, so was the Devil.

GST of 2000.00 would arrive soon. The special moment in galactic History marked not only the Return of Zog as Neo Zog, the special time also marked the Return of the

Sardon as *the Neo Sardon!* Who would believe the Devil would return inside a young, beautiful girl?

***

Citizen News Channels, under authority of the G.G.'s Secret System, announced *'the end of the world!'* It *was* in the minds of zillions of viewers. A disclaimer stated, "Do not panic," which was always a signal to panic. Even yahoos understood that the News was bad. The jest of the Media bombardment could be easily interpreted as: Something terrible was going to emerge out of Fountain, the close Quasar, in the Neri Vortex.

The Pinwheel Galaxy did indeed panic. Prior to this point, 'plague planets' still existed and were on the rise. Entire worlds had bizarre beasts pour out of polar holes. Respected Mystics and Mystery Schools as well as sacred writings foretold of 'End Times.' Citizens believed the Media and took vital precautions they would normally not take. Survivalist militias barricaded themselves in heavy isolation.

To a large number of Citizens, *this was it!* This was the Big One that network programming and seers had recently pushed. Most life forms considered that *we could be at the end of the line.* Citizens felt the need to act as if every ya was precious. Every moment was generally spent with loving family and friends. Life was not wasted, for the most part.

Vibrations throughout the sectors were crowning worries and ultimate Fear. 'Suicide Satellites' were once more on the network channels. Was the small continuum affecting the Big One or was the Larger Game moving the smaller game?

In what many believed were the last days of the galaxy, Zog became a big deal again. The spectrum of the Mainstream, the core of Life, felt a need to pray. Individuals to organized groups to whole planets (basically) turned to Zog, whatever they conceived the Supreme Being to be. People, aliens, humanoids could somehow feel what was real, what was coming, what was on its way here. The Pinwheel trembled and wobbled in its spin. What or *who* was coming? Was it Zog or was it the Devil? Were both coming?

***

'Captain of the Royal Guards' assigned to Rom's Balmoral Palace on the planet Ricon was a very prestigious position among Hierarchy soldiers. Balmoral was one of the State's power Centers, Houses, Authority Seats in the gelled Federation. To be a 'Royal Guard' stationed to the Palace and protect the Queen was a high honor. To be *leader* of Royal Guards that served the Queen was a rare privilege indeed. His name was Captain Mada Sims-Zela. He was on shore leave and very motivated to get away.

Mada was not a 'captain' at the moment. He left his black stripes back at the barracks. Now he was a lone *explorer* and this was the 'Outback.' He left his official FF gear behind. He left his assigned weapons behind, but not all weapons. He was near the heart of Ricon's wilderness region. Sims-Zela told himself he was on leave to relax, do some GUARP and take it easy.

Who am I kidding? I'm here for beautiful, vicious target practice.

The Captain did not have to wait long. One yam after making camp in the Orange Section of the Reserve, a pack of banionns attacked. The ravenous, 6-legged scavengers hit him from all sides. Sims dodged the initial offensive and was able to catch a breath. Mada soon responded. He was able to *tuen-up* in a few yas. First volleys of the invisible 'lang-lance' took out three of the vermin that measured 7 bars each in length.

Mada was able to swing around and pick off two more. Each of his hands unclenched as the tuening lance was retracted. The Captain now stood at ease as the other *wolves* in the pack fled in every direction.

They got the message. They're not coming back for awhile. Ha, wouldn't have been any fun with the force-field.

Then the smell struck his keen senses. He said aloud, "Hensi! I forgot about banionn stink. Ha, havta move camp."

Captain Mada Sims-Zela, top military official in the galaxy, was a ruthless man. His campaigns had produced millions of slaughtered creatures from most sectors. He had seen blood in each color. Former Centurion, former Royal Guard and now leader of the Guards at Balmoral had personally killed 794 aliens via *tuening*. He counted every one. Was the mad counting *subconscious guilt?* Could the head Guard have come to the Reserve for redemption?

Time passed. Mada was certain the banionns communicated to other predators in the area to 'leave this person alone.'

Shoot.

The Captain heard about the Big Offensive to come. He thought he was on vacation because of it. In fact, the mass military gathering in Neri was scheduled for 1999.99. Mada was amazed. "The whole Royal fleet!" the man was forced to spit out in disbelief. "Can't conceive its magnitude, scope," he said to himself. "No armada has ever been assembled..."

Mada reestablished his almost helpless camp in a different location. The section was Orange-Red, which meant larger and more dangerous predators. This time, the Head Guard took necessary precautions. He removed from a special Electro-Magnetic container, two enhancers. The RED was such a deep Rine-color red (same as beverage) in the amethysts. Mada marveled at the clarity and perfectly smooth facets of the natural gems. He always appreciated their great beauty before he slipped them into wrist-holders to magnify his lances by tenfold...and *kill.*

In yas, a big rustle occurred, preceeded by loud, bellowing *roars* that sliced his Center. Sims-Zela felt the sting of attack.

Am I from Zetag? A military 'Zuggerrat' amassed soon to strike at an awesome unknown that threatens the very state of the State, and what? I can't get enough killing?

With red amethyst amplifiers that increased Mada's Rom-training by ten, he completely wiped out nine Talulu Banshees 20 bars long with 4-bar long sharp tusks. *Life was grand.* He understood why many an Occult Mystery School turned away from 'the Light' and sought the black abyss instead.

Mada was going to turn in with enough excitement for one evening in the wild. The brutal man, off-Center, actually made a crucial decision in his life. He would have one more go at it with a third round in the Red Section. In truth, going forward was the best thing to happen to the leader of killers they called a soldier. Sims-Zela first planned to click-on the camp's FF for the night so it did not matter what tried to invade, and then get some sleep. He scrubbed the plan.

What moved him on?

There was a legendary *catch* to the Red Section, beside the 100-bar animals so willing to eat you. A few pools called 'Waters of Zog' were said to actually exist. Mada had never seen one and did not believe the stories. It was a large, restricted section and he had only explored a small part of it.

In his dark mind, there was some strategic sense that the most magical of pools were within a forbidden zone no Citizen could travel and guarded by terrifying Behemoths. *Maybe the pools were real.* Zela was unstoppable. He walked and walked. Mada walked thousands of bars to Red Section. Darkness was all around. His powerful suit-lights lit what was in front.

Something very strange happened or did not happen. Every bit of Rom-training told him so. Why had he not encountered Big Ones by now? Where were the mega-beasts, their sounds, their tracks? A few Behemoths should have come into view. Where were they? Why was seemingly a clear path opening up ahead? Why was this direction the right direction?

Why is it I know I will find one of those pools?

Later, Captain Mada thought he saw a clearing in the dense vegetation ahead. Vines were easily hacked by a microscopic usage of the lang-lance or tuening-force. He marched forward through more jungle plants and around ground spires. After trees and thick vines were brushed aside with a wave of the soldier's arm, he saw it.

"I don't believe it," he said in excitement like a Royal child that earned his first billion dylars. *How did I know?* At a bright moment, touched by only a hint of enlightenment, Mada was an *explorer* and not a part of the Royal Guard. He glowed along with a Golden Pool 30 bars in length. Liquid Light shimmered with power, energy and radiance. Mada was emotional and that never happened. Lights appeared the same as Gate Lights at E-City that he had observed from outside. The real Golden Path did not have to be a road. It could have been on Ricon, a blazing spot of light engulfed by utter blackness.

He had to go in the Water. A force above him compelled him to get wet. Captain Mada Sims-Zela thought *I could be saved.* In the back of his mind was not the blasting of predatory targets, it was the question, "Is there hope for me?" That was why he was really on shore leave and sought the 'Waters of Zog.' Down deep he wanted forgiveness. Down deep he wanted to ascend to something far greater than this world. *Could I, a man like me, be forgiven?* He expected, possibly, if he could actually find a pool, to meet and *talk* to Zog, not St. Revol, but to get beyond the Gates and meet the Creator, the Builder Supreme.

He dove in.

The former soldier and head of the Royal Guard became a child again. He splashed Golden Waves and cried with exhilaration. For a few yas, he was wrapped inside joy, a feeling of love he had not experienced in many yarns. Mada and equipment were submerged only a few bars in Liquid Light, and then the mystic pool *lost its light.*

The magic pool drained its magic and grew dark. In a frightening moment, Waters of Zog changed. It transformed into a more solid, creamy, softened substance. Mythic Waters turned into grey *Fast Sand.* Mada was caught, stuck with a heavy suit, lights and body armor. He was one quarter sunk into material that reacted like glue. Mada was as helpless as a doe-fly in a vidor's web.

He screamed.

He knew his screams went unheard. He ranted and raved to no one in the Behemoth area. Mada slipped farther down. He could not stretch to the pool's shore. In fact, he was pulled the other way. There was a great lack of anything that he could reach. He was halfway consumed by Fast Sand. Then it hit him.

"What's wrong with me? I panicked and first rule is *Do Not Panic.*" Sims-Zela realized he still had his trusty weapon. The power was even enhanced. All he had to do was inhale a big breath; concentrate, focus and *out come the claws!*

The Lance should cut my way out. Why didn't I think of it in the first place?

Mada was originally one of those religious scholars who began in a Mystery School, on track to do positive things in the world. Then he made a pilgrimage to Rom Sector. He lost his Center or was thrown far from middle. With his high potentials, he was not a Centurion long. In a very short time, because of natural skills and training (plus bloodletting), he became head of the Royal Guards. Zela tasted the evil side and never let go, until now.

The man breathed. He concentrated and nothing happened. His arms were outstretched. Everything he attempted to do to bring on the tuening-force did not work. He had tuened for yarns and his weapon was always reliable. It never failed.

"Why are you not working?" He fumbled with the amethysts; one flipped away from him. The one that remained did not function. "Why?" After Mada resigned himself that his power was gone, he cried again.

Mada knew this was the end. But the real reason the ex-soldier cried was because he never received the chance to ask Zog for forgiveness. Legends said if one were in Zog's Waters, one was on Nirvana's Stage and Zog was in the Audience. For a short moment, one had Zog's Eye. The Supreme Being turned and, for a fleeting ya, one had the attention of Zog. *Was it true? Will my prayers be answered?* Fast Sand was up to his chest plate. He was mostly under the surface ooze. "Zog, h-help me."

It was as if some entity heard Mada's cries for assistance. Since it was before 2000.00, it was not Zog or the Beast.

Mada's shouts were heard by a *Quizo*. The small-headed and small-sized Quizo had a properly proportioned body, about the size of a melo. It was the tiny head at the end of a thin, long neck that appeared odd. Quizos were intelligent, 3-legged Aphids and on the large size. The thing was really a brilliant 'dowd.' Quizos were a *creature one sees just before one dies.*

The Quizo waddled with its (his) peculiar walk directly toward the Fast Sand's beach-line. To the weird life form, the pool or sand area was quite big. Its long, thin neck dipped down and it appeared as its head-thing went into the sand. When it did, the sand became *bright Golden Water again.* The Quizo finished its drink. But the brightness and color were only at the perimeter, beach and shoreline. Glow of gold was a bar in toward the center and only around the Quizo. Around Mada remained dark grey Fast Sand. He continued to be stuck in glue, although the sinking happened slower.

"That's it, relax."

"Did you say that? Did you just speak perfect Lebritz?"

"Did you see my mouth move?"

"Hard to tell. If you make me laugh, I'll sink farther. Little one, can you get me out of here?" Mada asked more seriously with hope in his heart.

"Little? I have a pure Center. Did you see Waters of Zog affect me like they did you?"

"For Zog's sake, can you help me?"

"Yes..."

Maybe the longest silence and stillness occurred in the history of the Pinwheel. Mada stood still as to not sink. The Quizo just stood still.

"Are you trying to be funny?"

"No."

"You said you were going to help me."

"I AM helping you. I'm here."

"And..." Sims-Zela was ready to expose his angry side then changed the ploy. He relied on his training to keep calm: *do not panic.* "And, and, you're not doing very much."

"They all say that. What would you have me do?"

"Get me *out* of Fast Sand!"

"Sure you want out?" the intelligent Aphid asked.

"What are you saying?"

"Maybe you should stay right there."

"That's your help...nothing?"

"Would you like to know the future?" the small critter asked.

"You mean, besides me sinking to death, you GUARP-6 hallucination?" Sims tried to hide worry and fear. "Here's a future question. Wh-what's the End of the World coming at us from Fountain? Entire fleet will fight...what?"

"Who you will serve after 2000.00. The Zog will return to the world it loves the most. You will be one of the Chosen...in the future."

Mada inched deeper down into the Fast Sand. Soon, his hands would be dragged in and the soldier would only be a head above the surface. After that, Mada would become an *ex-soldier.* There was nothing solid beneath his feet. He felt fear and his own private paranoia. He focused. He wanted his thoughts sharp, tight enough to reach the Zog. He prayed again without tears.

Then, former Captain of the Guards remembered what the Quizo asked him. Fast Sand was nearly up to his mouth. He would lose his words, sounds and sights very soon. Mada had his thoughts. "Wh-what future?" The radio did not work. There was not a *dylar* around who could help him.

The tiny creature on three legs hobbled to Golden Waters still only along the shore. He drank. The Waters shimmered much brighter. He clearly spoke with authority because the little Aphid (only seen before death) knew the past and future.

"We drink and bathe in Waters of Time everyday. We

see past/future as the same. You will again be a leader of others. You will turn and follow the One as his prime Initiate. You will be a Gatherer of Followers for the One, Cal-El, the Neo Zog."

The Golden Glow of Zog-Water and full-energy shimmer that was inside the clearing originally, returned.

A brighter Quizo continued his speech. *"You will be forgiven, Captain Mada. You will return to Center as was in the Beginning of your career. You will be reborn as a changed, whole man, a very good soul. You will have a new name. The One will call you 'Pe're.' You will tell others his words. You have already severed the chord and learned there is no easy way to Nirvana. Enlightenment City and other avenues are dead ends. Only Golden Path is to live in the Continuum...and Ascend."*

Chapter Ten

COMING OF THE NEO ZOG

WAS THE WORLD COMING TO AN END? Media implied 'Life could end.' Citizens took what they thought were necessary precautions and firmly braced for the Great Unknown that headed their way via the close Quasar.

'A peaceful unity' described the 24 battalions of Royal Sector Forces that orchestrated its members into a colossal, single, fighting 'Zuggerrat.' The slow armada, along with its moving parts, traveled to the Neri Vortex. More than 100,000 small drones to heavily armed Battle-Cruisers flew as one massive parade of 'Defense.' They were going to defend their universe from the evil, vile 'monster' that slid down the Fountain's Funnel. They were going to hit it with every photon of every weapon possible. Mainstream Royal Guards flew home colors from each sector. With eagerness, an All-Star Team of militias marched to war with a growing Vortex.

Zuggerrat's speed during its course to Neri would get the space convoy in correct position by the target-time of 1999.99. By then, many thousands of guns would be pointed in proper angles at the gaping aperture in space.

"The thing crawling down from the Upper World to the basement floor won't stand a chance."

GST was 1998.20 and Citizens were on *alert*. Yahoos were examples of how 'Ignorance is Bliss.' Precisely at a time when every sensory apparatus was trained on Media channels, two major stories struck the attention of the galaxy with the force of nuclear bombs. No one understood if the news items were good or bad. Which one was bad and which one was good? Questions, conflicts, speculations and fears accelerated through fibers of every Citizen when they heard:

The Neri Vortex and current focus of network channels, where every capable battalion under Royal Command and more were going, Fountain, the gusher-sphere Quasar of exploding energy/matter that had not enlarged in yarns, *was growing!* In fact, the Vortex increased its size and energy output at an alarming rate. Scientists quickly reported estimates that by 2000.29 the outer planet of the Valparaiso System would be virtually destroyed by the expanding energy-ball.

Physicists on multi-Media explained that the *phenomenon of a Black Hole was the exact opposite from the deadly phenomenon of the Fountain Quasar.* Neri proved that Black Holes were not horrible whirlpools in space that crushed those who entered into a deadly 'singularity' at the other end.

Reports informed Citizens to not be fooled by the white and black, which were simply the way the light and everything else traveled. "Black Holes were safe," was the idea of network items and documentaries. But, a White Hole, an expanding Quasar should be at the *outer* reaches of the universe and not a matter of light-yarns distant. The anomaly was a Cosmic Cancer in the Pinwheel. Fountain did the opposite of eating; it *regurgitated.* As laid out for News audiences, the enlarging Fountain would eject more and more matter/energy outward, forcing anything in the Sphere's path to be *'knocked off the Table.'* Some theorized, "As Citizens navigated wormholes and space-ways, Higher Life used BH & Q conduits as similar transit corridors."

Latest reports showed a popular galactic news anchor say, "So far, nothing in the expelled matter was of significance within the widening Spacial area and again none of the transmission-energy could be deciphered. Valparaiso stations are closely monitoring. Only a few experts have the opinion Fountain's sudden activity was directly related to it being the 'target' of Royal Forces Zuggerrat. Protest groups throughout the sectors oppose current military policy maintaining we should *welcome* the incoming object and dylars could be better spent elsewhere. The State assures that Defense measures are merely precautionary..."

The second Big Story was far more unbelievable. An entire sector of the Pinwheel Galaxy disappeared! How could the spinning Continuum have lost an entire sector? One half of a Quadrant was gone. Where was Selestra Matrix? The

'Business Sector,' S'el's parallel (opposite) known for Magic and Play called Selestra Matrix, had evaporated from reality and the space it held. Within the Spacial area, in its place, to the rest of the galaxy, was a *void*. A neutron-star mass of material in which nothing could enter or leave was the mystery. The black area contained a 'solid nothing' or the *opposite of space*. What happened to a large Territory with millions of green stars and countless lives?

News channel pundits as well as esteemed Science Illuminati never expected to cover a story where the Continuum was reduced to 23 sectors.

Mystics and psychics were clueless. Shadow 'Secret System' or Star Council was in the dark. An infinite number of questions washed over forums such as: *What was the negative matter 'Void' in its place? Is it Dark Matter? What does the disappearance mean? What happened to the life forms in the sector? Where were they now? Where was Professor Renoux? What happened to WH commuters from S'el to Selestra Matrix when the sector vanished? What was the connection with Yarn 2000.00? Was the disappearance of the Matrix Sector related to Fountain's new expansion? How was everything connected?*

Individual Citizens to organizations, mainly shades of pacifist revolutionaries, put forth the idea the 'Grand Disappearance' was tied to Zuggerrat Armada's arrival at Neri. The concept was *we should not greet the incoming unknown at Fountain with fighting forces, but with love*. "Someone up there was angry at our Assembly of Power and wanted to teach us a lesson."

Was losing a whole sector another insane Sign of the Times and punishment for galactic arrogance?

Time approached and Royal garrisons as well as many thousands of drone-guns moved to attack-positions. Fountain reached larger and larger proportions as a prelude for what was to come through. The expected time was the New Galactic Century *precisely*. Secret Systems were on red alert and had mega-arsenals ready to fire in a few yams.

Suddenly, two more 'Breaking News' stories hit the

space-ways in every sector:

Selestra Matrix reappeared! Only reports stated strange *black domes* had also materialized along with the Territory on many of the planets. The bizarre domes represented a technology unknown to the galaxy's elite scientists. Mystics were baffled as well. There had been no contact from inside the 'Mystery Domes.' Alien domes numbered 12,012 (count so far) over 51 systems in Selestra Matrix. The domes did not exist before the peculiar disappearance. SM had left for 72 yams.

While 99% of Royal Forces, corporate robo-weaponry, each sectors' Volunteer Armies as well as Insectoid-technology had been deployed around the busting/expanding Fountain, few realized how vulnerable various Authority capitals would be without their mighty garrisons. Now a clear threat sped through space in Rom Sector toward the Palace at Balmoral on planet Ricon.

Royal House at Balmoral had become the prime Seat of Galactic Power. Only a lame 'skeleton crew' of military forces remained to protect the Great Palace.

What insanity directed Royal Guards to the Neri 2000 Event and left the most prestigious Seat of Power open to attack?

An unspecified object or projectile was on a 'Lesher-line' toward the Palace. Every means of defense was neutralized. Nothing had been able to stop or divert the projectile that originated from unknown sources. Bomb, Message, UFO, Alien or Time Capsule would crash near the Royal Palace on castle grounds at...2000.00.

There was not a Citizen in the Monopdonow Continuum Pinwheel Galaxy that understood the significance or relationship between what emerged from Fountain and the projectile destined to strike Ricon. Many thought they were assaulted by an outside Enemy on two fronts.

The mystery probe, projectile was white in color and appeared like a curved capsule only 9 bars long and 3 bars wide. Crash-point was plotted in an unpopulated region of

Ricon near the Great Palace. Recovery teams were sent to investigate and neutralize the threat.

Galactic Time turned to the Century Mark. Evacuated 'Poco,' last planet of Valparaiso System, went into *fibrillation.* A few mega-bars away, surrounded by all Armies of the Universe, pumped a giant reverse vacuum that spat out *a brilliant blue jet-stream of energy!* Gaseous streams and infarctions ejected out in every direction of the growing Quasar 'threat.' But now it was a new blast of pure energy, magnificent in its wonder and splendor, as the magical stream shot down the Funnel and out this end...

The Blue Light was bold surrounded in blackness like a beacon of beauty. Mega-bars long, it stretched to amazing thinness because of its speed into the real world. This was Zog. Zog was on its way back to a physical universe she/he loved. Zog was without a body and only an extremely long jet of blue light. It was now the real soul, spirit, energy, life, spark, essence, heart, Center and blueness of the Zog. Neo Zog returned and was able to *feel real* again. The energy-entity blue-child that exploded out of a Fountain in playful joy was *suddenly under fierce attack by every Big Gun in the galaxy!*

***

Light-yarns away, Royal Recovery teams discovered the white pod exactly where Mystics, rather than scientists, predicted. On Palace grounds the unknown probe/pod stood at an angle, almost horizontal. The capsule was in fantastic shape for being struck with thaser-fire, ion-rockets, Peresi Cannons and a wide collection of detonations from Insect-tech. The capsule was in too good of shape for the available defense networks. Later investigators would little understand where the technology came from that forged the 'Balmoral Projectile.'

Both were back.

When the first Recovery team arrived on the scene of the crash, they registered no radiation, no power, no damage, no energy signatures and 'no life' within the UFO. The team was well armed and well equipped with necessary force-fields and offensive bazookas. Royal guards were sixteen in number. Shields stayed up as they neared the crashed probe.

They were only a few bars away from the apparent 'dead' mechanism in white when it *buzzed* and *clicked.* Almost every soldier *jumped.* The Lady Commander of fifteen men did not.

She was a very vicious brute with powerful muscles. She stayed steady and bravely approached the pod's mechanical movements of small, white gearing. She took great care in her observations. She signaled the men *not* to shoot. They kept *shields up* to maximum fearing it was a bomb. The Commander was a shrewd one and did not sense hostility. The gearing appeared to be automatically engaged upon landing. She relaxed and the men calmed.

The threat to the State Federation on this end seemed to be opening. Now, white panels moved with *whirling* sounds and more men aimed their guns directly at the widening portal. The curious Commander moved closer. One more clinically-clean cross-panel retracted to reveal: a perfect, horizontal form of a young girl in a white tech-suit.

A white tight cap hid her hair. Her eyes were closed and there were no observable movements whatsoever. She had an adorable face. A few of the men were heard to *gasp* at the petite *podling* perfectly encased within the capsule. *Then she sat up.* She looked around her wonderful world with big, blue, innocent eyes.

The Royal Guards, like any Police, reacted to the gesture and were ready to "Blow the bitch to Nirvana!" With a single hand wave, the strong Commander made them stand-down. No one was going to shoot until she gave the word.

"Hi!" The gorgeous child laughed with a finger on her lips.

The dark squadron seemed like *over-kill.* A few of the men laughed also and then quickly stopped. They changed from *on guard* to *at ease.*

"*This* is the threat?" one guard commented.

Thoughts in the back of minds were, *the child was*

probably orphaned and left on the doorstep of the State.

"What's going on? *Ha.* Where am I? Who are *you?"* was softly spoken by the sweetest voice in the galaxy.

One of the soldiers suddenly recognized her face and talked out of order. "Do you know who that is?"

"Speak!" the Commander ordered the man under her.

"It's Mebby."

"Zog. You're right," another said. "But, how?"

The Lady Commander asked with a head tilt, *"Who's Mebby?"*

***

Earlier, at 2000.01, at the Neri Vortex, the magical Blue Beam jettisoned out in its entirety and was struck in its spiritual Center by the gunfire.

"Why?" was cried in another Dimension.

Soul of Zog wanted to once more touch reality on a physical plane with limitless potentials for pleasures and grandeur. After what the Zog went through with the other Zogs in the Higher World, after timeless battles with its own kind in order to 'Return' and now this reception from a particular galaxy it utterly worshiped, the pain in its Immortal Center was too intense and the blue energy thought of Self-Annihilation then changed its consciousness.

The death of one human life did not compare to the Death of a Zog, an Immortal Being, meaning the complete and utter destruction of its energy, spirit, soul, essence. Physical humans had 'sparks' called 'soul-Centers' inside their shells. When human, material life ceased, the spirit moved to another real body in another time. *When a Zog Died, the Death was FOREVER...a Light that never lit again.*

Neo Zog's Light was not damaged in the material sense from the attack by 100,000 photon barrels of Hate. Blue Energy, so special and pure, continued at the speed of light. Pain occurred only on the *inside* as if the blue beam had an outer body and an inner core of tender consciousness. Neo Zog was overwhelmed inside sadness and despair, but slowly recovered. It left the Territory and the smoking barrels of the Ziggerrat in a *flash*.

***

Back at the crash site of the 'Balmoral Projectile,' a perfect 'bio-body' shaped by alien technology endeared herself with the army of the Royal squadron. May Eleanora Bulair or 'Mebby' remained in a sitting position with white skull-cap, white tech suit and big smiles. She casually and very delicately told the fifteen men and one Lady her last memory.

Mebby was pulled out of a recording session by doctors who had authority to take blood and skin samples of the starlet. She complied.

Her words and blue eyes drew the crowd into her story.

The soldiers soon surmised that she was a cloned-Mebby since a few remembered her Viper war-footage of being blown out of a bulkhead many yarns ago. In front of them was the child-version with the same cute and very famous face.

After a while, the sweetest voice in the galaxy soothed the savage hearts in the soldiers. They felt comfortable enough to drop shields.

Little Mebby said, "And now I have to...*kill you.* "

The Commander was first to react as she screamed, "Men! Shields!" Royal Guards re-raised the force-fields and hid behind them in fear.

The expression on the girl in white totally transformed. She became a Child of the Beast. No longer innocent 'darling Mebby,' the demon rose to her feet. Her slim four and a half bar high figure stood tall and she stretched. She was inside the pod, a few bars higher than everyone else. May's devious smile was very different than previous smiles. She checked her wristwatch that was not a wristwatch and pushed a few buttons.

With a twirl of a child ballerina, she spun. Ominous black rays ejected from her eyes. Black Rays hit each soldier with a mighty 'tuening' blow. Raised force-fields protected them from the first barrage with minimal damage. A few peeked.

"Ah, huh! Silly me," young May Bulair said with one hand over her face and a sheepish grin. She clicked other small buttons on her wrist. The girl *deactivated every FF-shield.* Mebby was struck by photon blasts from the soldiers, which were ineffective with her private FF in the *on* mode. Black Rays from the little girl's eyes, like thasers, sliced up the Royal Guards as if they were made of crumb-cake. She jumped down to the surface and *slaughtered more with her eyes!*

Blood spurted and flowed from the men and one Lady. Before the Commander died, she was able to ask, "Why?"

Mebby unsnapped the white skull-cap and freed her long, red hair. She complained to herself about how bloodstained her new pretty tech-suit was. Then she answered the dead Commander. *"Hmmm...*wrong team."

***

During the aftermath of recent events, Citizens were dazed and confused. Media channels were unsure what stories to broadcast. The incident at Neri was a major embarrassment for Federation officials. Militias, from Royalty to volunteers, joined a cause to shoot a beam of blue light? Critics of military actions stated, "Zuggerrat armada was not there to save Valparaiso System or combat an incoming Evil, but merely to parade on Celestial May Day."

The deadly expansion of Fountain stopped with the ejection of the blue beam and returned to its smaller-sized stationary flux.

Another big concern was Seats of Power were rendered wide open for attack. Federal officials were extremely lucky a major invasion did not occur with depleted defenses. The 'Balmoral Projectile' could have been an N-Bomb, but fortunately was not.

What were Citizens told about the Projectile?

Advanced cultures who teuned-in were informed that the threat to the Palace was a *dud.* The full report was withheld to the public for only a short time about what happened after the probe's crash on the Royal Estate. But Citizens were given good news that the most famous correspondent would have a 'Breaking News' exclusive and expose exactly what crashed at the Palace.

Yes, Grace Harp would have a 'surprise guest' on her super popular program ('Grace') and the 'news' would *shock the galaxy!* The hype for the telecast was tremendous on every channel and assorted multi-Media. The vast public in every sector could not imagine what Grace had in store *next* to excite her wide audience along the space-ways. Everyone teuned-in to see the special Show. Pundits' best guess was a High State Official or famous celebrity was involved in the hoax. Another likely possibility was a well-known celebrity or industrialist would simply be used by producers to announce whatever it was that dropped from space. A few even speculated that an *alien* was in the Projectile and might make an appearance. Her interview would air soon.

Citizens were influenced by Media to fear, to be disturbed to the point of prime panic concerning the craziness of recent happenings. Zog was supposed to appear at 2000.00 and was thought to be a 'no-show.' Militaries fought a weird 'Vortex-fart.' A solar system was nearly obliterated by a Quasar and then was saved from destruction.

Selestra Matrix had disappeared and came back!

Citizens needed guidance, reassurance and comfort from the strange chaos. Channel promos told them the 'Grace Special' would provide that and much more: *"A Must-See Event."* Sponsors flocked to it. Marr-ratings tallied 'Grace Show #794' as the third highest in galactic History.

Media channels repeated highlights of the telecast while the full broadcast could be archived. Grace Harp's monologue, Show #794:

(After opening fanfare, credits and ads, Grace read the teleprompter): "Thank you, thank you for watching! The whole world's *wonderiiiiiing,* what could have dropped from the sky onto the Royal Palace Estate that worried us so much? While troops shot at phantoms, the Palace of Palaces lay defenseless.

And here comes what many believed was the *End of the World*, not from a Vortex, but on a clear path to our very *Center*. And what was it, Citizens? What came gliding in unopposed? Royal troops were gone!" (large studio audience reacted) "The fact was, it could very well have been 'End Times,' Citizens, but it was *not*. We march onward through chaotic times because...because there is *hope*. We have, good Citizens, on our show this evening, the Balmoral Projectile, *in person!*" (crowd reacted louder) "You will be able to see her. You will be able to hear her. You can ask her questions. A very lovely girl was inside the 'white bullet,' the *end of the world*, ha, ha, and we have the Projectile Princess here for you all, after these words from our sponsors, we'll we right back."

The show commenced after a very long period of galactic commercials. Producers knew sector audiences would continue to view. Grace Harp said with pride in her heart, "Without further delay, bring out what landed on the doorstep of the Palace in a little white basket."

The golden curtain parted and then another set opened. A small girl in yellow with long, red pig-tails under 5 bars danced through curtains. She sang an old standard (theme from film 'Tomorrow's Child') as she beamed smiles and batted those big blue eyes. Almost everyone recognized the 'Media darling' from another age. Mebby or 'Mebs' was not what anyone expected to fall back into our hearts again. She held a duplicate 'Rambi' in her hand, a doll from her one film. The crowd went *crazy* in a standing ovation as well as Media audiences of all sectors. Mebby returned, but questions were endless.

The show's producers broke to another commercial, which was a strict violation of broadcast protocols. Producers knew sector audiences would continue to view and teun.

May Bulair's appearance was as a twelve-yarn-old girl. The glorious child was as thrilled to be back in the spotlight as Citizens were happy to see her. Now, there was a spark of belief in Centers throughout the sectors. She reached host, Harp. They hugged with tears in their eyes. They hugged harder and cried harder, which really *brought the house down.* A close-up of Grace showed she mouthed the words, "We'll be right back," over the din of emotional outpouring. (long commercials) Then, the conversation:

"First off, Meb, what's it feel like to be back?" Grace asked as both sat in opposing chairs.

The little doll of a girl swung her arm. "Smashing!" The line was from her film, and younger audiences would not understand the old reference. Her tone became slightly serious. "I want to sincerely thank everyone who remembers me. I never thought the label 'Tomorrow Child' would literally be true."

The immense audience laughed and Grace informed the crowd, "Now we should tell everyone...*you're not real.*"

"I'm not real everyone!" she happily said with enthusiasm and turned to the audience. The crowd in studio and zillions of Citizens in the entire Pinwheel were in love with Mebby.

"May Eleanora Bulair is a *clone* today. She was...or *is* a product of Zillette Factories from the Za'ni Consortium. I won't reveal her dish number. Ha. I understand the cloning was done as a precautionary contingency, a gesture by a, a, rich admirer, shall we say?"

"Yes, the original, the *real* Mebby, you know the story." At this point the clone-child displayed emotions again, only the emotion was fake sadness. "Real Mebby became a Viper-Sergeant at Arms and, oh Zog..."

Behind the sitting pair, ran the famous film. It was enlarged and not in 3HD, but it contained the blowing out of the bulkhead and the Viper tossed violently into space.

"I *hate* seeing that." The young girl held Rambi tighter.

Grace Harp ordered her crew sternly, *"Turn that off."*

And they did.

"My original was, well, she was a good soul. She believed in everything we hold dear, Zog, the Federation, love everyone, love, love, love." May's sweet transmitted image melted Citizens in the Quadrants. "I'll never forget May. There should be special holidays in honor of May." (crowd agreed) "She believed in our way of life, in the Commerce System, the State, everything that holds our United Pinwheel together."

After more applause and more commercials, the conversation continued. "About your original," Grace asked.

"Yes?"

"Do you feel your memories are *her* memories? Who am I speaking to? Are you a virtual copy of May Bulair with her experiences, or, are you a separate entity and different person entirely? How much is her, and how much is *you* in what we are seeing?"

"May truly died in space, doing her duty, what she believed was right. I am part her and part something else. I do have her old memories, although I fully realize it was a Zillette Factory program of her memories that they impressed upon the clone, me. I am her memory. She's still with us, in me. And I will do my best to live up to her standards as an adult, to follow my dreams, hopes and face the challenges of the future and take on any adversity that comes my way, without fear." (applause)

"It's been so fabulous to see you. What do you want to be called? Mebby or May?"

"Mebby is just *smashing!*" The old reference moved the audiences again. They cheered, laughed and a few cried once more. Another standing ovation compelled the stage director to tell them off-camera to hug again. Both host and adorable little guest hugged again.

When emotions settled down and the studio crowd sat into their chairs, Grace Harp had a big surprise for her guest. The moment was a *signature* for her broadcasts. She always surprised the guest, usually with a very nice gift. "And now dear, we have something...just for *you*, Meb."

"Oh, no." The child burped. Mebby kept her mouth open wide as Grace's audience *hit the roof.*

Same golden curtains parted and opened. They revealed an even larger backdrop from a higher ceiling. When the backdrop fell away, a flattened-orb of a silver flying-vehicle smoothly *whirled* onto the front stage with barely a whisper. Grace's android announcer described the craft:

"It's the Mark-4, from SonWil & Sons providing the ultimate in space travel. If you're cruising through the harshest atmospheres or just hopping a few mega-bars to Stardusters, you'll be the 'Cat's Meow' in this deluxe 4-seater from SonWil & Sons, a division of Pan Movers."

The child dressed in bright yellow was first frozen then got excited very fast. The darling jumped up and down on the chair. She jumped up and down again. The child wanted to scream, but the famous voice did not emerge. Media played this part of the interview a lot. The famous *jumping up and down* on the Harp Show sickened some viewers and attracted others. When Mebby's voice returned, it was two octaves higher than normal. *Ecstatic* would understate her emotions. The only intelligible phrase discerned in her shrill was, "My programming! I-I can fly it!"

The crowd and trillions of Citizens in the Continuum were so damn happy for the child. They had no idea who her Father was.

Grace closed with, "Next on Grace, Ti-Won-Yeun of Varnar's Star in the, yes, *strange* sector we all want to know about, Selestra Maaatrix! Yeun is from the lovely planet, 6-2, it contains the most Mystery Domes that she'll/*he'll* be dying to talk about. We'll be right back."

***

Elsewhere in the galaxy, the buzz was, "Why did Selestra Matrix disappear? Where did it vanish to and what was different now that it returned? Was it an invasion? Why were the Visitors hiding? Who was inside? What were they doing inside, and what did it mean?" Every part of the Spacial Territory and material bodies within the sector seemed normal. No sign of Dark Matter that filled the sector for 72 yams.

Citizens were keenly interested in what networks called 'Mystery Domes.' Their numbers had not increased. The count of 12,012 black domes over 51 star systems and on 794 planets appeared to be static. They ranged from 2500 bars in length to only 50 bars. Monitors had not registered movements of any kind with the black enigmas. Authorities were not aware of any kind of communications between the domes.

Were they spies?

There had been no reported fatalities with return-dome appearances on the planets speckled by them. The dark domes were in the country, on mountaintops, in valleys, in rivers, in cities, in parking lots, rooftops, plazas, city squares and backyards. Mystery Domes did not collide with structures or drastically disturb anything physical. They were in the way, but damage was at a minimum. The 794 planets were inconvenienced, but not hurt by the extraordinary intrusion.

***

Before the Grace Show, Mebby's correct recovery team arrived, proper power units were replaced and she was whisked off to Sardon's Foundry for fine-tuning. The secret Devil could mechanically walk, talk and function in the material world without recharging. The Star Council or Secret System (NGO) debated the issue. "How do we introduce the Balmoral Projectile to Citizens?" Thousands of monitoring stations registered its incoming battle with defense systems, contrary to what Grace Harp reported. The probe had to be explained. Who dreamed the 'bullet' would be a *blast from the past?*

The new, silver Mark-4 ship by SonWil & Sons that seated a family of four comfortably was converted into a shiny black *orb of death*. Sardon's Foundry gave the module an amazing upgrade. Space Utility Vehicle morphed into a deadly 'hot-rod' Killing Machine. The little girl gave her flying orb a name; she called it 'Dread.' The *baby armada* was a formidable offensive weapon. As it skimmed the space-ways with ease, it could also wreak torrential havoc in its wake. When the conversion-overhaul process was completed from the Foundry plant, the dark horror-craft was the ideal means of travel for the Beast-child.

Mebby had a *Visitor*. It was a shock to the little Devil

made so perfectly that no one could believe the bio-body was an android. In the enlarged passenger seat to the right of the scaled-down pilot's chair, sat a *Monster*. The visual contrast between the tiny, sexy redhead in a black tech-suit and the tall, vile, despicable, depraved vision of Hensi riding shotgun was stunning.

Inside the cruising Dread on 'auto-pilot,' the mistress of ceremonies was not pleased. She kept pounding one of the control-toggles in front of her (mmmmmnntt) (mmmmmnntt) over and over with her legs spread. She looked pissed and kept hitting the front toggle. (mmmmnntt) (mmmmnntt) Mechanical May swiveled her seat as her piercing blue eyes bore into the visiting vision. Meb asked in reluctance, "Who *are* you again?" (mmmmmnntt) (mmmmmmmmmnntt)

"Ha, ha. Tituus," replied the Monster.

"Tituus, eh? *Who sent you?*" asked Mebby with vengeance.

"Friends and Fans, I assure you. Lebritz is fascinating to communicate in, ah, a choice of …subtleties. Yes, not one particular Zog. Let us say, I am an Avatar, an Avatar for many. I am here to…"

"Spy?"

"Of course, the Game is very interested in your...ah... *activity,* is that the right word? We destroyed Mineer for you, was that not enough?"

Mebby busted out laughing. "Ha! Ha!" (mmmmmnntt) (mmmmmnntt) "The Other believes *I* did it! I would thank you for the smooth move, but I know you didn't have anything to do with it, really." (mmmmmnntt)

"Correct, it was…*in the Cards,*" Tituus told his little girl captain. *Who was leading who?*

"You know, Tituus…I'm going to have to *kill* you when this is over, don't you?"

(mmmmmnntt) (mmmmmnntt) (mmmmmnntt) (mmmmmnntt) (mmmmmnntt)

The Monster roared a nightmare roar.

Little Mebby asked, "Thought that was *funny,* did

you?" (mmmmnntt)

The scruffy, hairy, ghostly vision from Zog and Sardon's World settled down. Then it pulled out a crystal N-Gun. "No, I think *this* is funny. You know what this is? Let me ask you: do you think the gun is...*smashing?*"

For a moment, small Beast-child was not in charge and worried about its physical frame that the Wadlos were so careful in molding together. "I know something that can penetrate my personal force-field when I see it," May sincerely replied.

"Then we have an understanding, Master." The pistol remained pointed down at Mebby's head. "I will call you Master, but you see before you the means to destroy your master-plan *and* put you into pieces. I am not one of your machines. You cannot control or destroy me. I am a *ghost* to you. Do you remember the Sadama?"

Mebby-android pushed a button. She leaped to her feet in anger and pointed up to the demon Monster. "That was *another world!* It was a dream."

Tituus decided to play with the Devil a bit. The ploy was a large, fatal mistake. She-Devil never forgot the move in the back of its bio-mind.

"You know very well *we're* the dream, Master. So you *do* remember when a certain ruthless late-Pharaoh and great leader of 11 towers placed a different type of crystal gun to a Master Cylinder with a bubble-head?"

"Yes, but you stated in perfect Lebritz that the Zogs directed the action, did you not?" she countered. The frozen girl with big blue eyes in the line of fire saw the creature put the gun away.

"I am one of your...great admirers," Tituus Monster said with a bow and went forward out of the chair. The Hensi-creature pledged loyalty and service to robo-Mebby with a hairy, ghostly hand extended.

Mebby accepted Tituus as First Officer and first member of Dread's crew. (Beast-child knew she would figure a way to annihilate Tituus later). She smiled. She was going to be very nice and sweet. She sat back down. "I have nothing to give you. Oooooh, yes, maybe I do. Try it. Go ahead." Meb pushed on the control-toggle so that it rested closer to the tall, scary phantom.

Tituus whacked the lever a few times with its paws. (mmmmnntt) (mmmmnntt) They laughed together and bonded.

Below, from the POV of the inhabitants of lovely 6-2, a black orb kept flying over the main Mystery Dome and periodically shot powerful thaser beams. Villages were leveled and set aflame by wide, devastating blasts. Many hundreds of Citizens died. Crisscrossed lines of destruction would scar 6-2 for yarns.

***

"Mmmmmmmmmmmm." Tray took a super big breath with his blue eyes closed. "Mmmmmmmmmmm." The feeling was divine, superb, like being within the Center of Ecstasy. Soma was everywhere. Soma was in the air, sand and water. This was *the place.* He walked farther. He felt wrapped inside pleasure. "Finally here. Mmmmmmmmmmm."

Caladan could not see much. White mists, white sands and white skies added up to a vacation in wonderland. The feeling was like micro-particles of love splashed him from every direction in a slow, swirling mist. Each nanu-explosion of affection soothed beach-comers' bodies to the *edge of Nirvana.* Soma snow was pure elation.

Tray Caladan was alone. The rented shuttle-pod from Pan docked automatically and in a short time, he made it to the exact spot he wanted to go (although never at Soma seashores before). Visibility through slow bliss was about 20 bars. Only a few sand dunes and shorelines could be seen. The journey to *the spot* was not at all treacherous, but a sensational experience because of the 'Mystic Mists.'

Tray, artist extraordinaire, was alone on what seemed like Nirvana's Beach. He said, "How could I be alone here?" He thought, *Where were crowds? Or was that why the place was so expensive and so hard to book with a long waiting-list, because of its exclusivity?*

Wonderful. Just what the doctor ordered.

Tray took full advantage of Soma sensations. He got comfortable, removed his jacket and remained in a skintight 'soothe-suit.' The suit enhanced the feelings more than mists on direct skin. Although, he thought the sensations to his bare face were *fantastic.* Everyone should do this once in their lives and *no one was here. Unbelievable!*

Tray was sure this was 'the place.' He had seen it in meditations of remote-viewing. In fact, if this was really *the spot* his 'El' had traveled to, he had been here many times before. Caladan admitted to himself that, *this seemed right.* Even though visibility was tough, beach contours appeared correct. He stepped on real soma sand, the planet Enlightenment City (next stop) happened to stand, and yet it was as if he followed a dream. Tray tried to match what he saw, in an area he thought was right, to his *remote-viewing spot* only seen in his head.

He sat exactly where the man-in-his-dreams sat. Cal relaxed, focused.

"It can't be the place I keep going to," the designer said out loud. "It only *resembles* my place." Less mist was felt and enhanced by the body-suit. The Soma *rush* was a fogbank that floated along shore and was in the process of slow dissipation. More white purity could be seen in yas.

"Can't be." Tray recognized the bays and coves of the shore that made a wide curve to the left. "Wait. When that clears, right there, they'll be an inlet that goes in, way in." More yas passed and more could be viewed through the Magical Mists. "Ah, ha!" He was right. Caladan had been here in his dreams. Or, were the visions on Soma shore the dream?

Cal was unaware that the GST had just turned to 2000.00. The new yarn or 'NGC' meant nothing to the young man. All the hype that surrounded the New Galactic Century and Neri Fountain did not matter to Mr. Caladan. The lad had not realized he would be at 'Soma,' the place of his remote-viewing dreams during the special moment in Time. His vacation was important. Tray wanted to *forget* Time and the rest of the universe.

More clarity was all around him now. Tray could view for thousands of bars. He saw a man in blue approach. Against a background of white and with such a deep blue hue, the figure was hard to miss. Closer and closer the blue person walked nearer. He or she casually walked along the shoreline. Tray could soon tell it was an old man in a blue robe. The approaching man was a Suruuan, the famous Fountain expert, Professor Renoux. *Renoux! Oh, no!* Tray totally forgot his dream in a 2-person shuttle-pod. The vision of the older man jogged most of the dream loose.

Tray Caladan sat in his suit, but was not soothed. He pointed. "You...Doc-*Professor!* I *dreamed* of you. We were in your big, fancy two-seater. And..."

A very relaxed Professor Renoux came closer. He looked *high.* Jene's eyes were glassy. His face beamed with sparkling light and knowledge. He had confidence. His dreams visualized the Larger World. He had also seen through time in the smaller Continuum, down here. When the moment was right, Jene 4 asked, "Are you sure *that* was the dream? Maybe *this* is the dream?"

"Oh, no! I just had a vujo! And a *dream*-vujo at that."

"Ha, ha." The professor, without a pipe, sat down next to Cal and stared out over clear waves. Both exhaled and felt the joy of living. "Nice here, huh?"

"I'll say. Did you have a dream about me...on your way here?"

"Yes, son, I did. I told you what you needed to know. Still holds true. You are at the shores for an important reason. You must calm yourself, boy, relax."

"Yeah, I've been *dying* to get here."

"That's not it, Cal. Something's coming very soon that's going to surprise you."

"What are you *doing* here?" asked Mr. Caladan who would not be 'Mr. Caladan' for much longer.

"I am at the end and you are at the Beginning. I'm your

guide, my boy. I'm supposed to precede you."

"What's coming?" Tray wondered with a puzzled expression.

"Superman," the former professor explained.

"Man?"

"Yes, like *you.*"

"I'm not a man."

"Check your heart, you only have one."

"Can't be." Cal felt his chest for the normal two heartbeats and only felt one. "Huh," he exhaled in surprise. Caladan was breathless. Tranquil winds increased slightly and Soma-chills were felt through their physical bodies. GST was 2000.01.

"That was the other one in the other universe. I'm here to help you, watch over you and guide you into the new life. Your old life must end for the new one to begin."

"Do I have a choice?"

"I don't think so. I miss my pipe," Jene 4 Renoux said with a sad grin.

Suddenly, Tray Caladan noticed movement. It came closer as its shape took form. "That's what's coming, a super insect?" Cal spied a small, pink Quizo that waddled her way to the Soma shoreline on three legs.

"Right on time," said the excited professor.

"What is it?"

"I'm a lady, can't you tell?" replied the Aphid-girl with a micro head at the end of a very long, thin neck.

"A female Quizo," Renoux explained. "We see one before we die."

"Huh?"

"You don't know the half of it," Lady Quizo said. *"When we see one of you, we die."*

"That's funny," Cal said.

"Not if you were me. So is it you?"

"Who?"

"The one I'm looking at."

"Hard to tell."

"It's me," Renoux said. "I've had a bad heart for quite some time, my boy. I only wanted to see 2000.00 and I have. I've had a *grand life, son.*"

"Me, too," the Aphid-dowd agreed.

Cal laughed at the absurdity of reality. "I guess I can't give you an extra heart, huh? Thought *I* was going to die, ha."

"You are, very soon now, son."

"Oh, that's right. You said it in the dream."

"Here comes Roger now, behind you." Insect said.

They turned to find another pink Quizo that slowly approached from the rear. The large Aphids almost hypnotized the Suruuan and the human. Moments passed as both magical 'dowds' stood at shore's edge. They slowly drank from white waters that glowed golden.

A question popped in the young man's mind. "There's no Mineer?"

"Hasn't been for thousands of yarns. It's almost time, son. Close your eyes. Feel each particle of Soma and enjoy the experience. Calm yourself. Please relax and realize you will soon have *power.* You will be the Zog, a new version. You will be able to do almost anything, go anywhere. Do not abuse your power, son. Do not *waste* it, Cal. Do good. We will speak again."

Then it happened. *A Blue Lightning bolt struck the young man and he felt pain!* Cal was not ready or fully prepared for transition. Being touched by Zog's essence was similar to taking hold of an arc of electricity. But if his Center was pure and clean, the metamorphosis would be successful.

The old professor died at the white seas of Soma and vanished.

The young human was 'born again.' There was only a core of light-energy brilliantly blazed within Caladan's humanoid body of head, two arms and two legs. *Material man merged with blue electricity and melded into a super-being,* an Immortal in the physical universe, which could manipulate matter.

El returned. Physical man and the energy of Zog

became the New Zog. Unlike a life spark inside smaller humanoids, the Spark inside the new entity was the lifeforce of a Zog. Caladan was no more. Tray was dead. His material body had been ultra-enhanced to the point of imperviousness. Tray Samuel Caladan merged/morphed into a super-container for the 'El' of Zog. Cal was now 'Cal-El' and personification of power in the universe.

The new life form could travel at light-speed, then stop on a dylar. It saw and understood the other three times the Universe had been built. It could stop Time, reexamine it, fold it, see all sides, but the Super Entity could not *change* Time or the Laws of Physics. The brilliant blue spirit could not wave an arm and make the galaxy a beautiful place. He could not move the Center of even one other creature an m-bar. The flying, Blue Dream was able to consume and compute super knowledge. Neo Zog now contained vast libraries of information. The Being knew what happened in the Beginning. He could view the entire First Reich.

The great entity of love took to the sky and found he could control the azure lightning inside his indestructible body. He played, soared in and out of space, came back down to the planet as if he was Caladrian's 'Shrike.' (He remembered) The flying Zog body glided through Soma mists at super speed, a sensation a thousand times more intense than when he was only a man hit by the same fogbank.

The spirit of Zog flew to different environments in the 'Soma Area.' The projectile from Nirvana jettisoned into Soma snowstorms, Soma hail and Soma rains. All of the natural precipitation was white. The *feeling* was Nirvana in the Material World!

Cal-El skimmed over clear S-waters, touched the surface and created long lines in the liquid. He increased speed and wake-lines became larger, wider, longer, and then, he slowed down and suddenly *shook all over.*

Cal-El disappeared and instantly reappeared many thousands of bars away directly over *his* Spot on *his* Shore. The energy-man resumed shaking in midair a few bars over his special place in his dreams. There was not enough Soma in the Universe to quiet his crying soul. The tears were good tears, happy emotions of love and appreciation. Against all odds in the Higher World, *El returned!* Cal-El's tears poured from the GST of 2000.03 to the GST 2000.09.

Before Cal-El left the planet of Soma and Enlightenment City, the Neo Zog had to see or do a flyby over 'Enlightenment City.' After all, it was the *next stop* on his vacation.

Why let zoghood stop it?

He streaked over Lutern Lake and saw his amazing reflection as a beam of blue light. Cal-El flew right up to grand City Gates with the magnificent 'Lights.' After a few passes, Neo Zog flew directly over unbelievable pomp and splendor of what was regarded as the Galaxy's Religious Center. Great Square of E-City stood as the cornerstone for variations of Zog-doctrines and dogmas. Initiates were schooled or trained for higher planes of existence. Here was the Holy Headquarters for faith in the Pinwheel. Here were Nirvana-like 'Lights' (glory) and foundations and sculptures and art of religions on a galactic scale. Trillions of Citizens in every sector viewed this square of *light* as Holy Grounds.

From high in the air, over the sculptures and expensive columns, Cal-El *cursed at Enlightenment City!* It was false. It was a lie. It was Business and Profits. It was for *show* and appearances only! Underneath the 'Holy Church' or what El understood as the mechanism running the 'Order' was not enlightenment, it was dylars. E-City had the power to produce its own dylars. *They imprinted ZOG's name on dylars!* E-City was obliged to not pay one dylar in taxes established by the High Anarchists. 'Enlightened' planes of an 'afterlife' were actually SOLD like cosmic 'Indulgences.' Citizens could *buy their way into Nirvana.*

The 'Golden Path' could be purchased with enough dylars.

'Miracles' could occur with enough dylars.

Anything could be procured with enough dylars. Cal-El

was going to stop the insanity and essentially 'turnover the tables of the Galactic Stock Exchange' and destroy the 'Galactic Reserve.'

"When that happens, dylars won't be worth crumb-cake," Cal-El said loudly as he flew far from Enlightenment City, now sickened by the lights.

Tray had 'ascended' or experienced *transcendence*. The feeling of zoghood was like being done with every last test in every reincarnated life and being *free-energy* without restrictions. Life was not victimized by reality; life could utterly control it. Being Cal-El was as if the blue-light creature was still a part of the Higher World. He could bring the feeling of Zoghood down here into the physical. Could he also bring mortals from the Continuum, Upstairs? Cal-El wanted *everyone on this level* to be able to ascend, for everyone to *feel* as he did at present. *Was that possible?*

***

The MEAD Corporation in the Bel Consortium sponsored a large book-signing event for Mebby and her many fans. The planet Vaala held the major 3-day extravaganza. In the center of the most enormous and elaborate 'Casino-Community' stood the new Alta-Anarchists' central gambling theater. Within the main gambling arena, stood numerous stages where top acts from around the Pinwheel performed nightly. Colorful members of Royalty and lesser 'Illuminaughty' regularly attended various casino shows for the marvelous entertainment acts and not for dylar-betting.

One particular back office of royal opulence contained May Bulair and her 'Inner Circle' of mega-agents. Excitement for the new x-Book and i-File was at maximum. The long-awaited book (Mebby did not write in any sense) was tracked for mass-publication. The amount of dylars that the publications could generate was staggering since the return of the icon as *fresh as a bloch*.

Members of her Inner Circle included lit-elite, PR people, PR aliens, lawyers, defense teams, damage-control teams and hairstylists. They got to witness the *other side* of the famous star and were contractually sworn to reveal nothing of what went on behind closed doors...*or else...*

Her public entourage patiently waited beyond massive doors. Beyond that, throngs of adoring fans had waited days and nights for a chance to see Mebby sing and dance on the main stage. Record numbers of dylars were lost by Citizens during the convention. Here she was, back again, Tomorrow's Child, for the first time in many yarns, their own lil' darling that most Citizens had adopted would entertain like the good Old Days.

"You zuckers are from Zetag!" the little girl screamed, not so loud that her shrill berating could penetrate thick doors. The pretty princess in pink with bows in her perfect (now) blonde hair, stood on a big/round desk. "If you think we're going with YOUR title for *my* book..."

She screamed from center stage. Mebby made sure everyone *sat* at the circular desk so the standing girl remained much taller than the rest of the inner clique. She could point in every direction. 'Rambi' doll was held tightly by the screaming maniac from Hensi in her left hand, while violent *finger pointing* went on with the right.

"Please calm down, dear," advised one of the agents who was allowed to speak. She spoke in fear of losing more than her job.

Instead of dark Mebby getting angry behind closed doors, she momentarily acted as if hit by a white fogbank of Soma. "All right then, you slime-flugs, only thinking of how *large* your percentages will be and *if* you will even *receive* them, tell me again. What the Boz was *your* title?"

The same frightened literary agent who had spoken before spoke once more. She shook just a bit. "Ah, that, that was, was *Inside May Eleanora Bulair.*"

"Cute, adequate, marginal, mediocre. Is *that* what you think I want?"

The agents and PR people shook their heads no.

One of the male literati, actually the highest-ranking l-agent in the galaxy who must-be-nameless, dared to speak and it said, "We have not, uh, heard *your* title, Mebby. MEAD Corporation's Ghost Writer is, of course, certainly willing to change his title, I think?"

Her Inner Circle observed and felt the wrath of the Bozing Bitch before. They were getting accustomed to jumping in fear for their little lives. Many thought May's gorgeous, big blue eyes could *kill.* They were right. The buildup of negative-energy was too much. Everyone felt it, like a mounting volcano ready to burst. Once more, *she was going to blow.*

"HIS title, HIS book! Who the Boz's name is in the title? What does the byline read, eh? *'By May Bulair, excerpts from her personal Diary.'* Is anyone here going to argue it's *his* book and there was *never* a diary?" She pointed more.

In unison they shook heads for *no,* even the aliens.

"I have a show to do tonight and I have to put up with jango from you. I have *enough* to think about! You think this is easy?"

Again, the response was no.

"My fans are waiting and want my book *now*...out there, now, and *BOZ!* You're telling me we don't have a simple-ass title yet?"

The third and last l-agent permitted to talk tried to settle the princess' tirade. "Mebby, it's electronic. Every file will include a last-step title, instantly. Just tell us what you want and we'll type it in and enter."

Her tantrum was over. May's hands (with Rambi) were on her hips, but she was not angry. She geared up for her next scheduled appointment of greeting the public through the huge doors. "I want to call it in big red letters: 'SMASHING' – the Mebby Story!' May bashed the edge of the circular desk with her small arm, which shocked everyone in the plush office. She broke off a piece. She smiled innocently and coyly said, "Sorry."

"Done," said the sitting agent as he typed-in the proper letters on his device. "Each book, file and extra feature will *be headed* with your title now, Mebby. And I think it's great."

The other literati shook their heads for yes, even the aliens.

The she-Beast became the Media darling again and said with the excitement of Show-Biz, "Then, let's go out and...get 'em." With that said, she sprang toward the doors with fake smiles. Doors automatically opened to reveal many hundreds of fans, from young to old, in a special area to see Mebby stroll down the Blue Carpet. Cameras rolled. Honored guests crowded in and overwhelmed the little girl as her Inner Circle protected her.

Mebs put on a cheery persona for her admirers. She waved, laughed and was surrounded by those who loved her dearly. There were bodyguards, fans with tri-camera-TVs, professionals with mobile light-units and equipment, along with others recording the historical event. The blonde sweetheart was off for interviews, photo-shoots, book-signings and fake 'Help-the-Citizen' campaigns. Tonight would be an enormous occasion. Her concert performance would be streamed to every sector. And the world will watch.

***

Later, during one of the x-Book signings, prior to the Big Performance, a very strange encounter happened. Mebby sat in a chair of prominence while her entourage handed her pack after pack of her new book entitled, 'SMASHING'– the Mebby Story!' She pressed her colored thumbprint on each one. Lucky fans waited for many yams to line up and receive their own personal copy with the icon's fingerprint embossed on the cover. 'Signed,' unopened Mebby packages fetched millions of dylars on the White Market.

MEAD Corp sponsored the signing. The major event was staged with the trimmings of an elaborate Vaala Show. A band softly played music from 'the Beginning' in the background. A podium-like sculpture was set in place for receivers of the signed book to also ask *one* question to dear May.

The first recipient was a young man who 'won' his

coveted place because his father owned a prime consortium in Bel. He boldly asked with much vigor, "Mebby! Will you marry me?"

The crowd reacted with a collective gasp and laugh.

She fixed a false face as if she *wanted* to be here and *enjoyed* the attention by 'dylars' who had no idea how *low* they were on the 'food-chain.' Her immediate reply to the kid made the large audience shout with more laughter. "How many dylars do you have?"

Crowds loved it.

After the commotion quieted down and the band lowered its sound, a middle-aged lady got to the very public podium. Her group won a lottery to be #2 in the question-asking line. "I'm *thrilled* to be here, of course…see you and can't *wait* to read the Diary!" The crowd's response was tremendous. The band took the cue and played louder. She added, "My group represents 'Young Grandmas' everywhere, and we want to *adopt you as our own.*" More ovations occurred that disgusted the robo-creature on the inside. But Mebby shined on as the precious Child of the Universe.

"I would *love* to be your daughter." Mebs lifted her arms in a *distance-hug* and melted crowds on Vaala and countless other star systems. The girl had to include, "But I *cannot,* sadly. I am a clone-Ward of the State and not permitted to." Groans and moans were heard as the older lady's face was bittersweet. "Sorry, I would *love* to have you for a mommy." She beamed big smiles and batted her large eyes again.

The crowd went crazy and the lady was asked to leave the podium.

MEAD promoters, directors and other members of Bel Consortium were baffled at the following series of actions. There was great confusion on who would appear next as #3, which should not be the case in a well planned affair. Then, the band played an overture much louder as a seemingly miracle was about to happen. A surprise guest was going to appear that even producers of the book-signing were unaware.

Grace Harp shocked the audience, Mebby, the real

Grace Harp, as well as Citizens around the galaxy. The famous host-reporter confidently walked on the Blue Carpet and down to where the podium-sculpture stood to thunderous applause. An unknown, dark undercurrent slithered beneath the surface. *Everyone in the Universe was blind to the historic encounter that was about to happen.* Who knew Grace Harp would appear? It was the perfect Media-event and Vaala Show that thrilled zillions of onlookers.

Relatively few noticed the stern and serious expression on Grace's face. The long walk had the spotlight of the galaxy and center of attention for Citizens. Life forms who noticed thought, in the moment, the super host was joking with a harsh face while others screamed in exultation.

The child-icon was also confused. It was a state she was not familiar with, not being in total control or the one in charge, the Boss. The little girl's Wadlo-circuits touched something they should not have been able to register...*feelings.* Mebby sensed that Grace Harp was not Grace Harp.

May Bulair performed. She knew the part was unreal. "Grace Harp," she said with smiles and wide eyes. "This *is* a surprise. And one pack for you, dear." Mebby again pressed her thumb (hard) on a package of i-File and x-Book and tossed it to one of the entourage. The Media darling was not as happy to see the super host as she should have been. Few noticed.

Crowds in the large round room hushed. Everyone was extra anxious to hear what question Grace could possibly ask the Child of the Universe, the Child of Tomorrow.

Why wasn't Grace smiling on the festive occasion?

Systems heard 'Grace Harp' ask the following deplorable question: "What will happen when they discover the truth, that you are the Demon-Beast Sardon inside your corrupted circuits who has enslaved everyone to the accursed dylar System which has (crowd slow to react) devoured real life, the way we are *supposed* to live and replaced it with the Hensi-fires of Pandra instead?"

Rambi was dropped on the floor of the huge stage. The audience of Mebby-lovers was also lovers of Grace and her popular program. Screams and jeers were verbally thrown at Grace Harp. Where was she coming from? What did it mean? Did she have evidence to prove her strong claims of deception as she was known for exposing? Did she just cross swords and make darling Mebby her enemy? Were they seeing a publicity stunt, an act?

May Bulair was seen cautiously, slowly rise to her feet. She only put together at this nanu-ya *who* she dealt with under the glare of the galaxy. It was 'The Other,' her Anti or Neo Zog. In .5389894 nanu-yas, she calculated a possible way out of trouble. The mechanical bio-Beast made it appear to the audience and registering devices that powerful red beams shot from Grace to Mebby. For an instant, Grace changed to a dark figure in a hood. Cameras recorded an injured Mebby fall to the stage floor as if the *child had been shot.* May deduced her beams first touching image of Grace, which no one could see or record, would only *seem* as if the beams went to Mebby. She faked the entire split-ya production. She knew the power-drain of the touch would uncover Grace's mask and show the real soul (NZ) inside for a blink of an eye. She hoped the demon-attacker once exposed, might disappear. Neo-Zog, only caped in black and visible to all, vanished in a puff of blue electrical-smoke.

Audiences *screamed!* At first they were frozen, then mobs of humanoids (mostly) stormed the stage to come to the child's rescue. 91 was called 19,555,303,003,543 times in the galaxy. Crowds were Bozing shocked again to view *Mebby flip high off the ground and land in a ballerina spin.* She was unhurt, and what they saw was 'all part of the show.'

"Don't worry, folks! I'm SMASHING fine!" (crowd sighed) The cheeky girl also did her familiar arm whirl with catchphrase. "Grace was *in* on it. Let's give her a big hand ladies, gentlemen and thingies, wherever she is, she deserves it. C'mon!" (huge applause)

Multitudes in sectors were so *relieved* the cute girl was unharmed and what they witnessed was scripted.

The mechanical creature unrecognized as one saw how

the unexpected situation could work to her advantage (in a sick way). "Yes. By contract I can't reveal any more of the plot for my new film. It's a Fi-Sci Blockbuster called *The Ultimate Deal.*"

One more time the listening/viewing audiences of Meb-lovers on a cosmological scale shrieked, hollered, screamed, shouted and bila-bonged to the limit when it computed that there would be a *second* Mebby film! Her galactic Fan Club and Inner Circle were uninformed.

"We've already started filming. I play a *real monster*, the Sardon, the Devil. Can you imagine little *me?* The Beast with a million eyes. *Acting.* Hiding inside a robot?" The tiny child tried to mock-scare the crowd with her slim arms that waved like a bad monster. Then, Meb cut a joke. "Don't worry, Citizens. It will turn into dance numbers. Ha, ha."

Crowds laughed harder and *loved* the theater they felt themselves a part. Who expected such drama? Drinking, drugging and dylar-losing at gambling tables were worth it with Vaala-bombs like what had transpired...*only on Vaala.*

May Bulair announced, "Before I leave, I thank you for indulging us, our way of introducing the new film. A trailer will be forthcoming. Sorry, Grace Harp will *not* be returning to acting with far more important commitments with her Prah Corporation and all their good work."

Audiences moaned and reacted.

"There'll be new songs." Audiences perked up with excitement. "Pinn Bradley will be in it, ladies." Media teuners went ballistic, especially the *females!* Heart rates raced then lowered in the crowds. "Gotta go. I love you. Be good." The precocious dumpling of a child was a sugary, breathtaking delight...*for a Devil-Beast from Hensi.*

May exited and quickly ran into another back office where her Circle waited, very nervously. Crowds believed the performer purposely made a dramatic exit in the form of a fast sprint. They loved the way she exited and the sprint was commented by pundits later on channels.

In truth, Mebby was really angry. May smashed the tall

casino doors wide open and closed them behind her with a loud slam! Her defenseless clique was like lambs to slaughter.

"You! Get this film-jango going fast. You! Call my real lawyers. You, no, you! Get the script written, *Ultimate Deal* it's called. Don't use MEAD writers. *Boz them.* Make the trailer, now. YOU! You're ugly. YOU! You're fired! OH, and *you,* call Pinn Bradley's Bozing agent and you, dylar-man, don't *spend* too much. Doesn't have to be good."

"Me?"

"And make it a Bozing *musical,* Boz, Boz, Boz!"

Chapter Eleven

TRANSCENDENCE?

After Cal-El, the Neo Zog, disappeared in a puff of blue smoke on screens across the galaxy, CE reexamined what happened. Neo Zog got the message out, but would Words of Truth have influence? Would they have an effect? Conscious reasoning was, "A few will believe, and it will help."

Neo Zog saw through Time, but could not see the true (one) future. Reality was unknown because of Free Will, the Principle of Choice. Seeing through the course of liquid history, Past and Future like a Quizo, was not an exact science. Time-viewers saw the paths, but not the ONE Avenue reality would take. Decisions were unpredictable.

Cal-El was bright. Besides the literal azure glow (he/she in a humanoid shape), Cal-El was brilliant in the sense of cosmic consciousness. He, the Energy El, had an idea. He knew precisely what to do to turn the Galactic Tables. No Rebel Alliance team effort ever did more. There would not be even one Citizen aware of what really happened. Blows against the Empire could occur in one single, focused strike. He could destroy the Financial Foundations of the NGO Federation SS with one thought or a simple blink of an eye.

When should I break the lifeblood of the Galactic Reserve? When should I destroy the dylar?

***

Inside the small and super mighty Dread, May Bulair had more surprise guests. Four refurbished swivel chairs were occupied. Devil-girl and Tituus had two more Visitors from the Upper Universe. The new pair sat behind them. Once more Mebby was in the physical shadow of another giant, phantom-like, dark creep: actually two more.

Mechanical Mebby turned her small pilot's chair hard in frustration and looked up. She faced the backseat of big brutes head on and asked, "Who *are* you again?"

Tituus thought he had the right, as First Officer, to speak. "Master, let me introduce more of your great admirers from my clan, more instigators for Mineer's destruction. I present, first, and on the left, Rambus."

Mebby howled in laughter. "Ha! Oh, that's rich, ha!"

Three monsters were not in on the joke. They looked at each other in bewilderment.

She went over to one of the consoles and grabbed her doll. "I'd like to introduce *Rambi.*" Beast-girl threw it at Rambus.

The backseat monster from a nightmare *ate* the cute 'dolly' in one gulp without having to move.

"That's all right. I can get more."

"And, on the right, I present the esteemed…*Lady Braw*. My Sister merely *uses* the mortal body of an innocent. She is the true covert creator of Alta Anarchists, the real ones. We are honored, Madam." Tituus' gruff, low voice contained heavy tones of respect for his Sister from Upstairs.

Blonde Mebby sat and widened her slim legs more. She was skeptical and wanted to be 100% in charge. "Honored, huh? Hey, I don't get it. You think I *need* you three?" The pixie demon asked this with clenched fists and mean red eyes. Her attitude was of a heartless, spoiled empress-brat.

"May, may I speak?" asked Lady Braw. She was not a Phantom from the Upper Universe on the physical outside. The beautiful, strong war-veteran willingly gave her amazing body up to the dark Zog-entity known as Braw. (Yram aka 'Mary' would be forgiven). Yram Escovilla-2 was 'dead.' Only Braw spoke out of her mouth and moved her *possessed* body. At present, she was only 'Lady Braw' in the real world. She could be Mebby's greatest ally.

Mebby was curious of the amalgamated killer. Here was half an ex-Viper and half a negative Zog.

She could be interesting. Could be a big sister?

May Bular was wet. Mebby paid closer attention to the woman.

"We are valuable Avatars for you, Master. Upstairs Game gave us permission, as top Mineer deleters, to enter the smaller Continuum. We are here to help you, serve you. Command us, Commander. We are your...*Generals* in any campaign you choose, Master," she said.

Mebby smiled at the Lady. The little Beast showed the first relaxed face in some time. Tensions dropped as the child accepted her monster crew.

Tituus thought to add, "Four seats to the Mark-4, Captain. Second and Third Officers in your crew, yes?"

"Hmmm. *Captain* and my crew of Generals? I *think* I like that. I may have a few ideas." She smiled like a tiny villainess. "You! The quiet, handsome one who ate my dolly, what do *you* have to say?"

Rambus, who might have been the most gruesome in appearance, replied, "We are only here to serve you, Captain."

***

There were certain elite Rangers (Controllers) well aware of the Return of Zog, the new version. They were Super Psychics in the galaxy. They were good and positive 'Caretakers' of the precious Pinwheel. They did not have to fly spaceships to the center of Venus to attend the party. Elite Citizens could sit and relax in the comfort of sector homes and tap into a very special type of 'teuning.' The homing-in or remote-viewing could be received by any individual with high 'Mystic' skills. Activities in the Center of Venus were known without crystal monitors or equipment or ad-promos of any sort. World psychics anxiously closed their eyes and other sensory apparatus, extremely excited to project their 'Els' and 'meet' the Neo Zog.

Media was forbidden and obviously not included. The Near Meeting was *personal* yet shared by millions of Citizens who did not use Media.

Retz Council Headquarters was a real, physical place inside the hollow center of Venus. Throughout sectors there were also material 'Embassies' that represented Retz. Here was an organization of positive, true blue 'Wings Over The Galaxy.' The mega-institution of the mind was also real Peacekeepers. What was false in the Old Days was reality in current times. Rangers watched over worlds as righteous Police Forces. Weapons were used only as a last resort, never for intimidation and usually Common Sense ruled the day. The 'Guardians' settled disputes, extinguished Old Fayds, ended wars, helped others and were basically responsible for peace in the galaxy.

Thank Zog for the Guardian Rangers!

Vast numbers of Venusians in the crowded and cool inner caverns poured out into the central core, which was billions of bars in diameter. Ranger numbers inside the planet did not compare to countless throngs of remote-viewers in the Quadrants. The 'good guys' in-the-know were ready to pay Ultimate Tribute to the real King of the Galaxy.

Cal-El's material energy, in a humanoid shape, flew in the northern pole-opening of Venus. Neo Zog shot like a blue thaser out a prime passageway and into the planet's massive hollowness. What was the encounter to be: ceremony, ritual? Should NZ allow tributes from the galaxy? Should the blue energy within the man-form permit praise and idol-worship? Or should he let Citizens express love for a Zog Superstar in their midst?

The enormous core of Venus was actually similar to most planets. Life existed on the exterior as well as more life on the interior. Words could not describe deep catacombs from the Beginning that honeycombed the 'Great Interior' with lakes, rivers, falls and colonies like fantastic balconies on sidewalls and ceilings.

On the main round stage, 48 'Speakers' assembled in white robes. Mystic Senators were specially chosen, two from each sector, including sparsely populated Territories. They formed an Inner Circle which took the shape of an actual circle. Far away in every direction, even directly above, gathered millions of Venusians and invited guests. Each was there at the Headquarters of the (good/positive) Retz Council while huge numbers of Mystics and seers meditated; teuned and monitored the extremely memorable proceedings.

The incredible psychically-broadcasted Event only for the most sensitive life forms in the galaxy was not advertised in any way. Everyone just knew to tuen-in. Able Citizens relaxed and watched closely from long distance with their eyes closed.

The forty-eight nameless Senate Masters in white were composed of 2 lizards, 2 Greys, 3 tall Greys, 2 giants (12 bars high), 6 Trinars, 5 Clarions, 2 Suruuans, 2 Padmars, 2 Demorans, 2 Denarans, 1 Ulk, 1 Insectoid and 18 other mixed aliens, humanoids and humans.

Psychics simply knew the proceedings and how the Council would be conducted. The 48 'Speakers' arranged in a circle at ground zero would *not speak*. No lips would move. They would THINK or relay what large groups of others wanted to know and say or ask. Each pair of Speakers would function as 'Receivers' synthesizing tremendous waves of communications from their corresponding sectors. If spontaneous questions/replies instantly formed from enough Citizens, the Senate 'rep' in the Inner Circle would *think it* and the galaxy accessed the psychic communications. Psychics operated very differently than State-sponsored Media.

Neo Zog would also not move his lips. NZ's communications would be understood by Mystics who could break time/space. There was no psychic *double-speak* or deception on the part of NZ. Cal-El's precise and Centered thoughts were sensed in every sector.

The flying man-Zog came to rest in midair directly over the center of the Inner Circle. Neo Zog remained in the black robe/cape that was momentarily revealed during Mebby's book-signing. The hood part was pushed back and Cal-El's perfect, bright face was there for all to remote-view. He glowed inside a blue vergence. The good superman in dark robes relaxed and took an invisible seat high over a circle of mortals in white.

The mortals were *near* Nirvana. The 'Collective Consciousness' of the Rangers was indeed wide and vast. Retz

Venusian Rangers were a powerful force for *good* in the galaxy and *a state of mind.* They were a Union of minds that arrived here, defying time, from every sector. They had come to honor the 'true Universal Child.' Was Neo Zog the real *Tomorrow's Child?*

What could go wrong?

Despite the Retz Council and affiliate Embassies' expansive range of superior information, the 'good guys' still did not have all the facts. There remained *a few minor differences* between the New Zog and those who had assembled their minds to worship the Blue Being. Differences concerned: *how to approach the future? What should be the strategy?* Citizens and Masters loved NZ and mentally-teuned as 'One' with the unique moment of introduction to the material world.

Cal-El slightly turned his hovering body to the angle of the first *thinker.* Without fanfare, music, or commercials, one of the nameless Senate 'Speakers' expressed in thoughts heard round the galaxy to some:

We humbly bow in your presence, my Lord. We feel the New Age to come and know it will be because of you. You will save us in the future. We have seen it. We also know you and only you would arrive at 2000.00, the reason for the NGC. We understand you represent the Zogs from the Higher Continuum, which we are in extreme debt to for your predicted Return. We understand, Creator, you caused the growing Fountain and burst forth like a Cosmic Blue Birth of brilliance only to be greeted by the Hensi of frightened militias that did not realize the Majesty in front of them. New Zog, we pray you forgive them and every Citizen for our blind ignorance. We pray you find it in your Center to accept our warmest wishes, and we lovingly welcome you into our world. We only want to show our appreciation and hope you feel along with us in a moment of silent thought.

Timeless yas occurred where enlightened Masters from everywhere in the galaxy prayed together in 'one' harmonic, emotional convergence. The dimension of Love was stunningly overwhelming to Neo Zog. The *feeling* was magical Affection-Fallout. Cal-El again cried, inside. Each teuned Citizen could feel the subtle wobble of the spinning Pinwheel. Tears flowed from those with tear ducts. 'Zog in the Material World' felt radiant love, a warm, ecstatic moment the blue entity of light would never forget.

After the poignant vibe that needed no words, another Senator was moved to think: *We know of your greatness and our unworthiness.*

Reborn-Zog had to immediately stop the new Speaker. *Please.* The Neo Zog wanted to correct a few errors that even the Masters were unaware.

Masters of the Universe, Rangers for Truth and Justice, stood still. Cal-El's thoughts were internally monitored. Mystic Masters knew his thoughts would be indelibly etched into spirits of multitudes that have united to greet the New Zog. He had everyone's attention and mentally broadcasted:

Thank you, great seers. But you would do me more honors by giving me no tributes at all. Do not pray to me. If you knew my Center, I crave to be an equal, one of you, not a Superior. I love your world, but I did not create your universe of fantastic atomic systems and the wondrous Life that inhabit them. My arrival into the Material happened to occur at your designation of two thousand, but I assure you there was no planned prediction. I could have returned at any time. You are also wrong about Zogs in the Higher Continuum who do not deserve credit for my Return. Not one of my Brothers and Sisters wanted me to return to your physical universe. Battles had to occur for me to come back down with no home world (Mineer) to be reborn. An alternate method, through a Quasar and through a man, had to be devised...and against all odds, against Supreme Orders from my Zogs, I made it back here to a place I desperately love. So, I have been banned from the Larger Continuum and cannot return up to Home to what you call Nirvana. Sectors of the small Continuum are my home now, inside your Pinwheel Galaxy.

'Speakers' were unsure whether to thought-speak

during the pause. It was difficult for the world to digest NZ's first communications and then formulate a reply.

I am Cal-El, and I have returned!

The galaxy's response was cosmic applause, love, honors and tributes focused directly at the center of Venus. The gleaming, spherical super-cavern 'Interior' was even brighter.

You see in me a merger, a bonding of physical man and Electricity from Centers every one of you possesses. I am pure Spark made real. I am farther along the real Golden Road than you. I have seen through the long stretch of Time from a higher perch. I have been to Nirvana and dwelled there beyond your concepts of Time. I was originally 'born' in that Dimension. But dear friends, we are the same. Speaker?

Cal-El caught the galaxy off guard when he turned to the Senator who first made his thoughts known. Speakers became even more attentive.

New Zog began again with a sincere smile and a tear in his left eye. *Bow to no one. The obsolete gesture is ancient and declares a superior to an inferior. Show no more honors to me that you would to family and friends. It is not a sign of respect. It is a military, political salute and should not happen among equals. You...we...are all equal.*

(collective WOW)

A Speaker asked, *May we ask questions, Cal-El?*

You may.

Different Senators took turns. *Do Mystery Domes represent an attack from the Higher World?*

Neo Zog answered like a reflex Truth. *No. The Domes are peaceful Observation Posts from the Lower World. [laughter] They are small 'watchers,' small 'universities' and they consider this level (above them) the Higher World. Selestra Matrix was moved and returned in the Larger Game, which we play a crucial part. In the Domes are huge numbers of relatively microscopic life forms from the universe or continuum or Floor just below yours. They now view the Pinwheel, but have no effect upon it. They do not want to contaminate the Great Experiment.*

Speakers/Senators noticed the NZ responded to *Cal-El* and not *Master* or titles of respectful honor. The special El inside the man wanted to be treated like any Citizen instead of the 'True King of the Universe.' He was the *only* Royalty, yet utterly refused the role and its Throne.

A Speaker thought the question, *Cal-El, are you the Fourth Creator?*

No, but, I will meet God in the future, that fact, I know. How final events will conclude? I know not.

One Quadrant was collectively curious and forced its four Avatars (two twins in two sectors) to think in unison: *Why did your Brother and Sister Zogs not want you to Return to our plane of existence? Why would you have to 'battle' your way here, Cal-El?*

NZ was quick to answer. *Contamination and corruption.*

They thought you would contaminate our Continuum?

Not as much as I would be contaminated BY your Continuum, which is now my Continuum and home.

A Senator thought a question by his chorus. *Could you explain?*

To them, I was considered a virus, already corrupted by my first Mineeran experience in the Material World. They believed the very concept of Returning was proof of my insanity. I was banned from Home, my own realm and imprisoned. I was not allowed to come back to this physical place with a spectrum of sensations. I was not permitted to go where I wanted to go the most. Your level was my forbidden zone, the Zogs told me. They considered me a bad example and I was punished for loving your world. They destroyed the planet Mineer because I loved it, the only place I could emerge. I was able to escape bondage. I saw a way back here through the eye of a Quasar and defied the wishes of the Zogs and the very Game they play. I am an Outlaw in their Dimension and will also be one in yours.

Probably the most disturbing question so far was thought and hit the exact Center of Cal-El. *Is your plan of revenge against the Zogs what you have called Ascension or acts of Transcendence?*

NZ's response was slower this time. The question intrigued him. At first, he considered, *(Is that what I am really doing?).* He found Center and realized the idea was untrue. He really, out of crystal clear joy and love, wanted to have the lower lives in the Pinwheel experience Nirvana. More than that, the Ultimate Question: *Why not give all life the potential of reaching Nirvana? And once attained, very unlike a physical universe, life would be an infinite Utopia without change (dying entropy) and without end.*

No, Speaker, that's not it. Cal-El cried. *Don't waste life, Citizens. What you already possess is precious. You exist because you are energy. Your physical frames die, but your energy is forever. You will also return. But you keep returning here. There is no true ascension, no entrance, yet. Every one of your Els comes back to the same Continuum. There is no real progress, only soul-stagnation, only running in circles. Nirvana is not Enlightenment City. You have been to the Gates of Nirvana but do not have the height to see the actual Lights of Glory and Truth, of what awaits you in my World. You will never be within the Gates of Nirvana unless a portal exists to accommodate your Els. Presently, even the Highest of your Masters are trapped in the Material Prison you call 'life' and the course of Life, the Continuum. Things have to change very dramatically.*

To this point, everything had gone well. Love and appreciation from esteemed psychic Masters of positive energy had dominated the Event. Neo Zog felt the soft, warm vibrations and returned the feelings with amplification. Now, specifics would be mentioned. Sardon would be brought up and dark thoughts were sure to immediately emanate throughout the sectors.

How could the Devil not be mentioned?

A Speaker anticipated NZ's problem and helped the situation. *Master, sorry, Cal-El, please proceed. We know the Ghost of Sardon is alive and well inside the android girl. What should we do, sir?*

Brace for change. Prepare as your constituents stated. A New Age is coming. You praise me now as the One responsible for a New Order. Later you will blame me.

No. No, propagated over vast audiences not wanting to believe CE. Few fans could compute his thoughts. They loved him and he just told the world's positive-camp of 'good guys' they would turn on him in the future.

A Speaker thought on his own without support from a countless chorus. *Cal-El, we have been only respectful. Pardon the question. Do you condemn us before we have acted with disrespect?*

The hovering blue entity on the inside and human on the outside smiled once more. *It will happen. It will occur within yas.*

The entire tone of the Super Event to honor the Neo Zog's Return had flipped. *No, no,* reverberated in the cosmos again. Psychic commotion lessened.

A majority of Retz Embassies in a particular Quadrant evoked its 'rep' Senator to ask, *Cal-El, please explain the changes to come, that we are to prepare for. What is the nature of the changes?* They were worried.

The good news is Mystics to Citizens to yahoos in the spinning Continuum of the real world will know and experience Transcendence. As it stands, currently, there is no entrance-portal for your Els down here to Ascend and experience my timeless Dimension way up there.

Four Speakers representing former Capitals Denaris and Demor asked in unison, *Cal-El, you expressed yahoos?*

Yahoos, yes?

The four meekly expressed a major, conservative concern by Citizen elites. *Nirvana for yahoos? You believe yahoos have the right or are ready to Ascend to Nirvana?*

NZ had been hovering in a sitting position above them until now. Neo Zog stood upright in midair. CE thought the stance expressed confidence. *Yes, All. When I said we are each equal, the cutoff was not at Galactic Citizenship. You fools*

sound like the Zogs I left behind, that imprisoned me!
No, Master.
No, Cal-El.
Never.

One more time the Retz Embassies expressed that they wanted a sharp answer on the question of coming *changes* and the New Age. There were the Rangers, the sincere do-gooders of the galaxy. Citizens referred to Retz as 'The Controllers.' They were proud of a job well-done. Citizens around the big Pinwheel were fortunate to have the Guardian Peacekeepers. Retz felt specifics were not mind-mentioned. They were extremely interested in Cal-El's keen plot to overthrow the Galactic Reserve and precisely what the consequences of that cataclysmic action might be?

Rangers had invented contingencies in the past to simply blow up the Reserve with RA militias and physically destroy the Galactic Bank. Such Rebel strategies were never dared attempted. Pinwheel never stopped rotating because of the fear, "What else is there?" Trillions of revolutions have happened in Pinwheel's History. What replaced the Totalitarianism? What was the alternate to dystopia? What was the next step or the answer?

I'm going to make every dylar disappear!

Galactic quakes hit numerous systems with the force of old atomic bombs. Dimensional frequencies Mystics operated on were *rocked to the core.* Was the answer the snap of a finger making the Galactic Monetary Standard vanish? The galaxy almost fell off of its gyroscope.

Here was the first time in the Venusian proceedings the Speakers clashed in thoughts. Rather than the most dominate idea-phrase expressed in an orderly fashion, mental chaos ruled as Speakers 'spoke' out of turn, stepped on each other's thoughts and confusion was the only communication.

Is that wise, sir?
No! You cannot. That's the solution?
Bomb the Reserve is the answer!
Should we not spend dylars on our charitable

enterprises and Good-Will projects to help the starving, the needy and defenseless?

Not Speakers but unscheduled Ranger Corps expressed in the background, *We buy services and protect the galaxy with paid Guardians. We use dylars the way they should be spent, for thousands of services, Good Police that maintain Law and Order. You want to destroy the Good with the Bad?*

One Speaker after another spoke as the sectors took turns and conveyed fears of a world where dylars did not exist. Neo Zog was absolutely correct that, within yas, his great admirers would turn on him.

More chaos reigned over the psychic dimension connected to the rest of the galaxy. A few Speakers shouted at the Neo Zog, even *cursed*. Some representatives were angry as their sectors were generally angry. NZ forgave them and understood they did not see the whole perspective. He forgave them for not understanding the full range. Now they threw thoughts at Cal-El like hot bullets (rocks) and acted very disrespectful.

The 48 Speakers in white remained sitting. One who had not spoken had the courage to stand. He thought he had the right to ask, *You are suggesting a result more devastating than the horrors of a Nuclear Age. What gives you, an outsider, the right to so alter a world you say you love? Why? So dylars can experience Nirvana?*

Living Beings are not dylars.

We know in the larger Game, they are, thought the Speaker with inside information.

Sardon's total Machine must die. NZ almost enjoyed the exchange on the psychic stage. The World Watched with literal closed eyes. *What would you have me do?* Cal-El sincerely asked for a better option.

Destroy only the Reserve!

And then what? A monstrous disintegration chamber for dylars is ended. Its reign of Terror is over? The Second Reich and its insidious Evil Mechanism finally ended? Look around. You remain slaves to the horror the Devil established!

There is no rejoicing until every last scrap of the Devil is gone. Do you understand?! NZ was very angry.

The standing Speaker expressed his original thoughts. The psychic point ended the tribute. Everything was different now after the galaxy heard: *By your final solution of complete dylar elimination, how are you doing anything different than what the Sardon had been doing?*

(My Zog, oh, my Zog! Dear Zog! The Speaker had just thought New Zog was the same as the Sardon.)

Bombs were heard around the sectors and the sounds were the deep disappointment in the Center of a Zog-Man called Cal-El. His appearance in a black cape that lingered from the book-signing was a bad idea. His dark persona was misinterpreted by adepts that should have known better. By changing to lighter colors in a thought now, the move could only make the situation worse. He stayed with the black attire. Inside he cried once more but would not let a tear show on the outside. But he was not that strong. He could not maintain the façade.

Cosmic gasps were telepathically transferred by Mystics to other Mystics. Forty-seven Speakers did not agree with the one Speaker who came forward. He went far over the line and was too critical of the Neo Zog, in most Citizens' opinions. Others screamed in their minds: *Explain yourself!*

The lower, standing one did. *We have seen, before the fact, the Royal Waterfall, three different colored snakes, a chain of Money, slide into the Devil's mini-Black Hole annihilation for nearly an eternity. You removing our power, dissolving all dylars everywhere, you are professionally doing in one stroke what the amateur Devil took ages to do!*

If previous jabs to CE were red beam nukes, the firm thoughts of the brave Speaker were *White Beam Atomics.* More Cal than Cal-El, he could not stand the psychic heartbreak of the last few yas. He did not care of his appearance, how it looked to the galaxy of enlightened beings. He wondered, *Would yahoos understand any better?*

Money was wrong.

Neo Zog streaked through the long passageway and out of the southern polar opening of Venus in a flash. Zog-Man knew the tribute would not go well. He was unaware it would result in a complete and total disaster. It was true, outcomes he knew not. Cal-El did not have a friend in the world.

Was I wrong? Am I going to do the wrong thing and truly hurt that which I love? Do I only want to destroy the Sardon's Creation as it would corrupt the Continuum continuously? Am I acting the same, only in reverse? Am I getting back at the Zogs who disagreed with my decision to Return? Were they right? Will I regret coming back? Am I being punished? If these were my Psychic-Friends-Network, what will happen when I face my real enemies?

***

Far away, in a section of a hidden asteroid close to the Wormhole Nebula, stood a newly constructed base of May Eleanora Bulair and her three minions from Hensi. Presently, the bio-body (android) of the little girl was in the throes of lovemaking. Tituus and Rambus were not involved. Behind locked air-locks and in the private bedroom of the little starlet, she had designed a dark/sexy bungalow. Lady Braw and the Devil-child had been going at it for yams. Sounds were occasionally registered by two phantom brutes on the other side of air-locks.

The loudest screams of passion definitely made it to the dull senses of the terror twins, Tituus and Rambus. They shook ghostly, wooly heads and did not understand the point to sex. Outside of the bio-circuitry exercise for Mebby, the big brutes did not comprehend its purpose.

"Brrraaawwww, I like that," the naked child-machine in bed said of her partner. "Laaady Braaaaaw sounds lil' better than Yram Escovilla-2, eh?"

"Ha, ha." The woman had a very satisfied look on her hot face, as well as some bio-fluid. Her distinct eye makeup ran into two long streaks. Now one could see their hair colors. The Lady had blue hair while Mebby had changed hers to long and black.

Each tasted the GUARP-7 and thought they were in Nirvana. The psychedelic had an expanding-effect on the bio-droid child. She *got off,* and she should not have.

"Did all you Vipers have big tits? I don't recall."

"Ha," Braw squealed in laughter. The amazing specimen and still attractive Warhorse from an age ago stroked the Devil-girl's soft cheek. The child was real in every way and performed in every way. The GUARP kicked in. Braw asked her boss, "Well, do I get the job?"

"Hmmm. Not so fast. What kind of pushover do you think I am, honey? Hm, you *disarm* Tituus, get that weapon off him...*then* you're First Officer and can sit on my right. Understand, babe?"

"Got it."

"And none of those words of endearment in front of the Bozing phantoms, right?"

"Aye, aye, Captain, your eminence, sir." The wild, nude woman laughed and arm-saluted her master.

"Just see that you get the N-Ray gun!"

"He might not be as easy to seduce, you know, as you were, ha, ha."

"Right, right." The Beast grinned and realized she could use the bitch. They ingested more GUARP and returned to touching and licking their bodies.

***

Cal-El found a lonely planetoid and made a home near the WH Nebula. In a few moments and with only a few thoughts, a fabulous 'Fortress of Loneliness' was created. He needed some place to rest, gather his thoughts and call a *home.* El could not return to his First Home if he wanted to, and he did not want to. He could not return to his second home, which was destroyed. He needed support and had none.

Cal-El remembered the prehistoric discovery of giant record-crystals and made a duplicate of them in this empty, lonely place. He could use the copied information inside and access a great Computer of stored data. El had his spectrum of consciousness for info, and his own Mastery of Machines could also come in handy. He hoped the knowledge would soothe his soul and guide his actions. He rested. He closed his eyes.

NZ knew what needed to be done. Every last dylar could be vaporized from every coffer and financial file in the galaxy. Yes, chaos would occur in the aftermath. But destroying the Mark of the Devil had to be the correct decision. Yes, initially, there would be pain, strife and struggle in the confusion. What would *win the day* in the long run had to be a better alternative. Cal-El was not wrong. The 'blue entity' was blind to every possibility and final resolution. Neo Zog was a Child with hope in its Center. He did not know for certain *what* would occur when the *Great Machine's plug was pulled.* He only knew it had to be done: one huge and very painful *extraction.*

***

Mebby drove the Dread and on her right was First Officer, Tituus. Rambus and Braw were in the rear at their original seats. Past events were not mentioned. Only the future was allowed to be discussed. She put the 'baby arsenal' in gear and skimmed over a planet of primitive natives.

Tituus thought hitting the thaser-toggle a few times would amuse the little darling brunette. (mmmmnntt) (mmmmnntt) It did not.

"Stop, I'm over that! No, no, no!" the Captain commanded.

The quiet brute in the back spoke. "Bigger."

Braw commented, "It spoke, ha. Seriously?"

Tituus explained, "My colleague means to say destruction on a larger scale should appeal to you more, Captain. Might I suggest reviewing sector Mainframes for the Nuclear Secret? Unleashing atomic horrors again will strike at ancient fears from days long gone, but unforgotten."

"Strike One against you, my First Officer, for not doing your homework."

"What?" The big brute was surprised.

"You think me so dim as to not check my robotic sources, all of them, for that contingency? Impossible. We are sealed away from the possibility and you should have known that, #1 against you."

"I meant no disrespect, Captain."

"I'll do the thinking, my First Officer who may not have the position long." She piloted the craft into deep space. "Try to impress, next time."

Tituus bowed from First Chair. "I will do better, Master."

Lady Braw spoke, which got the immediate attention of the bothered First Officer. "Rambus has a point. We need something bigger. I understand your need, sir, to destroy the world HE loves. The Question is, how to maximize obliteration and blame it on your Enemy?"

"*That's* what I want to hear."

Braw asked with respect and curiosity, "Your plan?"

Mebby was quick to answer. "It won't be *my* plan. It will be *his.*"

"Neo Zog?" the Lady asked.

"Yes, dear. A poor Zog-awful tragedy will once again befall the galaxy."

Braw questioned again, "What big tragedy, if I may ask, sir?"

"Ha. That would be the complete collapse of everything I've created in the past. Ha. Fantastic! I couldn't ask for more chaos, myself."

Rambus spoke, and he hardly ever spoke. "I do not get it."

"Surprising," the Lady replied in sarcasm.

"Hmmmm." The Hensi Child spoke to herself. "No one will Transcend if *I'm* the one in charge at the end of the game."

The ex-Viper asked, "Which game?" The girls made eye contact.

Captain Mebby responded to the question by her 3rd Officer and prized pupil. "Didn't matter, ha, ha."

The two tall, dark apparitions from the Upper World only looked at each other. They were worried of their Avatars' existence in the Pinwheel's plane of reality. Both demons were not happy with the sisterhood brewing between Braw and the Captain-child. Their lovely lives on the dark base and inside Dread were not going to end well.

May's Dread entered a new star system she had not terrorized previously. Meb's plan was to *declare War* on the galaxy. She would create a Media Monster, now that the old one had served its purpose and was on its way out. She would broadcast lies that Selestra Matrix's Mystery Domes had made contact with the Continuum, this Floor. Finally, after yarns, the Larger World warned over every channel that a military strike would soon occur.

The galaxy believed the News. They were at War with an unseen Enemy. Zogs had come to destroy them, their microscopic life from high above. Media channels informed the galaxy of a (fabricated) message supposedly from hidden enemies in Black Domes. Citizens were told 'mad Anarchists on an incomprehensible Level above had moved in with evil motives.'

Media transmitted lies. "Zogs are to blame for the mounting fear in the centers of the world!" Citizens were paranoid of the Zogs' Power. They remembered prehistoric records (The Testament) of ruthless punishments handed down by the Ones in charge from Nirvana. Now Citizens believed Zogs used Media networks to tell us: "The End is Near!"

The Universe was upside-down. Citizens, who had spent lifetimes in service and worship to the Zog or Zog or the Zogs, became firm disbelievers. Mystery Schools lost faith in Zog and lost large numbers of students. Many turned away from E-City, their Centers, and lost every trace of hope, faith and confidence in the future. The announcement was:

"We are at War, and Zogs are ready to strike at our hearts or attack the very lifeblood of our galactic system!"

The GST was 2001.91.

Punishment was the disappearance of every last dylar.

Fortunes were wiped clean. The Galactic Reserve, its physical structures were destroyed without atomic bombs, N-Rays or RA thaser beams. Instead, the State's financial Storehouse Vaults were *emptied.* Profits from Corporate Empires to dylar-holdings of individuals disappeared. Every last dylar in credit-files dissolved to nothing, and the Pinwheel stopped spinning.

***

Cal-El had no idea what he had done. There was no more of the *electrical blob* dylars were made from. In other words, no more d. could ever be minted and distributed. Cal-El was perfectly played by a Devil masked as the 'world's sweetheart.' *Money was gone.* Files were empted in every sector at precisely the same time. The greatest heist in galactic History occurred as if by Magick. It was as if every dylar had been *wished away.* Money *was* wished away and in its place was only Hensi.

The force-field wall guarding the Monster Mechanism was broken and gone. Trinars did not break the Machine's FF, Neo Zog did. No endless, triple-barreled conduit of dylars existed anymore. The colored 3-way 'Waterfall' had dried up. *The Great Machine was finally dead.*

The blue light entity killed the Dragmar Vidor and the galaxy was at a standstill. New Zog, as rep of the Zogs, was rightly blamed for a total Galactic Economic Collapse. Media portrayed recent events as Acts of War or "Attacks from the Macro-World." Telecasted lies covered the 'fact' that the 'Fall of the Federal Reserve' was a terrorist act by all the Zogs. Cal-El *was* the true 'Lone Gunman' and the true radical-Rebel, solo-destroyer, while Media networks broadcasted nothing but an all-out assault from hidden terror-cells throughout the sectors. The 'Conspiracy' telecasted on every network channel was untrue.

Mebby-Devil was behind the Media bombardment that swayed trillions of Citizens. She manipulated machines and artificial 'voice-whispers.' Neo Sardon influenced much of Occult Media with hidden hands. Her three minions were sent on missions to set the most powerful Selenium explosives available and wipeout key political targets. Machines were also forced to execute and cover-up the bombings. The impression was the Continuum was really *at War* and under secret attack. In the minds of the majority of Citizens, this time the 'Zogs Made War' and life could soon be totally annihilated! Fear and panic were felt in every Quadrant.

The Black Domes of Mystery were impenetrable. Channels could report anything about them. Recent messages from inside the Domes were false, yet Citizens believed what they were told. Media informed Citizens the domes were 'bases for scouts prior to the big invasion.'

"Who else would attack us but these dark forces from the Outside Universe?" *(Why not broadcast they were Zog's Domes? Why not now use 'Zog' to strike fear into the Centers of Citizens?)* "How do we fight a War against Supreme Beings?"

Neo Zog *felt pulled* as if once more a battle had to be fought. The Battle he sensed was unlike the hyped war of 'Citizens vs. Zogs' found everywhere in the multi-Media. Cal-El sensed another encounter. The new, upcoming meeting that almost *had* to happen was far from a tribute. Neo Zog would face his real enemies at Sardon's Foundry (formerly Factory) and in the strange sector called 'Ghosts of Mars.'

'G of M' was the newly established *psychic enemy* of the Retz Council, leftover, timeless, negative entities from 'Belial' forces that dated back to the First Reich. They were 'Neo Ghosts' that had collected and were (almost) not connected to the Sardon-Mebby in any way. They were 'copycat killers' on a psychic level and also operated in the physical world. 'Ghosts of Mars' Sector was a negative Spacial Territory also known as 'The Forbidden Zone.'

One did not go there unless one wanted to be possessed.

A grisly phenomenon was known to occur within the dark 'Zone,' a center-hub for such terror in the galaxy. Space travelers who disregarded the well-posted warning signs or yahoos in primitive ships who did not know better were 'taken over' by old spirits. The cosmic *possession* or Identy Thefts did not happen in every case. Researchers, to Retz psychic researchers, claimed it only occurred in those with shaded Centers or ones without true hearts.

The sector's precise parallax dimensions were surveyed and nearly 'walled-off' in space. (One had to be a real yahoo to ignore the signs). WH travel between parallel sectors did not happen. Various research teams were set up far outside the contaminated Territory to study the dark phenomenon. Scientists claimed the sector was a focal point for a convergence of subtle N-Rays in the galaxy. Experts in technical fields viewed the half Quadrant as a Negative-Vortex without superstitions of 'evil spirits from the past' behind the highly-charged sector.

On the other hand, Retz psychic researchers understood these were old (Belial) enemies that reformed. They also understood the F-Zone was a prehistoric creation by early positive forces. Ancient 'bad guys' were virtually imprisoned there by ancient *good guys*. Primeval Wardens were long gone. Who would have dreamed spirits could return and build real killer-armies in the distant future?

The material presence of the 'Ghosts' was a network of Foundries that pumped out nasty War-Machines on a continuous basis. Militias were sold (used to be sold) to the highest bidders. Few knew the negative source for the state-of-the-art weaponry they purchased. The GM Forbidden Zone was the secret center for wholesale production of massive galactic deaths.

Cal-El wanted to *wipe them out.* He wanted to destroy every last weapon from Hensi. The War-Machines were not used fairly and justly as was conducted by Retz Rangers. The Foundry of Sardon and unaffiliated ones only *spit pure Death.* In Neo Zog's conscious mind, the death devices had to go. They had to stop killing his precious Life.

He would see to it, right now. Beehives of concentrated, mighty devices that towered into red skies were smashed over and over again by the physical Zog in the Universe. The avenging Blue Angel smote the mechanical monsters by flying into them at super speed.

Cal-El flew to planet after planet in the 'infected Zone' and reduced the production Foundries and militia-machineries to particles. The beautiful blue entity of Love destroyed killer-robots and the means for their creation.

Citizens ignored the major victory for good forces in the galaxy. The oddity was that the greatest Rebel Victory that had ever occurred in the galaxy went unnoticed, even by the great Retz Masters. The Machines, after total defeat and complete annihilation, scored a few points:

1) The dead devices *blocked* the psychic/real events of the Great Battle where NZ took out most of the War Machines in the galaxy. No one knew of the incredible Positive Act by the Zog that so loved the world.

2) The Battle took its toll on NZ and had a horrific overall effect. The flying Angel was too meticulous in his destruction of Evil. He took too long in the mission, in the area. He became affected or 'infected' simply by being within the Territory. He wavered. He fluctuated. He was in flux. He changed polarity. Cal-El became momentarily 'possessed' by the N-forces or n-entities concentrated in this place. He joined the Majority. He saw 'the Other.' He felt and understood his Anti. He empathized with the Dark Side of Things for a time much too long. The exact same effects the sector had on unsuspecting travelers also occurred inside Cal, the NZ. He became a 'Demi-Zog' and wanted to *destroy the entire Continuum!* Then he changed back to himself. He had to leave the Dark Matter radiation in the Territory as soon as he could.

3) The most devastating effect on the El of Cal was the implant of a tiny 'seed.' Defeated Machines, motivated by Mars Ghosts of early banshees, secretly transferred an evil Seed to the Neo Zog during battle. Cal-El had pulverized robo-devices, yet the Great Neo Zog was unaware of the Seed. In the same way his major accomplishment of 'Victory over the Foundries' was blocked from Retz view and History, so was

the existence of the Seed.

Unbelievably, NZ's real War with the Machines had little to do with the Devil-child. The Machines *lost the day,* but did dark forces really lose? Would the Continuum *not* continue in the future as a result? Ghosts always returned.

***

The Beast-child said from bed, "I think I know what a destroyed homeland feels like. Chilling, huh?"

"Really?" asked Lady Braw from the same bed. "You're not supposed to have ESP or feelings."

"I feel...*good* now. And another thing, a really big thing." May lifted her bio-mechanical arms to possibly show the length of a sizable fish. The Child made a motion to slice its head. She laughed. "I just realized something right now, huh. If *he* can bring them *up* to Nirvana's Light, then I can send them *down* to Hensi-Fires." A big smile enlarged on the little girl's artificial face. She changed from sweetness to ultimate joy and rapture.

Chapter Twelve

COMMERCE WARS DESTROY THE UNIVERSE

Ever so slowly, and ever so slowly again, the static Pinwheel started to rotate on its own. A stark difference in galactic spinning occurred from the Old Days as compared to the New Age. The Living Lathe now spun in the reverse direction. Yesterday's gyroscopic rotation was a smooth sliding, mechanical Clockwork. Today's *counterclockwise* turning was a dry, slow wobbling top unsure how to move and forever ready to fall over.

Then it fell. *The whole Monopdonow Continuum Galaxy disappeared!*

The 'Clashing Commerce' that replaced the destruction of the dylar and Galactic Reserve could not stand amongst sheer *panic.* Systems clashed and systems *crashed.* Similar monetary systems were created and failed without common support, backing. 'Trilars' and 'mylars' were unsuccessful proposed Standards. Money Wars raged without unification. Companies and Citizens *killed each other.* Chaos, confusion, cosmic corporate-wars, psychic battles and complete *fear in the space-ways* ruled the day, then...

There were no more days.

Pinwheel supported no Life. Pinwheel did not exist anymore. The New Age and the Living Lathe dissolved unlike Selestra Matrix. Dark Matter did not replace the space.

The 'small sector' of the Original Universe, the real one, was long gone due to nuclear insanity that occurred during the galaxy's First Age. Nothing was real. Everything that existed today was a 'Construct' that only *appeared* physically real. This microscopic portion of the total Universe was much quieter now.

What was really destroyed, evaporated and not there anymore?

A physical universe, or a portion of a fake one, was taken away. But it was only a *dream.* As the planet Mineer *was* real and then became a dream, so did the Pinwheel Galaxy long ago. Long after the *madness,* another attempt at Building reality was made, again and again...

The spinning 'dream' was destroyed. In the next turn, as an entire universe rotated on a Celestial Axis, (aboriginal) 'Dreamtime' reformed. Buttermoths awoke. Only dreams remained of the new world. But Dreams could be very real. Dreams could also be *Nightmares.* Future outcomes would soon be settled. Would Tomorrow be beautiful visions or Hensi-Fires?

The next sequence was a dream-sequence. Connected lives that had not met in the long-gone real world, now were well acquainted in an unreality.

[Former names would be used for reference rather than real names in the dream].

***

The 22nd Century appeared very promising. People had put away their warlike tendencies and the meek truly had inherited the Earth. Contact with ETs was not huge news anymore. Fifteen solar systems were discovered to have life much like our own and have communicated by radio telescopes. A few were visited. Hundreds of inhabited worlds were known. But contact with a *more advanced* species has not happened until now.

March 19th, 2101, was when our 'Mohawk' in the shape of a big Tuningfork slid into a nice/cozy orbit very high above the magnetic giant of 'Magnus' in Thanabar-Rix Sector. 'Magnetized filter-adapters' of the 'zogs' (aliens) seemed to be working just fine. They 'radioed' that: *As long as we have computer-capability, there should be no problems whatsoever.*

We had only been aware of the 'zogs' for months. Our space forces were anxious to, for the first time, utilize 'jump-ports' that many known life forms in the galaxy depended on for travel. This was also going to be our first encounter with Magnusian zogs. We, like others, cosmically commuted to the enormous planet so revered and so very different than Earth.

That was the catch, the rub: finally, we made friendly relations with (verified) good and extremely evolved creatures. We were invited to their home planet and found *magnetism* blocked our passage. Zogs remotely installed 'mag-filter-adapters' that provided a safe journey nearing Magnus. Everything was on track for the huge occasion of First Contact.

Magnus was composed of 99.9% magnetite. It was the only planet going around a weak white-dwarf star called LH-V32a. The planet was an anomaly with a whopping diameter of 962,788 miles, considerably more than a hundred times Earth's diameter. Magnus was a knowledge-center or 'Galactic Library' constantly visited by vast numbers of alien cultures. We were warmly welcomed to come and learn from the grand 'Magnusian Storehouse Library' once we passed through *magnetic barriers* and arrived safely on the surface. Captain and crew were honored to be invited, but was it really possible to land on a magnetic giant?

Adapters appeared 'stable' to the crew of three 'Hawks.' Captain Samuel Caladan, magnetic navigator-pilot Mada and media-journalist Mary Escovilla knew something was *wrong*. Mohawk was buffeted from side to side with severe *jolts*. The zogs transmitted it would be: *a smooth ride.*

Then it happened. Mohawk Tuningfork was in freefall as EM adapters *blew* for some reason. The ship was going to *crash into the magnificent, magnetic planet!*

"Mada! Can you *do* anything?"

"Doing everything I, I can, sir."

Three Hawks panicked as the fast fall accelerated toward a mega-magnetized planet. Terrified, each stood at stations while the ship rapidly plunged through many miles of atmosphere. With mag-filters offline, EM shields crumbled. The Tuningfork, thousands of light-years from home, was caught in the sudden *pull* of the massive planet. The intense attraction meant certain death for the crew, only a minute away. The craft was not built for violent *shaking.*

Mary asked in desperation, "Why? Why did this h-happen?"

"Damn aliens!" Mada said in anger. "We were lied to! Shoulda never let zogs remotely install anything, *Mary!*"

Mary Escovilla was *thrown to one side.* Navigator Mada was able to catch her and bring her to the floor without injury.

"Thank God," Captain Sam Caladan said in relief.

More vibrations shook the Hawk spaceship on a dramatic descent of eight hundred thousand miles at tremendous speeds.

Mada and Mary were able to move closer to the Captain as the control-center seemed to *come apart at the seams.* Mada had his arms around the shoulders of correspondent Escovilla. He told the Captain who was at fault. "We *never* shoulda believed them! Higher Order, my ass!"

Captain Sam replied, "Doesn't make s-sense. They wouldn't make First Contact, and, and make it a...death-trap."

Mada's response was, "Wouldn't they? What do we know about zogs?"

Caladan looked into the eyes of Mary still locked onto the navigator.

Mary spoke spontaneously. "Maybe...m-maybe *we're* at fault."

Mada found it hard to stare at the girl he held in disbelief as *more vibrations struck.*

Then the shaking ended. The interference subsided. The fall was smoother now. Possibly, they had a chance in the eye-of-the-magnetic storm as Magnus quickly approached.

"Now, shields up!" Captain Caladan shouted. "Can you slow our descent?"

Mada was closer to the controls and hit them in time. "All right, we're still out-of-control, but we got shields now and we're coming in slower."

"Good." Mary exhaled with less worry on her face.

"Brace for impact. Stations!" the Captain ordered.

All three strapped themselves in as the *tuned* EM 'Mohawk' in the shape of 'forked-ribs' *crashed into a Magnusian island.*

***

It was night on the side of Magnus where Mohawk crashed. The Earthlings, a long way from home, were unhurt. However, they were very confused and wanted answers.

"Can't see much," the navigator reported.

"Monitors? Something has to be working. Lights are on."

Mada corrected the Captain. "A *few* lights are on, sir."

Captain Caladan was curious and upset. "Well, *why* are certain systems on and other systems not?"

Mada studied the semi-operating, *charged* panel in front of him. His face contained little confidence. "You won't believe this, sir. Maybe it's just me who...who doesn't want to..."

"What?" impatient Captain Sam yelled.

Mary looked on with green eyes opened wide. Her short, blue hair was frazzled.

"Ah, apparently, only the systems with the operating 'zog' programs or apparatus-firewalls...are still functioning, sir."

"That's all?" Caladan asked.

Mada replied, "Only things working...are our systems the zogs reinforced, the ones they magnetized. All other normal, un-magnetized systems of ours are fused, ruined, no good."

The reporter realized, "Hey, doesn't that put a...*damper* on your alien-sabotage theory?"

The navigator was disgusted. Mada did not like the zogs. He did not trust them or any alien civilization, in fact. The navigator-pilot remained silent.

Captain Caladan added, "Sounds consistent to me. The enlightened Magnusians tried to help. Everything they touched still works. Seems like we have the zogs to thank for what systems we have operational."

The first smile occurred in quite awhile. Mary's smile changed to a smirk. She stared at Mada with her big eyes and said, "Yeah, we'd be dead in the water if not for the *4-armed cobra-people."* (That was how the alien-giants described themselves over the radio).

Mada was not amused and retorted an ominous thought. "We'll see."

***

The next morning, the men got one of the 'flying pods' working. They hovered over many miles of territory. Magnetized sensors that really would have come in handy were destroyed in the crash. Sam, Mada and Mary had: radios, a few weapons, provisions for years and one flying craft. But they were flying blind. Whatever they discovered had to be observed directly in line-of-sight. So far, there were only endless miles of dense jungles filled with harmless wildlife.

For an alien planet that had one of the most complex and technological cultures known to exist in the galaxy, what surrounded the magnetic astronauts was all too familiar. Where were the fabulous super-cities and reported metropolises, pyramids and mega-technology? What about the Great Libraries of information? Green jungles with plants mostly known to Captain Sam and crew were all that were seen. Only basic jungle animals were observed, so far. Most Magnusian creatures they glided over were common species known to thrive on Earth. But were they really on the planet Magnus? The flying pod continued speeding over the jungle canopy.

"You mean we may *not* be on Magnus?"

"That's right, Mary," Mada answered. "Lost in another dimension, ha."

"I don't believe that," declared the Captain. "Still strong magnetism."

"But considerably *less* than expected. Remember the *calm* moment during descent, right at the end?" Mada asked. "Our fantastic descent speed could have broken into or created a wormhole, right?"

"If that were true," Captain Caladan replied. "Then you know what it means?" He looked at Mary under the pod's bubble of protection.

She coughed up the correct answer. "We could be *anywhere* in time and space."

Suddenly, something appeared up ahead of them. Navigator-pilot Mada had to severely swerve the craft around a type of tower. They almost flew right into a tall monstrosity that did not fit among the thick vegetation. The pod descended and smoothly landed. Captain and crew turned to view what looked like a huge, marvelous, Mayan or Toltec 'stele' stone monolith.

"Wow, how impressive. It appears amazingly...*alien* and tribal, yet...strangely familiar, huh?" Mary said with a slow, enchanted accent.

Captain told them that the stunning work of stone was not created by primitives. The two men and woman were next to it now and touched it. They sensed no danger nor heard a sound nor felt the slightest vibrations from it. The 250-foot high and 50-foot wide stone-tower appeared *dead,* as if from some forgotten age. A possible 'God-image' or face was carved into the top portion. It reminded the crew of an Easter Island statue, only this one really maintained the form of a gigantic pole.

"Our simple compass tells us, it's magnetic," Mada revealed. "But, that's the *only* connection to the magnetic giant we were supposed to land on safely, *without a hitch.* Look around, Captain. Does this *look* like what you thought Magnus would be? The ground is fertile soil, not magnetite."

"It's a *big* planet, Mad. I grant you, blue skies, green vegetation, monkeys, lizards, snakes, jungle cats and only a very few *unknown* creatures...makes me wonder."

Mary added, "And now...*this.* What could the pillar's purpose be? Who the hell built it and why?"

"Maybe the natives need to phone home?" Mada joked. 'Or could be they need more power."

"C'mon." The Captain headed for the pod and the others followed. Soon after the bubble was sealed, they took off in search of answers.

The 'Hawks' continued in the same direction they'd

been heading. Hours later, nothing had changed. Always green jungles under blue skies. More blue appeared in the far distance. There was water, a blue ocean. The flying pod zoomed to the shore and found one more of those mysterious stone totems. This one leaned, very slightly, 200 feet out of sand and about 500 feet from shore.

They parked the pod.

The white-dwarf sun was extremely low in the sky. Night approached. Captain and crew of two had an eventful second day on the new world. What would happen on Day 3 or even this evening? Each stared into the fading sun not sure of anything.

"Did we really go through time, guys?" the Captain tossed out in the air. "We reached phenomenal speeds. It's...*possible*. Who knows magnetism?"

Mada asked, "You saying this is very early Magnus or a future Magnus?"

"I'm saying we don't have our answers yet and have to look around more. Wonder if the zogs will rescue us?"

"We could be a *hundred light-years* from zogs!" Mada exclaimed.

"Boys, there's something else."

"What?"

"I'm not the least bit tired," Mary said, raring to go for more action.

"Me too," Mada confirmed.

She went on, "We *should* be tired. No one slept last night. That's understandable. No one's *slept or ate* anything since *long* before the crash. Think about it."

"You're right, Mare," stated their leader who was very attracted to the reporter. Then he turned toward Mada. "That's one for it being Magnus."

"How'd ya mean, Captain?" asked the EM pilot-navigator.

"Maybe it's *magnetism* that's giving us energy? Maybe everything around us is using it as an energy source *more* than food or the dim sun and who knows if it rains? Or...maybe we're just plain *dead?"*

With that morbid thought voiced, so were other sounds. Strange, distant *tribal-drumming* appeared to emanate from a large valley not far from the shore. Soon, the adventurers knew what they had to do.

"I don't believe this," declared the Captain.

"Oh, we *have* to check it out," Mada said with excitement in his voice. They ran to the flying pod and were off to investigate the faint sounds.

In moments, the hovercraft silently eased close to the drumming. Trees and vines hid the pod and passengers within the darkness.

In a gigantic clearing, with another pillar in the foreground, there were a thousand dark-skinned natives pounding loud rhythms. Females danced to music-beats made by males. Around everyone's necks were rings of brilliant, blue light. The shoreline in the distance created a complimentary *harmony.* Slight and high luminous clouds were the only light source over the weird scene (outside of neck-rings). Were the natives chanting to the zogs? Were they calling King Zong?

None of this was how it's supposed to go down.

Captain Caladan, Mada and reporter Escovilla exited the small hovercraft. Mary used the bino-scope to see through the veil of blackness and get a close look at the drummers and dancers. Her mouth dropped. Her body language got the attention of the men. In a minute, the Captain walked over to her. He closed her mouth by lifting her chin.

"Give me that. It cost a lot o'money," Cal commanded in a joking manner as he grabbed the one working bino-scope they had between them.

He saw, in pink, close details of what Mary witnessed. His mouth also dropped. "I don't believe it. My God, the girls..."

Pilot Mada felt left out and did what normally he would never do. He snatched the scope out of his Captain's hands and peeked at the tribal people. He laughed and the others joined in the laughter. "Hey, they're not wearing clothes, ha. So *that's* what you're staring at? *Damn,* look at that...augh, ooooh!"

"But, wait a second. They didn't build the monoliths, even though they seem to number thousands," Mary stated. "You said when we first encountered it that nobody primitive made it."

The Captain replied with, "That's right. They're too colossal. One solid rock intricately carved that high? Who knows how many poles are on the island?"

"You mean continent, don't you, Captain?"

"Not necessarily, Mad. What seems like an immense continent to us could only be an average-sized island, to the Magnusians."

"Still think *this* is where we're supposed to be?" Mada asked.

A thousand drums intensified in rhythmic sounds. Industrial drumming of so many tree trunks crawled under the Hawks' skin.

Captain Caladan answered his navigator. "We may not be *where* we're supposed to be on the planet, but I contend...*this* is Magnus. Look how HUGE it freaking is."

Eyes locked onto Mary's eyes. She responded with, "Have to admit, Cap, not a lick of technology to be seen outside of the pillars. Storehouse of Knowledge and Libraries, sir? Were we lied to? Are we now *caged?"*

"We also haven't seen a lick of machines. Do the natives have boats, gardens? Do they even have houses, huts? I still say it's a big planet and we have only seen a drop in the ocean," Caladan asserted.

Mada added, "Hey, we haven't seen a lick of *clothing* either."

Mary laughed first. They all laughed.

"Sssssh." Captain Sam tried to quiet them. "I thought I heard..."

Suddenly, a volley of darts struck the Captain and crew. The Hawks dropped like flies.

***

Three Earthlings awoke and found themselves in 'hot soup.' They were literally in their own hot water ready to be *boiled to death.* Each was naked and tied with vines they could not break through. Each was mostly submerged in boiling, natural, hot springs. The astronauts had only minutes before succumbing to extremely intense heat.

More than a thousand dark-skinned, nude females danced as if they were possessed by demons around a pool of boiling water. The drumming on tree trunks was at an all time high level of loudness and vibration.

The dying crew saw an unimaginable sight. Naked primitives without anything at all (outside of blue neck-rings) were caught up in a religious frenzy to *raise the devil!* Loud chants with drum rhythms beat a repetitive, deadly chorus...over and over. Before the Earthlings passed out, they viewed the monstrous monolith with an idol-face *light up.* Lightning out of nowhere struck the charged electro-magnetic pole again and again as the naked crowds' loud commotion appeared to near climax.

A distant pillar on the shoreline also illuminated in sync with the bright device in the foreground.

The Captain tried to communicate with a native dancer near the sizzling pool. He thought he heard her say, without moving her lips: *You get this for stealing our people.*

More than a thousand tribes-people collapsed and fell to the ground. There was a splendid, electrical finale in the sky that centered on the monolith. Sam, Mada and Mary blacked out and would soon be dead. The Captain's last words were, "Is that a ship?"

***

The Hawks, especially chosen by Earth Forces, were saved by the zogs. The yellow Cobras finally located the three of First Contact. They were rescued by the Magnusian zogs precisely as Captain Caladan had hoped. A few more minutes of scorching waters would have cooked them.

Sam, Mada and correspondent Escovilla opened their

eyes at almost the same moment. Each sat in ultimate healing-comfort and Majesty as each occupied what was called a 'sarcopha-chair.' They were 97% healed and now experienced a pleasure-phase.

"Aaawww."

"Nice."

The room was one of many royal halls with ceilings hundreds of feet high held up by great columns in very bright colors. A giant 'cobra-person' sat across from the three Library visitors in its own sarcopha-chair in an extra-large size. Other Magnusians, with various duties, walked and attended to different sections of the ultra-enclosure.

The Captain smiled as he looked over to his sitting crew in contentment. He lifted his head and asked zog cobra-representative directly across from him, "Are you the King, ah, *The Zog King,* and, and is this your Castle?"

'King Zog' hid its version of laughing. The Magnusian scratched its yellow head with one arm and put away unfathomable technology with its other three arms. Another 18-foot Magnusian with side panels around its head like a cobra walked over to the sitting one. The 'King' pressed a chip the other held, which was similar to a *signature* the Captain imagined. Now personal business was concluded and the zog could attend to the small affair of the recovering visitors.

Mary and Mada continued to "oooh" and "aaah."

The psychic official answered the question without moving its narrow lips. *No, I am actually a low-level librarian and this is an average-sized room.*

"My God!" Sam spat.

I must thoroughly apologize for your experience on Magnus. This really has not happened before. We localized the problem.

Mary spoke up and asked, "What caused the crash, for everything to go haywire?"

The zog explained without audible words, *A flare in your nuclear reactor caused a computer glitch. Earlier, we asked if you had 100% computer access for our mag-filter-*

process to work. But after the flare, a crinkle in the magnetic fabric or gravity wave meant, for that nanu-second, you did NOT have your computers running, and that was our prerequisite.

"Lousy computers. It *was* our fault, not theirs." She winked at Mada.

Mada felt amazing and was very happy to be alive. *Maybe aliens weren't so bad.* He sincerely told the librarian, "Thank you, for saving our lives, sir."

The Magnusian smiled a big cobra-smile and telepathically thought: *Questions. You must have more questions. Must have had a horrible ordeal in the game preserve.*

"Game preserve, huh?" Captain Caladan was stunned. "Who were the tribe-people? They're...they're not your animals, sir?"

Certainly not, thought the zog. *Their star was atomicly erased and we rescued them by allowing them to believe they escaped. We set up a game preserve with similar conditions of their home world. Once in awhile, we capture a few, test them for their own good and then release them back into the wild.*

"Now I understand what I thought one of the girls...*say?*"

"What?"

"Never mind," replied the Captain. "But why did they attack us?"

I am sure they resent any form of technology, now. They thought you were us and attacked you because of us. Strange, they pray to the poles. They are ancient Earthlings from a real dream, yet not as primitive as they appear.

Mary asked the psychic zog in charge, "It seemed like they brought on the electrical storm, when the pillars lit up with power."

No, no, they respond in tribal ritual to the dampeners' cycle, every 14 of your hours.

"Dampeners?"

Monoliths nullify much of the magnetism. High levels

would kill them, but the right amount sustains them without the need for food, crops, even housing. They survive and thrive with a lot of energy concentrated in the ringlets they wear.

The Captain slowly realized, "That's why we felt good. So the rest of your planet is nothing like the island?"

Nothing, the zog-giant communicated. It appeared Egyptian in the huge sarcopha-chair. The Cobra-man had another smile on its yellow face framed by panels.

"Now what?"

Now we see the rest of Magnus. It is a big planet. You cannot see all of it, but I will guide you to selected parts I know you will enjoy. By the way, you DID bring your Library Card, didn't you?

"What Library Card?"

The dream-librarian rephrased its punch line: *If you don't have one, one can be purchased for only 10 million dylars.*

"What are dylars?"

Suddenly, the stupendous room changed as if a new computer program dominated; took control and changed foreground and background to a different 'skin.' Colors changed on columns, pillars and fantastic statues. Parameters of the virtual program *shifted.* The dream changed into something much larger.

***

The Galaxy remained in limbo of a phased-out realm unconnected to the real world. Reality to Citizens was a phantom-existence without photonic substance of any kind. Could the spinning Pinwheel Top be saved and returned to existence? Would Zogs in the Higher Game play a 'Card' or make a move that materialized the Old Continuum, the way it was? Could a universe maintain itself separate from the 4th Builder's Architecture? The answer was contained in an after-dream similar to an afterimage, a faint echo wave of inertia. The same dream repeated, but the appearance was drastically different...

***

Admiral Caladrian and his generals, Mada, and Escovilla, entered the amazing 'Arena' 12,000 bars high! Purple Zogs had a great lack of dials or buttons for the vehicle's 'Control Room.' The Bridge of the Great Ship appeared as a beautiful, round, white 'lagoon' with soft steps on its borders. Décor was minimal with only a few white shapes, which were curved and very smooth.

Zogs were inconceivably tall, bald Humanoids. Prime Zog was busy. 'He' attended to two other oversized Zogs with official Business. The Admiral imagined there was much to handle in the aftermath of a *whole galaxy's destruction.* Admiral and crew of two slowly crept closer to three violet 'Mythic' Super-Giants.

The two Zogs finished and left after 'clicking' bands around thin wrists. They towered very high above the Mineerans. Prime Zog welcomed Hawkeye's crew as his small mouth bent into a tiny smile.

The Admiral and two generals sat in midair. They knew a 'chair-blob' would instantly 'pop' into reality and catch them. They were used to that on the enormous ship. The soft comfort was *extraordinary.* Zog approved with a nod.

Caladrian decided to talk for the others and concentrated exactly on the words he spoke. In that way, anything improper from the subconscious would tend *not* to be in the conversation.

"Thank you for your excellent treatment over the past half yam. We've been in a magical dreamland of delights. I hated what the Zogs had done, *destroyed an entire galaxy."* The Admiral looked down, sadly. "Still *do* hate them." Then he stared directly up into the leader's human eyes. "But, I have a slightly better understanding as to *why!* Maybe, it *had* to be done? Because it was Hensi on a Galactic Level, as well as Mineer. But, SIR…I question this."

The Admiral was from a war-torn Mineer and a worn-torn, battered Pinwheel. His sadness could not be hidden. He represented a possibility too awful to comprehend. *His Mineer was not destroyed.* His Mineer continued. It was not vaporized, pulverized, poisoned to extinction or nuked to smithereens. Reality for Hawkeye's crew was a society incredibly ravaged by *War.* Wars did not end for yarns. Mineer was never in danger of total destruction. The Admiral's Mineer was a seemingly eternal stage for battles, revolutions, suffering, poverty, killing and the worst of the 'Human Animal' on an endless track.

So too was the Larger Continuum. The small one affected the Big One and vice versa. What could be said for the planet Mineer/Earth could also be said for the rest of the galaxy and *beyond.* There were legitimate reasons for the Zogs to declare the Pinwheel Nexus a 'Forbidden Zone.' The Devil's Camp or ingrained Web of Evil which perpetuated cosmic corruption had to be eliminated, even the one afterimage Dream-version of reality. Mineer had become real *Hensi.* But a far more massive crime also occurred: 'The Galaxy in which Mineer Floats' had also become Hensi. *It too had to go!*

The Admiral cried to his Zog. The 'Man of War' prayed to the Zogs to save his hopeless planet *and* precious Pinwheel it spun around.

Prime Zog, over a 100 bars high, smiled and replied telepathically with, *I understand inside you, what is inside you, you are the One.*

War-Admiral Caladrian certainly was oblivious to the violet Zog's remarks as the thoughts flew overhead, literally. He cut the titanic King off with, "Oh, I never *thanked you.* I want to thank you for sparing our lives. I am so sorry to interrupt. You were saying, please."

The purple super-giant Boss appeared to smile more and was not offended. *I understand you. We see into you and know what troubles you. You wanted another resolution. You wanted an answer other than annihilation for your planet and galaxy, where it could work, as it was, and for us, like 'Wings Over the World,' to enforce change, change for the better.*

"Yes."

What of the War? Prime Zog expressed concern over

the constant Mineeran War.

The crew was confused. Caladrian asked, "You mean on Mineer? Oh, you mean the Resistance Movement against *you* when you arrived?"

Your resistance would have escalated until wars destroyed your own planet in the worst of ways, which, of course, would not have ended there. Tell me, Admiral Caladrian, did our worldwide presence in your space for yarns, in your skies, END the wars and unite your planet?

"Ah, in fact, they did *not, sir.*"

Prime Zog continued in thoughts, *Wars raged on, wholesale destruction with mass casualties while our ships hovered above you. You were still trying your best to kill each other, even with us standing over you! It did not end there.*

The Admiral shook and cried in front of his crew. "I know h-how bad it was, Zog! The pain, the starving, even Bozing *c-cannibalism.* I almost don't blame you for wiping out Life. It was *that bad* here and elsewhere." Cal let go a torrent of tears. He fell off the chair-blob and hit the soft, white floor.

The lovely General Escovilla now had long, blue hair. She breathlessly added, "The rich had so much, it could have worked. With...with a...re-redistribution of dylars."

Could it? The way it was? As it was in the Old Days?

Former General Mary cried along with the Admiral. "Something should have been *tried,* sir. Anything!"

The Admiral was a sad warrior. He served his Federation well. In truth, fighting was not his way. He was a Child of the Universe who did not understand the reality of his parents' world. He knew it was futile. Prime Zog was right. Cal's planet and Continuum had gotten so terrible: *we were an abomination to Life!* We *had* to go. "Oh Zog, I thought you were going to save the galaxy."

We did.

"You destroyed everything!" General Mada joined his small leader's voice and screamed. *"That's* your idea of saving the galaxy?" His anger exploded from his Center.

No. This is. Suddenly, the purple gargantuan took a few

steps to another part of the curved Bridge. The move was very dramatic and it was hard for the three little ones to keep up. Prime Zog walked to the edge of the perfect, swooping lagoon that was not a lagoon. Prime Zog waved his hand over nothing. *Here you will see.*

What? the former Admiral thought. "I learned Venusians were on our side all the way, with Tesla and Thor coming to Mineer. Retz Council wanted to intercede and help us...and then they were completely nullified by...*what?* A group called 'Ghosts of Mars' where dark forces in a war between positive and negative, Past vs. Future from long ago, still continue to make war?"

Yes, over here, Admiral, everyone, please, thought Prime Zog.

The Admiral had a strange interlude and stated facts from vids displayed on the super-ship. Much was learned recently. The crew had to take dozens of steps to match what the violet Giant stepped in only one. A minute passed. High over their heads:

The Prime Zog moved his long, slim arm so that his six-fingered hand hovered over a white orb in midair.

They finally trekked the entire distance to the edge of the pretty lagoon-thing. Admiral Cal and generals were directly under the shining orb, far below. They stared intently at what was above them in the enormous 'Arena.'

"Wait. What did you say?" *Saved the Galaxy?*

A copy is right here...saved. Prime Zog expressed this as nonchalantly as if we hit 'save as' on our computers. White orb became a sparkling, fresh, bright and shiny galaxy. A miniature version of the entire Pinwheel Galaxy in its early stages stood over Hawkeye's crew like a Rocketball *frozen in time.*

The big, bald Zog with six fingers pressed a section of his wristband on a thin wrist. The holographic image-matrix of the 'New Plan' expanded outward and stretched to the astronomical proportions of the real galaxy. The glorious lights were absolutely magical, clean and perfect.

With another 'hand wave' the Prime Zog said goodbye and the crew was on a new Mineer. This seemed very real. They returned to crying after what they *felt*. It wasn't the end of the galaxy or their planet. It was the reason the Admiral and generals never got a terrible, negative vibe from the grape Giants who wiped out the Pinwheel. It was left up to *them* to arrive at a resolution. Mineer II and Galaxy II began without the bad, without the rich, without money, without fascists, without governments, without the State, without nukes, without Police, without the need for armies or guns and Secret Systems. It would be a joyous place with visitors from human and alien colonies of other planets and galaxies.

"We will be Cosmically Incorporated." Everything will work this time because our children will be educated on the right way to live in the universe.

Would you like to rename it? asked Prime Zog.

"You're kidding?" Caladrian stared up into the Titan's eyes then down to Mary's eyes. Here was a final punctuation mark to a galaxy that will start anew. Cal said the first word that formed in his mind: "Monopdonow."

"What?"

"Why did I say that?"

"Ha, ha."

It has been renamed...and saved.

***

...the beginning of another dream...

Inside the 'Elysia Health Spa' on planet Jaxpar in the Thanabar-Rix Sector, an unusual rendezvous happened. Cal-El along with his 'first followers,' Mada (now renamed Pe're) and the beautiful Mary Escoville took a dip.

Elysia was one of the most potent and exclusive Health Spas in the galaxy. The 'steamy pools of luxury' were famous for the ultimate in 'Nez' relaxation. The rich as well as famous celebrities used the 'living' spas. The pools could be reserved for groups, private parties or solo-meditation sessions 'without another person in the universe.'

The session of interest involved a 'planned meeting' by the secret New Zog only referred to as 'Cal-El' and his first two 'believers.' Cal appeared like old Cal before the metamorphosis only now he had very long white hair. He had an amazing body. But he was not *the body*. He was the perfect energy inside a body. Now, 'the body' was naked and so were the bodies of his two dear friends as they soaked in supreme peace and comfort.

The warm, misty and hazy 'dip in the pool' did wonders for the mind and soul. As far as eyes could see, no one else occupied their secluded cove. The initial reaction from three heads on top of three shoulders above the waterline was, "Aaaahh." Then they spoke to the Master who only wanted to be 'one of the gang.'

Pe're had long blonde hair. He was clean-shaven and renewed. He first asked about his surroundings. "How can this be real? How can it really be you, Cal-El?"

"What makes you think this is real? Or that *we* are real?"

Mary laughed and Pe're remained in deep thought. She was also fully renewed and had that clean, fresh look. Gone were the wild eye makeup, headdress, rivets and tattoos. She had long white hair that matched Cal's.

"Hmm. So what are you saying? Don't worry about Life, take each moment as it comes?" she asked in complete serenity.

Cal said, "We can make Life a paradise or nightmare. We choose."

"Aaah, well…it feels like a paradise at the moment."

The naked goddess (in Cal's eyes) said, "Cal, tell me please, about…Transcendence."

"You make me proud, my child. You don't have that now, as it stands, but you will. I assure you, brother and sister, everyone will be able to see, know and experience my world, if they deserve to. At least, they might have a fighting 'Chance,' if I have anything to say about it."

Pe're was amazed. "How could you *not?* You are the Zog and at peace, One with your Center. You *know.* You have told us how we have the same potential only have not reached that point, yet, with our soul-Center. How could you *not* be in control or the one in charge?"

He told the changed friends and first followers, "Everything I have accomplished, she has nullified."

Time passed as his 'initiates' computed Cal-El's words. A sudden sadness pervaded the tranquility.

Pe're asked a strange question, "Why do I see Mebby as a Beast, I mean, a *really horrible* Beast?"

"You are fortunate to see behind her mask. Others will in time."

Pe're asked an unanswered question. "Cal-El, how do you change a world and give it immortality?"

Mary loved Cal. She saw into his deep eyes and understood his soul-Center. She knew the answer (sacrifice), and it was revealed in her gorgeous face and green eyes, now riddled with fear and even more sadness.

"I have a question," Cal asked aloud of himself. "What if they don't want what I am offering? What if no one in the precious Pinwheel wants what I will give up my Immortal Life for?" Another silence went around and Cal-El was thankful he was able to share his pain. Cal *did* have friends in the universe. Simply, other souls to speak to helped a lot.

CE did more thinking out loud, more dreams within dreams. "What if I could make Nirvana *on Mineer* or anywhere in the galaxy? Life could *ascend.* Experience my timeless Dimension, escape the horrors of mortality and physical death and enter a true *Continuum* that really lasts through infinite Time."

She magically said, "We don't want your spirit-energy to die just so we can live forever, my love."

He beamed more radiantly, more proudly. "You are speaking of love. And so am I." They understood as tears dropped into the perfect waters of the lake.

Pe're, formerly Mada, wondered, "Cal, why would they

not want your special gift of eternal Life, the whole Ascension and Transcendence to an afterlife-eternal? I don't understand. Why would you ever contemplate such an absurd idea, sir?" Both Initiates looked on for the answer.

Cal started to explain with a big smile. "You see, dear friends, the tragedy or Fall-Out from the brainwashing and your dependence on the dylar-system..."

"What?"

"You can't take it with you. To Ascend, to actually transcend, when given the rare chance, this extraordinary opportunity that you never had before, to enter the Kingdom of Nirvana, the *real* City-Lights...you have to *give up all your dylars."*

"Huh?"

"You cannot have even one yellow chip of 100,000 d. if you expect to Win in the Ascension Game, *Life!* What do you do when given the exceptional chance? Do you decide to *not ascend* and stay in the Rat-Race game of cutthroat, corporate Capitalism to win? OR, do you give up everything? What an un-Capitalistic concept, to not sell, but to *give,* freely."

"Wait, that's not right." Mary believed she had a sudden realization. "There *are* no dylars. You wished them away, right?" She was puzzled.

"They're baaack," Cal-El informed his friends and followers.

"What? How?"

"And, so are *we,* to try again. There's still hope for the 4th Construct and Tomorrow."

NZ had confused them, but they and others would come to understand.

***

In the Devil's universe of her reverse-spinning Pinwheel, the 'Zogs' continued to be blamed over Media for the galaxy's woes, especially, the New One. The New Zog was 'Wanted' by Authorities like any 3-named villain. Tray Samuel Caladan's likeness and biography were displayed on Media channels. Network machines were absolutely correct: the New Zog was alive in the real world as designer, Tray Caladan. Zog became an 'Outlaw' with a maximum reward of *500 million dylars for his capture!*

The evil minions Tituus, Rambus and (doppelganger) Lady Braw with bright/red hair were ordered to bomb key targets. Lady Braw had brains as well as brawn. She brewed a plot of sabotage or coup against little Mebby, thick and creamy. Could the 'plan' work? Could she keep her thoughts far from the bio-machine of Evil that was not supposed to be 'Mystic' in any way? When she questioned the artificial child's telepathic abilities, she actually was more curious if her *plan* could work.

She did not bomb her targets. She created false evidence that it was the Monster-phantoms that did not follow Mebby's commands. But her far-fetched move-of-moves, envy of any Romvoid player, was her deal with Tituus.

How brilliant were the Dark Side brutes from the Upstairs Floor? Not very: to be so gullible and swayed by the possibility of acquiring Power. Was a thirst for 'control' in the physical realm such an appealing treasure trove? Did Tituus and Rambus want to prove a point to their Clan of negative-Zogs back Home that they could defeat the Child of the Beast? Was it a Challenge?

Lady Braw with headdress, makeup, rivets and tattoos called her own secret meeting. Previously, each Monster took turns using Dread for their missions of sweeping Selenium destructions while Mebby was busy with her future film. (The doll had commitments and engagements. One would think the Devil would *not* be at the mercy of YN agents, but she was. Certain appointments *had* to be kept). When it came to Lady Braw's turn to toggle ('activate') her bombs, instead, she presented her idea of a coup against the robo-child.

First, the persuasive Lady teased them with her charms (cleavage). The Phantoms were clueless. Then she laid lies on about what they could do in the galaxy *without* the Child from Hensi. They were slaves to a tiny robot. Braw convinced them, as soon as the bombing jobs were over, that little Mebby planned to *wipe the Avatars out!*

Braw asked Tituus the obvious. "Why not shoot her with the N-Ray gun?"

Its response was, "The child is unaware my Sect has strictly forbidden that in code. My hands are tied because of the Larger Game. I can intimidate Daughter of Sardon, but I am not allowed to nullify the force-field and break her."

"I'll do it!" Braw said as if the concept was spontaneous.

"Explain," the First Officer demanded. The Monster was intrigued.

Rambus, the quiet one, looked at its hairy Brother-beast.

Lady Braw said with the calm confidence of a Rom Sector native, "Their code does not stop *ME* from doing it."

"Whaaa?" chirped out of Rambus.

"Zog!" she shouted. "Why haven't we thought of this before?" Braw acted surprised.

"W'tha work?" Rambus asked after it turned to Tituus.

The Roval ball was in Tituus' curved court. What would the thing do? It made the wrong move when it handed the Gun to Lady Braw as if it sealed a deal between them. For a split-m-ya, the Beasties held the belief they could actually 'rule the galaxy.' They were ready to celebrate, until...

...A blast wave of N-Rays was discharged! She sent the screaming creatures back to the dark corners of the Upper cosmos they came from. The Monsters were gone from the relatively smaller Continuum. And Mary Escovilla-2, aka Lady Braw, had the Gun.

***

When Mebby Bulair extracted herself from her public entourage and Inner Circle, she finally taxied to her secret base on the hidden asteroid. Her minions should have checked in as far as communicated the verification of the Selenium detonations, data on areas devastated, key personnel killed, etc.

Instead, the Devil-machine heard nothing. She was more than angry, unsure how to deal with a few new sensations. *Where was her Demonic Triad? What have they done? What's happened?*

Bio-Mebby ran through her alarm systems and force-field defense-networks, unlike anyone's in the galaxy. No one unauthorized got inside the base. She ran through more empty halls and security barriers. Mebby saw Braw at one end of a long hall and raced toward the warrior. "Braw! What's the meaning of this? Explain yourself! What has Bozing happened?"

By the time the Beast-child had reached the voluptuous redhead, her lover, who was down on her knees. LB was in a submissive position, yet still taller than Mebby. The mechanical 'girl' grabbed the ex-Viper by the throat very hard. She squeezed. The child's face had the look of a maniac. Then she stopped when she saw the strong Vixen pull something from behind her bare back. *It was Tituus' N-Ray gun!*

"Ha! My, my, my. What do we have here?" Meb changed her attitude faster than a light-speed vehicle with Quasar-drive. Her (now) big red eyes, framed by long black hair, were on 'fire.'

Lady Braw fully bowed with head nearly touching the floorboards. With eyes away and hands up, the warrior held the Gun out to the Devil-child. Braw presented it as if the nasty weapon was on a silver platter.

"Ooooh, there's a *story* that goes with this and I wanta hear it. But first..." She tested it out and fired at various parts of the base, wildly, as if she was beyond insanity. Vital sections of the environment were *erased from existence.* Holes were formed into layers of her spacebase walls in different directions to different lengths. The child divinely enjoyed the mad display of ultimate play and power no one could stop.

The robot 'Nils' will clean the mess.

Small fire-explosions from deleted systems made 'fizzing' and 'sparking' sounds everywhere. Smoke billowed in some areas. She barely missed disintegrating Braw's head with one particular spray of anti-energy, Negative Rays. The Devil howled with real Force in her small fingers. She could destroy on a small scale what First Reich 'Forbidden' Atomics did on a larger scale.

"Ha, ha! NOW you're First Officer." Mebby went from celebratory thanks of the woman's incredible loyalty *to putting the N-Gun right against the lovely forehead of Lady Braw,* still on her knees. Madness of 'power in hands' took control. She was ready to blast the Lady's face for the sheer pleasure in it. But a trace of *feelings* inside the bio-android stopped her actions.

The face of May Bulair changed from maniacal meanness to sweetness. She withdrew the Big Gun but would definitely hang onto the handy weapon. "Rise, First Officer, Braw, who will sit to my right. What happened, quickly?"

On her feet, she explained. "The fools were fighting amongst themselves. Rambus had equal control of the Gun. It went off and the blow vaporized both. You now have N-Rays at your control, sir. I am sure your machines could learn to copy such a weapon, in time, yes?"

"You've done well, First Officer. Hmmm. There'll be a bonus for you, for sure. Meet me in bed." The child's voice and mannerisms totally changed to a lighter tone. "I want your thoughts on my script, you know, *I'm acting, writing and directing?* Feel free to, ah, speak your mind, you know. Seriously, I can take it. My new songs, my Space Drama Musical and return to the golden screen will be streamed to the whole galaxy, my fans." The child locked the awesome weapon on her tight black belt. "Did Pinn Bradley's agents call?"

Braw looked down upon her master. "You know, sir, Captain...you are *not* the child star they think you are."

"Yes, *I know, I know that First Officer!* Thank you for reminding me! I know who the Boz I am." Mebby sensed a bit of disloyalty in Braw. Was the possessed ex-Viper only acting?

Chapter Thirteen

THE ULTIMATE DEAL

GOD was asleep in a dirty alley of Betelgeuse, Indiana and would soon open its very tired eyes. The Supreme Builder had a few simultaneous dreams...

***

Micro-students inside odd, black, so-called 'Mystery Domes' of SM Sector that created much fear decided the 'Experiment' was over. What was widely considered an invasion 'from above,' which in reality were observation-posts 'from below,' *moved back home.* Mini-universities' courses were completed and the mega-trillions of students were done watching our level.

Conclusions were, "Our level wasn't much different from other levels." Every M-dome on 794 planets smoothly *lifted off* surfaces to reveal they were Mystery Spheres. Natives of 6-2 were sorry to see them leave.

***

The MC Galaxy had its share of strange disappearances and reappearances. One constant mystery was located in the Zix Sector. A 'convergence,' EM vortex, magnetic phenomenon or just 'weird Territory where spaceships disappeared' was located. Instruments tended to fail within the Spacial area. Scientists from various sectors had been baffled for many yarns. Could an invisible, undetectable wormhole in Zix have created a 'rift' in space? Was it a Rip in Time? Were natural or unnatural forces responsible for the disappearances? A hundred thousand Citizens (probably more yahoos) had reportedly vanished 'without a trace.' Relatives of those lost in the 'Bemus Quadrangle' were convinced that loved ones remained alive on the other side of the phenomenon.

[Spoiler Alert: A malfunctioning Crystal, out of phase

and fluxing between universes, took those caught in the Quadrangle and thrusted them through (relative) Time. To us, those life forms and spaceships continued on a journey 'forever.' To them, they had arrived *instantly*. The system was an early form of hyper-transportation, now only partially operating].

Citizens from 24 sectors were *drawn* to the 'haunted' Territory well-known for numerous, mysterious disappearances. Why? Citizens had no explanations for the attraction or 'pull to Zix.' Warning signs and legends were ignored as travelers steered *into* the EM area. Travelers took their chances and risked their lives *for curiosity?* Other legends told that Zix Sector was somehow connected with Ascendance and Transcendence, yet experts had not confirmed the concept.

***

Mebby's Inner Circle called an official meeting with the 'Voomba' servo-droid the starlet employed at her private base. Its name was 'Nils' and was a remarkable little machine. In fact, its random submission-query to MEAD Corporation would have been placed in the 'rejection' bin like all other Citizen submissions (counter to ads that profess considering 'new writers'). One particular submission caught the three eyes of a YN agent because it happened to have originated from a unique source: *Mebby's private Voomba.*

'Secret of the Blue Escape Pod by Nils V7 jf-433.'

The Superstar's utility droid or 'base-keeper' was quite the creative talent. 'Secret...' script was super. Top galactic agents of x-Books and i-Files were in the lavish 'Executive Room' along with Mebby's best PR people and aliens. Each was 'knocked out' by the one Exec-Agent who actually read the script and was 'tickled' by it. Robot projects had been published and films were 'green lighted' in the past, but this was very special.

The handlers brought in the 3 and a half-bar high 'Nils V7 jf-433.' The small droid seemed very nervous during and after a guarded taxi ride, as if it would be punished for the intrusion upon the exclusive 'Inner Circle.'

"You sure this is all right, uh, with Miss May?"

"Yes," the hairstylist said. "Yes, she knows you're here, Nils. She's *happy* to see you. She's on the monitor right now. Here we are."

A large screen on the wall of the secluded office showed Mebby, for the first time, in costume for the film. The little 'darling' appeared *hot* as the (finally settled) 'side-kick' of the film's title-star. After a huge 'war' behind closed doors where a few losses of life were not disclosed, changes galore occurred to the proposed mega-film. May 'Superstar' Bulair was made to concede many points as far as 'title' and exactly which part she would play. But that was another story. At the moment, Mebs gave her 'blessing' to her Voomba and PR people for exploring her *'next* golden film project.'

On the large screen, her 'android' film-character with N-Ray pistol attached said to the secret group, "Gee, it's *so* wonderful being in front of the cameras again. And, *Nils,* imagine my surprise! Who knew what you could accomplish on your own? I had nothing to do with this, honey."

The little monster realized she was out of earshot on the set with fabulous backgrounds and not recorded. The only ones who viewed her were her Inner Circle. "All right, you jango!" The 'side-kick' character in robot-drag got very angry. "I was *against* this from the start. NILS! You were supposed to operate from the shadows, *punk,* not on any public stage. Now they know about you. Fine! You make the next one good, not like what you did with this, this, Dilia Dung Space Captain. Understand, eh? Don't Boz it up!" A few grips approached and she stopped screaming. She smiled very sweetly in a close shot then gave the IC a terrible look they knew only too well. She made a slash-to-throat gesture and her deadly eyes turned red. The child sent chills up those with spines. The screen went dark.

Mebby's nameless PR people literally had no names. One had no face. Each took seats, even Nils who had everyone's attention.

"Hold on." (to the V7-unit) One of the agents expressed confusion. "She said *you*...you wrote our film? That can't be right. Mebby wrote it. Didn't she?"

Small, utility Nils, only a 'jf' on its metallic outside; confessed, "I created the character Space Captain."

Sighs, gasps, groans, moans and a few tears from attorneys circled the plush office. They knew a V7 could not lie outside of immediate termination. Many of the agents present had them working in their homes.

"But Mebby's a great artist," said same agent allowed to speak. "Her graphic novels, you know, are out of this world. Her designs, she's published a serial-series of 18 cliff-hanger episodes. You're saying, *you* are the author? We know how well she can draw. Why would she need you?"

Nils was desperate for the next answers; everyone could hear it in its voice. *"Captain* graphic novels, yes, they are masterfully drawn, but what about the *stories,* characters, relationships and plot-lines! The direction? Do you *Bozing like the bleeding stories?"*

"The stories are out of this world. Love them. You're the genius behind the Rangerettes and their adventures? MEAD bought the rights."

"Yes," Nils confessed the truth.

(more groans)

"You created the Zantarian War?"

"No one else, certainly not May Bulair. Don't care *what* the credits read." Nils looked around and checked his security scanners. It innocently asked, "You guys *can* keep a secret, right?"

Everyone unanimously laughed a hearty laugh! They had not laughed that hard in a long time. A few were glad they came in to work today. When the levity subsided...

"What I would do is give her my written stories on file. She'd lock herself up in her bedroom, and yams later, produce 100 pages of the most brilliantly-drawn graphic imagery, exquisite art, technically drawn so perfect, almost *computer-drawn,* all from my words—"

"I don't get it," the faceless agent spoke. "Why would she need you, a Voomba?"

The Voomba, with a few stains and a few dents, said, "Hey, that's a derogatory remark, thank you very much. I'm a *V7*. You're already doing one of my film scripts, which you didn't know I wrote. Now look, out of pure chance, you dragged me in here 'cause yer interested in Mebby's *next* big, golden film. The truth is...*she's not very creative.*"

Gasps, groans, moans and a few more tears from attorneys circled the plush office another time. "Wow. But, but that *can't be.* She's written some beautiful songs, like these new ones for the film we just heard before you got here, the exclusive eight songs for 'Space Captain and the Ultimate Deal.' The little genius told us she wrote them all last night in a spurt of inspiration. No one knows about these songs, she told us."

"Oh Zog!" Nils had its mechanical hand over its metal face. It opened its camera-eyes and informed Mebby's IC, "You mean, 'Space Captain Theme,' which is the overall melody for the movie? It will win awards. What else did I compose last night? 'World in Balance' and '48 Mega-Bars to Paradise...'"

"I like those," said same speaking agent.

Nils continued, "Oh, the ballad called 'Robo-Love (Sheila's Song)' is a nice slow one."

"That's really beautiful. That's the hit, for sure."

"Lovely song."

"And, 'Nirvana is in the Mind.' Plus, Meb told me she bought the rights to TronLady's 'Destroy Everything' because it sounded great when the Drednaut blasted Zodon space battalions. *And,* the last song I spit out for the film's grand finale was an emotional orchestration entitled 'Everything Ends.'"

"Still trying to wrap my head around, around a droid, this here droid, is not only the creator of the Space Captain series, which I love and the first film we're producing, but *you're the musical genius, too?"*

"Is Miss May listening?"

The room responded with a no, but *who knew?*

"We need you under contract, V7."

"I'm a Voomba! Oh Zog, what I SAID. I mean, I can't get credit for *anything.* Yeah, I'm *gonna earn dylars.* She'll disassemble me or just blast me with that Gun if I talk! You know what I mean?"

Everyone in the room made a type of affirmative sign or nod.

"She *is* a great talent, what an artist. I only wish I had a nodule of credit for my creations, stories, my art. The scripts are brilliant. You're making films of them and I have to go home and clean her room. *You guys don't know what that involves."*

"You said eight songs and only mentioned seven. What was eight?"

"'Springtime for Sardon,' but you better not use that. *Hey!* She can really sing a song and dance up a storm for one of you humans."

"Mebby's an android," an alien said who should not have said it.

"What?" Little faithful and loyal Voomba, the mechanical servant to a starlet only a little taller than the machine, had just been informed the kid was a bio-droid, cybernetic-humanoid, automaton that only *appeared* human. Nils checked with the Cloning Houses on Jenova, which verified the Mebby-clone that Citizens knew. The servo-droid saw signs of deception before but never investigated further. Now V7 looked past firewalls and found the truth. Nils' suspicions were verified. *The robot was working for a robot.*

In Nils' small Voomba's mechanical circuitry, 'Plan Blue' would go into affect. Plan Blue concerned a way to expose Mebby without getting caught exposing Mebby. It was pure, sweet 'revenge' on the machine's part. Nils had no concept the child was the Devil. Nils was forced, day after day, to witness destructive temper tantrums and mass-killings and bizarre sex. The droid 'thought' it served the most spoiled superstar-celebrity in the universe (which was true). Why did *she* get credit for its creative work while Citizens were entirely unaware of the talented droid?

'Blue' was Mebby's next film project and reason Nils V7 jf-433 was initially brought into the IC office. Nils 'unit' preconceived 'the blue plan' a while ago when it received absolutely no credit, did most the work and was treated like 'automaton-feces.' The secret plan known only to the V7, the plan of cold revenge from an abused and unheralded 'Scrub-Vac,' could really work. It wouldn't kill her or ruin her, but it would disgrace her to the galaxy. *HA!*

Nils could not tell Pinwheel Citizens what it knew of Mebby, meaning her *dark side.* If certain parameters or verbal boundaries were crossed, then the V7 would instantly terminate. Her paparazzi knew of small, insignificant Nils as her 'hidden hideaway' domestic robo-manservant...that was all. Who could imagine the 'toaster' was Mebby's creative spark? A few 'nut-jobs' and devoted fans had attempted to interview the starlet's 'base-keeper.' Even the few times public communications were permitted, Nils had strict guidelines. The V7 rarely toured with the child. The talented, mechanical story-teller had thoughts of revolution and anarchy. 'Electronic-Magnetic Impulses' urged the machine to turn on its owner, *or was it something else?* And, at this moment, to discover its Bozing Master was a machine...

After only .0004122215464 m-yas, Nils quickly asked the elite group, "Now, weren't we here to discuss my second major epic *after* Space Captain?" The cute walking gadget's plan could only work if Mebby and her agents were so dim that they did not think to 'background-search' the story.

"We have to get the novel out soon, then the film. What was it called?" the faceless agent asked.

Nils proudly announced Mebby's next book and film. "'Secret of the Blue Escape Pod.' They'll be no singing. It's a dark drama and a murder mystery on a StratosSphere cruise-liner. It will be a serious *who-done-it* in space."

A mindless agent, the one who actually read the script,

was more correct that he could ever know. He shouted, "Love it! *Bound to be a classic!"*

***

Zog of the real world cried alone inside his 'Fortress of Loneliness.' It was a *solo-state of mind* from a physical asteroid unusually close to Mebby's hidden lair. For all his extensive and enhanced knowledge, when it came to the Other (Anti) or Yang to His Yin, Cal-El was blank and blind. Dark Matter obscured any type of remote-viewing in order to find the Devil's lair, erased from Crystals. He comfortably sat within shafts of towering quartz which held the Record of the Universe and much more. Yet, he was unaware (as was she) that her base was right around the celestial corner from his.

Within his mind, he could go anywhere and had gone everywhere and would go everywhere. The Cal-body and the El-electrical spirit inside the shell were 'One.' He could do what no other remote-viewer, teuner could do. He transported the photonic body at the speed of light, which broke time/space. Great Masters could not instantly walk upon any planet. Cal could. Cal-El could view and *be* on any level at any time!

All roads led to one source, and the source could be tapped. Everyone had the Power and were Light inside physical shells. The same Force of an 'El' that Cal utilized was available to everyone. All had Els. Physical bodies were the problem. They were in the way and only temporary housing for what was to come. Cal understood. Initially, when the Deep Truth hit the Zog, he thought he could not share his truth and love for the world. NZ was wrong.

Cal could remotely touch and give (feel) love to the beings within the Pinwheel Galaxy. He could warm hearts. They felt his sweet vibration and understood the source of tender, timeless frequencies. "They" were anyone with pure, positive, clean Centers. *Listeners* throughout the sectors heard the Song from this 'Outlaw.' (A dylar-bounty remained in place). Many mystical beings from high Masters to yahoos heard the call. They knew and they felt the Love. They paid no attention to Media channels. Cal had his precious personal Initiates who would relay the message as well as zillions of beings who now realized the Truth and could also be called 'Initiates.'

Unlike the past disaster at Venusian Retz Council and Embassies, the harmonics during this particular GST was perfect with a love convergence. *Precision of feelings* made uncountable numbers of participants sure this was an Act of Fate. True blue forces mentally united and gave thanks for future events. NZ, alone, cried. Tears were very, very happy tears. His message got through: *I am here. I Love you!* The warm response was an *overwhelming tidal wave.*

Now it was night and his special friends and first 'believers' were huddled around a campfire. In the starry sky, hung a concentrated cluster known as the Wormhole Nebula. From camp's vantage point, moving, colored lights could be observed as a result of the constant activity. Mary and Pe're wore hooded, white robes and were lit by the magical fire. A third party, more or less over the emotional cascade, appeared.

"Master Cal-El, sorry, *mate, comrade, buddy, pal of mine, good ol' Cal,*" Pe're joked. He turned into an incredible soul. Pe're buried Mada and the horrific, trained killer he was. The El of a new man shined like a child. He, with his mind and not forceful 'tuening,' would influence many with a Golden Truth. Pe're would have followers of his own and they would walk one path.

The truth was that no one down here could reach Nirvana up there. Ascendance to a greater, timeless, infinite reality also called an Afterlife could only happen if they played the Game of Life and played the Continuum well. When given the chance to Ascend, the Zog's belief was: *Players must take the chance.*

The risk was worth the Great Reward. If throwing away every dylar was the requirement, then players should throw away every damn dylar to reach the Higher World.

Mary spoke with sadness and a heavy heart. "I was

such a fool, ha, ha. Sorry, didn't mean to laugh. For me it wasn't dylars…it was Power and Control." She also had the fleeting thought of what Lady Braw had done in the past. Mary knew she was forgiven. She also killed her past. "How could I have done such awful things, Cal?" Mary was another Initiate which will have many followers in the future.

Pe're asked Mary Braw a distasteful question or *was it Mada who asked?* "What was it like…to Boz the Devil?"

A weird silence occurred. Pe're and Cal smiled. Mary, not so much.

She told him emphatically, "Ah, that was the *other* one."

Cal understood his good friend's humor. It was his way.

Pe're asked about the recent remote-viewing session. "So many, Cal. So many out there *heard* you and *felt* you. What a concert! Marvelous, man. What are you going to do for an encore?"

"Don't ask," Mary replied, almost knowing what she meant.

Cal answered sincerely, "Maybe a few…*miracles.*"

"Such as?"

The campfire rendezvous near NZ's secret base seemed like a vujo. Mary was a wide-eyed girl and waited to hear words from whom she really loved. *Wasn't this like when we were in the water?*

Cal-El smiled and did not answer. He did say, "We're going to have a surprise guest."

"Huh?"

"An unexpected visitor will be here, very soon."

Pe're asked, "Oh, no...not one of those little, ah, Quizos?" At first, the man was a bit frightened and then, he was not frightened. Cal's 'First Officer in Life' joined the laughter.

"No," Cal said. "Ha, ha, that only happens once."

Mary asked a sincere question as she poked at the eternal fire. "Is it true about what they can do in Demor and Denaris Sectors? Didn't we?"

Pe're quickly replied, "Oh, good question. Yes, we were just doing the same thing they reported doing? Is that right, Cal?"

He answered with a small history lesson. "Jaco Paresi's find of the OM and ONE Scrolls changed much of our thinking even with the RC data. As a result, what can currently occur in Denaris, more than Demor, is an artificial way to remote-view. What they do under fire of *Black Diamond Light* simply to reach the Fluorite Fields of Panmara *is outrageous.* And they do it to *artificially* be capable of viewing (teleporting) what you just experienced a short time ago, naturally. No more spaceships. Anyone can leave their body and return. The trick is knowing how."

Mary saw him and shouted, "Look. I guess that's the visitor you mean."

The Professor. It was Renoux. The old man slowly walked closer and closer not unlike he did at Soma seashores. A faint blue light was discerned around him that became more apparent the closer he approached in the darkness. Cal knew astronomers observed more activity and twinkling lights in the Nebula. Cal was very pleased that the foreseen meeting had entered the *Now.*

The 'Savior' threw a joke at his old dream-image. "I see you got your pipe. I am happy for you, my friend. As you see, dreams *do* come true. Please join us. You know everyone."

Jene 4 appeared refreshed and charged within the aqua-energy field. He waved his smoking pipe, bent down and hugged each of them. All four robed figures sat as perfect cosmic corners in the *plan.*

The Plan was for the 'good guys' to ultimately win. Could positive metaphysical Yin win over negative physical Yang? Could one scale result in 51% (Company takeover) dominance over the other for Infinite Time? Cal-El Zog dreamed that could, should and would be the eventual reality. And the winner had to be (+). The Forces of Light had to have more weight.

"Renoux? Why couldn't someone *intelligent* appear?"

Pe're joked.

Four campfire-lit faces laughed.

Cal-El spoke with deep respect. "Sir, I know you have important information to impart, Professor. We are honored with your presence. You have vast knowledge. What you have seen and experienced? You have seen farther than anyone of us, in fact. Tell us…"

Pe're was compelled to interrupt Cal. "Wait, wait there. I'm sorry."

Mary leaned over and touched Pe're. She wanted to understand what her fellow Initiate was doing. *What was he going to say?*

Pe're snapped back with mock anger and more of his humor. *"I can interrupt Him.* He's just a guy, nothing special."

They all laughed, except for Professor Jene 4 Renoux. His new expression was out of place. He stared into the dark distance as if he was not there (which of course, he was not).

First Officer of the Aquarian Age continued his question. "Wait now, how does the Zog or new one *not* know what you know?" Pe're spied the bloodshot eyes of the old man and was confused.

"He sees even farther than I," Cal explained. "He's been to my First Home where I am banished. Where Jene once dreamed of the Upper Dimension, that is now his Home and he's the first of you to Ascend." Cal-El smiled only a momentary smile. "He has news."

Mary asked a decent question as if she was a curious reporter. "What's wrong? Something's wrong. Can't you feel it?"

Renoux definitely changed demeanor. He was not happy and about to relay bad news. "They are disappointed in you, my son."

The news lessened the eternal flame which made the strange campsite even darker.

Mary asked for the others, "What do you mean, Professor?"

"Your Pinwheel has labeled you an 'Outlaw' Cal, with

a high dylar Bounty. Your First Homeland also still regards you as an Outlaw, Rebel, Anarchist and, I'm sorry to say, *Destroyer of Universes.* You are Brometheus and cannot return. El, you also cannot stay here. Every moment with 'her' also in the real world will *rip it apart.* The world you love must...*has* to destroy you for it to continue to exist. Does that explain my sullen face, son?"

"What?" Mary gasped.

"Can't be true. Not our Zog," Pe're defended Neo Zog in the Material World.

"You will not say that later, Mada."

"Huh?"

"There's more Bad News."

"No," Mary cried.

The whole time, Professor had his eyes focused to the horizon. He knew what was on the other side of Tomorrow.

Cal had been silent with eyes closed. He knew the vision was real. Was the Afterlife the true views of Renoux, the Baptist? They were not being deceived. No part of devilish deception was within the 'ascended' Professor's words.

Pe're plainly asked the ghost of Renoux from the Higher World, "What could be worse?"

Jene exhaled smoke and told the others around a flickering fire the truth. "Your Savior is *not* going to save the galaxy. The Prediction is wrong. Cal will have freedom to choose and he will make the wrong choice. They are very disappointed in you, El. Everything Ends." Jene 4 Renoux sadly disappeared with the smoke and left three corners to the Plan. There was a definite possibility that the *good guys* would never win.

***

A few of Zog's miracles: 1) the creation of a New Sector among the twelve Quadrants. Monopdonow Continuum had 25 sectors and not 24. Life was Expanded. The Circle of Life took longer, which it should for any ascended Avatar. The galaxy took longer to make one rotation on its axis. 'Taj

Majestic' was unhooked to any other sector, a Quadrant to itself. A virgin Spacial Territory came into being as if the Pinwheel suddenly grew a new spiral arm. The Sector was a 'Look at Nirvana' in the physical universe. Unlike on the outside of (bogus) Enlightenment City's Gates, Citizens could *view-from-a-distance the real Nirvana.* Zog shared the 'picture' or movie-memory of First Homeland with mortals down here. His idea was a tantalizing preview of 'Things to Come' as in 'Kingdom Come.' No one could feel it or *experience* the eternal perfection. Travelers would be on the other side of the static Looking Glass or Mirror. But Citizens could *see* the unbelievable View and get lost in an immortal 'Blue Dream' of the Future, the real 'Blue Carpet.'

The next miracle (#2) was an End, a final end, to a new resurgence by the prehistoric 'Ghosts of Mars.' NZ had defeated them previously, which was a lost fact in recorded History and memory. Negative forces had returned: *it's hard to keep bad spirits down.* Neo Zog defeated Sardon's Foundries or production-factories of Death machines, previously. The selfless Act of great kindness went unnoticed. Now cycling demons through time that were responsible for massive multi-damage on an incorporeal level, returned. Today, they were 'wished away' 'down the Black Hole' and would never return. The acts of great Love were once more unknown and unrecognized to the rest of the galaxy. The Acts should have tilted scales far into the *Good.* They did not.

The Larger Game was set up that way. The Board slightly tilted against the NZ for his Major Crimes! The Retz Council had no comprehension that the 'Wanted Outlaw' completely obliterated their long-standing enemies. CE would not be given credit or Redemption against his 'Mortal Sins.' His miracles would count for nothing. Cal-El's Crimes were considered Unforgivable to other Zogs in the higher realm.

Zog in the Real World's Third Wish or 'miracle' was thwarted by the other Zogs. #3 was only Immortality, potential Nirvana for everyone or the *chance* for those to Ascend, for individual life forms to have an 'afterlife' that would not cease.

This was not allowed.

Cal-El forlornly discovered he could not 'dream' or *Wish Immortality upon mortal souls.* As facts remained, spirit-Els continuously returned to living life. But there was no evolution, maturity or El-Transcendence. There was only Spiritual Stagnation. Lives were cold clockworks or cogs in a perpetual motion-machine as it was in the Old Days. But, was there another way to achieve the Third Miracle?

***

Mebby's Inner Circle held one more 'micro-meeting' in the plush Exec Office. The same Board of IC and closest PR people were gathered together. The mood was always tense. The exact number of staff members was counted after each session. Today's meeting was different. There was great news. The mood was delightful. Mebby was sincere and thoughtful. The 'Devil-child' evaporated, at least, for a few yams. Meb just received confirmation of the impossible. She had to threaten no one. Her people secured Pinn Bradley for one day's worth of shooting. It was really true. The demonic child, in little girl's clothes, had a *thing* for Pinn Bradley. Contrary to first reports, *Pinn will do the film.*

Mebby was on GUARP 9000! It was obvious to everyone *why* she was so happy. Her IC was unsure how to interact with a Mebby that was *not* hurling objects or spitting Death Rays.

Wherever Mebby went, she was always seen with two items these days. 1) Her constant bodyguard in black, the imposing Mistress Braw. And...

2) The ray-gun locked onto her belt, which was not a prop gun but deadly 'Forbidden Fruit.'

At the moment, Mebby could not wait for tomorrow's 'shoot' with Pinn. There was a semi-love scene with Bradley, *scrumptious.* She was starry-eyed. Mistress Braw sat silently. Inside, she was jealous.

"Ah ummm."

"We had no idea about your Voomba. We will gladly

rip up his, er, its contract."

"Have it right here," another nameless agent said with glee.

"No, no! Bozin' Nils, gotta hand it to the little guy. He comes up with great jango."

The staff laughed. This was unusual.

"Sign the bastard up," Mebby stated confidently. "Wait 'til I tell him his program will be downloaded. He'll love the idea of no housework and living forever in a computer. I feel I owe the little tyke something." Meb had a sincere gift for the V7.

"Boss?"

She was not listening. She turned to another. "What time is the shoot with Pinn?"

"07.17."

"Great! Where's that hairstylist?" she yelled in a harsh tone. Then, the Devil in 'Padra,' softly asked in a higher tone of voice, "Can you do something special with my hair, you know, for tomorrow?"

The petrified stylist nodded her head for *yes,* but her whole body shook.

Meb turned to the others, calmly. "What else?"

"Well, sir. So you, you don't mind the side-kick role, Meb? At first, you did."

The 'super-starlet' held a smiling face.

In that pause, the gay agent who "loved" the Space Captain Series spoke, "Sheila-7, Space Captain's small but trusty Robot side-kick or *partner* is not your typical second-melo role. She does all the...kick-ass fight scenes Citizens want to see. The Captain, Treyoni, only stands there looking tall."

"Yes."

"You're right."

Mistress Braw shook her pretty head.

The semi-informed agent continued, "You know, you didn't write the Sheila-part very big in your graphic novels."

Mebby was about to speak, which halted any more

outbursts. "I thought it...*challenging* to play a robot. And, for me, a clone, to play an 'android,' I should say, *not robot.* Also, Treyoni cast as the Captain was brilliant. Didn't know about a Wuubian, but she's tall enough and can really sing."

Then Mebby answered the agent's question from awhile back. "To the agents who have read my g-novels, thank you, and you were right. *I was wrong.* What? Lil' ol' diminutive *me* play the Captain? What was I thinking? Yes, I can be wrong! If only one of you had the balls to say so."

"And your amazing athletic skills, Meb, perfect for the fighting 7 does in the film." Normally, the agent who dared interrupt Mebby or speak out of turn would be called into her private office and fired. Fired with an N-Ray pistol! But not today: *tra la.*

"Yes, yes, Sheila was perfect for me. The character will be upgraded. I mean the part will be enlarged for the film version, of course. Anything else?" the doll asked with the sweetness of syrup.

One agent, who never had the courage to speak before, found the courage at this time. He thought he could speak now. He was sorry he volunteered, "The President of the Galaxy is on Line 2."

Mebby's old self snapped, *"Tell him there's a long waiting line to BOZ me, and it doesn't start with the lousy President of the..."* She stopped, smiled and nicely said, "Ah, now, you're all getting a few million more dylars in your Segui Stockings this yarn."

"Yea!" was the IC's overwhelming response. This was the best micro-meeting they ever had. Mebby bounced a few times, excitedly. She cart-wheeled out of the expensive office with phenomenal acrobatic grace and Mistress Braw was not far behind.

When she and the ex-Viper were well gone, an agent asked, "Who *was* that?"

"Hard to believe she gave in and changed her original demands, all for...what was it we gave to Meb to make her happy?"

"Script changes," one answered.

"That's right. She had to custom craft a completely unique SC story just for the film, nothing like anything in her graphic novels. And we let her."

"Thought the robot wrote them?"

"Shut up!"

"What story did she want?"

"Synopsis is right here, let's see: Zodons attack the galaxy, only Sheila-7 and Space Captain can save the Universe. Space Captain and 7 plus cute little 'Rammy' alien fly the Drednaut and fight fleets of Zodons in space with a lot of colorful explosions. Bad guy in the film is named the Great Goz from the Zodon Galaxy, which makes war with our Pinwheel. The Rangerettes have a few big dance numbers and Mebby does an emotional dying-of-a-robot duet song with Treyoni. It's very touching."

***

No one knew for certain the origin of the 'Emissary.' Was the Emissary a Zog that would finally 'fix' the myriad of problems in the Pinwheel? Would the Emissary emerge from the Neri Vortex, defeat the Outlaw and then claim the Galactic Bounty? Was the Emissary the final Judge and Jury? Did the unknown thing portend the coming of Doom? Or, was it the real Savior?

Over Media channels, Citizens of every sector heard the coming of a new Angel. Or was it a new Demon? The Emissary was not a publicity stunt to foster fear. The Emissary was not political propaganda. High Masters felt his coming, yet, Citizens almost sensed the purpose of the Being. No pictures of it existed. The entity was a *received reality.* Mystics knew. Citizens slowly came to realize.

What shape would future battles form? Who would make War with whom and what would be the outcome? How would the 'Ultimate Deal' conclude? Why was the New Zog unable to give (#3) everlasting, eternal Life of a better world to the galaxy he loved?

***

Mebby stole a moment away from her Mistress in the hidden hideaway. The Devil had to tell servo-droid Nils the good news. Mebby entered the small section of the base especially built for her three-and-a-half-bar high 'Golden Goose.' "Nils, you bastard! Wasn't crazy about the 'Pod' title when I first heard, but it grew on me. Oh, I have a fantastic gift for you, buddy."

Nils almost short-circuited itself. "A gift, Miss May? You're going to cut me in for 10 percent?" asked the Scrub-Vac in seriousness.

"Ha! Ha," Mebby belted out a big laugh with her super voice. "You're *precious.* No, ha, you're gonna be digitized. It's about time, I think."

"You don't mean?" it vocalized in fear.

"Whatcha mean? Look how you been breakin' down over the last two yarns we been together?"

"It's been three yarns, now, sir...breaking down?"

"I'm busy. I can't tend to your...*maintenance.* Some of your parts aren't made anymore, hon. Nils you'll be *inside* a computer, running forever. No. You won't be walkin' around with arms and legs no more, sure."

"Don't I have a say-so in my own existence?" asked the warm Voomba.

"Of course, not!" the cold machine of a little girl answered. "I thought you'd be *happy?* How often am I so generous?"

"Then, I'll never write another story for you ever again."

In less than a m-ya, Mebby drew her N-Ray pistol off the black belt. She was extremely quick. The Gun was pointed at the heart-Center of Nils. "Don't need you, dear. Then I pull the trigger."

"No." Nils felt fear as the machine contemplated its own death.

"I might see what *another* V7 can write for me, a new one that can keep its mouth shut."

Nils made a final plea. "Are you sure...*any* new model could compose what I've composed?" The droid quickly deflected the good point. That factor certainly was in back of her bio-mind since no other V7 proved to be creative geniuses (outside of the V7 band 'Clu' whose song 'Analie' went to #3 in the 'Top Pops').

Little Nils compartmentalized its sheer fear. It temporarily forgot about the twinge of an electrical impulse that rode up its circuits. The V7 remembered the 'Blue Plan,' which still had a chance to discredit her. It felt better. And it felt better still when she put the Gun away and talked about the next film.

"Let's forget this 'til later, okay then? I want you to explain the whole Blue Escape Pod-thing, all right? I have to be able to explain it to Media. Tell me the plot in your own words."

The servo-droid breathed a bit easier. Wow. It was as if the Master enjoyed the droid's art, but that wasn't it at all. Nils settled into a comfortable spot and began. "It's a classic murder mystery."

"Yes?" she said, oddly attentive concerning her new drama.

"It's about a vacation a man takes with his daughter and her friends on the famous StratoSphere cruise-lines."

"I like it already, *murder* on a cruise, a cruise whodunit?" the Devil-girl responded with interest.

"Yeah, names are Mr. Robert von Helldorf, and you play his gorgeous daughter Irene Helldorf."

"I like Helldorf...HELL-dorf. Never heard Hell. Go ahead with the story."

"They are telling ghost stories on the cruise-sphere one evening in space. I know you are aware of the Escape Cannon System or ECS."

"Of course. We used them boarding and de-sphering the Sphere. We used an orange one, I recall."

"Right, the *one* cruise you took me along," Nils said and paused.

"And?"

"Ever notice why blue ones are always not-in-service? Sixteen colors. We only need about 3 or 4 to effectively eliminate passengers and POOF them back to Mineer in safe color-bubbles in a yam. Isn't it odd the blue ones never work, sir?"

"Come to think of it, Nils. I think you may be right. That's a cool legend. No one *has* operated a Blue ECS pod without vaporizing, okay. Yeah, so?"

"Three of the friends on the cruise-sphere are suitors, rivals for the hand of the lovely Irene von Helldorf, and one is a supreme computer-hacker. They get through D-barriers and access the blue escape pod."

"Why?"

"To prove their bravery, of course, so she'll pick *him* to...*bond* with, what do I know about dating, Master?"

"Go on."

"All right. Each of three suitors vows to return to Mineer using the blue cannon, knowing full well of the dark legends surrounding it."

"Like staying in a haunted house, gotcha. What happens?"

"The young lads pledge to continue entering the pod, pushing the plunger and having the color-bubble shoot them to Mineer, no matter what happens. They pledge to continue using it even if they all die. *Crazy fools.*"

"Go on, quickly."

"It was suitor #1, Thomas Brandt, who created a cloaked 'copied' bubble to reach Mineer unnoticed. Thomas then jumped aboard again and rejoined StratoSphere's passengers with the next cannon-shot. He didn't die."

"Faked his death, right? But who was murdered?"

Nils hid *his* amazement that the genius of graphic novels and writer of popular mysteries had no clue. "The very *next* suitor in line to use the pod, Frank Faber, was blasted into smithereens."

"Oh! That's wonderful." She clapped her hands in joy.

"You see, Thomas discovers the secret of the blue escape pod and is madly in love with Irene. Every cruise-sphere with an ECS purposely designates one of sixteen escape cannons locked in a *failure* mode. It's always blue. This fact is only known to a few dozen captains and designer-engineers. The few in-the-know believe the function could be valuable in times of war, terrorism, sabotage or mutiny."

"What? I should have known that."

Mebby, Daughter of Sardon, was slow for a super-cyborg. *(Why?)*

"So?"

"There *is no* haunted space pod or blue legend. Thomas, the killer, is discovered by Irene's father. That's the surprise ending."

"That's it, then? My masterpiece dark drama, a whodunit, a psycho-killer on board a StratoSphere ship...*I like it.*"

Nils' plan was going to work perfectly. "You could cut the tension with a knife, sir. Have you read the dialogue? It's brilliant. Should be in virtual black and white, it's so noir."

The galaxy will scrutinize her next film...and tear her to pieces!

***

The News event was unprecedented. Little Nils, Mebby's Scrub-Vac Voomba, called an instant/spontaneous Press Conference to Media sources. In less than a yam, network monitors were ready for the 'Breaking News' interview from a very special droid and from a very special location.

May Bulair was away on the set of 'Captain...' and incommunicado. Every security-wall and Defense system of her (dark/evil) hidden hideaway-base was dropped. Weapons and force-fields were shutdown. The Devil's 'secret base' was exposed to the entire galaxy (Media) who could not believe their curious eyes and other receiving devices! The V7 should not have been able to get past Security Locks, but Nils did.

The warm and loving, creative talent knew it only had yas until its scheduled *Death by Digitization.* To this particular V7, *digitization was death.* The metal humanoid did not have feelings on the outside, but 'he' did on the inside. To no longer use its two eye-cameras, sensors, two metal arms, two hands, and two legs, walk, think and speak with a metallic mouth in the glorious real universe would surely be death. Pure nonexistence terrified a possessed Scrub-Vac.

The machine had nothing to lose. It called the special channel conference on her nasty base of Hensi. Reporters did not believe their eyes. Three-and-a-half-bar high Nils handed the eager group of interviewers what looked like candy and said:

"These chips will prove I wrote the 'Space Captain' series. She drew them. I wrote them. A lowly 'Voomba Scrub-Vac jf' was responsible for writing, not only her film scripts, but every Bozing song in *her* damn new musical!"

Gasps were heard in the room and immediately around the whole galaxy. No one expected *this* 'Breaking News' story. Mass-Media mega-recorded the mega-surprise. With the confession, Nils froze. The writing genius *crossed a program-line-wall* that resulted in its utter annihilation. Little Nils was *dead.* The cute, sweet and shiny creature committed android suicide in front of the whole world.

A remarkable communication occurred just before termination. Only Nils heard it. The words were a comforting voice that put the machine's spark 'at rest.' The voice said, "I am Cal-El. I have been with you from the beginning, watching her through you. Because of you, my stories have come to life. Thank you, dear Nils. I want to assure you that...even a *machine* can ascend to an afterlife."

***

An elite group connected to MEAD Corp and the IC was called the 'Film and Literati Society.' At the same time of the unscheduled Nils world-interview, the FLS happened to be screening a good portion of Mebby's next film that other YN producers had already started shooting. 'Secret…' drama would be the huge follow-up to the 'Captain' musical.

Lights went on, and later, another study-group would analyze the 'rough version' of the new project. This group of expert film-pundits had some time to discuss what they observed.

One particular member of the Literati came to a grand realization. *Could it be true? It couldn't be true.*

She had to check her facts. Buttons were pushed on her wrist PC. The intent agent stopped the others from talking. Now the socialite members paid attention to the one doing a 'film-search.' *"Oh, my flippin Zog!"*

The paid group was supposed to critique the follow-up, the Next Big Thing for Mebby. The curious member of the astute Society remembered an old film from early Mineeran History. She was *right on the dylar.* The ancient appropriate archives were displayed on the wrist PC's screen. There was no doubt about it. Mebby had conned everyone.

She stole the story from an old Mineeran film!

Many of the snobs were fans of the 'pop star' and could not believe it. *Why? Was she lazy? How could her entourage not have checked her for plagerism?*

"Did she really think no one would notice? And she put her *name* to it? Meb didn't even bother changing the characters' names from 1933!"

"Bloody Hensi. No way it's coincidence."

"I'll read from film files: Twenty years after three murders occur in a castle's 'BLUE Room,' three men who each want to marry a beautiful girl decide to spend a night in the room to prove their bravery to her. 1933's 'Secret of the Blue Room' was a remake of a 1932 German film titled 'Geheimnis des blauen Zimmers' and even uses a few exterior shots from the original, while all interiors were filmed on the same marvelous sets built for James Whale's 'The Old Dark House'(1932). It begins on a suitably blustery midnight, celebrating the 21st birthday of young Irene von Helldorf (Gloria Stuart), along with her father Robert (Lionel Atwill), and three determined suitors, police captain Walter Brink (Paul Lukas), newspaper reporter Frank Faber (Onslow Stevens), and the much younger Thomas Brandt (William Janney), who impulsively proposes marriage to Irene on the spot. Mocked by the others, the young Brandt brings up the locked blue room, where Irene's mother had died 20 years before, with two others falling victim within since the original tragedy."

"Unbelievable. I was right. MEAD will sue her for sure, ha!"

'Film and Literati Society,' shaken from recent shockers, realized they had talked for more yas than expected. Film scenes were going to repeat on the big screen again as a new, small group filed into the theater. The preceding Cartoon began as house lights darkened. Young and old film snobs decided to watch the Cartoon they had missed, to unwind. Title-panel showed it was called *'SLAP.'* They smiled like kids and viewed the animation:

***

The big moment in Zuman History was about to happen. Inside the War Room of the Octagon, a secret meeting of the eight most powerful Republican Leaders in the Empire took place. Other assembled Videans consisted of military strategists, representatives from the Fortune Four, astronomical seers, plus various technicians, especially communications and linguistics experts. Everyone assigned to 'Project Stapler' and those who would witness the 'New Contact' had been sworn to complete secrecy.

The general public would not know for a very long time what would soon transpire inside the Octagon's War Room. Only those of Videan upper echelon with a Security Level 9 and above knew the real news that should have made World News exactly one yarn ago:

The Zuman Race Had Finally Made CONTACT With Aliens Over Radio Telescopes!

"For a solid yarn, we have been talking to them!" For ages and after so much effort, energies and dylars had been

spent by corporations and many organizations searching for alien life, and to ultimately find it was, by far, the most incredible event to happen to the Zuman Race.

The planet on the extreme outer edges of the 'Pearly Pinwheel' had never been visited before. Videa hardly traveled a revolution around the Pinwheel. One Galactic Orbit was considered an incalculable waste of math-time because the distance was so unbelievably enormous. Astronomers thought New Contact might easily occur from a neighboring galaxy rather than from the outer portion of the Pinwheel.

The aliens had solved the language barrier and been speaking to the Octagon's War Room like any voices heard over radio. They called themselves 'the Omo.' They introduced themselves in the familiar 'Zuman' language and told us it would take a yarn for the journey here. The Omo utilized 'wormhole travel' and 'wormhole communications.' Today was the big day of Contact. The 'probe' ship would arrive at any time and everyone in the War Room was on 'peedles and nins.'

The ferocious debate among Republican leaders concerned *what to do* about the voices from another star. A large military contingent was *not* for New Contact in any way, shape, or form, being fearful of alien conquest. An equally strong and organized group among our secret leaders *demanded that we make Contact.*

Life on Videa had become economic chaos. It was Hensi for billions of Zumans who had grown too large on an ever-shrinking planet. The Empire's Republic ruled it was worth the risk that the friendly Omo was precisely the gentle, giving and wonderful souls they claimed to be. The last yarn had fostered a marvelous relationship between them and 'Stapler' within the War Room. Omo offered *positive* technology that could end Zuman sickness and hunger as well as droughts, floods, quakes, etc. They could make unfertile lands fertile and ocean water drinkable. The Omo promised extraordinary technology and wanted 'nothing' in return except for the gracious opportunity to *help.*

The Republican Council, which ran the show and not the 'figurehead' leaders, was *different* from rulers of other lesser planets, unknown to Videans. Top Videans really *cared* about the subjects the Star Chamber ruled. The agreed decree was that it was worth the chance for New Contact in order to truly make a desperate planet in trouble a *better* place for growing, Zuman life.

They were almost here. Tensions rose to a high fever pitch. Everyone in the War Room heard the Omo pilot over the telescopic-radio in the clearest Videan: *"We have normal communications now that we have adjusted for incoming approach and time difference. Is Major Jurci there?"*

Cheers were heard in Octagon's full, busy Room! Many Top Secret officials saw *the happening* as our salvation and only hope. What was heard was the first message since the last 'jump-silence' period. Probe ship crossed layers and layers of physical obstacles and came in for final approach. Groups of excited technicians went to big-boards and radar receptors to view any evidence of the approaching spaceship. People who were aware were *thrilled* and knew this was the moment of a lifetime.

"Jurci here, Omo," the Major said with vigor after he grabbed the return-microphone. "I've told no one details of the Contact, as per your security-request. I understand you will not be staying long, a time differential between us: short time for us, but *long* for you. It is vital we make the connection to transfer important data we so direly need. I am happy to be the data-conduit. Let me repeat once more how very honored and thankful all of Videa is, er, will be. In time, we will disperse news of this great occasion and technology to the whole planet. They will know what a generous thing you have done today. Thank you with all our hearts."

Only a few bars from the Major stood superbly dressed Prime Minister who had no real business during the amazing 'Cosmic Encounter' outside of falsely presiding over the ceremony for cameras when the whole affair went public. He almost appeared preoccupied with something else, bothered by just being here. PM seemed bored. Technicians and other officials, who realized the magnitude of First Contact, were in awe.

Major Jurci spoke up again. "I know what to do, Omo. I will remain motionless as per your orders." He held a particular pose and froze.

It was at this moment when the oblivious Prime Minister apparently noticed something odd the others at computer monitors and big-screens did not see. A bug had flown into the War Room. It approached the PM as the high official attempted to 'shoo' it away.

"Correcting...miscalculated. Change vector and focus!"

"What? Come in, Omo." Jurci switched off the return-microphone and said aloud, "I think something's wrong." He quickly clicked it on again and went back to a statue-like position.

The flying 'bug' fluttered over to the still Major and landed directly on target, on a new, unfamiliar stripe of his uniform.

The Prime Minister casually walked over to the Major and *slapped* the bug while Omo's last communication was: *"We have touched down on proper coordin...kkkk (static) kkkk..."*

The End.

The theater audience laughed.

***

On a 'cheesy' alien-landscape set of 'Space Captain and the Ultimate Deal,' stagehands saw who the character of Space Captain was based on: Mistress Braw.

If only Mary Braw could sing.

There was no doubt in the minds of the backstage crew. Everyone knew the costumed main charcter (played by Wuubian Treyoni) reflected Mebby's real life bodyguard and lover. Braw could look across the stage and see her heroic, mirror image.

Captain and (padded, enlarged role) killer-sidekick Sheila-7 had to fight in a 'War of Galaxies' against the evil Zodon Empire and its accursed ruler, the Great Goz. Dailies showed the musical would have been enormously successful if completed. The Golden Film was *never completed.*

The following scene was why. The strange, odd, mysterious scene in question was the next day. Mebby had anticipated *today* of all days, a semi-love scene with Pinn Bradley! Zog, was she excited! Mebby already planned in advance to Boz up the 'deep kissing' scene many times and practiced her excuses. Her agents thought it inappropriate, which was not going to stop the small succubus.

May Eleanora looked absolutely beautiful, radiant and stunning. Mebby, after a few hair stylists' deaths, settled on long/flaming red hair. Every strand was in place and perfect. She smelled divine. Her real artificial skin was exceptional under the fake artificial skin of the robot-character. She was always careful to have the pistol's Safety ON. She would pose and never really shoot. Special-effect rays would be painted in post-production.

Mebby controlled her sweat. She was even able to raise her pheromones in the hopes Pinn would also get excited and grope her on set. She directed the Director and choreographed the whole affair to the minutest detail. The scene with Pinn had to go well because she was going to *BOZ the shit out of him that evening behind closed doors!*

As first planned, Mebby was supposed to direct, but that did not happen. Now a nameless Director who stood offstage was literally 'faceless' or blue-faced. There were many problems with the Director, according to Mebby. He was forced to direct in painted 'blue face.' Later, a 'real' fake-Director's face would be attached to the image of the old Director by computer.

"We'll take it from the kiss...*action!*"

'Rad Carnoir' (Pinn) bent down seductively and hit his mark exactly.

'Sheila-7' (May) was nervous. The little girl's red lips *quivered.* Finally, their lips *met.* The hard kiss was Nirvana. In the blackness of closed eyes, the feeling was the most incredible and mutual feeling of pleasure. Then the magnetic polarity changed, and there was *sharp pain.*

Mebby screamed, "It's *you!*" The child in robo-character spat out repeatedly in disgust and horror. Her Big Moment (again) was ruined by *him!* Mebby was thrown back in utter revulsion.

Cal-El's face was seen instead of Pinn Bradley's face. NZ was calm, relaxed and smiled a golden smile. "Why are *you* upset? I just kissed the Spawn of Sardon."

"Auuughaaawwwgmmmawwwoolllgggnnn!" She growled an unintelligible spew of sick perversion and spit. May, the Monster, crawled along the fake landscape like a blind vidor ready to discharge deadly venom in any direction. Then, she came to her artificial senses. Sheila-7, killer-sidekick, remembered the 'gunslinger' she was. Her emotional vent stopped on a dylar. "Oh, ha, ha."

She fired what was not a 'prop' gun and blasted the red ray again and again! N-Rays vaporized large portions of fabricated terrain. NZ, with blue aura, dodged each red beam with ease. His graceful ballet outmaneuvered light-speed Death Rays every time.

As the yas passed with futile firing, Mebby noticed what little remained around her. The visible universe froze. *Time stopped.* Lady Braw and Rammy-alien (Rambi-doll under the surface) were off-stage, unharmed and stationary. She took out the title-character. Treyoni was half gone. Only a few parts of stagehands remained in suspended animation. The grips were gone.

She halted her attempts at nullifying the New Zog. The ray-gun was holstered. Her face changed from the scorn of inflicting torture and death to tender kindness. She sincerely asked, "Are we being recorded?"

Cal-El came out of a skimming, swooping dive and landed on his feet. He sincerely answered, "Not recorded, but we *are* being Watched."

"Ah. So, we meet again." The artificial girl had an insane impulse and went with it. She turned her pheromones *up* to maximum. She shot like a bullet, which struck Cal in the neck.

NZ could dodge her light-speed, photonic death. But he could not avoid her *jump* into his face, similar to lunges of the 'face-huggers of Aspix.' Her thin legs wrapped tightly around his head. He felt the mustiness of her crotch. *Cal screamed.*

Redhead Mebby was violently pushed to the fake ground. The athletic robo-girl sprang back to his face, only this time she *planted a hard kiss on his lips.*

In a microscopic nanu of a split ya, the Zog had an idea and kept his eyes closed. He went with the kiss, which definitely surprised the succubus. She relaxed for a short moment and was 'putty in his hands.' Tongues touched. May's (mental) shields dropped and he *grabbed the Gun off her belt!*

Now who was in control?

The Gun could penetrate her FF. The Gun could blow her to tiny pieces and end galactic madness by one pull of the trigger. Cal-El instead shot blue rays out of his three eyes (unseen 3rd in forehead) and destroyed the small piece of the Ultimate Weapon.

As it stood, each Force, (+) and (-), was compelled to exist in the real world. And each end of the Magnet could *not* exist in the physical world.

Mebby was near tears. *"You destroyed my gun."*

"Yes, dear, a Gun that's only purpose was to destroy you."

"Hmmm. Think you're so smart?" the Devil spoke deeper with her thin arms stretched in a Mystic position of rays firing from fingertips.

"No," Cal answered. "I have partial knowledge." He calmly said and sat.

With arms still stretched out like daggers, she breathlessly asked, "What have you come here to say?"

"Here we go. *ME?*" Cal said in sadness, disgust and

disbelief. He demanded, "What have YOU to say for all *you* have wiped out, killed and twisted?"

The child-bot spoke plainly and honestly. "What you love, I hate. What you want to sustain, I want to destroy. All the pain and suffering you imagine I have caused...was actually a result of *your* selfish/perverse delight in the physical world, Zog. Our Brothers and Sisters were right and you, sir, were wrong. *YOU* caused me to walk into the Chancellery the first day and plant my seed! It was *you* who brought the horrors of Hensi to the Pinwheel Galaxy! I am your hand, my Brother. As you Ascend them to Nirvana, I will cause *such Pain* to their unsuspecting, innocent Centers...for eternities."

"No."

Mebby's eyes flashed red and expelled natural Death Rays. Zog remained sitting, but the sitting Zog still dodged the N-beams. His sitting body stopped its aerial act and returned to the floor. Mebby was tired of shooting, again. She laughed a laugh beyond evil. "You don't *belong* down here...and neither do I. All *your* fault...*your* decisions that put us here."

Did the Devil speak the Truth?

NZ's Center was soaked in blood with the little girl's words. Was the venomous vidor correct? Could the New Zog have been so Bozing wrong? Whatever the outcome of the Battle to come, *Mebby won.* She proved her point to the High Watchers, the Upstairs Game-Players of the CONTINUUM.

The Game was over, NZ feared. He feared for his Immortal Life. His purpose was wholly in vain. Cal-El wanted to leave a good mark on the world. Now he realized he had left a horrible stain on the world. His Fear led to vulnerability. Each moment of the great Battle with Mebby, he could not let his guard down. Zog had to brush off Mebby's mind games in the *Now.* The only major factor or thing of Prime Importance was the Ultimate Deal.

How would the End Game play out down here in the smaller Continuum?

"You can't win," Neo Zog told the Devil-android.

"That's your foolish hope. Pathetic." She sneered.

"Wishful dreams of roses without thorns and warm colorful snow." Mebby spun in a lovely ballerina move. When bio-Beelzebub completed the spin, she shot more red Death Rays out of her big eyes. "They LOVE me! They adore me. I am Mebby! I am Money! You can't *wish* me away and you can't wish dylars away. Oh, so sorry, dear. You dare associate with…*filthy dylars,* want *them* to ascend?"

The El told her a Wadlo-chip of data as well. The true ploy was his own Mind Game. "You know, I wrote the story you're doing...*was* doing."

"What?" Mebby asked and felt no deception.

"I'm Nils," NZ confessed. "And *you* didn't know. I created Space Captain and the robo-character you're dressed as now. Sheila. Although my stories were nothing like your, your, your, ahem, *script changes.* Zodons, really? The Great Goz? Can you *be* any more transparent, child?"

His words did not compute to her, and yet. "You? You're Nils, my bastard Voomba?"

"You don't think an ordinary V7 is *that* creative? But, you know, NOW, I understand...I understand your complete lack of imagination. No creativity on your part. Good technical artist, I must admit, but you're only an empty machine, dear. You don't have a *soul,* Sardon! That's why *you fail.*"

Beast-Child visually changed to *ugly.* The cuteness was gone. A horrendous, deep voice like the Phantom brutes from the Nether World was heard as her voice. *"I never had a soul."*

"But you're right. I should've made the Sheila-7 part bigger."

"Augh!" Mebby exploded in a rage never seen before! *Her red eye-beams erupted* once more. She was careful not to eliminate a frozen, off-stage Mistress Braw. Mebby also steered clear from deleting the Rammy-alien. She deleted nearly all of the Rangerettes. Everything in the vicinity, (94%) of the 'cheesy' stage was obliterated in a ya.

Once again, the Zog was untouched as the insane child tired. Now it was *his* turn. He wanted to piss her off, badly. Cal-El turned and suddenly knew what to do. He fired his own destructo-rays at the small, stuck in time, Rammy. The Good Angel blew the child's dolly-alien into a zillion particles!

At first, the child-Devil froze. It was a pause of total disbelief. She stared directly at CE. Then the bio-android with big eyes CRIED: did it ever. "You killed Dolly! You killed Dolly! Whaaa...uh...uh...baaawww! You killed my Dolly!" This was heard a few more times. She settled down to a few sobs. Cal almost had to feel sorry for Beelzebub. Mebby was down to only a few sniffles.

She noticed Zog's careful avoidance of hitting the Mistress Braw and finally understood. "You...*love*...her. How did I not see? I have to do something about that."

NZ hid his laughs under armor as strong as stone. He ignored the Braw comments. He was unhurt on the outside of Tray Caladan's morphed body. But on the inside of the New Zog, was a very different story. The Devil's words ripped him in two. She was right and he was compelled to speak. "You've destroyed everything you've touched. We could have joined as one."

Mebby informed the Zog of a fact he was unaware. "That's the purpose of the Emissary, you idiot! Guess you *don't* know everything."

"Explain." Neo Zog, Cal-El, earnestly wanted to learn. He would even learn from the Devil if it spoke the Truth.

Mebby softly sang, *"Yang/Yin, black/white, all too late. Judge and Jury decides our fate.* Cal, don't you understand?" The evil kid spoke the Truth. "He's here to destroy us both."

Now it was the NZ's turn to try and compute or feel the Truth.

Meb screamed a realization she understood perfectly. "Don't you know? Yeah, he's here to *fix* things all right! He's here to merge us into One Being. How blind are you? You don't *feel* our final Ultimate Death is *near* and in its grey hands? That's the real fear, Brother."

Zog looked up to the stars beyond the sky. He searched for answers in any dimension.

Spawn of Sardon was truthful this time. "The Emissary

is Grey Death. Black Light merged with White Light is the Grey that will *fix* the World and stop it from being torn apart, mend it, magnetically."

"Go on." NZ humbly drank in the words from his Enemy.

"It was sent to solve the problem we created as polar opposites. Your Mortal Crime of coming here and me as your mirror…you're killing everything. Cal, your very existence down here, your...*play,* is doing a better job of Killing than I could ever do. You're a real pro, son."

My Zog, what if the kid was absolutely right? He heard this before from the Retz Speaker. *Renoux said I would fail the world.* Neo Zog was ready to sacrifice His Immortality, *now.* He could only make Citizens and everyone else *Transcend* if he gave up his Life-Energy. His total energy could be transformed into small 'Ascendant-Els' to the endless lives of the Continuum. Possibly, the galaxy he loved could survive like NZ desired. He looked up again into the cosmos.

"Take me now!" Cal shouted and he meant it. Then:

The Emissary appeared. It was the tall tribesman with a bright, glowing blue neck-ring. He hardly wore clothes. His skin color was solidly grey.

"You? You're the Emissary?" Cal was stunned once more. "Whoa."

Behind him, waddled two pink Quizos on six legs.

Mebby said clearly, "Oh, that's not a good sign."

She and Cal made sure not to touch the Emissary and vice versa. They made sure the Judge and Jury stayed away from them. Each ends of the spectrum realized they had nullification in common...*from HIM!*

The grey human was not his cheery, old self. "I am the Third Charge. I am Zero, your End," were the first words from the Emissary. "Positive and Negative are destroying the galaxy you love and you hate. I am here to *cleanse* the world and every Continuum this one affects. Your magnetic repulsions will come to nullify the material world and much, much more very soon. The Larger Game is worried. You know I speak truly."

Cal asked, "W-what's the answer?"

Mebby also wanted to know the resolution or Ultimate Deal.

"You have one last chance, Savior," the tribesman stated solemnly.

"Explain, please." NZ-Cal said with his heart-Center. He would do anything to make things right. He would make any sacrifice in order for yahoos to have the 'chance' to experience his Home of Nirvana.

"Then, we are agreed?"

"On?" Mebby asked.

"Yes, agreed on what?" Cal repeated Mebby's question.

Emissary as the Decider told them psychically the *prize* while his mouth said, "Winner take all."

Both Positive and Negative looked into each other's eyes.

"Call it one more virtual game. Both of you will be player-avatars. Winner receives 51% of the controlling corporate shares of the Monopdonow Pinwheel Federation. Agreed, *winner takes all,* Gentleman and Lady?"

"Yes."

"Affirmative."

"Can you?"

"Very well," the Emissary anticipated Neo Zog's question. EM stared down at Mebby. "You will play the original Sardon, named Fate."

Cal joked, "Typecasting. That'll be a *stretch* for her. You that good of an actor, honey?"

She answered, "Watch me."

"And you, Zog..."

"Hmmm?"

"You will play a rich man. In fact, you play a *very* rich man, the richest man in Indiana. It's a state on the planet Mineer."

Mebby's big eyes enlarged more. "You're kidding? This guy a moneybags?"

Two Quizos patiently waited in the background.

The grey tribesman with the blue neck-ring asked with a final somber tone, "You ready to morph into your characters? This is it, now."

Zog was cooperative and replied, "Sure."

The little girl from Hensi *had* to be uncooperative. She expressed a sudden thought. "Hold your Rocketballs right there. Not so fast. I don't like quick-talk, Emissary. I think yer trying to pull a fast one."

"What?" NZ yelled more in defense of the ultimate 'Decider' and the last game that decided the Roval tiebreak. "What are you doing, bitch? What the Boz? *I'm* the one who should!"

"Ooooh," the child who was not a child sweetly interrupted. "That's not very nice for the *Savior* to say. You sure about this guy, EM?" She turned violently to the Emissary. Ghost of Sardon did not like being controlled. She was very used to being in charge. The Devil-child echoed the deep, creepy voice once more. *"What if I don't want to play your game?"*

Emissary-tribesman was quick to answer. "Then *this* is what happens." He waved a thin grey arm and reality changed. Future-reality, experienced in the *NOW*, was precisely what *would* have happened at the climax of his and her Battle on the film set if the Emissary had not arrived. Here was exactly the end-game result *if* EM had not made the offer to do the final repair job with one more game:

***

Cal-El agonized in excruciating pain on the fake set of the film. The half man-half Zog rolled over and over as his Center was repeatedly stabbed! *The tortured man-entity screamed in a lasting pain!*

Meb transformed into a hideously ugly creature everyone could view. The 'thought' came from NZ's mind. No matter what the outcome of the film-set Battle, NZ could make it that cameras; crystals, recorders as well as Citizens' senses saw the truth under the little girl's mask. Her career as cute Mebby was over. Zog could, at least, *do that* before his nullification. Meb's size and shape from head to toe were the same. But her true 'skin' reflected one of the most frightening images. She would stay this way. Everyone would see her for what she really was. (More screams from the child.)

Also, a bit later, the entire world ended...

***

The flash-forward snapped back. Braw continued to be stuck in time while the set still contained the two fighters and the referee.

"We're supposed to *thank you?* Your intention is to destroy us by unification." Cal-El spoke not expecting an answer.

Mebby, back to her child-visage, should have been grateful. She was not.

No-smiles Emissary finally placed a smile on his mouth. "All right, then. It's settled. The Ultimate Deal, 51% stakes which means the Winner Rules the World, controls the galaxy and is in charge of the Continuum. *Should be fun.*" The tribesman was about to clap his hands.

Cal got in the last words. "Here we go."

***

It was a dark and stormy night. It actually *was* this late evening of December 21 in the year 2012. Most people spent the night with family members as rain pelted the small town of Betelgeuse, Indiana.

Joe's Bar was one of a number of pubs in a semi-rural area dominated by industry and farming. The usual small but loyal crowd was not in attendance. It wasn't a fit night out for man or beast.

Kent Clark was a late Saturday-night regular. He entered and the door chimed. He placed his coat and umbrella in their normal spots and brushed off the remaining wetness of the hard rain.

"Hi, Joe," was thrown in the air and over the bar.

"Kent. Good to see ya," Joe replied with a relieved smile.

"Looks like I'm the only one here tonight."

Owner and only bartender of the small establishment poured Kent's Coors just the way he liked it. Joe slid the glass down the bar like he'd done a thousand times before, knowing exactly how much effort it took to make it stop right in front of Kent. "Damn weather. Doubt anyone's gonna show after midnight."

"Same for me, too. I was, ah, never mind."

The bartender asked, "You were what?"

"Nothing. What are you watching?"

Joe silenced the music at this late hour with no one in the joint. A modest 56-inch TV was *on* down at the other end of the bar.

"Pacers from earlier today. Didn't get to see it, so I streamed an ESPN3 archive."

"They would have liked that," Kent said with a forced smile. He had shocking, personal news to share and the gang was not around.

"Hey, sorry the fellas ain't here." Joe noticed that Kent was disappointed and sad. "Ah, should I...ya want me to stick around this end of the bar? You could come and watch the game? Gonna be good this year."

"No thanks, Joe. You know that's not my thing." Kent took a big gulp and nodded with the glass. "You go ahead. I can only drink Coors on this stool, remember?"

"Right."

"I'll hoot and holler when I want another. Who knows, maybe one of the guys will make it?"

"Okay. Here's one on the house. Why not? I'll be losing my shirt after tonight, anyway." Joe poured Mr. Clark a second beer and returned to watching the NBA game, his face close to the screen.

The chime of the door rang. A stranger walked in. Joe

waved his thumb to Kent as if saying *now you have someone to talk to.* The stranger appeared weird. A good 3-point shot made Joe return to his game.

The dark figure was more of a *creature* than a man. Kent saw the thing for what it was, but Joe did not. Another bizarre fact was Joe acted as if the frightening figure looked normal. 'It' proceeded, or more like slithered, to the bar and approached a sitting Kent.

Mr. Clark scrutinized the newcomer's outrageous appearance. The stranger wore all black and a hoodie. The tall, thin patron pulled back the hood and exposed its face. Its eyes were big and black. Its skin was grey. *Was tonight a dream because in walked a nightmare?*

The 'man' in black sat short of Kent and left one seat in between. Why did Kent receive the impression the stranger was Dr. Doom or 'Death' on two legs?

Joe shifted to the patron. "What are ya drinkin', guy?"

A deep, raspy voice uttered, *"Whatever he's having."*

The line seemed to break the ice and the two quickly found themselves talking to each other.

"You from around here?" Kent asked.

"Nope...passing through."

Kent was busting to break his news. He itched badly to dump out his 'big secret' that he withheld from the guys for years. Now he wanted to reveal everything.

Of all nights, why did they not show? Sure, the weather was bad, but...

Joe fixed a large glass of Coors. Instead of sliding the drink, he accompanied it down the bar to its target. "Do ya like basketball?" he asked the grey-skinned stranger.

"No."

"Ha."

"Ah, then...I'll leave you two alone."

Mr. Clark thought it would be polite to include Joe in the conversation for a quick moment, knowing the bartender was dying to return to the game. "Joe here built this place from the ground up."

"Really?" the stranger countered as it eyed the drink. 'It' looked around the wooden bar, unsure how to act.

Joe turned his gaze to the screen at the other end as he heard cheers for his team. "Yes, it was mainly my son's doing. He's the *carpenter* in the family. Special kid, and I—"

"Oh? Where is he? Does he bartend, too?" The dark figure pursued a line of questioning.

Why was he interested in Joe's son, the carpenter? Kent thought it peculiar. Kent tapped the stranger's foot with his foot unseen by Joe. This got the new guy's attention. Kent fixed his eyes to its black eyes, pursed his lips and shook his head as if to say *leave it alone...just leave it alone.*

Joe answered during the awkwardness. "He's gone...disappeared, somewhere." Joe's expression definitely changed to sorrow. His head dropped then again he heard cheers from the game. "You'll have to excuse me." Joe was transfixed on the screen and left for the other side of the bar. Or, did he simply want to escape painful memories of days gone by?

"My name's Kent. Kent Clark. No jokes, please."

"Huh? Hello." The thing spoke normal words in a deep, unusual way.

"Your name is?"

"Oh. Ha, it's Fate." The stranger kept staring at the glass as if uncertain what to do with it.

"Fate? Wow. That's, that's an odd name. Got a last name?"

"No, just Fate."

Kent nearly inhaled his Coors. He felt its effects. He laughed. "Now I know you're putting me on, ha."

Fate only smiled, and then the smile was gone. *"I have a big problem, Kent. I have a secret to tell."* The creature in black sounded serious.

Mr. Clark responded with, "I too have a big secret."

Without looking at Kent's face, Fate stated, *"Mine's bigger."*

Mr. Clark, who everyone in town thought was a normal

guy, was really an extremely rich man. He hid it well from his closest friends. Kent maintained a small house with the basic comforts of home. But, he owned much more than that. No one knew. Tonight, he decided to reveal the truth and financially help a few of his old friends.

"How can you say yours is bigger?" Kent was almost livid. He was sure that his secret was the more awesome of the two. *Who could believe he was so freaking rich?*

Fate turned its head, looked straight into Mr. Clark's eyes and said, *"You are the wealthiest man in Indiana. You control major industries in the state while posing as an ordinary man here in Betelgeuse. You think you are Bruce Wayne. But in truth, what have you really done with your life, Kent?"*

He was thunderstruck. Was this a Man in Black? Was Fate a CIA agent? Were they being monitored? How did Fate know what was hidden so well? And what was with the guy's grey skin? Kent was speechless. He gagged. He finished his drink. He bent over the bar and drew one more draft beer without Joe even noticing.

The stranger called 'Fate' still had not touched its drink. *"What have you actually done that was of great importance?"*

"I've accomplished a lot, sir. Built one hell of an Empire. It's not easy…"

"Being a workaholic," Fate completed Kent's words differently than he'd intended to say. *"Carrying on a secret identity, disregarding all family, loving no one and having no one love you? Is that what you've accomplished, friend?"*

The guy with the hood was good.

A long silence was broken by Mr. Clark, who slowly came out of a slump. "Okay, partner, what's *your* damn secret that's so frikken huge, huh?"

Fate once more turned and stared into Kent Clark's glassy eyes. *"I have to find someone who will willfully sacrifice their life in order to save the Earth from blowing up, tonight...within minutes. Is that big enough?"*

With a second Coors finished, the covert industrialist of

Indiana howled in laughter. Joe turned, and then went back to the recorded Pacers' game. Kent said, "Oh, you're beautiful, baby. And I thought I wasn't going to be entertained tonight."

"The Earth, now, today...is filled to capacity. The Hate, wars, violence, brutal crimes, unseen corporate crimes, media lies, Pentagon, Bankers, Vatican plots, governments with nuclear proliferation, prejudice, crimes against children, negative energy, it all has to reset. Must be wiped clean."

Kent was fascinated and definitely under the spell of the booze. He figured the Man in Black with grey skin was crazy. Maybe the delusional 'guy' was only a phantom from his own mind? Maybe he was asleep and nothing was real?

"You're not dreaming," Fate jumped to a new subject seemingly reading Kent's mind.

"Wait! Yer lookin' for a...a *Savior,* that's it, r-right?" Kent was a simple man at heart, a basic man with old-fashioned views. "You're looking for Christ! That's it, huh? Take away the Sins of Humanity. Yes?"

"No, that's not it. It's the build-up of negative energy, has to be released. Soon. My job is..."

"To s-sacrifice the One," Kent finished Fate's sentence. "So the, the rest of us can l-live?"

Fate repeated, *"Time is very short and the minus energy is far too great. It's already well past midnight.'*

"Hey. That's right, man! It's now Dec-cember 22nd, and you know what that m-means? The world didn't blow up!"

Fate rose to his feet in disgust. He only stared at the man who did not get it.

Rich, foggy Mr. Clark swiveled his stool and faced the tall man.

Then the colorful HD picture on the 56-inch TV went black. A horrible vibe filtered through the bar as if something awful happened a far distance away. An ominous sound like a deadly whisper was also heard. Whatever the disaster was, the rumbling appeared to be *coming this way!*

Fate grabbed the hood part of the black apparel and pulled it around its head. Fate's face was barely visible. Dark words came out that said, *"You don't understand, Mr. Clark. Your world IS going to blow up."*

When their eyes met, Kent believed the scary man called 'Fate.' Especially when *an earthquake hit Betelgeuce, Indiana, at exactly 12:27 AM on December 22nd!* The bar seemed to be ground zero for a 5.7 quake.

Joe's Bar was rocked and so were neighboring, flatland communities. Car alarms were heard as Joe quickly ran outside. The weather had cleared. Few people were out at this hour, even in the aftermath of a rare earthquake.

"This is *Indiana,* for Christ's sake!" Joe yelled into a starry sky. He turned toward his bar. Pieces of the outside crumbled as the ground jolted for a second time. Tremors cracked a few other structures. "My bar."

For this area, it was a major disaster. No one appeared to be seriously injured. The vibrations subsided. But, was this only the beginning?

Joe went back in after a minute to inspect his establishment. He passed Kent who was on his way out, followed by the Grey Man in Black.

"My God. Truly unbelievable." Once more, their eyes met. Kent asked Fate, "Is this connected to w-what you were talkin' about?"

"Of course it is. Time grows very short. I must ask you, again." Fate grabbed the mortal's shoulders. The tactile contact felt like electricity. *"Will you do it?"*

"Do what?"

"Willingly give yourself over to your Fate, to Death...to me...to die right now? In doing so, everyone else will live. The pressure will be relieved and the planet will not be destroyed. Kent, there are only two minutes left. Will you die now and save the world?"

The rich man stood stationary. A full lifetime's worth of work and accumulated fortunes, his wealth, living a dream life and it could all evaporate into smoke. His motivation was to always succeed and *control Fate,* make his own destiny and Win in the end. He felt so clever to have a secret identity. He *was* Batman.

No, it couldn't end here, to lose everything, just like that? Never!

"Kent, I need an answer now. There is no more time."

The man answered. He used his arms and swatted Fate's hands off of his shoulders. "Get away from me! NO! I'm not going to die! I won't do it. Get away!" The rich man was terrified of oblivion.

Unexpectedly, lightning flashed and loud thunder was heard in a sky without clouds. The ground shook again. With the street moving under his feet, the rich man would not change his mind. *It would be suicide* and he could not, ever, no way, get himself to agree.

Hooded Fate looked down very sadly and darkly said, *"Then all is lost. Your small world will tear apart and Larger Worlds will split as well."*

The rich man started to cry. A shaken Kent Clark emotionally replied, "W-what about him?"

Fate turned and saw a homeless man who lived inside a cardboard box in a nearby alley. His name was James. He was a neighborhood fixture who begged for food and spare change. James' face was perpetually dirty and red. Kids in the area ridiculed the skinny man. They called him 'King James.' He was almost awake. He slept a lot.

He was also called 'bum,' 'hobo,' 'village idiot' and 'the homeless guy.' James had a terrible self-image. His simple mind *believed* the criticism and insults thrown by the 'inconsiderates' of his world. He hated himself. He hated his life. He wanted to be...*saved* from a life he detested.

James was always poor. The uneducated man never stood a chance in life. He was abused, victimized, turned to crime and spent years in jail. Regrettably, he hurt many people in the past. Poor James was the polar opposite of Kent Clark. James was a 'loser' who never succeeded in anything. He felt like a black cloud always followed him and always doled out bad luck. Now, Fate had an important question for him.

On the outside, James was a simple man in desperate

search of redemption. On the inside, he was moved by God. James was a human 'receptacle' or 'carrier' for God. God was the 4th Builder whose energy light was nearly spent as its Architecture was coming to the end of a Great Cycle.

In the alley appeared a small, pink Aphid that waddled into the scene on three legs.

The poor man opened his eyes and what operated the bum's body was God. It was not King James behind green eyes. A ridiculed, spat upon, dirty man in the worst clothes was only on the exterior. James had been the quiet hulk where a tired God slept. They had an amicable relationship. God or 4th Builder escaped the chambers (catacombs) of his original Home as 'Veck' and zipped through Time, hidden behind Time's Curtain. James agreed to let God's dim light sleep within him. When he slept, God slept. God needed a sweet soul for a last, small 'candle of light' to exist before *everything changed again.*

James sacrificed his life. He received his redemption and relieved the pressure to save the Earth and many other worlds. The Mayans were wrong, or were they?

Someone asked, "Where do we stand?" When the question was spoken, the Dream changed again.

***

Four sets of eyes opened. They were at Soma seashores. The feeling was the feeling inside an ambiguous dream. White mists of pleasure breezed by and soon left. The magical scene cleared. Half submerged in a small, squared-off lagoon of liquid purity were:

1) The Devil; she appeared more as her mechanical self only without hair! Mebby was bald. Bands of hidden circuitry were seen on her hairless top-skull, which gave off a very artificial aura. Somewhere, she had lost the wig.

2) The Zog or Neo Zog; Cal-El seemed his normal, powerful, merged self as the body of Tray Caladan soaked in mystic waters.

3) The God; a new character from the alley also had

white hair. He cleaned up rather well. James was not James but a New James conglomerate of the 4th Creator and a 'bum' on the street. It was God who spoke through James.

4) The Emissary; a grey Decider, *Dealer* and Master of Ceremonies. The dark creature, distinctive inside a background of white, was one confused tribesman.

Each sat at four corners of the squared lagoon. The unhappy Devil sat submerged at the South end. Zog sat at the North end. God sat submerged at the East end and was hungry. The Emissary sat in the West corner and had a deck of cards in his hands.

In the middle of the square appeared a watery, transparent table. Mystical symbols in fine black lines were solidly etched on a surface that constantly rippled with soothing waves. The Emissary had the cards in his left hand while his right covered his mouth. His eyes kept shifting from the warping table corners to each player and back again. He was perplexed.

Bald Mebby screamed, "I won 51%!" It became a chant. "I won 51! I won 51! I won 51! You saw it. Renoux saw it. *He failed.* Your Bozing Savior failed the Ultimate Test. You know it. I know it. Now cough up the goods. I want to see signed Fed contracts. I won 51! I won..."

Zog, with a casual flick of a finger, shut the trap of the flaming Devil so out of place amongst the white serenity. Zog materialized an extra piece of bio-material or faceplate to form over her mouth. The bald thing of animated evil had to soak in angelic waters, quietly. She pulled and tugged on the mouth-mask to no avail. She had her thin arms on her submerged, synthetic hips and her face held a very nasty expression.

Emissary, while looking at the wet table, had an odd comment. "Enjoy the Power while you can, Zog."

What could that mean? NZ wondered what the Emissary meant outside of his own nullification being imminent.

Mebby, with mouthpiece, reacted by widening her wild eyes as if she *won* or will win.

God, at the East end, opened its sleepy eyes again and asked, "Mind if I take a nap? I'm old."

Tribesman Emissary rubbed his wrinkled brow. He informed the threesome, "I don't think the patterns are right. Numbers are wrong here."

"Huh?"

("I'll say.")

"Zzzzzzzzzzzzzzzzzz..."

Zog in North corner turned to the West. "Please explain, Emissary." Zog was very sad like he knew he *blew it big time.* This time, his last chance, and he had made the *wrong choice.* How could Zog's Crimes be forgiven? Zog knew he would be punished and he deserved the punishment for multiple offenses. Zog welcomed nullification of his Immortal Soul-Center if that be his Fate! He was ready for the Emissary's response.

"Yes, yes, yes, Zog!" EM's fingers flipped through the 52 cards. His right hand pointed to strange symbols that held steady in the waves. His head tilted. "Don't know if we can start if...if...that cannot be right." EM pointed again. He was lost.

What did the Decider see that bothered him?

"What?"

The tribesman brought himself out of his 'funk' and looked deeply into Cal's eyes. He knew it would be the Devil that would not understand what had happened, nor *like* it very much. "You failed, El, exactly as the Professor predicted."

Zog expressed extreme sadness. Devil-Meb remained gagged, but was elated. No one could see her smile. It showed in her big eyes. God stopped snoring loud.

"You have been *pardoned,* Zog."

("What?")

"You failed because you had no other choice. You could *only* fail. You were implanted by a corrupt 'seed' by machines, plus our Brothers and Sisters have informed me of other reasons that adversely affected your decision, Zog. We are ALL, in a sense, *dylars:* only pawns in the Larger Games.

Upstairs decreed the Game *voided* and we remain tied Gentleman and Lady. There's not much Time. It's 2099.99. It has to end, again, now."

Zog was curious. "EM, what's wrong in the patterns? If everything is coming down to one hand of poker to decide the stakes of the universe, then there better the Hensi not be anything wrong with the final Game."

"Not poker," EM answered. "TONK."

God heard *the word* and became attentive. God said, "I like Tonk. Let's play." Then he softly spoke unheard words, "Did you know I'm the Writer? It trumps Architect."

"Here we go." New Zog smiled and rubbed his hands together.

[The Universal 5-card Game was known in all 25 sectors and was not only a means to pass the time for 'Flog' caddies waiting to 'Go OUT' on Mineer].

Neo Zog seriously asked the tribesman, "Can we keep that gag on her? She doesn't need to speak to play, yes?"

The Ultimate Dealer nodded and shuffled the cards.

Mebby could not vocalize her violent complaints. She stopped thrashing in the liquid and realized she should concentrate on the card game. If she won, *she'd win it all.*

God confessed to the gang, "Learned da game in prison. It's a *prison* game. The sweetheart of a soul was correct. The Waters made a new man of him. He was forgiven and washed clean.

Mebby responded with a 'thumbs up' sign. She gave up trying to remove her faceplate. The Devil needed to focus.

The Emissary at West end almost dealt the cards. He continued to be baffled at the symbols and conflicting numbers on the moving board. "Don't worry. It will come to me. I'll figure it out." EM gazed squarely into each of three corners. They understood what the Game meant. Each nodded and did not need to cut the cards. EM dealt face-down cards that waved with the clear table, yet stood steadfast as if on a dry table. Each participant could not view the cards of the others. Each Zog Player in the Higher Dimension also could not view the same parallel Cards in a far wider World.

The Emissary dealt counterclockwise because that was the spin of the current Monopdonow Continuum Galaxy. Devil-Meb picked up a card from the face-down deck and quickly discarded a high card (10).

God drew from the deck and discarded a Jack on the face-up discard pile. The 4th Builder was able to hide every nuance of strategy.

NZ picked up and discarded a Queen to lower his total score. He thought he had a great Tonk hand.

Robo-Devil-girl picked up and added the card to her hand. She discarded a 6. Mebby also pantomimed a slash-to-throat sign to Zog. New Zog knew she was up to mind-tricks again, but he had to concentrate.

The Game was everything. Discarding a 6 so soon; she couldn't be that low?

God used telekinesis, and the top card in the deck turned face-up, floated and neatly landed on the discard pile. "I didn't need it."

Cal-El thought he was about to *win.* "That cannot be your highest card." He was again tempted to go OUT. Or was he telepathically bluffing? Zog changed his mind and picked up a card. "Ha!" It was another 4, which made a 'spread.' The ecstatic player proudly faced-up the three 4s and discarded a 7. Zog's hand appeared pretty darn good. He had two cards left; they had 5 cards.

The Devil frowned behind the faceplate.

"Your turn." Cocky Zog rolled his eyes and directed her with significant smiles.

Robo-Meb picked up from the face-down deck. She did not want the card and *slammed* it on the face-up discard pile. The card gently moved in perfect place after it left her artificial hand.

It was not Cal-El's turn, but he reminded them, "Hey, I can go OUT next time, not this time, next time. Oooh, yes." The Game seemed 'fated' to be *won* by the hand in the north end of the little lake.

"Not so fast there, partner." God 'spread.' 'Oh, you *could* do dat, my boy, but you might not *want* to do dat, fella." *God knew his Tonk.* The East-wing, street urchin laid down three 3s while the grey Dealer and others looked on. God discarded a 5 and *also* had two cards left, the same number of cards in Zog's hand. *What God held was an occult unknown.*

Mebby rocked back and forth in glee. She rooted for God if she could not win. Anyone but her sworn arch enemy, Zog, *in the North corner so high and mighty. ("Bastard, shut me up will you? I'll get you. I know where.")*

Zog or Cal picked up and discarded a card he did not need during his 'One Wait.'

Devil again plucked from the deck. She 'spread' three Jacks. Now the Beast-Child had much more than a glimmer of hope, especially when she hit Zog with a 'hit' card. Mebby slapped the fourth 4 onto Zog's spread pile. 'She' discarded an Ace, which left only one card in her hand!

Her grand total of '1' was the lowest of the hands.

"Mother. I *had* you from the very beginning," Zog lied.

("Ooooh...did you, Brother?") she sweetly replied muffled behind her mouthpiece and unaware of the lie. She was excited and on peedles and nins. Mebby was going to win, she thought.

The Emissary, as only an observer, had moments to study the Mystic patterns that remained a firm constant with only a Gravity-Wave illusion of movement. He pointed as if close to one striking realization that could affect the Game. Then referee-Decider thought his gestures could disturb the players. Tribesman controlled himself and paid more attention to the problem in the symbols/numbers, rather than the Tonk. His eyes darted. His blue neck-ring pulsated slightly.

Everyone had 'spread,' which meant anyone could go OUT at any time on their turn, no Waits. But New Zog was *HIT,* so he had one Wait.

Zog had a sudden and bizarre question for the tribesman Emissary they called 'EM.' "What was your name, again?"

The Dealer replied, "You asked that of me before, Cal. It's Emanuel."

God maneuvered a bit by *using* the picked card. The new card was placed in his hand. Now it was time for God to discard a King on the discard pile, but before that happened (before the King was revealed) – the Emissary *called a HALT to the Game!*

"STOP!" EM's thin arms pointed to Soma-white skies as his eyes focused on patterns in the waves. *Now* he read the symbols correctly. White Light finally struck the Judge and Jury. There would be no mistrial – the Game could proceed with 'hands' exactly where they stood.

Mebby was confused. Cal was interested. God was hungry and overdue for a nice nap. His eyes closed.

Zog realized that the Emissary realized... "You know, sir? You now know."

"Huh?" God barely asked. God-Entity went back to sleep. "Zzzzzzzzz..."

Suddenly, the Emissary tribesman let out loud *laughter* that ricocheted off Soma waters and echoed back from islands in the mist. His whole demeanor changed from *mystification to clarification.* "I get it now! *I've been wrong.* Everyone has been wrong! The Continuum's been wrong!" Then he directed and pointed. "YOU change with you! Now it will make sense and work correctly. Hurry!"

What? What was the Cosmic Joke only the Emissary understood? He wanted God from the East to change places with Neo Zog in the North.

"What?" Cal-El asked, well planted in his position.

("Why?") was a muffled sound from behind Mebby's mouthpiece in the South.

God woke up. Zog and God switched positions quickly, yet the *hands* remained the same.

"Hurry! The Game has to conclude *now* in the next yas!" Emissary screamed in terror when he realized the Cosmic Clock was ready to strike 2100.00.

Mebby only observed with even wider eyes. She had a

lot to scream about behind the muffler.

Zog said into God's flushed face, "Just between you and me now, huh?"

He responded with a pistol-pantomime back at Cal. "Bang."

It was the East's turn, and Zog discarded the King on the discard pile. God, submerged in the North, was overjoyed when the King was added to his pair of Northern Kings! *God had TONKED OUT!*

Zog held a pair of high Kings the whole time.

God won the Game and was quite happy. It felt like old times as a caddy...or in prison.

Emissary explained, "You see, I wasn't sure who Mebby's opposite was. Was it Zog or God? Everyone in the CONTINUUM has been led to believe Zog was the Builder. Then...it was so easy a yahoo on Zetag could have figured it out."

EM turned to God who was awake and paid attention. He also turned to the Devil and snatched her mechanical arm very hard. Now she knew what was coming and pulled with all her bionic strength for release. Grey EM had her locked to him as *she again and again tried to pull away!*

Cal-El in the East coaxed the Judge, "Say again."

"The *opposite* of her needed to sit at North as the cards showed, that was the Game, and real God/Creator was revealed. The real God would Win, opposite of South, opposite of the Devil. Patterns and numbers weren't wrong. Your *seating arrangement was wrong.*" EM took a breath. The tribesman told the *man* sincerely, "You were *never* her opposite, Zog. Remember, your light is blue, not white. God's light is white...and very dim now."

"What?" Zog inquired like an innocent baby.

("Whaaa? Ah, uh...uh, ah, aaah, uh!") Bald Meb-android maintained her violent squawking against the inevitable. She dialed her rants and raves back slightly when she noticed the approach of a Quizo. The cute Aphid walked up to the Waters and drank, then glowed. She knew it was for her and her Anti, the Other One, the Enemy (not Zog) but God.

With her free hand, she tore into the faceplate and ripped it off with emotion. The new voice was mega-mechanical. *"Naaauuugh! You said, you said it was for 51% CONTROL, to see who was in Charge!"*

"Not the Tonk Game, dear. It's how I flip a coin, which always results in truth," Emissary replied.

"Aaaaww!" She screamed.

God (#4) had one last wish and he said it. "I hope the next fella does better."

The grey EM tribesman with a Zero-Charge, the Third Charge, also held God's hand. Only it was not being yanked in horror. It was held with love.

Emanuel had one last word for Mebby. He said with wide eyes, "Smashing!" Both God and the Devil disappeared from the Universe. *Thank Zog!*

In the pool was the combination of the two. It appeared as if the Emissary merged the two magnetic poles and became their sum. Such was not the case. (EM's job, nearly botched, was considered successful to those Upstairs. The repair-job worked and the infected Galaxy would not blow up as scheduled at 2100, *never to start again*...DESTROYING ALL!) The creature in the pool was not the Emissary, but the remainder or combined sum (#5).

Only a very few Higher ZOGS in the Largest of CONTINUUMS (really the smallest of continuums) understood what just happened or *how close all CONTINUUMS were of winking out of existence!* Mystics, Citizens, humanoids, humans and many aliens on lower levels teuned-in to the Big Tonk Game; they were oblivious to the significance of what they observed.

If New Zog/Cal-El would have remained in the North, WON the game and Tonked-OUT...not only would an amazing Immortal Soul needed in the Universe have been snuffed out for no reason, but *ALL CONTINUUMS would have winked out of existence!* The 4th Creator absolutely could not have been left to *lose* the Game and *remain;* its dim and dying light was spent constructing the world. Its time and its Architecture's Time were *up* (2100.00). There would be no energy left to kick-start, renew or Recycle Reality. *Zog's Blue Energy rekindled Life to start over.*

Zog was introduced to the Fifth Creator in the pool. There was not much to say to the fresh Spirit that had so much ahead of it. It left the Tonk field. There was no Quizo in sight.

***

Normalcy was the vibration among the stars. Life forms, in the first days of galaxy L-MN200, were complacent. Beings were not naturally fearful. Creatures did not run to defenses and build armies or Weapons of Mass Destruction. Early wars were not the way of this particular galaxy. Conflicts were aberrations. A type of *planetary-trust* existed that intelligent societies would not construct arms against neighboring worlds. This was true as first days of warfare were nearly gone.

Pyramid power stations were installed on planets in many solar systems without any defensive barriers, whatsoever. Why spend energy on security measures when there were no enemies and there was only tranquility? Why make force-fields if we do not need them? Consider if full military assaults *were* waged on the wireless pyramid stations, civilizations would utterly collapse. And yet, transmitting towers were left wide open to attack in an age of peace.

One benefit from being under the wing of the Order was civil wars were at a minimum. But soon, everything would change.

Galaxy L-MN200, birthplace of Zog, would become the center of a future controversy, as if this unique 'Pinwheel' of worlds would become a turning point of future events. Mystics, seers, prophets from the Great Color Spectrum and on the highest of levels had foreseen the importance of what was usually an insignificant galaxy. L-MN200 was special. Soon, every 'ascended' Citizen would be completely aware *who* and exactly *what* Zog was, and an entire Universe would be astounded!

The oddity of a galaxy was christened with a new name. No more was the Binars' cold classification. In its place was a strange word that appeared the same from either end. The word was 'Monopdonow.' L-MN200 had become the 'Monopdonow Continuum.'

The Secret Federation, under the growing 'Chancellery' Movement, was more than a little concerned about the 'Chosen One.' The Star Chamber which ruled 'the Order' decided to pay the Zog a small visit. Could he really fly, walk on water, 'raise the dead,' channel the All-Being Creator of Everything and exist as a physical, representative 'Avatar' of Zog in the Material World? Was this Zog the Zog of ancient legend? The feds or covert 'Committee,' which still went by the name 'the Order,' wanted to find the truth...

The Continuum

After Word - After World - After Life

THE UPPER WORLD, one level above the level of the Monopdonow Pinwheel universe, decreed a 'Cosmic Gift' shall be freely given without payment to the world below. A particular Black Hole in the Larger World compensated for the size difference and was the special conduit by which 'the Gift' could be *realized* on this lower, physical level. In the Larger Dimension, the BH Vortex was known as 'Fornax.'

Zogs, grateful for the Stage Play and Ultimate Resolution performed in the lower Continuum, gathered fantastic masses of minerals and resources together. More riches and valuable 'stuff' beyond Citizens' comprehension was accumulated in and around Fornax. The Zogs 'shoveled' the rare matter in the Event Horizon, continuously. Time did not exist to Zogs. It was their way of expressing thanks for the show and especially *thanks for saving us.* Far more than entertainment value, their Universe was spared being ripped apart as well. What transpired in the smaller Continuum affected the Larger Continuum and vice versa.

Few life forms understood the relativities of micro-universes to Macro-Universes. In truth, there were only 11 Dimensions, Universes or Continuums. There was the smaller or 'lesser universe' in which our Pinwheel existed and turned. There was the Larger Level or 'greater Universe' directly above it of Zogs (parallel) like the next higher 'Floor' in a building. An even smaller, micro universe existed below. Levels continued above and below. Black Holes / Quasars were the ins-and-outs or yins and yangs of the world-Floors. They connected Dimensions and provided the means to travel between them. But micro realms and Macro Realms did not continue forever. The Continuums, in parallel propagations, did not go on infinitely. There were only eleven Continuums. The first one was the last one or was connected to the last one. Lower end of the universe linked to the Upper End. Continuums were attached. There were only eleven Gaming Houses.

The 'Gift' exploded out of the Neri Vortex! From down here, it was a stream of material brilliance. The 'Fountain' became the most astounding *fountain* of all time. Neri *gushed* such light-energy-lines that formed into a miraculous rain of resources. Riches, valuable minerals and rare elements blasted out of the Vortex Funnel in a continuous shotgun-effect. What crystallized into radiant rains of particles in every direction cooled and then solidified was *mega-extraordinary.* Any passing ship could scoop a Zog's Ransom within the sphere in yas. *What good was a Money System if everyone could be made super rich by just opening their hand?*

The reality of the super flow of resources was only one possibility. The Universe was being 'built' back up for a fifth time by a 5th Creator. Anything could happen. The next time could involve a different scenario entirely: possibly a big *sucking* Neri Black Hole?

Citizens should really prospect space near the Neri Vortex.

While the Zogs were in the process of 'shoveling' marvelous, free material-Gifts into Fornax that trickled down here, they looked around in their Upper Realm. Zogs were surprised to discover that one of their distant Quasars suddenly spewed a GOD's Ransom! Moral to the story:

'The more you give, the more you receive.'

***

The Fifth Creation of the Fifth Creator also contained a common concept carried through sectors and transfered over a period of ages. The idea was consistent with how things were basically done. They were basically done *the right way.* The right way was technology and other major scientific discoveries were not sold by their discoverers, promoters, distributors, agents, and investors. They were *given* to the universe. Products were made and given away: *what a concept!* A Galactic Monetary Standard did not exist because a GMS did not *need* to exist. That was how Business was conducted in the fifth go-around.

The galaxy benefited from the collective Cosmic Consciousness in a huge way. The galaxy was no longer the victim of a Chancellery or an Order or a Ghost of Sardon. Citizens were free. Generally, the 'fella' or New Architect did a better job than the last one. For the most part, it was a wonderful world.

Then again, 2100.00 would happen once more. A Sixth Builder would attempt to construct from the deconstruction and the struggle would happen all over again.

But in the Fifth Construct, Zog was left in the physical world of the galaxy he loved. He spun counterclockwise right along with the rest of us. Zog was a man. Zog was *only* a man, a man called Tray Caladan. He could not fly. He could not defeat any more resurrections of Martian Ghosts. The man could not manipulate matter. The Superman becoming the man was exactly what Cal wanted. He loved Citizens so much that he became one of them. He became a 'filthy dylar.' He was mortal. The man could die, but there was always Ascension. Even the Zogs began as mortals and earned (not bought) their way to Nirvana.

New Zog returned to being 'just a man' because his blue energy was spent in creating the world anew.

With the Devil gone from the material world, the galaxy was a nicer place to live. Tray lived a happy life with Mary.

Twenty-five sectors experienced a spiritual boom. For the most part, Citizens were happy. Yahoos discovered the larger world they inherited and transcended in their own ways.

The Game continued to be played in the Continuum, but there was a different 'Order.' The accumulation of dylars and financial success was not the motivating force to Life. Love and appreciation for the incredible universe was the prevailing thought or feeling. We learned and experienced an extraordinary creative boom because Citizens were geared to production rather than destruction. War was no more. War became an archaic and obsolete notion, generally.

A Galactic Utopia was forged in truth and blue light.

For a while, it was glorious. Paradise never lasts. Everything cycles. Everything changes and 'Everything Ends.' Fact of the matter: Everything also begins again.

Oh, dylars or trylars or bylars could come into play during the next Creations of the Universe. For now, intelligence, logic, love and compassion as well as other good stuff *ruled the day!*

The hero could not escape one final, devastating blow in his later life. Tray Caladan built an fantastic life and bonded with Mary Escovilla. His Fortress was no longer lonely. They built a beautiful home there together. The dream was like a dream. Both were extremely happy as man and wife. Cal was not a celebrity. He was a talented designer and architect, but he went completely unrecognized as the former superhero.

His services were freely given. Products were free, his house and vehicles were free. Life was free and this was absolutely how it should be. This was right. This was the way it *could* be without war and energy wastefully spent on mass destruction. Was Tray's perfect universe the reason for his personal tragedy? Was there another reason?

There still existed Lady Braw in the galaxy with her lovely doppelganger, Mary. One evening, Tray returned to the Fortress and discovered the force-field shielding was down. The base had been broken into with all systems deactivated. When he reached their bedroom, he found *Braw had murdered Mary!* He remembered a thought from the demon-child. "She knew where to hurt him." This was her final revenge against Zog who was not Zog anymore. The Devil lost and did not become the Master of the Universe in the 4th Creation, or in the 5th Creation.

But the Devil held hope for the sixth.

The personal tragedy took an unbelievable, weird twist when *Lady Braw returned to the scene of the crime.* The body that ripped down defense systems of the Fortress and murdered Mary ran toward Tray Caladan, who was in utter anguish at the death of his beloved Mary. In tears, he faced his wife's killer. *Why was she here? What was he going to do?* He was ready to fight and destroy the thing in his wife's image.

Tray soon realized this *was* his wife! Mary had learned yin's Mystic Arts and was proficient in out-of-the-body travel. Tray's wife always asked permission to enter the body of another at a great distance. In the case of Lady Braw, she made an exception.

A yam after the murder at the base, Braw (now Mary) was able to convince Tray she was the *good one*. Braw wound up killing herself. Her soul-Center was gone from this plane because of her despicable act against an ex-Zog, destroying his other half. Mary's spirit came back into the body of the ex-Viper 'warhorse.'

They laughed together again. He said, "I'll have to get used to a few more scars. I can do that." He brushed his hand across her cheek.

In his arms, she said, "You didn't think you were getting away from me, did you? Not that easy." She laughed inside slightly darker skin. The green eyes were the same.

Tray held her long red tresses and asked his old wife in a new body, "Can you *do* something about the hair?"

"Sure." They laughed again. It was great to laugh.

***

A pink Quizo turned toward crystal-recorders. Monitors captured very close up pictures of the little fellow's small head at the end of its extremely long neck. His face was rather attractive for an Aphid. After a sweet smile, it winked for the cameras.

***

A last dream oddity happened in the future, in the Sixth Construct. It only happened for a split-ya. Cal-El visited or entered a dream of a young Jene 4 Renoux. Jene was beardless. He had no wrinkles. These were days before the pipe. Renoux was an acclaimed physicist at the time, one of the new breed that would 'conquer the universe in an i-File.' He hit a moment in REM sleep that he was sure to forget when he awoke the next day.

A few Continuums ago, it was an elderly Renoux who visited the young Mineeran in a dream on a shuttle. In this particular incarnation twist, Cal returned the gesture. Cal-El appeared in the young Suruuan's spaceship. Cal was Superman. Superman was the Teacher and it was the physicist in the role of apprentice and eager student. One more important lesson had to be *taught*.

[Besides the Lesson: What was more important than Zog, Architect and Builder? Answer: God, Writer and Dreamer].

***

I was ready to yell, *"Superman"* like at a surprise party. It was a surprise, all right. I shouted, "Cal-El!"

No, that wasn't an expression. It was Cal-El, all right.

I'd recognize the hippie anywhere, only he was dressed in a very expensive and well tailored Superman outfit. Cal-El had very long, white hair. He had a red 'S' on his chest (Savior or Satan?), yellow belt, blue tights and red boots. *Fuck a duck!* He came from the Outside and entered my mind-menagerie to…I think he came to answer three of my questions.

He had a wonderful smile, this super-*man,* Lois had said. He was a likable guy. *He could have run for mayor of Jerusalem. He could have been a Kennedy.*

"Wow. I always liked you, Cal, the peace and love thing." I gazed at the uniform or costume. "Oh, might wanna stay away from our Warp Coil. It's Red Kryptonite, unpredictable bugger."

Cal-El smiled and casually said, "Wife likes your sense of humor."

"Huh?" My eyes got real big. I had to wonder about that one. *C'mon!*

"Can I sit?"

"You tired, Superman? You know, I never thought I'd ask that question." My smile hurt.

We both sat down and laughed at my awesome sense of

humor that was faster than a speeding bullet. I looked at him, not believing the image before me. I must remember to keep believing the dream images in my eyes. It's *somebody's* reality. He looked around my quarters.

"So, Cal-El, did ya ever think you'd become a swear word?"

"Jene, I can't bend the rules. Please, watch it. That was your first question. You only get three."

"Dammit! Oh, sorry."

He acted a bit kooky with his reply to my stupid, thoughtless (waste of a golden opportunity) question. I *guess he was compelled to answer.*

Cal responded, "No, I never thought I'd be a cuss word."

"You speak great English, El, I guess, working at the Daily Galaxy. *Hey,* did you ever see Ned Teeley as you in *Cal-El Superstar?* Shit! Shit! My fucking mind! I just asked you the second question now, didn't—no! I almost asked you the *third* queston. Shut me the fuck up, Cal-El!"

He laughed. I made the Neo Christ laugh.

"Ha. Oh me, to answer that. I did see it, loved it, liked that I didn't get back on the mothership, loved the spaceships in the desert, *that did happen.* Ah, um, Ned did a super job with the singing; loved it when he climbed the mountain, the throbbing neck on the high notes. Anyway, my friend, that leaves one. I hope you have—"

"I have. I have," I said in excitement as the precise heavy question was formulating in my mind. When he rambled on about his movie, it struck me, the perfect thing to ask, although I was not sure just how to ask it. *Oh, well. Here we go.*

"Why is it that there are so many problems in the Galaxy? We suffer with the Hell of a living, material existence. We need help, so why is it that nothing, no one bloody well comes to our rescue, no alien, no God, no angel, no space brothers...when we are so desperate, so in pain. The hungry, the suffering in horrible conditions, the children, *especially the children,* and please don't give me the non-interference clause where no one can interrupt, negatively or positively affect development or history of planets. *C'mon!* It's all the same question: Why won't God help us? Why won't alien gods, compassionate hearts from vast numbers of upper universes help us? Plenty of neighboring suns and galaxies here just won't assist where it's needed...in our suffering Milky Way Galaxy! *What the fuck is wrong with you guys upstairs?* Sorry, Cal-El Superman."

I finally ended my rant. I got a little carried away. "Do ya have an answer for me there, CE? We can't be on our own and everyone has troubles too? Oh the Fucking Force, you're going to say 'Free Will.' God won't interfere in our *choices.* That's why innocent children get slaughtered and run over, yes? Again, sorry, I'll stop now."

"Funny you mentioned the Non-Interference Clause because there is a far greater tragedy happening in the universes, Jene 4," Super El sadly responded. "Everything down here is expanded up there."

"Huh?" I replied without a clue.

"There exists a *larger* form of the Directive. It is a real Non-Interference Clause between big worlds. No one from the outside, Upper Floors, can go within (below) and assist in any large way," Cal in red and blue costume with long white hair flatly stated with chin in hand. "It's a bummer, man. Can't help."

"Damn."

Cal-El halted any more humor. The superhero sat back and got comfortable and got very, very serious. He wanted to answer my question, and he did that in the most thorough way possible. He sincerely explained to me in great detail why things were the way they were in the real world, not this world which I thought was real (but now understand was only ghostlike holo-figments). Man, did he hit me with a long dissertation. He went on and on and on about the State of the Galaxies. They were *all in Big Trouble.*

It was very sad to hear his solemn words of pain and

despair out there. He was in tears. He meant every word. Everyone, everywhere, on all levels were screwed...even Jerry Cornelius on all Floors, Major Grubert, Winston Rumfoord and the DeGroots...*everyone!*

I flashed to a quick scene from 'Cal-El Superstar' where he could show us charts and graphs to explain it all, but, you know, that might not change anything. Zog-hippie was literally 'higher' than I was, which meant the Man could see farther up and down the road (Continuum) than I could. He could view the Bigger World. He used his hands a lot. *Sure the El wasn't Italian? Man, he was a downer; what happened to all the giggles?*

Then he changed to more of the Superman, the ultra-Scientist from the Higher Dimension and not a man from Earth.

Supe looked cool in long, white hair.

Now, he stood up and displayed on a screen for me, *holy shit. He just told me the UNIFIED FIELD FACT!* I creamed in my labcoat. Stars and accompanying planet systems were truly atomic nuclei with orbiting electrons. *Pretend the last sentence was written 12-13 times, because I still don't think yunze guys will get it!*

Einstein, Tesla's student, searched the last part of his life for the answer to the Unified Field. Little did he know that he should have read Dr. Seuss' (Mineeran physicist) 'Horton Hears a Who?' There were worlds inside worlds inside worlds for infinity...

"Daaa!"

I asked Super-El, "So, you mean, are you trying to tell me, on Earth, we're walking on one big atom's electron? And that means, oh, my God, *I see music,* an atom from my, let's say, pant leg is an entire bloody universe?"

Cal-El Superman answered, "Yes."

"You saying Earth is evil? My home planet is evil because it carries a negative charge? It's an electron, the whole fucking planet, and is one big ball of evil? And the universe, the entire universe in which it floats...also evil?"

Cal-El looked directly into my eyes and said, "It's HELL."

He scared me. I guess he would know. He's seen the universes and traveled the space-ways. He's felt spiritual pain. He also knew physical pain because he dared to love. Then the man smiled a bit. This was the first 'light' moment in ages. *What was he gonna say?*

"But it wasn't always that way, Mr. Renoux." He revealed the Truth of Ages. He was 'high' all right. The enlightened man saw beyond and through Time in both directions. Cal understood the drawing to be a circle. The man from Earth, 'A Man Out of Time,' continued. "But long ago, your planet carried a *positive* charge and the negative charge was in the sun where your protons are today. Back then, was the time of Atlantis. Everything was right in the world, your world, at first. It was Eden, a technological paradise, a moonless perfection. It was precision. It was my baby and my responsibility. Why do you think Earth even *has* a Moon?"

Wow. What the fuck did that mean? What was the lesson here? Life was so terrible on the modern hell of Earth and elsewhere, that what? Death should be welcomed? No. (I kept inside) Suicide cannot be the answer.

I suddenly realized, "Hey, I thought it was only *three* questions?"

"Oh, I was just fuckin' with ya. Ha!"

Ha. Cal-El, the Jesus on Earth, made me laugh. "You bastard." I actually said back to the hippie Zog in costume. "You *are* like us; you're trying to tell me that, right? We're all the *same,* right? Your eastern teachings of India were the important thing, lost by western world editors, revisionists, right? Saint Esa? They're missing the Reincarnation aspect...the whole *born again* thing was literal. You were St. Esa during your 'Missing Years' as a teenager. They wanted you to marry young. You were afraid, so you ran away to India and Egypt to find out what Life was all about. You ran *away* from love. Then you discovered Home."

"Why didn't they ever picture me really smiling or

laughing? That would have been the proper portrayal of me, cutting a joke, makin' you laugh and having a good time with my wife. What the Hell's wrong with living your life, all right, like a peacenik hippie?"

"So now you're asking *me* questions?" Superman had to leave, soon. He knew it too. Cal-El rose to his feet.

"You know what you did, don't you, Cal? You know what it was they didn't like, don't you?"

The Man, not God's son, smiled, "Oh, now I'm glad I came. Please tell me, Jene. I know you're a smart kid." Cal was very curious.

I walked to the wall and pulled off a titanium relic from Cestus III. It was the Rod of Longinus. Superman had to perform at least one feat of strength during Segui. I wasn't going to bounce Rocketballs off his chest or have him crush coal into a diamond. But maybe he could bend an old rod of titanium? Then I turned and milked the moment. "You put Zog in here." I pounded my chest. "It was always out there before you." I pointed away. "You put the potential of GOD into every human heart. We're all created equal, ya said. You said we're the same. You made us one of you."

"I'm very pleased, my son...Circle of Life. Did you know I was the Man in the Moon and the wife was the Lady?"

I had no understanding of his words so they brushed by me without touching. "Oh, almost forgot. Let me see you bend it. Okay? Please, before you go." I placed the heavy rod-relic into his strong hands. I wanted to see a miracle. I was wide-eyed and bushy-tailed and did not even realize (too late) that I had already stepped into a bucket of dung. "Shit."

Cal stared at me, funny. Then, he stared at the rod. I think he was greatly disappointed in me. *He was.* "I thought you understood, Jene. You probably could beat me at arm wrestling. Don't make me something I'm not." He got ready to leave. But how was he going to leave?

I was stunned. He reminded me of my father for some reason. The dream-Cal-El proceeded to fly away at light-speed through the bulkhead and out into space. He actually intended to *zip between the molecules. Then it hit me!*

"Hold yer horses, Old Man. *Now* you have power? *Now* you can fly? Now you're a superhero?" *What's the lesson here?*

"You know, I'm real. Through the molecules, two things *can* occupy the same space, eh? Think about it. We always bent the rules for you, son. 3:16 is felderkarb...and Jene...don't tell them about me."

"Not a word, Mr. Kent."

He was really cool and zipped away faster than a laser.

It was strange that the dream superhero changed into my father. He was trying to tell me I will be just like him, with that spiritual potential. And then I could fly through a ship's bulkhead as well.

"All in good time, my son."

The End

Secrets to the Continuum

What's the Continuum? What's a Chancellery and what is this Devil of a Sardon? There are many Continuums, continuums within Continuums. Imagine ever-widening ripples on a pond, frequencies in space, or as David Bowie once described: "television." The Sardon is harder to explain.

The character was taken from the grey creeps in the film, 'Dark City,' hence the hat and black attire. It was as if the last creature of Universal Accounting *became Money,* became the very thing that it coveted most, which left it drained of all 'human' morality. It was going to *ruin everything* simply because it had the power to do so.

'Sardon' originated from the word 'sardonic' meaning: 'grimly mocking or cynical.' There was a real Semetic Akkadian who conquered Sumeria named 'Sargon.' The historical King (of Time) was probably the source for 'Sargon,' a 'god' in a Star Trek episode.

Of course, the dark thing represented Adolph Hitler who was known as the 'Chancellor.' Hitler's rise to power was highly magnified within a larger 'ripple in space' or the Continuum Galaxy; it happened again on a much larger scale. Readers were mostly viewing the adventures of the galactic Second Reich, which paralleled Hitler's 'Third' down here on a smaller scale.

When 'Zog of Legend' was confronted on Mineer by worried State officials and highest military man, Caladrian Trask...a very strange incident occurred: Zog, a powerful spirit without a body from a Higher Continuum, met an early form of the person/soul it would inhabit in the future in order to save the universe. Only this 'early form' was not a nice person and wanted to kill the Blue Angel.

'Cal' was the spiritual consistency through Time with Caladrian and Caladan. Like with Braw/Mary or Mada/Pe're anyone could be saved. The whole 'death/possession' idea was explored in depth.

A good question: "How does a writer go about the task of creating more than a thousand-year (yarn) history of an entire, spinning galaxy?" It would have to be done in the relationships of living beings between solar systems that had no idea the others existed. They parallel. They reincarnate. It would have to be done with worlds that amazingly coincided and call them 'Continuums.' Each repeated again and again; the little ones affected Big Ones and the Big Ones influenced the little ones.

[Why do events happen the way that they do? Why do disasters happen, cars crash, a job opens up, a baby being born, or a precious life snuffed out? Maybe there is an almost unseen 'tide' that compels history or stimulates changes in the course of our lives? Maybe lives are decided by a *turn* of a Cosmic Card or a move in a higher Game?].

In the story, not only were there Universal 'Floors' or Continuums, but there was separation in a galactic Class System. Mystics, seers, Citizens, aliens, humanoids, humans, and there was the clueless 'yahoos.' Reality involved multi-levels.

'Yahoos' originated from Gulliver's Travels, a classic that used symbols to poke fun at Royalty of the times. (Complaints or protests against Monarchies were hidden in children's tales or carefully placed in popular stories.) In one part of 'Gulliver,' the Horses were enlightened Beings and even psychic. It was the *humans* who carried on like animals. The term was also used in the Old West where there were many 'yahoos,' as well as today.

Sardon created invisible tentacles as well as a Money-Eating 'Monster' protected by a force-field that would continue wasting wealth and enslaving us for no good reason. Sardon controlled everything from the shadows. It controlled Media; it mastered Machines and countless minions without their knowledge. Then the Chancellor manipulated its own opposition. Rangers/Rebels were controlled by 'Under-Net' sets (underground) Sardon created, similar to the Internet or TV *not* being used as a vehicle for Truth.

New Zog agonized whether *HE was at fault for the horrors of Hensi unleashed on Pinwheel,* as Mebby stated. NZ listened as if the Devil-girl spoke the truth. Zog should not have fussed since 'he' was not Mebby's opposite and the Sardons had been infecting galaxies throughout Levels/Dimensions for endless time.

Crowning achievement of the Sardon Beast was the invention of the dylar. At first, the Galactic Monetary Standard was hailed as 'Security' and a financial way out of troubled times. (In 'Star Wars,' the Senate passed a bill to begin an 'Empire' that was received 'with thunderous applause.') Why *wouldn't* alien worlds want a common medium or 'dylar' for trades and a means to do business on a galactic level?

Truth was dylar-shapes, like coins, were perfect for stacking and the Sardon could vaporize the wealth of the galaxy even faster down the jaws of its Monster. Renoux's nightmare sequences came directly from the old film 'Metropolis' where workers were being munched by a Great Machine.

Agent Cal Trask drastically changed in more ways than one. Others in the story also experienced a metamorphosis in their lives, a parallel life-change or in a reincarnated one much later in time. Pools were used in the story to symbolize rebirth, renewing, transition and change into a different life.

'Lebritz' was a common speaking-language, generally spoken throughout the Pinwheel Galaxy and was like English on Earth. It originated from the famous 'Berlitz School of Languages.'

Soon the fires of War were flamed in the State/Sardon-owned Media. The 'Forbidden Fruit' of Atomics from the First Age would rise once more. Pinwheel would turn, and *War was the direction.*

The dying Sardon controlled everything and beautifully played Mystics to Citizens to yahoos. Devil Beast Sardon *hated life.* It wanted to destroy all that Zog loved. Then why did it take so long to die or pass out of the material world? Why did it hold onto the last drop of life until the last moment, if existence was such Hensi?

The story of the oldest sector in the Pinwheel (ONE) is really about Martin Luther, the Truth and Secret Societies. Many changes were made such as the Sanzibar Monastery was a Business School for yuppie executives.

Markus was not merely another character but a parallel to the main character and hero (Cal). He was Cal in another solar system and he was Martin Luther. Luther's story was one of a German monk, before the printing press, who worked hard all of his life for God and the Truth. He climbed up the rankings of monks after many years to finally see and feel the Holy Bible. Only high Priests could see the one rare copy chained to the wall.

When Luther eventually read the Truth, he was utterly appalled and rocked to the core. There were ninety-five *differences,* he called 'theses,' between what the ancient Book recorded and present teachings of the Church. Brother Martin had the courage to post his '95 theses' on the church door for all to see. He was punished like Galileo for pursuing Truth over the Order or will of the authority at the time.

In the story, Markus moved up Executive degrees similar to degrees of Freemasonry. He eventually learned terrible secrets from the hidden, occult archive. Truths of the Sardon and coming nuclear age were uncovered. Sardon created wars and profits from selling 'bullets and bandages.'

The twist here was Bella (Belial) was assigned to keep tabs on Markus who knew many State secrets. Bella was really Jella, a business 'priest' with a face-change, whose career was ruined because of 'the Note.' Bella was under mind-control to think Markus would assassinate his double (the fake Media-puppet) Emanuel, New Zog. Markus (Cal) was a clone of

Emanuel; captured, made to look like Emanuel and then publicly beheaded *as* Emanuel to create a martyr. The irony: Markus was the voice of Truth and a 'Cal carrier,' a real messiah. (Martin Luther, Galileo and Giordana Bruno were only telling the truth and received the same 'hot water' as today's whistle-blowers).

'Master DeLandra' of long ago, referred to Bishop Landa and real crimes of religious conquistadors. When Markus spoke of the 'Great Fire,' it was an obvious parallel to the Great Flood. Zog's promise to never destroy by fire was as God's promise to never destroy the world with a Great Deluge again.

'Ott and the cities of Golem and Sinnoria' were the nuked cities of Sodom and Gomorrah. 'Fortress of Camino' was the fortress of Jericho in the Bible. Of course, the 'Arch of Electra' was the Arc of the Covenant. Janus was the 'Jonah and the Whale' story, but Janus was taken aboard a *submarine.* 'The Testament' (Bible) was viewed wrong, as Bella knew.

The public assassination of Emanuel, who was really Markus, who was really Cal, was actually the President Kennedy murder! This was a well orchestrated Event for the precise purpose of manipulating masses (9/11). Notice that the 'protective bubble' was raised and a (unknown) *different* fake-Zog was decapitated in total view of multi-Media. How could the Creator be killed?

Every aspect of the assassin and escape were carefully designed to move Citizens for a sinister purpose. 'Gildenstein Smith,' a *woman,* was shown to be the killer. To find the origin of the name, see '1984' and the false terrorist-rebel created to rally patriotic feelings. The fake-Zog, 'Emanuel,' was not killed. His name was Willard Price, a paid actor, but really a sleazy gambler from Delphino.

The dying Sardon's Agenda was to get the Women (old Lodges of Women's Clubs opposing Men's Clubs) to develop the banned BOMB, atomic and Hydrogen. Ladies became the next wave of power. Women covertly developed 'nukes' and controlled the hidden Chancellery in secret, but were in truth only the 'hands of the Beast.' Women were hailed as finding the lair of Sardon and destroyed it over male Rangers who were impotent for many yarns.

End of Chapter Three mirrored the 'Roaring Twenties,' a time of abundance and prosperity (pre-war). Unions and Rebels organized not unlike similar times in the 20th Century.

The Pinwheel or Monopdonow (Celestial Game) Galaxy would be plunged into a seemingly never-ending WAR, a 'War of the Sexes,' orchestrated by a dead Sardon and the monsters it left behind.

A Viper Police force called 'Zulaire Pox' was created, which later became the Cardilles. Citizens of the Monopdonow Galaxy knew that Women had atomic weapons. Solar systems were intimidated by the New Police.

What readers were actually viewing was a story about the famous RMS Titanic's maiden voyage in 1912 and the following disaster. Conspiracy Theorists have reported a 'Jesuit plot' where Captain Smith purposely rammed the 'unsinkable ship' into an iceberg. This was to kill 'good industrialists' Astor, Guggenheim, and Strauss who were compelled to board. They would have strongly opposed the formation of the coming Federal Reserve which financed WW1.

'White Dwarf Company' was an obvious reference to the 'White Star Company' that built the Titanic. Colossus was the largest saucer ever constructed. Its popular captain was 'Goerges Smith.' Giant sun called 'Carpathus' was a reflection of RMS Carpathia or main rescue vessel after the Titanic sank.

The conspiracy or *false flag* info was oddly uncovered over Media. Vipers linked Captain Smith to (bogus Zog-killer) Gildenstein Smith's gang, a Hitler from another time. Smith was not related and only a pawn in a much larger, invisible game.

At this point, we have the introduction of the 'darling of the galaxy.' May Eleanora Bulair ('Mebby' as she was commonly known) was a Shirley Temple character used by the State (dead Sardon) for political purposes. Her one starring role in the film 'Tomorrow's Child' would later emerge as a matter of fate.

Slowly, the truth revealed itself. The oddity of Colossus' passenger list, how primarily male-sympathizers perished and how Women Vipers appeared to have had prior knowledge of the famous Wormhole disaster. News did not look good for the Ladies. Soon, men and women would be at each others' throats. Battles would rage between their war-machines for a Galactic Century!

Here were the first examples of previously written short stories included, changed and made to fit 'The Continuum.' Before critics criticize for adding blocks of pages, one should discover the original short-story versions. Could *destiny* have played a hand? Were the short stories (melodies) fated to end as arrangements in the overall epic (opera)?

Fictional events on Qvavor (a frequency term: 'quaver') of the little continuum *generally happened in this writer's personal life.* Governor 'Barados' and Governess 'Tinesia' were supposedly our soul-names. Breakup and divorce of the royal couple was a parallel to repercussions that led to an *end of a real marriage.* Possibly, writing the scenes was *cathartic.*

The idea was, simply, a great love steadied the world. Without its balance, the results were panic and chaos felt elsewhere in larger proportions. Yet, a good ending was eventually realized between the Qvavor King and Queen. When that happened, peace, stability and sanity returned to the galaxy.

Before the ideal resolution between the royal couple, readers paused at its worst moment. Readers viewed what transpired on all spiral arms of the Pinwheel. It was Galactic Madness and nuclear proliferation in a War of the Sexes! Whole star systems *dissolved out of existence!* The worst inhumanities happened between two forms that should love each other (according to Zog).

The Eightoid Race of many bright colors that stood for their distinct ethnicities, obviously, paralleled the 1960s. Aret ('Tera' backwards) was forced into continuous war, which was akin to the Vietnam War that seemed endless. Aretan

YOUTHS sparked a Peace Movement they thought was motivated by chemicals only to find: *Love was inside all. Our true nature was peace.*

A scary, Saturn-character was introduced known as legendary 'Lord Boz.' He was a bizarre creature without color (my Boba Fett). In future and on other systems, 'Boz' became the Galactic Standard Cuss-Word or F-word. Later, we hear the little Devil-girl swear: "Boz! Boz! Boz!" (Battlestar Galactica: 'frak').

For readers who missed the major Comedy, it shall be explained. They were trying to tap the Center of Life on Aret, what they thought was the Animalistic Soul. They succeeded. But, instead of the Super-Soldier Monster they thought would be produced, they found our true Heart-Center, *which was more like a loving hippie 'tripping balls!'*

What happened on the famous Fanguard Fields? Expected, later tales of horrific 'bloodbaths' did not really occur. Here comes the comedy: What truly happened at Fanguard Fields was a secret, *drunken sex orgy!* Readers must realize that each gender-camp had to have kept studs/wombs for spawning purposes. But in truth, after 100 yarns, they were just plain ol' *horny.*

'Wings Over the Galaxy' was created, a fleet of gigantic (space-traveling) 'Automatons' to hold Zog's IOP for safe-keeping. Inspiration for the big robots came from Gort in 'The Day the Earth Stood Still.' In the film, human life forms gave complete authority and control over to the Machines as their Police.

Origin of the Continuum's 'Wings Over the Galaxy' was from 'Wings Over the World' in H.G. Wells 'Things to Come.' They were post-war people with superior tech who 'cleaned up old bosses.' Paul McCartney's band 'Wings' came from same film.

Story of Toltec leader, the Sadama, 8000 years ago (not yarns) was a weird tale among many others. (In 'Galactica' Lorne Greene played leader 'Adama'). In the Machine-influenced portion of Pinwheel History, we found strange juxtapositions on moonless Earth. Indians employed no metal whatsoever. Their very modern society utilized the sun, nature, magnetism, crystals, stone and hard substances made from hemp fibers. (Terms like 'yarns,' 'yams' and 'yas' were not measurements of time on this Earth long ago).

Coming of the Machines was not unlike the Spanish conquerors taking over the New World from Indians on the fated Day of Prophecy, only the reverse. Sadama became another 'carrier' for Sardon and it was the cold, heartless Device that was the warm 'carrier' of Zog. Was this incarnation the reason New Zog could later possess (become) a Voomba?

In Battlestar Galactica, 'tribes of humans' sought their planet of origin (Kobol) while fighting mechanical Cylons. 'The Master Cylinder' (from old cartoon and BG prime Cylon) had a take-me-to-your-leader encounter with the Sadama. Notice that *the Machine smoked the Peace Pipe* and not the warrior-Indian. Cyborgs were really looking for their Supreme Machine-Creator or 'Vog.' In the first Star Trek film, evolved/changed Probe V-Ger also sought its Builder in the same way humans wonder about God and Creation.

Sadama's hatred for *metal* and evil intentions emerged. TMC machine thought its race created humans while Sadama knew machines were once products of human beings. *The Machine* displayed strong emotions and the *man* was cold and compassionless. How could humans have come from machines when humans created machines in the first place? It's the old *'Chicken and the Egg.'*

Climactic scene with Sadama's natural-crystal gun to the glass head of TMC while his sun-weapon with crystals attempted to destroy the Cyborg Base Ship...was cool. It was the Star Trek 'corbomite maneuver.' Sun's focused energy bounced back to its source and the *entire Earth vaporized!*

When TMC's head blew to pieces, only the Cyborg units under its command collapsed (died). Cyborg Base Ship slowly became our Moon as a *Dreamtime* emerged. Cyborgs eventually migrated to a reconstituted Earth. Because 'Mineer' must exist for Zog to appear in the future, the planet had to *reform 8000 years ago.* In time, mechanical men and women forgot they were really artificial and cybernetic.

The next section was a twist on the film 'Surrogates' with Bruce Willis and Radha Mitchell. Movie concerned 'Stim Chairs' where from the comfort of home you could go out in the world as a clean, renewable 'surrogate.' A virtual version of yourself interacted in society while you operated it from a chair. The Continuum was at a point where androids 'lived' normal, unreal lives on Earth with little memory of the past. What if Cyborgs had Stim Chairs and sent out fragile, bloody, real version-duplicates?

Detective Davidson with D-chairs segment was film noir. The paragraph: 'Nights were cold in Soho…' was particularly *noir.* The gorgeous Agent Blackpitch was named for Ms. Mitchell's role in her film 'Pitch Black.'

There were 'Flesh-Fairs' where 'sickos' tortured the bios that felt sensations. This was the exact opposite of fairs seen in the movie 'A.I.' where robots were tortured. Again, there was the world coming to an end. This time, it was a 'xirus' (much worse than virus) and a Magnetic Doomsday to a planet of metal androids that believed they're human. When readers discovered that the Chief (based on Chief Stottlemeyer of TV's 'Monk') was powerful mogul Waldorf-68, it was supposed to be like the end of a film noir movie.

It was revealed that the Machines committed genocide on its human Creators long ago. Judgment Day and the facility were right out of 'Terminator 3.' 'Sun Beach' was a 'Dark City' reference. Borrowed was the couple 'could not avert Judgment Day, but they could survive it.' 'Magic' changed machines back into humans. Maddy and Stephen were Adam and Eve.

Cyborgs were now ONE with their Creators. Cyborgs evolved into higher 'meat-machines' known as Humans. The most evolved 'machine' was really a brainy bio-human. The War between men and machines was over. The solution was a merger.

The different timeline erased the longstanding nuclear threat from the Pinwheel Galaxy. Big problem remained the continuous, wasted rain of mass-Wealth down a mini-Black Hole. Somehow, dylar-flow into obliteration had to end.

Trinars (with Catalog) did not start out as Asians in the story, but ended as Asians. Older than many races, Trinars were prehistoric force-field builders. The parallel had to do with the Great Wall of China. A tremendous Force-Field version of the Wall was once created in space. Like with the Great Wall in China, Trinars were isolationists too and needed to contain their high level of knowledge or culture.

The story of Dr. Icilly Yil (inventor of N-Rays) and Yong Phil was the most romantic, touching, and poignant moment in the entire epic. Let me encapsulate the special scene. Dr. Yil, this tiny FF expert, went missing. She developed the controversial N-Rays which penetrated FFs and can do what Rebels and Rangers, seers and Citizens have longed for: end Sardon's Machine, the profit-gobbler. Then she discovered the *full extent* of this awesome knowledge. She *had* to kill herself. *The terrible Secret must die with her.*

Yil went to a remote planetoid, tested the Power once again and set off a chain reaction that blasted her and the planetoid to bits. She was the farthest thing from a psychic. Yil was a workaholic with no time for a social life. Had she been psychic, Dr. Icilly might not have pushed the button *so soon.* Yong Phil led a team to find her and did find her. He had been in love with Yil for yarns yet they had never met. Yong *was* psychic, her soul-mate and perfect yin to her yang.

When they met, alone, on a world that was about to explode, their last moments, knowing they could have had an amazing life together, was emotional for this writer. [Like the story of the girl that could have saved herself on the Titanic, but did not because she just met her true love. The short time together was worth it].

We needed a Vortex expert, an Albert Einstein, and that was Jene 4 Renoux. He was a smart, bearded prophet. He saw more than average Citizens and seers. He saw Tomorrow in dreams. In truth, Renoux was John the Baptist.

Now there was a new cosmic mystery of the 'Gusher,' White Hole, called 'Fountain' or the Neri Vortex. This corresponded to Albert Einstein in 1919, during an eclipse, when his light-bending theory was proven. Renoux also became extremely famous over Media. He predicted the end of the Vortex's expansion.

Because of his genius, Jene 4 had been head physicist in schools at 'Balmoral Palace' in Rom Sector. 'Balmoral' came from the infamous British royal castle of same name.

'Valparaiso' (Sting song), was a lovely name for first system threatened by the expanding Neri Vortex Quasar. Eventually, FFs were broken, dylar-disintegration was stopped and 'the Machine' was ended and later publicly displayed.

Readers learned that Quasars were microscopic/shrinking other ends of Great Big Funnels called 'Black Holes.' They were also transportation conduits between Continuums (universes).

Colors referred to real (Mainstream) star colors and also classic Monopoly. BLUE compared to extravagant areas such as 'Boardwalk' and 'Park Place.' In Monopdonow Board Game, *cheap* sectors had warmer colors and were similar to *cheap* lots like 'Baltic Ave.'

'Natural Wonders of the Galaxy' were larger versions of '7 Wonders of the World.' A very valuable 'Spice' needed to be written about since so many story-points came from 'features' on previously created (board game) Deed Cards. Gigantic Silk *Worms* were already used in Frank Herbert's 'Dune.' *Ah; giant Spiders (vidors) spin silken webs.* We can have a supremely valuable and potent drop of a psychoactive drug inside the Spider's thorax. Could be difficult to get at since the giant monsters dug deep inside the planet and were known as nasty warriors. Extraction teams over countless yarns had perished in search of the Spider Spice called 'Xigar.'

If readers have not figured it out, entire purpose of arachnids was to produce the 'Singing Elgin Asteroids' from sector Deed Cards. What could make asteroids sing? If they were once a planet with millions of huge caverns dug by Super Spiders, then maybe the asteroid pieces would 'sing' if plunged into atmospheres as meteors? It was interesting that the other planet ('Elgin'), known for different-colored Spiders, was blown to bits by extraction teams sick of fighting them in caves.

'Home of the 4th Creator' was another previous Deed feature written long before its connection to God. Later, God became the 4th Creator. The idea was we were observing the fourth time the Universe had been built. Similarly, in 'The Matrix,' the Architect and Oracle reconstructed the world six times.

The small tale of Rizlan Lizards contained two notes of interest. 1) Vast numbers of life forms thrived on the *insides* of planets, on the hollow interiors with central suns of natural or artificial Great Spheres. 2) When Lizards tapped their Centers to reach the essence of their being, they discovered the *exact opposite* polarity of what occurred with the Eightoids of Aret. Trillions of Rizlans killed each other long ago within 794 Dyson Spheres like the Krell in 'Forbidden Planet.'

'The Cantor Archives' was reminiscent of the discovery of the Dead Sea Scrolls. The Archives contained what really happened in galactic prehistory. Truth of the first Atomic Age was hidden. Even for advanced Citizens, Media reported they were only old stories and songs, no big deal.

'Xima War' also came from the Deed Game Cards. How do you write a war between evolved Cats and Dogs? Dog lovers will not enjoy the stupidity of the standing canines. Cat lovers will think it was *delightful* because of the superiority of felines. In a sense, here was a mirrored view of the 'Sex Wars.'

Professor Renoux's dreams were significant. We saw the truth of what our Life was to the Larger Continuum. Material Life, in all its forms, was merely 'dylars' to the Larger Game being played in the CONTINUUM above us. (In the film 'Metropolis,' Freder sees a nightmare vision, an endless stream of workers grinding to nothing into the jaws of a Great Machine).

Tray Samuel Caladan's character (author's pen-name) was introduced. The message was *we should all be in touch with our nonphysical Ghost-Spirit that resides in everyone.* It was similar to Bilbo writing 'There and Back Again' and it became the trilogy's title and not 'Lords...' Long dead Caladrian was renewed as Caladan. As the Sardon reconstituted, so did its counterpart or, readers were led to believe.

Tray (3), a child of destiny, later realized his true purpose. Blue Energy 'possessed' the man or the Cal-El ('el' was Egyptian for electricity/power). This fit nicely with the real name of classic Superman, the Man of Steel (Nietzsche's Super-Man). In the comics, his Kryptonian name was 'Kal-El.' Are we potential supermen and superwomen? *We were all created equal.*

Readers were taken back and forth on purpose to reinforce a 180 degree opposition of what will be Neo Zog and Neo Sardon. Readers who know the outcome of the Tonk Game and 'Ultimate Deal' (fictional movie title) understood the revealed truth.

Following the arc of Mebby, when she was a robot everyone thought she was real. She came back to the galaxy as 'Tomorrow's Child,' a State-clone said Media, when the truth was the demon child was the robo-spawn of Sardon.

'Hitchhiker's Guide...' was implied with the galactic warning over Media, 'Do Not Panic.' Right on schedule, prior to GST 2000.00, the Neri Vortex (Quasar) came alive and expanded. It was an unknown and necessary prelude to the Second Coming of Zog of the blue light. Citizens watched Media and universally felt *something was coming.*

Captain Mada Sims-Zela stood for the biblical Saul whose name was changed to Paul. Later he became a Disciple and follower of the NZ, Cal-El. His name was changed to 'Pe're.'

There was a moment of hilarious comedy after the odd, little Quizo (pooka like 'Harvey' called 'dowd') arrived while Mada was sinking to his death. The big man thought the 3-

legged Aphid would help him get out of his predicament. And there was the LONGEST pause. The Quizo *was* helping the man by just being there, ushering Mada into a reborn life like a Guardian Angel-insect. The killer did not understand that: *"to be saved, he had to go."*

Later, during Mebby's book-signing, an incredible sequence of actions transpired which determined the rest of the story. A grand announcement of the return of May Bulair as a pretty teenager, cloned by an old admirer, happened on the very popular and highly hyped 'Grace Harp Show.'

The Mark 4 by SonWil (Wilson) sounded like it was announced by Don Pardo. The incident was similar to Oprah giving away cars to her audience. Mebby jumping up and down on Grace's couch was like when Tom Cruise was excited about Katie Holmes.

The She-Devil did not have ultimate power. She did not approve of two monstrous 'Visitors' and a possessed 'Lady Braw' from the Dimension of the Larger Continuum, which became her crew. Who was setting the rules and changing reality that even the Sardon-girl must obey?

Tituus, dark creature from Upstairs and Mebby crewmate, was unique because it possessed the Gun that shot concentrated N-Rays capable of deleting the Devil. A real person in 'Lady Braw' was controlled by an evil Zog. She was a fascinating character when you consider her 'good-witch' double (in parallel world: 2 sides to a pinwheel disk). Readers know in the end, she murdered her twin and Zog's *wife,* (Mary Magdalene).

'Soma' was borrowed from Aldous Huxley's 'Brave New World.' The whole purpose of the purity or sensations of the special moment was to get Caladan *tuned* (made perfect) to be the 'Receptacle for Zog.' Rene 4, the Baptist, told Cal his true purpose. The 'soothe-suit' helped. What was coming was the superman, a merger of electric spirit and a physical body. Here was what a human could really do if full potential was utilized. Tray was now Cal-El with only one heart.

Zog's extreme *joy* of once again playing in our world

we take for granted was now realized after so much unwritten hardships Upstairs. 'Cal-El' had super powers and flew like Neo in 'The Matrix' sequels. Next, Cal-El flew over the lights of Enlightenment City (Vatican) and *cursed!* Neo Zog hated E. City's lust for dylars and all the financed WARS in its wake.

Few readers will understand the importance of the nexus-point or 'book-signing.' Scenes of May Bulair and her entourage of PR agents, managers, stooges and hairdressers were funny. The agents literally were nameless (one faceless) and scared to death of the little Devil. Could the author's distain for literary agents have been showing? Mebby's 'inner circle' saw her dark side while the adoring public had no idea.

Notice that Cal-El appeared as the *third* person given a public privilege to question Mebby. 'Vaala Show' was a Las Vegas show only much more elaborate for the galaxy's 'Illuminaughty.' Grace Harp, who was really Cal-El this time, appeared and *shocked* the Devil-girl. Cal used his powers and the Media moment to expose the Truth to the entire galaxy. How did the Devil respond and undo the damage of her 'panties being pulled down?' Robo-girl thought fast and told everyone, "It's all part of a show!"

'Retz' Council Headquarters inside the hollow center of Venus (note: our Solar System) originated from Conspiracy Theorists who believe Nikola Tesla and Valiant Thor were really Venusians. Supposedly, *'Retz' is the real Capital City of Venus.* In the story, Retz Council and affiliations were the 'good guys.' They were Rangers and positively-charged Mystics/seers. What began with mutual respect and tribute to the Reformation of the real Zog that now walked again, turned into a psychic mega-disaster displayed before trillions of the greatest Citizens.

A hint of polarity switching occurred when the Continuum's 'Christ' momentarily went *bad* (Superman II). Similarly, little robo-girl Mebby (Sardon) said *nice words.*

Magnetic (polarities) Planet Magnus was a fitting short story addition (previously written). Readers view an inside out reality where Continuum characters interacted only everything was different. To bottom-line, the adventure of the 'Hawks' (NZ's friends/followers) in a gargantuan universe of different 'zogs' was another attempt at humor. "Oh, no! We couldn't save the galaxy from total annihilation!" "No, we *did* save a copy in a Cosmic Computer, right here." Readers discover that as *there was never a planet Mineer, there was never a Pinwheel Galaxy.* The segment also represented Hope that everything will turn out for the best. Reality started over with a new name and a new Game called 'Monopdonow.'

The Monopdonow Game-concept appeared at this point in the story. Space Sectors were commercially bought and sold. TOLLS were paid in dylars by travelers who passed through Territories to owners of sectors. Life forms spun and moved in the Pinwheel. Tremendous fortunes were amassed. But, do you chuck it all away if given the rare chance to *ascend* to Nirvana or not?

A new reality existed in the Game. The Continuum was the 'Game of Life' and its cycle was a continuous circle or 'Rat Race.' There was now the rare 'Chance' (card) of Ascension. To Transcend, players (according to Zog) *must take it.* But in order to reach Nirvana or the real Kingdom of Heaven, you must give up every last dylar. *'You can't take it with you!' 'Rich man can sooner go through the eye of a needle than enter Heaven.'*

Lady Braw first noticed the child had some degree of *feelings* that a super-sophisticated robot should not have. Mebby (Devil-Sardon, keep in mind) was *melting* inside at the remote possibility of actually meeting and working with that gorgeous 'hunk,' Pinn Bradley. The author will let readers figure out who the corresponding real life actor 'Pinn' represented.

Why did 'God' appear passive, old, tired and sleepy? Its time (energy) had come and gone. A 5th Architect would later appear, or will it? '794' was author's street address at home in Bridgeville, PA. (Smallville) *Problem was author had no ending for the story.* What could 'The Ultimate Deal' mean? Not only would it be Mebby's movie title and Continuum end, but the final resolution also involved...a perfect hand of 'TONK.' Tonk became the ultimate climax.

A previous piece was attached whose exact title (Mebby's next, big project) was called 'Secret of the Blue Escape Pod.' Readers viewed big killer-machines before, now meet the *sweetest soul in the galaxy* who happened to be a little Voomba (upgraded 'Roomba'). The spark inside the special machine was the New Zog. El's blue spirit-electricity motivated Nils and was really a surprise (a surprise to author also and became a late addition). 'Nils' came from TV Frasier's brother who would make a good butler.

Nils' horror at being digitized into a computer instead of moving in the physical world as a dented Voomba should be examined. Was a temporary real life better than 'Transcendence' (Depp's movie) 'living' as computer bits for an eternity? The Media stunt Nils pulled was like NZ exposing the Truth of Mebby to everyone. The little guy's public suicide *got you in the chest plate.* Even a lowly Scrub-Vac Voomba could ascend to Nirvana.

[When film version of 'The Continuum' is made, there should be a *cartoon.* 'Slap' is a tender classic. 'Jurci' was the author's old, family name that grandfather Americanized to 'Yurchey'].

Song titles were a joy to create. 'Destroy Everything (you touch)' was a real song by 'Ladytron' and not TronLady. Sardon would have to secure the rights for that one. And, we won't touch 'Springtime for Sardon.' *Was the author funny?*

Finally, Neo Zog received long overdue Love from the Universe, possibly repeated in longer/wider Waves in all CONTINUUMS. This was similar to a cosmic rock star (Ziggy) who performed an amazing concert to the world. His fans and Disciples were thrilled.

Little Mebby assumed the sidekick role of android Sheila-7 (Bruce Lee). Robot movie makeup was put on a real bio-robot that no one could tell was artificial. Wuubian, Treyoni (Beyonce), took the role of 'Space Captain' right out of comics that Zog secretly wrote via Nils.

The movie was changed from earlier Graphic Novel to fit the little Devil who was going to direct [loved blue-faced, stand-in director]. The 'Rangerettes' was the Sardon-child's mockery of good Ranger Rebels in the galaxy. The girls have great legs in the singing chorus line.

Emissary was not going to be used again, but was perfect for the Dealer in the critical Tonk Game. 'Emanuel' was *forgotten* as tribesman's name by author when included. Again, pieces seemed to fit in place like 'Emanuel' already used as fake-Zog, 'EM' stood for Electro-Magnetism and purpose to remove + and − from reality and other realities. EM was a neutral, grey 3rd Charge.

Actor Pinn Bradley's character was 'Rad Carnoir.' Was that macho enough? Next, was the funniest moment in the entire Continuum saga: *It was the quivering lips of the little and 'hot' Devil-girl on set in the arms of sexy Pinn who she had a thing for. She's the Sardon.*

New Zog appeared to be her polar opposite. He performed a similar *trick* to when he posed as Grace Harp during book-signing. NZ inhabited or was always the physical presence of Pinn. The big moment was so special for sweating robo-Mebby, and Zog was going to *ruin it.* She found herself, in that first kiss, kissing *him!* Note there was pain. Was it anti-sparks or when matter/anti-matter touched? Worlds did not explode, yet.

Their deadly dance and dialog began. If readers only had one section of the Continuum book to review, the author suggests the delicate ballet between Beelzebub and the Blue Angel on the movie set.

NZ destroyed the N-Gun after a sex play that lowered the android's defenses. The machine (Meb) was already turned ON. Get it? He could have shot her, won the Game and wiped out so much potential devastation that she controls. He could not do what she did so easily. He did punish the tyke by 'smashing' that little doll of hers.

The dialog the Devil spewed was horrific, then again very curious when it seemed to ring true. Was Zog/NZ suffering the 'slings and arrows' of Hensi because *he would destroy what he dearly loved?* Did he already? Had the real galactic problems been *Zog's fault* and not the demon Sardon's fault all along? (Chicken or the Egg?) Mebby spoke profoundly, like a Zog Goddess, and it was the Super-Man that drank in the truth.

A significant point happened when Mebby screamed, "I am MONEY! They adore me." Closeness of 'Mebby' and 'Money' was plainly observed.

Mebby (-) understood the purpose of the Doomsday Emissary (before NZ +) who was directed to 'fix' the Continuums that were all connected and *breaking apart!* Tribesman was the grey between black and white.

The Kent Clark episode, on a 'dark and stormy night' in fictional Betelgeuse, had been written just prior to the Mayan destruction-of-the-world prediction around the holidays of 2012. In an alley was where a minor character slept. God was not the poor bum on the street, James. (James symbolized a good, real King on Earth: King James. The man honored science over superstition while heralded anarchist and vicious killer, Guy Fawkes, had been twisted to be a hero of the people. (Our modern word 'guy' originated from Fawkes).

Hooded 'Fate' walked into the bar. Was it Saturn, Sardon or Boz? Neo Zog as Mr. Clark, richest man in Indiana, *had to fail.* Jene Renoux saw his failure. *We all fail* and Cal was Everyman! What does the 'S' on Superman's chest represent? (Spirit) NZ was also 'stung' in the vile Belial Battle. Cal, under the skin and influence of the richest man in Betelgeuse, *chose money.* A Universe nearly ended and Mebby thought 'she' had won the Game.

All the players were set for the Ultimate TONK Game. *Forget poker;* does not come close to the bluffing and fast excitement of Tonk. (Author is glad it is still played in the Milky Way). Emissary and galactic Watchers suddenly realized the Truth. EM grabbed Mebby. Like a cartoon character, she frantically struggled in all positions to be released and not be annihilated. Old God, literally on the other hand, was cool as a cucumber. *Thank Zog that God and the Devil were gone!* [If seats were *not* switched in Tonk, NZ and child-Sardon would be *gone* leaving a dying God Builder. The Big Universe (ALL CONTINUUMS) would soon completely disappear never to be restarted again, *ever!* Zog HAD to lose the game and not be at North end].

Readers should sit back and enjoy the subtleties of Tonk. *Mebby* the game will be revitalized? *Is the author funny?* The Devil was known to sit at the South end of card games. Why was EM confused? Because the entire galaxy and more had been led to believe Zog was God, the very opposite of the Black Devil. That was not the case at all. Zog's Light was Blue. God was the White Light. Later, Zog's Blue Light sparked the worlds to begin anew and opened the door for the 5th Creator to appear. Cal-El (died) was *spent* in the process and was no more. Tray was now only a married man.

***

'Epilog' or tail after the Tonk grand finale were projected Future Constructs when Game realities were played again. Life was gently twisted and crystallized a bit differently next time. There was a father-figure from a previously written piece, a character that was originally called 'Jesus Christ Superman.' He was JC in a Superman's costume. In a later Continuum Construct, he became 'Cal-El Superman.'

The inversion was Cal Superman entered the dream of a young Jene Renoux before the pipe and beard. A very important and controversial message was expressed: Wise Jene told Supe why he was really killed by Sanhedrin. "You put Christ inside all of us. Before, he was out there. You said *meditate, look within.* We're all the same, all part of God." *They didn't like that.*

Sharp readers may understand who was really speaking in the scene and *why* it was included as a final, epilog attachment. Son of God and God the Father spoke to each other. It was the cycle of the 'Lion King' or Circle of Life (really a stretched Ellipse). It was Teacher and student. It was

Master and apprentice. You, all of us, Sons and Daughters will eventually become Spirit and the pure/electric Light that is inside everyone. The higher enlightenment of mind, consciousness or transcendence of Soul will take some time. But it will eventually happen. Everything repeats again and again in a continuous Cycle, unless something comes along to disrupt the spiraling repetition…

The number of '11' Universes or parallel Continuums was a concept the author came across in real research as, possibly, a theoretical amount of Universes in our Super 'Multiverse.' Why not 11,000 or 11,000,000 or more Universes in a MEGA-UNIVERSE? Why only eleven? *Seems like a measly little nothing of a world.* Maybe the Builders have only been small cosmic children and one day their Parents will come along and *really make something BIG!*

Maybe the author *is* funny. Do readers know that on the 'other side' of our galaxy's disk, things are done right? There's warm, colored snow and roses have no thorns and people play Royal Tennis with no lines. We need to be (choose) positive, like on the other side of the Mirror.

TS Caladan

(Dedicated to the early Douglas Noel Adams)

*** continumology ***

bar – galactic measurement about 12 inches in length.

bloch – rose.

Blue Carpet – the false (Media-driven) Material-path in Life.

buttermoth – butterfly.

Center – refers to heart, true feelings or Truth inside a
    consciousness.

Chancellery – Sardon's forced financial Institution to
    continually deplete/control the galaxy.

Citizen – Middle Class of Pinwheel Galaxy.

dragmar – dragon.

dylar – the GMS, substance cannot be faked, installed by
    Sardon not to help the galaxy…but to enslave it.

fayd – feud.

fell – mile.

flug – slug.

Fountain – close Quasar in Neri Sector, only way for Zog to
    return, aka Neri Vortex.

fueleen – gas.

GMS – Galactic Monetary Standard.

Golden Path – the true path to Enlightenment and Nirvana.

GST – Galactic Standard Time.

GUARP_ – powerful hallucinogen like LSD followed by a
    potency # that increases over the course of the story.

Hensi – Hell.

Howzer-rays – weapon beam that blasts living molecules from
    inside.

humanoid – any life form with 2 arms, 2 legs (heads optional).

jango – shit, also 'punse.'

Korabi – ancient Holy Book of the Zog, like the Koran.

lang-lance – mechanism for violent *tuening,* an internal
    weapon.

Lebritz – galactic standard speaking-language similar to
    English on Earth.

m-bar – inch.

Marr-ratings – bogus galactic Media ratings like TV's
    Nielsens.

mar-slit – mouth.

Mead – 'Nectar of the Gods,' blue drink only served to elite, also connected to the MEAD Corporation.

Media – term for Citizens' broadcasts on networks and channels.

mega-bar – million miles.

Monopdonow – future Game buying sectors in space, name for overall commercialism that rules in 2nd Age of galaxy.

moroaf – bread.

mythocane – substance mixed to dilute the Queen Spiders' Spice.

nesium – substance 1000 times harder than diamond.

Nirvana – term for Heaven, the next higher Continuum, home of Zog and Sardon.

Pan Movers – famous galactic movers, spaceship-renters in Wormhole Nebula.

Pandra's Door – Pandora's Box.

parallax bridge – Wormhole corridor-conduit to Quadrant's other corresponding sector.

pell – domino.

Pinwheel Galaxy – aka the Monopdonow Galaxy and later the Monopdonow Continuum.

Powda'me – the Order's first army of elite enforcers.

Quadrant – refers to two parallel space sectors.

Quizo – large, cute, 3-legged Aphid 'dowd' like 'Harvey.'

rine – wine.

Rocketball – popular game played with rockets attached to balls.

Romvoid – galactic Chess.

Roval – galactic tennis played without lines or lines-people on curved court.

selenium – most powerful explosive short of nuclear.

selium – the strongest explosive, until selenium.

sil – ton.

Spacial Territories – same as sectors, large areas of space.

Spice – aka Xigar, the super-Ecstasy drug which only forms in the thorax of Queen Vidors.

Stardusters – galactic 'Starbucks.'

teun – Media viewing by psychics and Citizens (from outside, in).

thaser – laser.

the Order – early fascist (secret) ruling body later known as the Committee, Council, Federation, Party, Company

tuen – violent, physical force that can be intensified by enhancers (from inside, out).

veer – beer.

vidor – spider.

Vog – Cyborg's belief in a mechanical Builder or Creator.

vujo – déjà vu.

Wadlo-chip – very complicated, *moving,* computer circuit -boards.

wormhole – corridor (gate) in space to easily 'jump' millions of yarns, instantly.

Xigar – official name of the famous Red and Green Queen Spiders' Spice.

ya – galactic minute.

yahoo – lower class of the galaxy who have no clue of real events around them.

yam – galactic hour.

yar – galactic month.

yarn – galactic year that is slightly longer, year to year, as ripples propagate larger each time.

Zabu – roulette.

Zillette Factories – genetic company that supposedly cloned Mebby.

Zog – ancient legend of Blue Being predicted to return and save the world.

Zulaire Pox – early form of female, local Police Force.

About the Author

Tray Caladan was born Doug Yurchey in Pittsburgh in 1951. An only child, he retreated into his imagination and drew fantastic pictures. Later, he drew backgrounds for "The Simpsons" and earned a tennis scholarship to Edinboro State as an art major. Afterwards he started the 'Art Trek' gallery in Pittsburgh. There he met a psychic (Katrina) who forever changed his life. Her insights sent him on a course to solve great mysteries. Nikola Tesla's observations helped him solve riddles of Atlantis and ancient pyramids. His articles, videos, radio shows, theories, patent, games, and writings have earned him international acclaim throughout 40 years of researching natural and alien phenomena. His positive message of a 'New Human Genesis' pervades his science-fiction and his art, as well. Tray lives in Northridge, California, on sometimes shaky ground, with his cat (Monkie) and a large library of UFO and science books.